BEAUTIFUL DARKNESS

BY

KAMI GARCIA &
MARGARET STOHL

LITTLE, BROWN AND COMPANY
Boston ◆ New York

Little, Brown and Company
Hachette Book Group
237 Park Avenue, New York, NY 10017
Visit our website at www.lb-teens.com
Little, Brown and Company is a division of Hachette Book Group, Inc.
The Little, Brown name and logo are trademarks of Hachette Book Group, Inc.
First Edition: October 2010

The characters and events portrayed in this book are fictitious. Any similarity to real persons, living or dead, is coincidental and not intended by the authors. To the extent any real names of individuals, locations, or organizations are included in the book, they are used fictitiously and not intended to be taken otherwise.

Library of Congress Cataloging-in-Publication Data

Garcia, Kami.
Beautiful darkness / by Kami Garcia & Margaret Stohl.—1st ed.
p. cm.
Summary: In a small southern town with a secret world hidden in plain sight, sixteen-year-old Lena, who possesses supernatural powers and faces a life-altering decision, draws away from her true love, Ethan, a mortal with frightening visions.
ISBN 978-0-316-07705-7 (hc) / 978-0-316-12636-6 (international ed.)
[1. Supernatural—Fiction. 2. Psychic ability—Fiction. 3. Love—Fiction. 4. South Carolina—Fiction.] I. Stohl, Margaret. II. Title.
PZ7.G155627Bf 2010   [Fic]—dc22   2010007015

10 9 8 7 6 5 4 3 2 1
RRD-C
Book design by David Caplan
Printed in the United States of America

For
Sarah Burnes, Julie Scheina,
and Jennifer Bailey Hunt
because for some silly reason
they wouldn't let us put their names on the cover.

We can easily forgive a child
who is afraid of the dark;
the real tragedy of life is when
men are afraid of the light.

— PLATO

⋈ BEFORE ⋊

Caster Girl

I used to think our town, buried in the South Carolina backwoods, stuck in the muddy bottom of the Santee River valley, was the middle of nowhere. A place where nothing ever happened and nothing would ever change. Just like yesterday, the unblinking sun would rise and set over the town of Gatlin without bothering to kick up so much as a breeze. Tomorrow my neighbors would be rocking on their porches, heat and gossip and familiarity melting like ice cubes into their sweet tea, as they had for more than a hundred years. Around here, our traditions were so traditional it was hard to put a finger on them. They were woven into everything we did or, more often, didn't do. You could be born or married or buried, and the Methodists kept right on singing.

Sundays were for church, Mondays for doing the marketing at the Stop & Shop, the only grocery store in town. The rest of the week involved a whole lot of nothing and a little more pie, if you were lucky enough to live with someone like my family's housekeeper, Amma, who won the bake-off at the county fair every year. Old four-fingered Miss Monroe still taught cotillion, one empty finger of her white-gloved hand flapping as she sashayed down the dance floor with the debutantes. Maybelline Sutter was still cutting hair at the Snip 'n' Curl, though she had lost most of her eyesight around the same time she turned seventy, and now she forgot to put the guard down on the clippers half the time, shearing a skunk stripe up the back of your head. Carlton Eaton never failed, rain or shine, to open your mail before he delivered it. If the news was bad, he would break it to you himself. Better to hear it from one of your own.

This town owned us, that was the good and the bad of it. It knew every inch of us, every sin, every secret, every scab. Which was why most people never bothered to leave, and why the ones who did never came back. Before I met Lena that would have been me, five minutes after I graduated from Jackson High. Gone.

Then I fell in love with a Caster girl.

She showed me there was another world within the cracks of our uneven sidewalks. One that had been there all along, hidden in plain sight. Lena's Gatlin was a place where things happened—impossible, supernatural, life-altering things.

Sometimes life-ending.

While regular folks were busy cutting back their rosebushes or picking past worm-eaten peaches at the roadside stand, Light and Dark Casters with unique and powerful gifts were locked in an eternal struggle—a supernatural civil war without any hope of a white flag waving. Lena's Gatlin was home to Demons and danger and a curse that had marked her family for more than a hundred years. And the closer I got to Lena, the closer her Gatlin came to mine.

A few months ago, I believed nothing would ever change in this town. Now I knew better, and I only wished it was true.

Because the second I fell in love with a Caster girl, no one I loved was safe. Lena thought she was the only one cursed, but she was wrong.

It was our curse now.

Perpetual Peace

The rain dripping off the brim of Amma's best black hat. Lena's bare knees hitting the thick mud in front of the grave. The pinpricks on the back of my neck that came from standing too close to so many of Macon's kind. Incubuses—Demons who fed off the memories and dreams of Mortals, like me, as we slept. The sound they made, unlike anything else in the universe, when they ripped open the last bit of dark sky and disappeared just before dawn. As if they were a pack of black crows, taking off from a power line in perfect unison.

That was Macon's funeral.

I could remember the details as if it had happened yesterday, even though it was hard to believe some of it had happened at all. Funerals were tricky like that. And life, I guess. The important parts you blocked out altogether, but the random, slanted moments haunted you, replaying over and over in your mind.

What I could remember: Amma waking me up in the dark to get to His Garden of Perpetual Peace before dawn. Lena frozen and shattered, wanting to freeze and shatter everything around her. Darkness in the sky and in half the people standing around the grave, the ones who weren't people at all.

But behind all that, there was something I couldn't remember. It was there, lingering in the back of my mind. I had been trying to think of it since Lena's birthday, her Sixteenth Moon, the night Macon died.

The only thing I knew was that it was something I needed to remember.

The morning of the funeral it was pitch-black outside, but patches of moonlight were shining through the clouds into my open window. My room was freezing, and I didn't care. I had left my window open the last two nights since Macon died, like he might just show up in my room and sit down in my swivel chair and stay awhile.

I remembered the night I saw him standing by my window, in the dark. That's when I found out what he was. Not a vampire or some mythological creature from a book, as I had suspected, but a real Demon. One who could have chosen to feed on blood, but chose my dreams instead.

Macon Melchizedek Ravenwood. To the folks around here, he was Old Man Ravenwood, the town recluse. He was also Lena's uncle, and the only father she had ever known.

I was getting dressed in the dark when I felt the warm pull from inside that meant Lena was there.

L?

Lena spoke up from the depths of my mind, as close as anyone could be and about as far away. Kelting, our unspoken form of communication. The whispering language Casters like her had shared long before my bedroom had been declared south of the Mason-Dixon Line. It was the secret language of intimacy and necessity, born in a time when being different could get you burned at the stake. It was a language we shouldn't have been able to share, because I was a Mortal. But for some inexplicable reason we could, and it was the language we used to speak the unspoken and the unspeakable.

I can't do this. I'm not going.

I gave up on my tie and sat back down on my bed, the ancient mattress springs crying out beneath me.

You have to go. You won't forgive yourself if you don't.

For a second, she didn't respond.

You don't know how it feels.

I do.

I remembered when I was the one sitting on my bed afraid to get up, afraid to put on my suit and join the prayer circle and sing *Abide With Me* and ride in the grim parade of headlights through town to the cemetery to bury my mother. I was afraid it would make it real. I couldn't stand to think about it, but I opened my mind and showed Lena....

You can't go, but you don't have a choice, because Amma puts her hand on your arm and leads you into the car, into the pew, into the pity parade. Even though it hurts to move, like your whole body aches from some kind of fever. Your eyes stop on the mumbling faces in front of you, but you can't actually hear what anyone is saying. Not over the screaming in your head. So you let them put their hand on your arm, you get in the car, and it happens. Because you can make it through this if someone says you can.

I put my head in my hands.

Ethan—

I'm saying you can, L.

I shoved my fists into my eyes, and they were wet. I flipped on my light and stared at the bare bulb, refusing to blink until I seared away the tears.

Ethan, I'm scared.

I'm right here. I'm not going anywhere.

There weren't any more words as I went back to fumbling with my tie, but I could feel Lena there, as if she was sitting in the corner of my room. The house seemed empty with my father gone, and I heard Amma in the hall. A second later, she was standing quietly in the doorway clutching her good purse. Her dark eyes searched mine, and her tiny frame seemed tall, though she didn't even reach my shoulder. She was the grandmother I never had, and the only mother I had left now.

I stared at the empty chair next to my window, where she had laid out my good suit a little less than a year ago, then back into the bare lightbulb of my bedside lamp.

Amma held out her hand, and I handed her my tie. Sometimes it felt like Lena wasn't the only one who could read my mind.

I offered Amma my arm as we made our way up the muddy hill to His Garden of Perpetual Peace. The sky was dark, and the rain started before we reached the top of the rise. Amma was in her most respectable funeral dress, with a wide hat that shielded most of her face from the rain, except for the bit of white lace collar escaping beneath the brim. It was fastened at the neck with her best cameo, a sign of respect. I had seen it all last April, just as I had felt her good gloves on my arm, supporting me up this hill once before. This time I couldn't tell which one of us was doing the supporting.

I still wasn't sure why Macon wanted to be buried in the Gatlin cemetery, considering the way folks in this town felt about him. But according to Gramma, Lena's grandmother, Macon left strict instructions specifically requesting to be buried here. He purchased the plot himself, years ago. Lena's family hadn't seemed happy about it, but Gramma had put her foot down. They were going to respect his wishes, like any good Southern family.

Lena? I'm here.

I know.

I could feel my voice calming her, as if I had wrapped my arms around her. I looked up the hill, where the awning for the graveside service would be. It would look the same as any other Gatlin funeral, which was ironic, considering it was Macon's.

It wasn't yet daylight, and I could barely make out a few shapes in the distance. They were all crooked, all different. The ancient, uneven rows of tiny headstones standing at the graves of children, the overgrown family crypts, the crumbling white obelisks honoring fallen Confederate soldiers, marked with small brass crosses. Even General Jubal A. Early, whose statue watched over the General's Green in the center of town, was buried here. We made our way around the family plot of a few lesser-known Moultries, which had been there for so long the smooth magnolia trunk at the edge of the plot had grown into the side of the tallest stone marker, making them indistinguishable.

And sacred. They were all sacred, which meant we had reached the oldest part of the graveyard. I knew from my mother, the first word carved into any old headstone in Gatlin was *Sacred*. But as we got closer and my eyes adjusted to the darkness, I knew where the muddy gravel path was leading. I remembered where it passed the stone memorial bench at the grassy slope, dotted with magnolias. I remembered my father sitting on that bench, unable to speak or move.

My feet wouldn't go any farther, because they had figured out the same thing I had. Macon's Garden of Perpetual Peace was only a magnolia away from my mother's.

The twisting roads run straight between us.

It was a sappy line from an even sappier poem I had written Lena for Valentine's Day. But here in the graveyard, it was true. Who would have thought our parents, or the closest thing Lena had to one, would be neighbors in the grave?

Amma took my hand, leading me to Macon's massive plot. "Steady now."

We stepped inside the waist-high black railing around his gravesite, which in Gatlin was reserved for the perimeters of only the best plots, like a white picket fence for the dead. Sometimes it actually was a white picket fence. This one was wrought iron, the crooked door shoved open into the overgrown grass. Macon's plot seemed to carry with it an atmosphere of its own, like Macon himself.

Inside the railing stood Lena's family: Gramma, Aunt Del, Uncle Barclay, Reece, Ryan, and Macon's mother, Arelia, under the black canopy on one side of the carved black casket. On the other side, a group of men and a woman in a long black coat kept their distance from both the casket and the canopy, standing shoulder to shoulder in the rain. They were all bone-dry. It was like a church wedding split by an aisle down the middle, where the relatives of the bride line up opposite the relatives of the groom like two warring clans. There was an old man at one end of the casket, standing next to Lena. Amma and I stood at the other end, just inside the canopy.

Amma's grip on my arm tightened, and she pulled the gold charm she always wore out from underneath her blouse and rubbed it between her fingers. Amma was more than superstitious. She was a Seer, from generations of women who read tarot cards and communed with spirits, and Amma had a charm or a doll for everything. This one was for protection. I stared at the Incubuses in front of us, the rain running off their shoulders without leaving a trace. I hoped they were the kind that only fed on dreams.

I tried to look away, but it wasn't easy. There was something about an Incubus that drew you in like a spider's web, like any good predator. In the dark, you couldn't see their black eyes, and they almost looked like a bunch of regular guys. A few of them were dressed the way Macon always had, dark suits and expensive-looking overcoats. One or two looked more like construction workers on their way to get a beer after work, in jeans and work boots, their hands shoved in the pockets of their jackets. The woman was probably a Succubus. I had read about them, mostly in comics, and I thought they were just old wives' tales, like werewolves. But I knew I was wrong because she was standing in the rain, dry as the rest of them.

The Incubuses were a sharp contrast to Lena's family, cloaked in iridescent black fabric that caught what little light there was and refracted it, as if they were the source themselves. I had never seen them like this before. It was a strange sight, especially considering the strict dress code for women at Southern funerals.

In the center of it all was Lena. The way she looked was the opposite of magical. She stood in front of the casket with her fingers quietly resting upon it, as if Macon was somehow holding her hand. She was dressed in the same shimmering material as the rest of her family, but it hung on her like a shadow. Her black hair was twisted into a tight knot, not a trademark curl in sight. She looked broken and out of place, like she was standing on the wrong side of the aisle.

Like she belonged with Macon's other family, standing in the rain.

Lena?

She lifted her head, and her eyes met mine. Since her birthday, when one of her eyes had turned a shade of gold while the other remained deep green, the colors had combined to create a shade unlike anything I'd ever seen. Almost hazel at times, and unnaturally golden at others. Now they looked more hazel, dull and pained. I couldn't stand it. I wanted to pick her up and carry her away.

I can get the Volvo, and we can drive down the coast all the way to Savannah. We can hide out at my Aunt Caroline's.

I took another step closer to her. Her family was crowded around the casket, and I couldn't get to Lena without walking past the line of Incubuses, but I didn't care.

Ethan, stop! It's not safe—

A tall Incubus with a scar running down the length of his face, like the mark of a savage animal attack, turned his head to look at me. The air seemed to ripple through the space between us, like I had chucked a stone into a lake. It hit me, knocking the wind out of my lungs as if I'd been punched, but I couldn't react because I felt paralyzed—my limbs numb and useless.

Ethan!

Amma's eyes narrowed, but before she could take a step the Succubus put her hand on Scarface's shoulder and squeezed it, almost imperceptibly. Instantly, I was released from his hold, and the blood rushed back into my limbs. Amma gave her a grateful nod, but the woman with the long hair and the longer coat ignored her, disappearing back into line with the rest of them.

The Incubus with the brutal scar turned and winked at me. I got the message, even without the words. *See you in your dreams.*

I was still holding my breath when a white-haired gentleman, in an old-fashioned suit and string tie, stepped up to the coffin. His eyes were a dark contrast to his hair, which made him seem like some creepy character from an old black and white movie.

"The Gravecaster," Amma whispered. He looked more like the gravedigger.

He touched the smooth black wood, and a carved crest on the top of the coffin began to glow with a golden light. It looked like some old coat of arms, the kind of thing you saw at a museum or in a castle. I saw a tree with great spreading boughs, and a bird. Beneath it there was a carved sun, and a crescent moon.

"Macon Ravenwood of the House of Ravenwood, of Raven and Oak, Air and Earth. Darkness and Light." He took his

12

hand from the coffin, and the light followed, leaving the casket dark again.

"Is that Macon?" I whispered to Amma.

"The light's symbolic. There's nothin' in that box. Wasn't anythin' left to bury. That's the way with Macon's kind — ashes to ashes and dust to dust, like us. Just a whole lot quicker."

The Gravecaster's voice rose up again. "Who consecrates this soul into the Otherworld?"

Lena's family stepped forward. "We do," they said in unison, everyone except Lena. She stood there staring down at the dirt.

"As do we." The Incubuses moved closer to the casket.

"Then let him be Cast to the world beyond. *Redi in pace, ad Ignem Atrum ex quo venisti.*" The Gravecaster held the light high over his head, and it flared brighter. "Go in peace, back to the Dark Fire from where you came." He threw the light into the air, and sparks showered down onto the coffin, searing into the wood where they fell. As if on cue, Lena's family and the Incubuses threw their hands into the air, releasing tiny silver objects not much bigger than quarters, which rained down onto Macon's coffin amidst the gold flames. The sky was starting to change color, from the black of night to the blue before the sunrise. I strained to see what the objects were, but it was too dark.

"*His dictis, solutus est.* With these words, he is free."

An almost blinding white light emanated from the casket. I could barely see the Gravecaster a few feet in front of me, as if his voice was transporting us and we were no longer standing over a gravesite in Gatlin.

Uncle Macon! No!

The light flashed, like lightning striking, and died out. We were all back in the circle, looking at a mound of dirt and flowers. The burial was over. The coffin was gone. Aunt Del put her arms protectively around Reece and Ryan.

Macon was gone.

Lena fell forward onto her knees in the muddy grass.

The gate around Macon's plot slammed shut behind her, without so much as a finger touching it. This wasn't over for her. No one was going anywhere.

Lena?

The rain started to pick up almost immediately, the weather still tethered to her powers as a Natural, the ultimate elemental in the Caster world. She pulled herself to her feet.

Lena! This isn't going to change anything!

The air filled with hundreds of cheap white carnations and plastic flowers and palmetto fronds and flags from every grave visited in the last month, all flying loose in the air, tumbling airborne down the hill. Fifty years from now, folks in town would still be talking about the day the wind almost blew down every magnolia in His Garden of Perpetual Peace. The gale came on so fierce and fast, it was a slap in the face to everyone there, a hit so hard you had to stagger to stay on your feet. Only Lena stood straight and tall, holding fast to the stone marker next to her. Her hair had unraveled from its awkward knot and whipped in the air around her. She was no longer all darkness and shadow. She was the opposite—the one bright spot in the storm, as if the yellowish-gold lightning splitting the sky above us was emanating from her body. Boo Radley, Macon's dog, whimpered and flattened his ears at Lena's feet.

He wouldn't want this, L.

Lena put her face in her hands, and a sudden gust blew the

14

canopy out from where it was staked in the wet earth, sending it tumbling backward down the hill.

Gramma stepped in front of Lena, closed her eyes, and touched a single finger to her granddaughter's cheek. The moment she touched Lena, everything stopped, and I knew Gramma had used her abilities as an Empath to absorb Lena's powers temporarily. But she couldn't absorb Lena's anger. None of us were strong enough to do that.

The wind died down, and the rain slowed to a drizzle. Gramma pulled her hand away from Lena and opened her eyes.

The Succubus, looking unusually disheveled, stared up at the sky. "It's almost sunrise." The sun was beginning to burn its way up through the clouds and over the horizon, scattering odd splinters of light and life across the uneven rows of headstones. Nothing else had to be said. The Incubuses started to dematerialize, the sound of suction filling the air. Ripping was how I thought of it, the way they pulled open the sky and disappeared.

I started to walk toward Lena, but Amma yanked my arm. "What? They're gone."

"Not all a them. Look—"

She was right. At the edge of the plot, there was only one Incubus remaining, leaning against a weathered headstone adorned with a weeping angel. He looked older than I was, maybe nineteen, with short, black hair and the same pale skin as the rest of his kind. But unlike the other Incubuses, he hadn't disappeared before the dawn. As I watched him, he moved out from under the shadow of the oak directly into the bright morning light, with his eyes closed and his face tilted toward the sun, as if it was only shining for him.

15

Amma was wrong. He couldn't be one of them. He stood there basking in the sunlight, an impossibility for an Incubus.

What was he? And what was he doing here?

He moved closer and caught my eye, as if he could feel me watching him. That's when I saw his eyes. They weren't the black eyes of an Incubus.

They were Caster green.

He stopped in front of Lena, jamming his hands in his pockets, tipping his head slightly. Not a bow, but an awkward show of deference, which somehow seemed more honest. He had crossed the invisible aisle, and in a moment of real Southern gentility, he could have been the son of Macon Ravenwood himself. Which made me hate him.

"I'm sorry for your loss."

He opened her hand and placed a small silver object in it, like the ones everyone had thrown onto Macon's casket. Her fingers closed around it. Before I could move a muscle, the unmistakable ripping sound tore through the air, and he was gone.

Ethan?

I saw her legs begin to buckle under the weight of the morning—the loss, the storm, even the final rip in the sky. By the time I made it to her side and slid my arm under her, she was gone, too. I carried her down the sloping hill, away from Macon and the cemetery.

She slept curled in my bed, on and off, for a night and a day. She had a few stray twigs matted in her hair, and her face was still flecked with mud, but she wouldn't go home to Ravenwood, and no one asked her to. I had given her my oldest, softest sweatshirt and wrapped her in our thickest patchwork quilt, but she never stopped shivering, even in her sleep. Boo lay at her feet, and Amma appeared in the doorway every now and then. I sat in the chair by the window, the one I never sat in, and stared out at the sky. I couldn't open it, because a storm was still brewing.

As Lena was sleeping, her fingers uncurled. In them was a tiny bird made of silver, a sparrow. A gift from the stranger at Macon's funeral. I tried to take it from her hand just as her fingers tightened around it.

Two months later, and I still couldn't look at a bird without hearing the sound of the sky ripping open.

⊰ 4.17 ⊱

Burnt Waffles

Four eggs, four strips of bacon, a basket of scratch biscuits (which by Amma's standard meant a spoon had never touched the batter), three kinds of freezer jam, and a slab of butter drizzled with honey. And from the smell of it, across the counter buttermilk batter was separating into squares, turning crisp in the old waffle iron. For the last two months, Amma had been cooking night and day. The counter was piled high with Pyrex dishes—cheese grits, green bean casserole, fried chicken, and of course, Bing cherry salad, which was really a fancy name for a Jell-O mold with cherries, pineapple, and Coca-Cola in it. Past that, I could make out a coconut cake, orange rolls, and what looked like bourbon bread pudding, but I knew there was more. Since Macon died and my dad left, Amma kept cooking and baking and stacking, as if she could cook her sadness away. We both knew she couldn't.

Amma hadn't gone this dark since my mom died. She'd known Macon Ravenwood a lifetime longer than I had, even longer than Lena. No matter how unlikely or unpredictable their relationship was, it had meant something to both of them. They were friends, though I wasn't sure either of them would've admitted it. But I knew the truth. Amma was wearing it all over her face and stacking it all over our kitchen.

"Got a call from Dr. Summers." My dad's psychiatrist. Amma didn't look up from the waffle iron, and I didn't point out that you didn't actually need to stare at a waffle iron for it to cook the waffles.

"What'd he say?" I studied her back from my seat at the old oak table, her apron strings tied in the middle. I remembered how many times I had tried to sneak up on her and untie those strings. Amma was so short they hung down almost as long as the apron itself, and I thought about that for as long as I could. Anything was better than thinking about my father.

"He thinks your daddy's about ready to come home."

I held up my empty glass and stared through it, where things looked as distorted as they really were. My dad had been at Blue Horizons, in Columbia, for two months. After Amma found out about the nonexistent book he was pretending to write all year, and the "incident," which is how she referred to my dad nearly jumping off a balcony, she called my Aunt Caroline. My aunt drove him to Blue Horizons that same day—she called it a spa. The kind of spa you sent your crazy relatives to if they needed what folks in Gatlin referred to as "individual attention," or what everyone outside of the South would call therapy.

"Great."

19

Great. I couldn't see my dad coming home to Gatlin, walking around town in his duck pajamas. There was enough crazy around here already between Amma and me, wedged in between the cream-of-grief casseroles I'd be dropping off at First Methodist around dinnertime, as I did almost every night. I wasn't an expert on feelings, but Amma's were all stirred up in cake batter, and she wasn't about to share them. She'd rather give away the cake.

I tried to talk to her about it once, the day after the funeral, but she had shut down the conversation before it even started. "Done is done. Gone is gone. Where Macon Ravenwood is now, not likely we'll ever see him again, not in this world or the Other." She sounded like she'd made her peace with it, but here I was, two months later, still delivering cakes and casseroles. She had lost the two men in her life the same night—my father and Macon. My dad wasn't dead, but our kitchen didn't make those kinds of distinctions. Like Amma said, gone was gone.

"I'm makin' waffles. Hope you're hungry."

That was probably all I'd hear from her this morning. I picked up the carton of chocolate milk next to my glass and poured it full out of habit. Amma used to complain when I drank chocolate milk at breakfast. Now she would have cut me up a whole Tunnel of Fudge cake without a word, which only made me feel worse. Even more telling, the Sunday edition of the *New York Times* wasn't open to the crossword, and her black, extra-sharp #2 pencils were hidden away in their drawer. Amma was staring out the kitchen window at the clouds choking the sky.

L. A. C. O. N. I. C. Seven across, which means I don't have to say a thing, Ethan Wate. That's what Amma would have said on any other day.

I took a gulp of my chocolate milk and almost choked. Sugar was too sweet, and Amma was too quiet. That's how I knew things had changed.

That, and the burnt waffles smoking in the waffle iron.

I should have been on my way to school, but instead I turned onto Route 9 and headed for Ravenwood. Lena hadn't been back to school since before her birthday. After Macon's death, Principal Harper had *generously* granted her permission to work at home with a tutor until she felt up to coming back to Jackson. Considering he had helped Mrs. Lincoln in her campaign to get Lena expelled after the winter formal, I'm sure he was hoping that would be the day after never.

I admit, I was a little jealous. Lena didn't have to listen to Mr. Lee drone on about the War of Northern Aggression and the plight of the Confederacy or sit on the Good-Eye Side in English. Abby Porter and I were the only ones sitting there now, so we had to answer all the *Dr. Jekyll and Mr. Hyde* questions in class. What prompts Dr. Jekyll to turn into Mr. Hyde? Were they really any different after all? Nobody had the slightest clue, which was the reason everyone on Mrs. English's glass-eye side was sleeping.

But Jackson wasn't the same without Lena, at least not for me. That's why after two months, I was begging her to come back. Yesterday, when she said she'd think about it, I told her she could think about it on the way to school.

I found myself back at the fork in the road. It was our old road, mine and Lena's. The one that had taken me off Route 9 and up to Ravenwood the night we met. The first time I realized she was the same girl I'd been dreaming about, long before she ever moved to Gatlin.

As soon as I saw the road, I heard the song. It drifted into the Volvo as naturally as if I had turned on the radio. Same song. Same words. Same as it had for the last two months — when I turned on my iPod, stared at the ceiling, or read a single page of *Silver Surfer* over and over, without even seeing it.

Seventeen Moons. It was always there. I tried turning the dials on the radio, but it didn't matter. Now it was playing in my head instead of coming out of the speakers, as if someone was Kelting the song to me.

> *Seventeen moons, seventeen years,*
> *Eyes where Dark or Light appears,*
> *Gold for yes and green for no,*
> *Seventeen the last to know...*

The song was gone. I knew better than to ignore it, but I also knew how Lena acted every time I tried to bring it up.

"It's a song," she would say dismissively. "It doesn't mean anything."

"Like *Sixteen Moons* didn't mean anything? It's about us." It didn't matter if she knew it or even if she agreed. Either way, it was the moment Lena usually switched from defense to offense, and the conversation veered off track.

"You mean it's about me. Dark or Light? Whether or not I'm going to go all Sarafine on you? If you've already decided I'm going Dark, why don't you admit it?"

At that point, I would say something stupid to change the

subject. Until I learned not to say anything at all. So we didn't talk about the song that was playing in my head, same as it was in hers.

Seventeen Moons. We couldn't avoid it.

The song had to be about Lena's Claiming, the moment she would become Light or Dark forever. Which could only mean one thing: she wasn't Claimed. Not yet. Gold for yes and green for no? I knew what the song meant—the gold eyes of a Dark Caster or the green eyes of a Light one. Since the night of Lena's birthday, her Sixteenth Moon, I had tried to tell myself it was all over, that Lena didn't have to be Claimed, that she was some kind of exception. Why couldn't it be different for her, since everything else about her seemed to be so exceptional?

But it wasn't different. *Seventeen Moons* was proof. I'd heard *Sixteen Moons* for months before Lena's birthday, a harbinger of things to come. Now the words had changed again, and I was faced with another eerie prophecy. There was a choice to be made, and Lena hadn't made it. The songs never lied. At least, they hadn't yet.

I didn't want to think about it. As I headed up the long rise leading to the gates of Ravenwood Manor, even the grinding sound of the tires on gravel seemed to repeat the one inescapable truth. If there was a Seventeenth Moon, then it had all been for nothing. Macon's death had been for nothing.

Lena would still have to Claim herself for Light or Dark, deciding her fate forever. There was no turning back for Casters, no changing sides. And when she finally made her choice, half her family would die because of it. The Light Casters or the Dark Casters—the curse promised only one side could survive. But in a family where generations of Casters had no free will

23

and had been Claimed for Light or Dark on their own sixteenth birthdays without any say in the matter, how was Lena supposed to make that kind of choice?

All she had wanted, her whole life, was to choose her own destiny. Now she could, and it was like some kind of cruel cosmic joke.

I stopped at the gates, turned off the engine, and closed my eyes, remembering—the rising panic, the visions, the dreams, the song. This time, Macon wouldn't be there to steal away the unhappy endings. There was nobody left to get us out of trouble, and it was coming fast.

⊰ 4.17 ⊱

Lemons and Ash

When I pulled up in front of Ravenwood, Lena was sitting on the crumbling veranda, waiting. She was wearing an old button-down shirt and jeans and her beat-up Chuck Taylors. For a second, it seemed as if it could've been three months ago and today was just another day. But she was also wearing one of Macon's pinstriped vests, and it wasn't the same. Now that Macon was gone, something about Ravenwood felt wrong. Like going to the Gatlin County Library if Marian, its only librarian, wasn't there, or to the DAR without the most important daughter of the Daughters of the American Revolution herself, Mrs. Lincoln. Or to my parents' study without my mom.

Ravenwood looked worse every time I came. Staring out at the archway of weeping willows, it was hard to imagine the garden had deteriorated so quickly. Beds of the same kinds of flowers Amma had painstakingly taught me to weed as a kid were fighting for space in the dry earth. Beneath the magnolias, clusters of hyacinth were tangled with hibiscus, and heliotrope infested the forget-me-nots, as if the garden itself was in mourning. Which was entirely possible. Ravenwood Manor had always seemed to have a mind of its own. Why should the gardens be any different? The weight of Lena's grief probably wasn't helping. The house was a mirror for her moods, the same way it had always been for Macon's.

When he died, he left Ravenwood to Lena, and sometimes I wondered whether it would have been better if he hadn't. The house was looking bleaker by the day, instead of better. Every time I drove up the hill, I found myself holding my breath, waiting for the smallest sign of life, something new, something blooming. Every time I reached the top, all I saw were more bare branches.

Lena climbed into the Volvo, a complaint already on her lips. "I don't want to go."

"No one *wants* to go to school."

"You know what I mean. That place is awful. I'd rather stay here and study Latin all day."

This wasn't going to be easy. How could I convince her to go somewhere I didn't even want to go? High school sucked. It was a universal truth, and whoever said these were supposed to be the best years of your life was probably drunk or delusional. I decided reverse psychology was my only shot. "High school is supposed to be the worst years of your life."

"Is that so?"

"Definitely. You have to come back."

"And that will make me feel better how, exactly?"

"I don't know. How about, it's so bad, it'll make the rest of your life seem great in comparison?"

"By your logic, I should spend the day with Principal Harper."

"Or try out for cheerleading."

She twirled her necklace around her finger, her distinctive collection of charms knocking against each other. "It's tempting." She smiled, almost a laugh, and I knew she was going with me.

Lena rested her shoulder against mine the whole way to school. But when we got to the parking lot, she couldn't bring herself to get out of the car. I didn't dare turn off the engine.

Savannah Snow, the queen of Jackson High, walked past us, hitching her tight T-shirt above her jeans. Emily Asher, her second in command, followed behind, texting as she slid between cars. Emily saw us and grabbed Savannah by the arm. They stopped, the response of any Gatlin girl whose mamma had raised her right, when faced with a relative of the recently departed. Savannah clutched her books to her chest, shaking her head at us sadly. It was like watching an old silent movie.

Your uncle's in a better place now, Lena. He's up at the pearly gates, where a chorus a angels is leadin' him to his everlovin' Maker.

I translated for Lena, but she already knew what they were thinking.

Stop it!

Lena slid her battered spiral notebook in front of her face, trying to disappear. Emily held up her hand, a timid half-wave. Giving us our space, letting us know she was not only well bred but *sensitive.* I didn't have to be a mind reader to know what she was thinking either.

I'm not comin' over there, because I'm a lettin' you grieve in

27

peace, sweet Lena Du-channes. But I will always, and I do mean always, be here for you, like the Good Book and my mamma taught me.

Emily nodded to Savannah, and the two of them walked slowly and sadly away, as if they hadn't started the Guardian Angels, Jackson's version of a neighborhood watch, a few months ago with the sole purpose of getting Lena kicked out of school. In a way, this was worse. Emory ran to catch up with them, but he saw us and slowed to a somber walk, rapping on the hood of my car as he walked by. He hadn't said a word to me in months, but now he was showing his support. They were all so full of crap.

"Don't say it." Lena had rolled herself down into a ball in the passenger's seat.

"Can't believe he didn't take off his cap. His mamma's gonna kick the tar outta him when he gets home." I turned off the engine. "Play this right and you might make the cheer squad after all, sweet Lena Du-channes."

"They're . . . they're such—" She was so angry for a minute I regretted saying it. But it was going to be happening all day, and I wanted her to be prepared before she set foot in the halls of Jackson. I had spent too much time being *Poor Ethan Wate Whose Mamma Died Just Last Year* not to know that.

"Hypocrites?" That was an understatement.

"Sheep." That, too. "I don't want to be in their squad, and I don't want a seat at their table. I don't want them to even look at me. I know Ridley was manipulating them with her powers, but if they hadn't thrown that party on my birthday—if I had stayed inside Ravenwood like Uncle Macon had wanted . . ." I didn't need her to finish. He might still be alive.

"You can't know that, L. Sarafine would have found another way to get to you."

"They hate me, and that's how it should be." Her hair was beginning to curl, and for a second I thought there was going to be a downpour. She put her head in her hands, ignoring the tears that were losing themselves in her crazy hair. "Something has to stay the same. I'm nothing like them."

"I hate to break it to you, but you never were, and you never will be."

"I know, but something's changed. Everything's changed."

I looked out my window. "Not everything."

Boo Radley stared back at me. He was sitting on the faded white line of the parking space next to ours, as if he had been waiting for this moment. Boo still followed Lena everywhere, like a good Caster dog. I thought about how many times I had considered giving that dog a ride. Saving him some time. I opened the door, but Boo didn't move.

"Fine. Be that way." I started to pull the door closed, knowing Boo would never get in. As I did, he leaped up into my lap, across the gearshift, and into Lena's arms. She buried her face in his fur, breathing deeply, as if the mangy dog created some kind of air that was different from the air outside.

They were one quivering mass of black hair and black fur. For a minute, the whole universe seemed fragile, like it could fall apart if I so much as blew in the wrong direction or pulled the wrong thread.

I knew what I needed to do. I couldn't explain the feeling, but it came over me as powerfully as the dreams had, when I saw Lena for the first time. The dreams we had always shared, so real they left mud in my sheets, or river water dripping onto my floor. This feeling was no different.

I needed to know what thread to pull. I needed to be the one who knew the right direction. She couldn't see her way clear of where she was right now, so it had to be me.

Lost. That's what she was, and it was the one thing I couldn't let her be.

I turned on the car and shifted into reverse. We had only made it as far as the parking lot, and I knew without a word that it was time to drive Lena home. Boo kept his eyes closed the whole way.

We took an old blanket back to Greenbrier and curled up near Genevieve's grave, on a tiny patch of grass next to the hearthstone and the crumbling rock wall. The blackened trees and meadows surrounded us on every side, tufts of green only beginning to push through the hard dirt. Even now it was still our spot, the place where we had first talked after Lena shattered the window in English class with a look—and her Caster powers. Aunt Del couldn't stand to see the burnt cemetery and ruined gardens anymore, but Lena didn't mind. This was the last place she had seen Macon, and that made it safe. Somehow, looking at the wreckage from the fire was familiar, even reassuring. It had come and taken everything in its path, and then it was gone. You didn't have to wonder what else was coming or when it would get here.

The grass was wet and green, and I wrapped the blanket around us. "Come closer, you're freezing." She smiled without looking at me.

"Since when do I need a reason to come closer?" She settled back into my shoulder and we sat in silence, our bodies warming each other and our fingers braided together, the shock moving up my arm. It was always that way when we touched—a gentle jolt of electricity that intensified with our every touch. A reminder Casters and Mortals couldn't be together. Not without the Mortal ending up dead.

I looked up at the twisted black branches and the bleak sky. I thought about the first day I followed Lena to this garden, the way I'd found her crying in the tall grass. We had watched the gray clouds disappear from an otherwise blue sky, clouds she moved just by thinking about them. The blue sky—that's what I was to her. She was Hurricane Lena, and I was regular old Ethan Wate. I couldn't imagine what my life would be like without her.

"Look." Lena climbed over me and reached up into the crumbling black branches.

A perfect yellow lemon, the only one in the garden, surrounded by ash. Lena pulled it loose, and black flakes flew into the air. The yellow peel gleamed in her hand, and she let herself fall back into my arms. "Look at that. Not everything burned."

"It'll all grow back, L."

"I know." She didn't sound convinced, turning the lemon over and over in her hands.

"This time next year, none of this will be black." She looked up at the branches and the sky above our heads, and I kissed her on her forehead, her nose, the perfect crescent-shaped birthmark on her cheekbone, as she tilted up toward me. "Everything will be green. Even these trees will grow again." As we pushed our feet against each other, kicking off our shoes, I could feel a familiar prick of electricity every time our bare skin met. We were so close, her curls were falling into my face. I blew, and they scattered.

I was caught in her drag, struck by the current that bound us together and kept us apart. I leaned in to kiss her mouth, and she held the lemon in front of my nose, teasing. "Smell."

"Smells like you." Like lemons and rosemary, the scent that had drawn me to Lena when we first met.

She sniffed it, making a face. "Sour, like me."

"You don't taste sour to me." I pulled her closer, until our hair was full of ash and grass, and the bitter lemon was lost somewhere beneath our feet at the bottom of the blanket. The heat was on my skin, like fire. Even though all I could feel was a biting cold whenever I held her hand lately, when we kissed—really kissed—there was nothing but heat. I loved her, atom by atom, one burning cell at a time. We kissed until my heart began skipping beats, and the edges of what I could see and feel and hear began to fade into darkness....

Lena pushed me away, for my own good, and we lay in the grass as I tried to catch my breath.

Are you okay?

I'm—I'm good.

I wasn't, but I didn't say anything. I thought I smelled something burning and realized it was the blanket. It was smoldering from underneath, where it was touching the ground.

Lena pushed herself up and pulled back the blanket. The grass beneath us was charred and trampled. "Ethan. Look at the grass."

"What about it?" I was still trying to catch my breath, but I was trying not to show it. Since Lena's birthday, things had only gotten worse, physically. I couldn't stop touching her, though sometimes I couldn't stand the pain of that touch.

"It's burnt now, too."

"That's weird."

She looked at me evenly, her eyes strangely dark and bright at the same time. She tossed the grass. "It was me."

"You are pretty hot."

"You can't be joking right now. It's getting worse." We sat next to each other, looking out at what was left of Greenbrier. But we weren't really looking at Greenbrier. We were looking at the power of the other fire. "Just like my mom." She sounded bitter.

Fire was the trademark of a Cataclyst, and Sarafine's fire had burnt every inch of these fields the night of Lena's birthday. Now Lena was starting fires unintentionally. My stomach tightened.

"The grass will grow back, too."

"What if I don't want it to?" she said softly, strangely, as she let another handful of charred grass fall through her fingers.

"What?"

"Why should it?"

"Because life goes on, L. The birds do their thing, and the bees do theirs. Seeds get scattered, and everything grows back."

"Then it all gets burnt again. If you're lucky enough to be around me."

There was no point arguing with Lena when she was in one of these moods. A lifetime with Amma going dark had taught me that. "Sometimes it does."

She pulled her knees up and rested her chin on them. Her shape cast a shadow much larger than she actually was.

"But I'm still lucky." I moved my leg until it caught the light, throwing a long line of my shadow into hers.

We sat like that, side by side, with only our shadows touching, until the sun went down and they stretched toward the black trees and disappeared into dusk. We listened to the cicadas in silence and tried not to think until the rain started falling again.

Falling

In the next few weeks, I successfully convinced Lena to leave the house with me a total of three times. Once to the movies with Link—my best friend since second grade—where even her signature combination of popcorn and Milk Duds didn't cheer her up. Once to my house to eat Amma's molasses cookies and watch a zombie marathon, my version of a dream date. It wasn't. And once for a walk along the Santee, where we ended up turning around after ten minutes with sixty bug bites between us. Wherever she was, she didn't want to be.

Today was different. She had finally found somewhere she was comfortable, even if it was the last place I expected.

I walked in her room to find her lying sprawled across the ceiling, arms flung across the plaster, her hair spread out like a black fan around her head.

"Since when can you do that?" I was used to Lena's powers

by now, but since her sixteenth birthday they seemed to be getting stronger and wilder, as if she was awkwardly growing into herself as a Caster. With every day, Lena the Caster girl was more unpredictable, stretching her powers to see what she could do. As it turned out, what she could do these days was cause all kinds of trouble.

Like the time Link and I were driving to school in the Beater, and one of his songs came on the radio as if the station was playing it. Link was so shocked he'd swerved a good two feet into Mrs. Asher's front hedge. "An accident," Lena said with a crooked smile. "One of Link's songs was stuck in my head." Nobody had ever gotten one of Link's songs stuck in their head. But Link had believed her, which made his ego even more unbearable. "What can I say? I have that effect on the ladies. This voice is as smooth as butter."

A week after that, Link and I had been walking down the hall, and Lena came up and gave me a big hug, right as the bell was ringing. I figured she had finally decided to come back to school. But she wasn't actually there at all. It was some kind of projection, or whatever the Caster word was for making your boyfriend look like an idiot. Link thought I was trying to hug him, so he called me "Lover Boy" for days. "I missed you. Is that such a crime?" Lena thought it was funny, but I was starting to wish Gramma would step in and ground her, or whatever it was you did to a Natural who was up to no good.

Don't be a baby. I said I was sorry, didn't I?

You're as big a menace as Link in fifth grade, the year he sucked all the juice out of my mom's tomatoes with a straw.

It won't happen again. I swear.

That's what Link said back then.

But he stopped, right?

Yeah. When we stopped growing tomatoes.

"Come down."

"I like it better up here."

I grabbed her hand. A current crept through my arm, but I didn't let go, pulling her down onto the bed next to me.

"Ouch." She was laughing. I could see her shoulder shudder even though her back was to me. Or maybe she wasn't laughing but crying, which was rare these days. The crying had mostly stopped and had been replaced by something worse. Nothing.

Nothing was deceptive. Nothing was much harder to describe or fix or stop.

Do you want to talk about it, L?

About what?

I pulled her closer, resting my head on hers. The shaking slowed, and I held her as tight as I could. Like she was still on the ceiling, and I was the one hanging on.

Nothing.

I shouldn't have complained about the ceiling. There were crazier places you could hang out. Like where we were now.

"I have a bad feeling about this." I was sweating, but I couldn't wipe my face. I needed my hands to stay right where they were.

"That's weird." Lena smiled down at me. "Because I have a very good feeling about it." Her hair was blowing in a breeze, though I wasn't sure which kind. "Besides, we're almost there."

"You realize this is insane, right? If a cop drives by, we're gonna get arrested or sent to Blue Horizons to visit my dad."

"It's not crazy. It's romantic. Couples come here all the time."

"When people go to the water tower, L, they aren't talking about the *top* of the water tower." Which is where we would be in a minute. Just the two of us, a wobbly iron ladder about a hundred feet above the ground, and a bright blue Carolina sky.

I tried not to look down.

Lena had talked me into climbing to the top. There was something about the excitement in her voice that made me go along with it, as if something so stupid might be able to make her feel the way she did the last time we were here. Smiling, happy, in a red sweater. I remembered, because there was a piece of red yarn hanging from her charm necklace.

She must have remembered, too. So here we were, stuck on a ladder, looking up so we didn't look down.

Once we reached the top and I looked out at the view, I understood. Lena was right. It was better up here. Everything was so far away that it didn't even matter.

I let my legs dangle over the edge. "My mom used to collect pictures of old water towers."

"Yeah?"

"Like the Sisters collect spoons. Only for my mom, it was water towers and postcards from the World's Fair."

"I thought all water towers looked like this one. Like a big white spider."

"Somewhere in Illinois, there's one shaped like a ketchup bottle."

She laughed.

"And there's one that looks like a little house, this high off the ground."

"We should live there. I'd go up once and never come back down." She lay back on the warm white paint. "I guess in Gatlin it should be a peach, a big old Gatlin peach."

I leaned back next to her. "They already have one, but it's not in Gatlin. It's over in Gaffney. Guess they thought of it first."

"What about a pie? We could paint this tank to look like one of Amma's pies. She'd like that."

"Haven't seen one of those. But my mom had a picture of one shaped like a corncob."

"I'd still rather have the house." Lena stared up at the sky, where there wasn't a cloud in sight.

"I'd take the corncob or the ketchup, if you were there."

She reached for my hand and we stayed like that, at the edge of Summerville's plain white water tower, looking out at Gatlin County as if it was a tiny toy land full of tiny toy people. As small as the cardboard village my mom used to keep under our Christmas tree.

How could people that small have any problems at all?

"Hey, I brought you something." I watched as she sat up, looking at me like a little kid.

"What is it?"

I looked over the edge of the water tower. "Maybe we should wait until we can't fall to our deaths."

"We're not going to die. Don't be such a chicken."

I reached into my back pocket. It wasn't anything special, but I'd had it for a while now, and I was hoping it might help her find her way back to herself.

I pulled out a mini Sharpie, with a key ring on it.

"See? It fits on your necklace, like this." Trying not to fall, I reached for Lena's necklace, the one she never took off. A tangle of charms, each one meant something to her—the flattened penny from the machine at the Cineplex, where we had our first date. A silver moon Macon had given her the night of the winter formal. The button from the vest she was wearing the night in the rain. They were Lena's memories, and she carried them with her as if she might lose them without proof of those few perfect moments of happiness.

I snapped the Sharpie onto the chain. "Now you can write wherever you are."

"Even on ceilings?" She looked at me and smiled, a little crooked, a little sad.

"Even on water towers."

"I love it." She spoke quietly, pulling the cap off the Sharpie.

Before I knew it, she was drawing a heart. Black ink on white paint, a heart hidden at the top of the Summerville water tower.

I was happy for a second. Then I felt like I was falling all the way down. Because she wasn't thinking about us. She was thinking about her next birthday, the Seventeenth Moon. She was already counting down.

In the center of the heart, she didn't write our names.

She wrote a number.

⊰ 5.16 ⊱

The Call

I didn't ask her about what she'd written on the water tower, but I didn't forget it. How could I, when all we had done for the past year was count down to the inevitable? When I finally asked why she'd written it or what she was counting down to, she wouldn't say. And I had the feeling she really didn't know.

Which was even worse than knowing.

It had been two weeks since then, and as far as I could tell Lena still hadn't written anything in her notebook. She was wearing the little Sharpie on her necklace, but it looked as new as the day I bought it at the Stop & Steal. It was weird not to see her writing, scribbling on her hands or her worn-out Converse, which she didn't wear much these days. She had started wearing her thrashed black boots instead. Her hair was different, too. Almost always tied back, as if she thought she could yank the magic right out of it.

We were sitting on the top step of my porch, the same place we had been sitting when Lena first told me she was a Caster, a secret she had never shared with a Mortal before. I was pretending to read *Jekyll and Hyde*. Lena was staring down at the blank pages of her spiral notebook, as if the thin blue lines held the answer to all her problems.

When I wasn't watching Lena, I was staring down my street. My dad was coming home today. Amma and I had visited him on Family Day every week since my aunt checked him into Blue Horizons. Even though he wasn't back to his old self, I had to admit he was acting almost like a regular person again. But I was still nervous.

"They're here." The screen door slammed behind me. Amma was standing on the porch in her tool apron, the kind she preferred over a traditional one, especially on days like this. She was holding the gold charm around her neck, rubbing it between her fingers.

I looked down the street, but the only thing I saw was Billy Watson riding his bike. Lena leaned forward to get a better look.

I don't see a car.

I didn't either, but I knew I would in about five seconds. Amma was proud, particularly when it came to her abilities as a Seer. She wouldn't say they were here unless she knew they were coming.

It'll be here.

Sure enough, my aunt's white Cadillac made the right onto Cotton Bend. Aunt Caroline had the window rolled down, what she liked to call 360 air conditioning, and I could see her waving from down the block. I stood up as Amma elbowed her way past

me. "Come on, now. Your daddy deserves a proper homecomin'."
That was code for *Get your butt down to the curb, Ethan Wate.*

I took a deep breath.

Are you okay? Lena's hazel eyes caught the sun.

Yeah. I lied. She must have known, but she didn't say a word.
I took her hand. It was cold, the way she always was now, and
the current of electricity felt more like the sting of frostbite.

"Mitchell Wate. Don't tell me you've been eatin' anybody's
pie but mine. 'Cause you look like you fell into the cookie jar
and couldn't find your way back out." My dad gave her a knowing look. Amma had raised him, and he knew her teasing held
as much love as any hug.

I stood there while Amma fussed over him as if he was ten
years old. She and my aunt were chattering away like the three
of them had just come home from the market. My dad smiled at
me weakly. It was the same smile he gave me when we visited
Blue Horizons. It said, *I'm not crazy anymore, just ashamed.*
He was wearing his old Duke T-shirt and jeans, and somehow
he looked younger than I remembered. Except for the crinkling
lines around his eyes, which deepened as he pulled me in for an
awkward hug. "How you doing?"

My voice caught in my throat for a second, and I coughed.
"Good."

He looked over at Lena. "Nice to see you again, Lena. I was
sorry to hear about your uncle." Those were hard-bred Southern manners for you. He had to acknowledge Macon's passing,
even in a moment as awkward as this one.

Lena tried to smile, but she only managed to look as uncomfortable as I felt. "Thank you, sir."

"Ethan, come on over here and give your favorite aunt a hug." Aunt Caroline held out her hands. I wanted to throw my arms around her and let her squeeze the knot right out of my chest.

"Let's go on inside." Amma waved at my dad from the top of the porch. "I made a Coca-Cola cake and fried chicken. If we don't get in there soon, that chicken'll have a mind to find its way home."

Aunt Caroline looped her arm through my dad's and led him up the stairs. She had the same brown hair and small frame as my mom, and for a second it felt like my parents were home again, walking through the old screen door of Wate's Landing.

"I have to get home." Lena was clutching her notebook against her chest like a shield.

"You don't have to go. Come in."

Please.

I wasn't offering to be polite. I didn't want to go in there alone. A few months ago, Lena would have known that. But I guess today her mind was somewhere else, because she didn't.

"You should spend some time with your family." She stood up on her toes and kissed me, her lips barely touching my cheek. She was halfway to the car before I could argue.

I watched Larkin's Fastback disappear down my street. Lena didn't drive the hearse anymore. As far as I knew, she hadn't even looked at it since Macon died. Uncle Barclay had parked it behind the old barn and thrown a tarp over it. Instead, she was driving Larkin's car, all black and chrome. Link had foamed at the mouth the first time he saw it. "Do you know how many chicks I could pull with that ride?"

After her cousin had betrayed her whole family, I didn't understand why Lena would want to drive his car. When I had asked her, she'd shrugged and said, "He won't be needing it anymore." Maybe Lena thought she was punishing Larkin by driving it. He had contributed to Macon's death, something she would never forgive. I watched the car turn the corner, wishing I could disappear along with it.

By the time I made it to the kitchen, there was already chicory coffee brewing—and trouble. Amma was on the phone, pacing in front of the sink, and every minute or two she would cover the receiver with her hand and report the conversation on the other end to Aunt Caroline.

"They haven't seen her since yesterday." Amma put the phone back to her ear. "You should make Aunt Mercy a toddy and put her to bed until we find her."

"Find who?" I looked at my dad, and he shrugged.

Aunt Caroline pulled me over to the sink and whispered the way Southern ladies do when something is too awful to say out loud. "Lucille Ball. She's missin'." Lucille Ball was Aunt Mercy's Siamese cat, who spent most of her time running around my great-aunts' front yard on a leash attached to a clothesline, an activity the Sisters referred to as exercising.

"What do you mean?"

Amma covered the receiver with her hand again, narrowing her eyes and setting her jaw. The Look. "Seems *somebody* put the idea in your aunt's head that cats don't need to be tied up, because they always come back home. You wouldn't know anything about that, would you?" It wasn't a question. We both knew I was the one who had been saying it for years.

"But cats aren't supposed to be on leashes." I tried to defend myself, but it was too late.

Amma glared at me and turned to Aunt Caroline. "Seems Aunt Mercy's been waitin', sittin' on the porch, starin' at an empty leash hangin' on the clothesline." She took her hand off the receiver. "You need to get her in the house and put her feet up. If she gets lightheaded, boil some dandelion."

I slunk out of the kitchen before Amma's eyes got any narrower. Great. My hundred-year-old aunt's cat was gone, and it was my fault. I'd have to call Link and see if he'd drive around town with me and look for Lucille. Maybe Link's demo tapes would scare her out of hiding.

"Ethan?" My dad was standing in the hall, right outside of the kitchen door. "Can I talk to you for a second?" I had been dreading this, the part where he apologized for everything and tried to explain why he had ignored me for almost a year.

"Yeah, sure." But I didn't know if I wanted to hear it. I wasn't really angry anymore. When I almost lost Lena, there was a part of me that understood why my dad had come completely unhinged. I couldn't imagine my life without Lena, and my dad had loved my mom for more than eighteen years.

I felt sorry for him now, but it still hurt.

My dad ran his hand through his hair and edged closer to me. "I wanted to tell you how sorry I am." He paused, staring down at his feet. "I don't know what happened. One day, I was in there writing, and the next day all I could do was think about your mom—sit in her chair, smell her books, imagine her reading over my shoulder." He studied his hands, as if he was talking to them instead of me. Maybe that was a trick they taught you at Blue Horizons. "It was the only place I felt close to her. I couldn't let her go."

He looked up at the old plaster ceiling, and a tear escaped

from the corner of his eye, running slowly down the side of his face. My dad had lost the love of his life, and he had come unraveled like an old sweater. I'd watched, but I hadn't done anything about it. Maybe he wasn't the only one to blame. I knew I was supposed to smile now, but I didn't feel like it.

"I get it, Dad. I wish you'd said something. I missed her, too. You know?"

His voice was quiet when he finally spoke. "I didn't know what to say."

"It's okay." I didn't know if I meant it yet, but I could see relief spread across his face. He reached around and hugged me, squeezing my back with his fists for a second.

"I'm here now. Do you want to talk about it?"

"About what?"

"Things you need to know when you have a girlfriend."

There was nothing I wanted to talk about less. "Dad, we don't have to—"

"I have a lot of experience, you know. Your mother taught me a thing or two about women over the years."

I started planning my escape route.

"If you ever want to talk about, you know..."

I could hurl myself through the study window and squeeze between the hedge and the house.

"Feelings."

I almost laughed in his face. "What?"

"Amma says Lena's having a hard time with her uncle's passing. She's not acting like herself."

Lying on the ceiling. Refusing to go to school. Not opening up to me. Climbing water towers. "No, she's all right."

"Well, women are a different species."

47

I nodded and tried not to look him in the eye. He had no idea how right he was.

"As much as I loved your mother, half the time I couldn't have told you what was going on in her head. Relationships are complicated. You know you can ask me anything."

What could I ask? What do you do when your heart almost stops beating every time you kiss? Are there times when you should and shouldn't read each other's minds? What are the early warning signs that your girlfriend is being Claimed for all time by good or evil?

He squeezed my shoulder one last time. I was still trying to put together a sentence when he let go. He was staring down the hall, in the direction of the study.

The framed portrait of Ethan Carter Wate was hanging in the hallway. I still wasn't used to seeing it, even though I was the one who had hung it there the day after Macon's funeral. It had been hidden under a sheet my whole life, which seemed wrong. Ethan Carter Wate had walked away from a war he didn't believe in and died trying to protect the Caster girl he loved.

So I had found a nail and hung the painting. It felt right. After that, I went into my dad's study and picked up the sheets of paper strewn all over the room. I looked at the scribbles and circles one last time, the evidence of how deep love can run and how long loss can last. Then I cleaned up and threw the pages away. That felt right, too.

My dad walked over to the painting, studying it as if he was seeing it for the first time. "I haven't seen this guy in a long time."

I was so relieved we had moved on to a new subject, the

words came tumbling out. "I hung it up. I hope it's okay. But it seemed like it belonged out here, instead of under some old sheet."

For a minute, my dad stared up at the portrait of the boy in the Confederate uniform, who didn't look much older than me. "This painting always had a sheet over it when I was a kid. My grandparents never said much about it, but they weren't about to hang a deserter on the wall. After I inherited this place, I found it covered up in the attic and brought it down to the study."

"Why didn't you hang it up?" I never imagined that my dad had stared at the same hidden outline when he was a kid.

"I don't know. Your mother wanted me to. She loved his story—the way he walked away from the war, even though it ended up costing him his life. I meant to hang it. I was just so used to seeing it covered up. Before I got around to it, your mom died." He ran his hand along the bottom of the carved frame. "You know, you were named after him."

"I know."

My dad looked at me as if he was looking at me for the first time, too. "She was crazy about that painting. I'm glad you hung it up. It's where he belongs."

I didn't escape the fried chicken or Amma's guilt trip. So after dinner, I drove around the Sisters' neighborhood with Link looking for Lucille. Link called her name between bites of a chicken leg wrapped in an oily paper towel. Every time he ran his hand over his spiky blond hair, the shine got shinier from all the grease.

"You shoulda brought more fried chicken along. Cats dig chicken. They eat birds in the wild." Link was driving slower than usual so I could keep an eye out for Lucille while he beat time to "Love Biscuit," his band's terrible new song, on the steering wheel.

"Then what? You'd drive around while I hung out the window with a chicken leg in my hand?" Link was so transparent. "You just want more of Amma's chicken."

"You know it. And Coca-Cola cake." He hung his drumstick bone out the window. "Here, kitty kitty..."

I scanned the sidewalk, looking for a Siamese cat, but something else caught my eye—a crescent moon. It was on a license plate stuck between a bumper sticker of the Stars and Bars, the Confederate flag, and one for Bubba's Truck and Trailer. The same old South Carolina plates with the state symbol I had seen a thousand times, only I'd never thought about it before. A blue palmetto and a crescent moon, maybe a Caster moon. The Casters really had been here a long time.

"Cat's stupider than I thought, if he doesn't know about Amma's fried chicken."

"She. Lucille Ball's a girl."

"It's a cat." Link swerved, and we turned the corner onto Main. Boo Radley was sitting on the curb, watching the Beater roll by. His tail thumped, one lonely thump of recognition, as we disappeared down the road. The loneliest dog in town.

At the sight of Boo, Link cleared his throat. "Speakin' a girls, how're things with Lena?" He hadn't seen much of her, though he'd seen more than most people had. Lena spent most of her time at Ravenwood under the watchful eyes of Gramma and Aunt Del, or hiding from their watchful eyes, depending on the day.

"She's dealing." It wasn't a lie, exactly.

"Is she? I mean, she seems kinda different. Even for Lena." Link was one of the few people in town who knew Lena's secret.

"Her uncle died. That kind of thing changes you." Link should've known that better than anyone. He'd watched me try to make sense of my mother's death, and then a world without her in it. He knew it was impossible.

"Yeah, but she hardly talks, and she's wearin' his clothes. Don't you think that's sorta weird?"

"She's fine."

"If you say so, man."

"Just drive. We have to find Lucille." I looked out the window at the empty street. "Stupid cat."

Link shrugged and cranked up the volume. His band, the Holy Rollers, shuddered through the speakers. "The Girl's Gone Away." Getting dumped was the theme of every song Link wrote. It was his way of dealing. I still hadn't figured out mine.

We never found Lucille, and I never got the conversation with Link, or my dad, out of my mind. My house was quiet, which isn't what you want a house to be if you're trying to run away from your thoughts. The window in my room was open, but the air was as hot and stagnant as everything else today.

Link was right. Lena was acting strange. But it had only been a few months. She'd snap out of it, and things would be the way they were before.

I dug through the piles of books and papers on my desk,

51

looking for *A Hitchhiker's Guide to the Galaxy*, my go-to book for taking my mind off things. Under a stack of old *Sandman* comics, I found something else. It was a package, wrapped in Marian's signature brown paper and tied with string. But it didn't have GATLIN COUNTY LIBRARY stamped on it.

Marian was my mother's oldest friend and the Gatlin County Head Librarian. She was also a Keeper in the Caster world— a Mortal who guarded Caster secrets and history, and, in Marian's case, the *Lunae Libri*, a Caster Library filled with secrets of its own. She had given me the package after Macon died, but I had forgotten all about it. It was his journal, and she thought Lena would want to have it. Marian was wrong. Lena didn't want to see it or touch it. She wouldn't even let it into Ravenwood. "You keep it," she had said. "I don't think I could bear to see his handwriting." It had been collecting dust on my desk ever since.

I turned it over in my hands. It was heavy, almost too heavy to be a book. I wondered what it looked like. It was probably old, made of cracked leather. I untied the string and unwrapped it. I wasn't going to read it, just look at it. But when I pulled the paper away, I realized it wasn't a book. It was a black wooden box, intricately carved with strange Caster symbols.

I ran my hand over the top, wondering what he wrote about. I couldn't imagine him writing poetry like Lena. It was probably full of horticultural notes. I opened the lid carefully. I wanted to see something Macon had touched every day, something that was important to him. The lining was black satin, and the pages inside were unbound and yellowed, written in Macon's fading spidery script. I touched a page, with a single finger. The sky began to spin, and I felt myself pitching forward. The floor rushed up to meet me, but as I hit the ground, I fell through it and found myself in a cloud of smoke—

Fires burned along the river, the only traces of the plantations that had stood there just hours ago. Greenbrier was already engulfed in flames. Ravenwood would be next. The Union soldiers must have been taking a break, drunk from their victory and the liquor they had pillaged from the wealthiest homes in Gatlin.

Abraham didn't have much time. The soldiers were coming, and he was going to have to kill them. It was the only way to save Ravenwood. The Mortals didn't stand a chance against him, even if they were soldiers. They were no match for an Incubus. And if his brother, Jonah, ever came back from the Tunnels, the soldiers would have two of them to contend with. The guns were Abraham's only concern. Even though Mortal weapons couldn't kill his kind, the bullets would weaken him, which might give the soldiers the time they needed to set fire to Ravenwood.

Abraham needed to feed, and even through the smoke, he could smell the desperation and fear of a Mortal nearby. Fear would make him strong. It provided more power and sustenance than memories or dreams.

Abraham Traveled toward the scent. But when he materialized in the woods beyond Greenbrier, he knew he was too late. The scent was faint. In the distance, he could see Genevieve Duchannes hunched over a body in the mud. Ivy, Greenbrier's cook, was standing behind Genevieve, clutching something against her chest.

The old woman saw Abraham and rushed toward him. "Mr. Ravenwood, thank the Lord." She lowered her voice. "You have to take this. Put it somewhere safe till I can come for it." Pulling a heavy black book from the folds of her apron, she thrust it into Abraham's hands. As soon as he touched it, Abraham could feel its power.

The book was alive, pulsating against his palms as if it had a heartbeat. He could almost hear it whispering to him, beckoning him to take it—to open it and release whatever was hiding inside. There were no words on its cover, only a single crescent moon. Abraham ran his fingers over the edges.

Ivy was still talking, mistaking Abraham's silence for hesitation. "Please, Mr. Ravenwood. I got no one else to give it to. And I can't leave it with Miss Genevieve. Not now." Genevieve raised her head as if she could hear them through the rain and the roar of the flames.

The moment Genevieve turned toward them, Abraham understood. He could see her yellow eyes glowing in the darkness. The eyes of a Dark Caster. In that moment, he also understood what he was holding.

The Book of Moons.

He had seen the Book before, in the dreams of Genevieve's mother, Marguerite. It was a book of infinite power, a book Marguerite feared and revered in equal measure. One she hid from her husband and her daughters, and would never have allowed into the hands of a Dark Caster or an Incubus. A book that could save Ravenwood.

Ivy scooped something from inside the folds of her skirt and rubbed it across the face of the Book. The white crystals rolled down over the edges. Salt. The weapon of superstitious island women, who brought their own brand of power with them from the Sugar Islands, where their ancestors were born. They believed it warded off Demons, a belief that had always amused Abraham. "I'll come for it, soon as I can. I swear."

"I will keep it safe. You have my word." Abraham brushed some of the salt from the Book's cover so he could feel its heat against his skin. He turned back toward the woods. He would walk a few yards, for Ivy's benefit. It always scared the Gullah women to see him Travel, to be reminded of what he was.

"Put it away, Mr. Ravenwood. Whatever you do, don't open it. That book brings nothin' but misery to anyone who messes with it. Don't listen to it when it calls you. I'll come for it." But Ivy's warning had come too late.

Abraham was already listening.

When I came to, I was lying on my back on the floor, staring at my ceiling. It was painted sky blue, like all the ceilings in our house, to fool the carpenter bees that nested there.

I sat up, dizzy. The box was beside me, the lid shut. I opened it, and the pages were inside. This time I didn't touch them.

None of this made sense. Why was I having visions again? Why was I seeing Abraham Ravenwood, a man who folks in town had been suspicious of for generations because Ravenwood was the only plantation to survive the Great Burning? Not that I believed much of anything the folks in town had to say.

But when Genevieve's locket triggered the visions, there had been a reason. Something Lena and I needed to figure out. What did Abraham Ravenwood have to do with us? The common thread was *The Book of Moons*. It was in the locket visions and in this one. But the Book was gone. The last time anyone had seen it was the night of Lena's birthday, when it was lying on the table in the crypt, surrounded by fire. Like so many things, it was nothing but ashes now.

All That Remains

When I went to school the next day, I sat alone with Link and his four sloppy joes at the lunch table. While I ate my pizza, all I could think about was what Link said about Lena. He was right. She had changed, a little bit at a time, until I almost couldn't remember how things used to be. If I had anyone to talk to about it, I knew they would say to give her time. I also knew that was just something people said when there was nothing left to say and nothing you could do.

Lena wasn't coming out of it. She wasn't coming back to herself or to me. If anything, she was drifting farther away from me than anyone else. More and more, I couldn't reach her, not on the inside, not with Kelting or kissing or any of the other complicated or uncomplicated ways we used to touch. Now when I took her hand, all I could feel was the chill.

And when Emily Asher looked at me from across the

lunchroom, there wasn't anything left but pity in her eyes. Once again, I was someone to feel sorry for. I wasn't *Ethan Wate Whose Mamma Died Just Last Year.* Now I was *Ethan Wate Whose Girlfriend Went Psycho When Her Uncle Died.* People knew there were *complications,* and they knew they hadn't seen Lena in school with me.

Even if they didn't like Lena, the miserable love to watch someone else's misery. I had just about cornered the market on miserable. I was worse than miserable, lower than a flattened sloppy joe left behind on a lunchroom tray. I was alone.

One morning about a week later, I kept hearing a strange sound, like a grating or a record scratching or a page tearing, in the back of my mind. I was in history class, and we were talking about the Reconstruction, which was the even more boring time after the Civil War when the United States had to put itself back together. In a Gatlin classroom, this chapter was even more embarrassing than it was depressing—a reminder South Carolina had been a slave state and that we had been on the wrong side of right. We all knew it, but our ancestors had left us with a permanent F on the nation's moral report card. Cuts that run that deep leave scars, no matter what you try to do to heal them. Mr. Lee was still droning on, punctuating each sentence with a dramatic sigh.

I was trying not to listen, when I smelled something burning, maybe an overheating engine or a lighter. I looked around the room. It wasn't coming from Mr. Lee, the most frequent source of any horrible smell in my history class. No one else seemed to notice it.

The noise grew louder, into a confusing blur of crashing—ripping, talking, yelling. *Lena.*

L?

No answer. Above the noise, I heard Lena mumbling lines of poetry, and not the kind you send someone for Valentine's Day.

Not waving but drowning…

I recognized the poem, and it wasn't good. Lena reading Stevie Smith was only one step up from the darkest Sylvia Plath and *The Bell Jar* kind of day. It was Lena's red flag, like Link listening to the Dead Kennedys or Amma chopping vegetables for spring rolls with her cleaver.

Hang on, L. I'm coming.

Something had changed, and before it could change back, I grabbed my books and took off running. I was out of the room before Mr. Lee's next sigh.

Reece wouldn't look at me when I walked through the door. She pointed to the stairs. Ryan, Lena's youngest cousin, was sitting on the bottom step with Boo, looking sad. When I tousled her hair, she held her finger to her lips. "Lena's having a nerve breakup. We're supposed to be quiet until Gramma and Mamma get home."

That was an understatement.

The door was open a crack, and when I pushed on it, the hinges creaked, like I was walking into a crime scene. It looked like the room had been tossed. The furniture was upside down or busted up or missing altogether. The entire room was covered with pages of books, pages torn and ripped and plastered all along the walls and ceiling and floor. Not a book was left on the shelf. It looked like a library had exploded. Some of the charred pages piled on the floor were still smoking. The only thing I didn't see was Lena.

L? Where are you?

I scanned the room. The wall over her bed wasn't covered with the remnants of the books Lena loved. It was covered in something else.

Nobody the dead man & Nobody the living
Nobody is giving in & Nobody is giving
Nobody hears me but just Nobody cares
Nobody fears me but Nobody just stares
Nobody belongs to me & Nobody remains
No Nobody knows Nothing
All that remains are remains

Nobody and *Nobody.* One of them was Macon, right? *The dead man.*

Who was the other? Me?

Was that who I was now, *Nobody*?

Did all guys have to work this hard to figure out their girlfriends? Untwisting the twisted poems written all over their walls in Sharpie or cracked plaster?

All that remains are remains.

I touched the wall, smearing away the word *remains.*

Because all that remained was not remains. There had to be more than that—more to Lena and me, more to everything. It wasn't just Macon. My mom was gone, but as the last few months had shown, some part of her was with me. I had been thinking about her more and more.

Claim yourself. It had been my mom's message to Lena, written in the page numbers of books, scattered across the floor of her favorite room at Wate's Landing. Her message to me didn't have to be written anywhere, not in numbers or letters or even dreams.

Lena's floor looked a little like the study that day, books lying open all over the place. Except these books were missing their pages, which sent a different message altogether.

Pain and guilt. It was the second chapter of every book my Aunt Caroline had given me about the five stages of grief, or however many stages of grief people say there are. Lena had covered shock and denial, the first two, so I should've seen this one coming. For her, I guess it meant giving up one of the things she loved the most. Books.

At least, I hoped that's what it meant. I stepped carefully around the empty, burnt book jackets. I heard the muffled sobs before I saw her.

I opened the closet door. She was huddled in the darkness, hugging her knees to her chest.

It's okay, L.

She looked up at me, but I wasn't sure what she was seeing.

My books all sounded like him. I couldn't make them stop.

It doesn't matter. Everything's okay now.

I knew things wouldn't stay that way for long. Nothing was okay. Somewhere along the way between angry and scared and miserable, she had turned a corner. I knew from experience there was no turning back.

Gramma had finally intervened. Lena would be going back to school next week, like it or not. Her choice was school or the thing nobody said out loud. Blue Horizons, or whatever the Caster equivalent was. Until then, I was only allowed to see her when I dropped off her homework. I trudged all the way up to her house with a Stop & Steal bag's worth of meaningless worksheets and essay questions.

Why me? What did I do?

I guess I'm not supposed to be around anyone who gets me worked up. That's what Reece said.

I'm what gets you worked up?

I could feel something like a smile tugging at the back of my mind.

Of course you are. Just not the way they think.

When her bedroom door finally swung open, I dropped the sack and pulled her into my arms. It had only been a few days since I'd seen her in person, but I missed the smell of her hair, the lemons and rosemary. The familiar things. Today I couldn't smell it, though. I buried my face in her neck.

I missed you, too.

Lena looked up at me. She was wearing a black T-shirt and black tights, cut into all kinds of crazy slits up and down her legs. Her hair was squirming loose from the clasp at the back of her neck. Her necklace hung down, twisting on its chain. Her eyes were ringed with darkness that wasn't makeup. I was worried. But when I looked past her to her bedroom, I was even more worried.

Gramma had gotten her way. There was not a burnt book, not a thing out of place in the room. That was the problem. There wasn't one streak of Sharpie, not a poem, not a page anywhere in the room. Instead, the walls were covered with images, taped carefully in a row along the perimeter, as if they were some kind of fence trapping her inside.

Sacred. Sleeping. Beloved. Daughter.

They were photographs of headstones, taken so close that all I could make out was the rough stubble of the rock behind the chiseled words, and the words themselves.

Father. Joy. Despair. Eternal Rest.

"I didn't know you were into photography." I wondered what else I didn't know.

"I'm not, really." She looked embarrassed.

"They're great."

"It's supposed to be good for me. I have to prove to everyone that I know he's really gone."

"Yeah. My dad's supposed to keep a feelings journal now." As soon as I said it, I wished I could take it back. Comparing Lena to my dad couldn't be mistaken for a compliment, but she didn't seem to notice. I wondered how long she had been climbing around His Garden of Perpetual Peace with her camera, and how I had missed it.

Soldier. Sleeping. Through a glass, darkly.

I came to the last picture, the only one that didn't seem to belong with the rest. It was a motorcycle, a Harley leaning against a gravestone. The shiny chrome of the bike looked out of place next to the worn old stones. My heart started to pound as I looked at it. "What's this one?"

Lena dismissed it with a wave. "Some guy visiting a grave, I guess. He was just kind of…there. I keep meaning to take it down, the lighting's terrible." She reached up past me, pulling the tacks out of the wall. When she reached the last one, the photo vanished, leaving nothing but four tiny holes in her black wall.

Aside from the images, the room was nearly empty, as if she'd packed up and gone to college somewhere. The bed was gone. The bookshelf and all the books were gone. The old chandelier we'd made swing so many times I had thought it would fall from the ceiling was gone. There was a futon on the floor, in the center of the room. Next to it was the tiny silver sparrow. Seeing it flooded my brain with memories from the funeral—magnolias ripping out of the lawn, the same silver sparrow in her muddy palm.

"Everything looks so different." I tried not to think about the sparrow or the reason it would be next to her bed. The reason that had nothing to do with Macon.

"Well, you know. Spring cleaning. I had kind of trashed the place."

A few tattered books lay on the futon. Without thinking, I flipped one open—until I realized I'd committed the worst of crimes. Though the outside was covered with an old, taped-up cover from a copy of *Dr. Jekyll and Mr. Hyde*, the inside wasn't a book at all. It was one of Lena's spiral notebooks, and I had opened it up right in front of her. Like it was nothing, or it was mine to read.

I realized something else. Most of the pages were blank.

The shock was almost as terrible as discovering the pages of my dad's gibberish when I had thought he was writing a novel. Lena carried a notebook around with her wherever she went. If she had stopped scribbling every fifth word into it, things were worse than I thought.

She was worse than I thought.

"Ethan! What are you doing?"

I pulled my hand away, and Lena grabbed the book.

"I'm sorry, L."

She was furious.

"I thought it was just a book. I mean, it looks like a book. I didn't think you would leave your notebook lying around where anyone could read it."

She wouldn't look at me, clutching the book to her chest.

"Why aren't you writing anymore? I thought you loved to write."

She rolled her eyes and opened the notebook to show me. "I do."

She fluttered the blank pages, and now they were covered with line upon line of tiny scribbled words, crossed out again and again, revised and rewritten and revisited a thousand times.

"You Charmed it?"

"I Shifted the words out of Mortal reality. Unless I choose to show them to someone, only a Caster can read them."

"That's brilliant. Since Reece, the person most likely to read it, happens to be one." Reece was as nosy as she was bossy.

"She doesn't need to. She can read everything in my face." It was true. As a Sybil, Reece could see your thoughts and secrets, even things you were planning to do, just by looking you in the eye. Which was why I generally avoided her.

"So, what's with all the secrecy?" I flopped down on Lena's futon. She sat next to me, balancing on her crisscrossed legs. Things were less comfortable than I was pretending they were.

"I don't know. I still feel like writing all the time. Maybe I just feel less like being understood, or less like I can be."

My jaw tightened. "By me."

"That's not what I meant."

"What other Mortals would be reading your notebook?"

"You don't understand."

"I think I do."

"Some of it, maybe."

65

"I would understand all of it if you'd let me."

"There's no letting, Ethan. I can't explain it."

"Let me see it." I held out my hand for her notebook.

She raised an eyebrow, handing it to me. "You won't be able to read it."

I opened it and looked at it. I didn't know if it was Lena, or the book itself, but the words appeared on the page in front of me slowly, one at a time. It wasn't one of Lena's poems, and it wasn't song lyrics. There weren't many words, just strange drawings, shapes and swirls snaking up and down the page like some collection of tribal designs.

At the bottom of the page, there was a list.

what i remember
mother
ethan
macon
hunting
the fire
the wind
the rain
the crypt
the me who is not me
the me who would kill
two bodies
the rain
the book
the ring
amma's charm
the moon

Lena grabbed the book out of my hand. There were a few more lines on the page, but I never got to read them. "Stop it!"

I looked at her. "What was that?"

"Nothing, it's private. You shouldn't have been able to see that."

"Then why could I?"

"I must have done the *Verbum Celatum* Cast wrong. The Hidden Word." She looked at me anxiously, her eyes softening. "It doesn't matter. I was trying to remember that night. The night Macon...disappeared."

"Died, L. The night Macon died."

"I know he died. Of course he died. I just don't feel like talking about it."

"I know you're probably depressed. It's normal."

"What?"

"It's the next stage."

Lena's eyes flashed. "I know your mom died, and my uncle died. But I have my own stages of grief. This isn't my feelings journal. I'm not your dad, and I'm not you, Ethan. We aren't as much alike as you think."

We looked at each other in a way we hadn't in a long time, maybe ever. There was a nameless moment. I realized we'd been speaking out loud since I got there, without Kelting a word. For the first time, I didn't know what she was thinking, and it was pretty clear she didn't know how I felt either.

But then she did. She held out her arms and drew me into them because, for the first time, I was the one who was crying.

When I got home, all the lights were out, but I still didn't go inside. I sat down on the porch and watched the fireflies blinking in the dark. I didn't want to see anyone. I wanted to think, and I had a feeling Lena wouldn't be listening. There's something about sitting alone in the dark that reminds you how big the world really is, and how far apart we all are. The stars look like they're so close, you could reach out and touch them. But you can't. Sometimes things look a lot closer than they are.

I stared into the darkness for so long that I thought I saw something move by the old oak in our front yard. For a second, my pulse quickened. Most people in Gatlin didn't even lock their doors, but I knew there were plenty of things that could get past a deadbolt. I saw the air shift again, almost imperceptibly, like a heat wave. I realized it wasn't something trying to break into my house. It was something that had broken out from another one.

Lucille, the Sisters' cat. I could see her blue eyes shining in the darkness as she stalked onto the porch.

"I told everyone you'd find your way back to the house sooner or later. You just found the wrong house." Lucille cocked her head to the side. "You know the Sisters are never gonna let you off that clothesline again after this."

Lucille stared back at me as if she understood perfectly. As if she had known the consequences when she took off but, for whatever reason, she left anyway. A firefly blinked in front of me, and Lucille leaped off the step.

It flew higher, but that dumb cat kept reaching for it. She didn't seem to know how far away it really was. Like the stars. Like a lot of things.

The Girl of My Dreams

Darkness.

I couldn't see a thing, but I could feel the air draining out of my lungs. I couldn't breathe. The air was filled with smoke, and I was coughing, choking.

Ethan!

I could hear her voice, but it was distant and faraway.

The air around me was hot. It smelled like ash and death.

Ethan, no!

I saw the glint of a knife, over my head, and I heard the sinister laughter. Sarafine. Only I couldn't see her face.

As the knife plunged into my stomach, I knew where I was.

I was at Greenbrier, on top of the crypt, and I was about to die.

I tried to scream, but I couldn't make a sound. Sarafine threw back her head and laughed, her hands on the knife in my stomach. I was dying, and she was laughing. The blood was running all around me, rushing into my ears, my nostrils, my mouth. It had a distinct taste, like copper or salt.

My lungs felt like two heaving sacks of cement. When the rush of blood in my ears drowned out her voice, I was overwhelmed with the familiar feeling of loss. Green and gold. Lemons and rosemary. I could smell it through the blood, the smoke, and the ashes. Lena.

I always thought I couldn't live without her. Now I wasn't going to have to.

"Ethan Wate! Why don't I hear that shower runnin' yet?" I bolted upright in bed, drenched in sweat. I ran my hand under my T-shirt, over my skin. There was no blood, but I could feel the raised impression where the knife had cut me in the dream. I pulled up my shirt and stared at the jagged pink line. A scar cut across my lower abdomen, like a stab wound. It had appeared out of nowhere, an injury from a dream.

Only it was real, and it hurt. I hadn't had one of the dreams since Lena's birthday, and I didn't know why they were coming back now, like this. I was used to waking up with mud in my bed or smoke in my lungs, but this was the first time I had ever woken up in pain. I tried to shake it off, telling myself it didn't really happen. But my stomach throbbed. I stared at my open window, wishing Macon was around to steal the end of this dream. I wished he was around for a lot of reasons.

I closed my eyes and tried to concentrate, to see if Lena was there. But I already knew she wouldn't be. I could feel when she had pulled away, which was most of the time, lately.

Amma called up the stairs again. "If you're fixin' to be late for your last examination, you'll be sittin' on your sweet corncakes in that room a yours all summer. That's a promise."

Lucille Ball was staring at me from the foot of my bed, the way she did most mornings now. After Lucille showed up on our porch, I took her back home to Aunt Mercy, but the next day she was sitting on our porch again. After that, Aunt Prue convinced her sisters that Lucille was a deserter, and the cat moved in with us. I was pretty surprised when Amma opened the door and let Lucille wander in, but she had her reasons. "Nothin' wrong with havin' a cat in the house. They can see what most people can't, like the folks in the Otherworld when they cross back over—the good ones and the bad. And they get rid a mice." I guess you could say Lucille was the animal kingdom's version of Amma.

By the time I made it into the shower, the hot water rolled off me, pushing everything away. Everything except the scar. I turned it up even hotter, but I couldn't keep my mind in the shower. It was tangled up in the dreams, the knife, the laughter—

My English final.

Crap.

I'd fallen asleep before I finished studying. If I failed the test, I would fail the class, Good-Eye Side or not. My grades were not stellar this semester, and by that I mean I was running neck and neck with Link. I wasn't my usual don't-study-and-get-by self. I was already close to failing history, since Lena and I had ditched the mandatory Reenactment of the Battle of Honey Hill on her birthday. If I failed English, I'd be spending all summer in a school so old it didn't even have air conditioning, or I'd be looking at sophomore year all over again. It was the particularly penetrating problem a person with a pulse should be prepared to ponder today. Assonance, right? Or was it consonance? I was screwed.

This was day five of supersized breakfasts. We'd had finals all week, and Amma believed there was a direct correlation between how much I ate and how well I would do. I had eaten my weight in bacon and eggs since Monday. No wonder my stomach was killing me and I was having nightmares. Or at least, that's what I tried to tell myself.

I poked at the fried eggs with my fork. "More eggs?"

Amma squinted at me suspiciously. "I don't know what you're up to, but I'm in no mood for it." She slid another egg onto my plate. "Don't try my patience today, Ethan Wate."

I wasn't about to argue with her. I had enough problems of my own.

My dad wandered into the kitchen and opened the cupboard, searching for his Shredded Wheat. "Don't tease Amma. You know she doesn't like it." He looked up at her, shaking his spoon. "That boy of mine is downright S. C. A. B. R. O. U. S. As in..."

Amma glared at him, slamming the cupboard doors shut. "Mitchell Wate, I'll give you a scab or two all your own if you don't stop messin' with my pantry." He laughed, and a second later I could have sworn she was smiling, and I watched as my own crazy father started turning Amma back into Amma again. The moment vanished, popping like a soap bubble, but I knew what I'd seen. Things were changing.

I still wasn't used to the sight of my dad walking around during the day, pouring cereal and making small talk. It seemed unbelievable that four months ago my aunt had checked him into Blue Horizons. Although he wasn't exactly a new man, as Aunt Caroline professed, I had to admit I barely recognized him. He wasn't making me chicken salad sandwiches, but these days he was out of the study more and more, and sometimes even out of the house. Marian scored my dad a position at the University of Charleston as a guest lecturer in the English department. Even though the bus ride turned a forty-minute commute into two hours, there was no letting my dad operate heavy machinery, not yet. He seemed almost happy. I mean, relatively speaking, for a guy who was previously holed up in his study for months scribbling like a madman. The bar was pretty low.

If things could change that much for my dad, if Amma was smiling, maybe they could change for Lena, too.

Couldn't they?

But the moment was over. Amma was back on the warpath. I could see it in her face. My dad sat down next to me and poured milk over his cereal. Amma wiped her hands on her tool apron. "Mitchell, you best have some a those eggs. Cereal isn't any kind a breakfast."

"Good morning to you, too, Amma." He smiled at her, the way I bet he did when he was a kid.

She squinted at him and slammed a glass of chocolate milk next to my plate, even though I barely drank it anymore.

"Doesn't look so good to me." She sniffed and started pushing a massive amount of bacon onto my plate. To Amma, I would always be six years old. "You look like the livin' dead. What you need is some brain food, to pass those examinations a yours."

"Yes, ma'am." I chugged the glass of water Amma had poured for my dad. She held up her infamous wooden spoon with the hole in the middle, the One-Eyed Menace—that's what I called it. When I was a kid, she used to chase me around the house with it if I sassed her, even though she never actually hit me with it. I ducked, to play along.

"And you better pass every single one. I won't have you hangin' around that school all summer like the Pettys' kids. You're gonna get a job, like you said you would." She sniffed, waving the spoon. "Free time means free trouble, and you got heaps of that already."

My dad smiled and stifled a laugh. I bet Amma had said exactly the same thing to him when he was my age.

"Yes, ma'am."

I heard a car honk, and the sound of way too much Beater bass, and grabbed my backpack. All I saw was the blur of the spoon behind me.

I slid into the Beater and rolled down the window. Gramma had gotten her way, and Lena had come back to school a week ago, for the end of the year. I had driven all the way out to Ravenwood to take her to school on her first day back, even stopping at the Stop & Steal to get her one of their famous sticky buns, but by the time I got there Lena was already gone. Ever since then, she had been driving herself to school, so Link and I were back in the Beater.

Link turned down the music, which was blasting through the car, out the windows, and down the block.

"Don't you embarrass me over at that school a yours, Ethan Wate. And you turn down that music, Wesley Jefferson Lincoln! You're goin' to knock over my whole row a rutabagas with that ruckus." Link honked back at her. Amma knocked her spoon against the post, put her hands on her hips, and then softened. "You do well on those tests a yours, and maybe I'll bake you a pie."

"That wouldn't be Gatlin peach, would it, ma'am?"

Amma sniffed and nodded her head. "Just might be."

She would never admit it, but Amma had finally developed a soft spot for Link, after all these years. Link thought it was because Amma felt sorry for his mom after her invasion-of-the-body-snatchers experience with Sarafine, but that wasn't it. She felt bad for Link. "Can't believe that boy has to live in the house with that woman. He'd be better off if he was bein' raised by wolves." That's what she'd said last week before she packed up a pecan pie for him.

Link looked at me and grinned. "Best thing that ever happened to me, Lena's mom gettin' mixed up with my mom. Never had so much a Amma's pie in my life." It was about as much as he ever said about Lena's nightmare of a birthday anymore. He floored it, and the Beater went skidding down the road. It almost wasn't worth mentioning that we were late, as usual.

"Did you study for English?" It wasn't really a question. I knew Link hadn't cracked a book since seventh grade.

"Nah. I'm gonna copy offa someone."

"Who?"

"What do you care? Somebody smarter than you."

"Yeah? Last time you copied off Jenny Masterson, and you both got D's."

"I didn't have time to study. I was writin' a song. We might play it at the county fair. Check it out." Link sang along with the song, which sounded weird because he was singing along to a recording of his own voice. "Lollipop Girl, took off without a word, was callin' out your name, but you never heard."

Great. Another song about Ridley. Which shouldn't have

surprised me, since he hadn't written a song about anything but Ridley for four months now. I was beginning to think he would always be hung up on Lena's cousin, who was nothing like her. Ridley was a Siren, who used her Power of Persuasion to get what she wanted with one lick of a lollipop. Which, for a while, was Link. Even though she had used him and disappeared, he hadn't forgotten her. But I couldn't blame him. It was probably tough being in love with a Dark Caster. It was pretty tough sometimes with a Light one, too.

I was still thinking about Lena, despite the deafening roar in my ears, until Link's voice was drowned out altogether, and I heard *Seventeen Moons*. Only now the words had changed.

> *Seventeen moons, seventeen turns,*
> *Eyes so dark and bright it burns,*
> *Time is high but one is higher,*
> *Draws the moon into the fire...*

Time is high? What did that even mean? It wasn't going to be Lena's Seventeenth Moon for eight more months. Why was time high now? And who was the one, and what was the fire?

I felt Link smack the side of my head, and the song disappeared. He was shouting over his demo tape. "If I can get the backbeat down, it'll be a pretty rockin' tune." I stared at him, and he knocked me in the head again. "Shake it off, man. It's just an exam. You look as crazy as Miss Luney, the hot-lunch lady."

Thing is, he wasn't that far off.

When the Beater pulled into the Jackson High parking lot, it still didn't feel like the last day of school. For the seniors, it wasn't. They would have graduation tomorrow, and a party that lasted all night and usually gave more than a few people a brush with alcohol poisoning. But for us sophomores and juniors, we had one more exam until we were free.

Savannah and Emily walked past Link and me, ignoring us. Their short skirts were even shorter than usual, and we could see bikini strings hanging out from under their tank tops. Tie-dye and pink gingham.

"Check it out. Bikini season." Link grinned.

I had almost forgotten. We were only an exam away from an afternoon at the lake. Everyone who was anyone was wearing bathing suits under their clothes today, since summer didn't officially start until you had taken your first swim off the shores of Lake Moultrie. Kids from Jackson had a place we hung out, up past Monck's Corner, where the lake opened deep and wide into what felt like an ocean when you were swimming in it. Except for all the catfish and the swamp weeds, you could be out to sea. This time last year, I rode to the lake in the back of Emory's brother's truck with Emily, Savannah, Link, and half the basketball team. But that was last year.

"You goin'?"

"Nah."

"I've got an extra suit in the Beater, but it's not as cool as these puppies." Link pulled up his shirt so I could see his bathing suit, which was bright orange and yellow plaid. About as low-key as Link was.

"I'll pass." He knew why I wasn't going, but I wouldn't say it. I had to act like things were okay.

77

Like Lena and I were okay.

Link wasn't giving up today. "I'm sure Emily's savin' you half her towel." It was a joke, because we both knew she wasn't. Even the pity parade had moved on, along with the hate campaign. I guess we were such easy targets these days, the sport was gone, like shooting fish in a barrel.

"Give it a rest."

Link stopped walking and put his hand up to stop me. I shoved his hand away before he could start talking. I knew what he was going to say, and as far as I was concerned, the conversation was over before it started.

"Come on. I know her uncle died. Quit actin' like you're both still at the funeral. I know you love her, but..." He didn't want to say it, even though we were both thinking it. He never brought it up anymore, because he was Link, and he sat at the lunch table with me when nobody else would.

"Everything's fine." It was going to work out. It had to. I didn't know how to be without her.

"It's hard to watch, dude. She's treatin' you like—"

"Like what?" It was a challenge. I could feel my fingers curling into a fist. I was waiting for a reason, any reason. I felt like I was going to explode, that's how badly I wanted to hit something.

"The way girls usually treat me." I think he was waiting for me to hit him. Maybe he even wanted me to, if it would've helped. He shrugged.

I uncurled my fingers. Link was Link, whether or not I felt like kicking his butt sometimes. "Sorry, man."

Link laughed a little, taking off down the hall a little faster than usual. "No problem, Psycho."

As I walked up the steps toward inevitable doom, I felt a familiar pang of loneliness. Maybe Link was right. I didn't know how much longer things could go on like this with Lena. Nothing was the same. If Link could see it, maybe it was time to face facts.

My stomach started to ache, and I grabbed my side, as if I could squeeze out the pain with my hands.

Where are you, L?

I slid into my desk just as the bell rang. Lena was sitting in the seat next to mine, on the Good-Eye Side, like she always had. But she didn't look like herself.

She was wearing one of those white V-neck undershirts that was too big, and a black skirt, a few inches shorter than she would've ever worn three months ago. You could barely see it under the shirt, which was Macon's. I almost didn't notice anymore. She also wore his ring, the one he used to twist on his finger when he was thinking, on a chain around her neck. It hung on a new chain, right next to my mother's ring. The old chain had broken the night of her birthday, lost somewhere in the ash. I had given her my mom's ring out of love, though I wasn't sure it felt like that to her now. Whatever the reason, Lena loyally carried our ghosts with her, hers and mine, refusing to take off either one. My lost mother and her lost uncle, caught in circles of gold and platinum and other precious metals, hanging above her charm necklace and hidden in layers of cotton that didn't belong to her.

Mrs. English was already passing out the tests, and she didn't look amused that half the class was wearing a bathing suit or carrying a beach towel. Emily was doing both.

"Five short answers, ten points each, multiple-choice, twenty-five points, and the essay, twenty-five. Sorry, no Boo Radley this time. We're covering *Dr. Jekyll and Mr. Hyde*. It's not summer yet, people." We had been reading *To Kill a Mockingbird* in the fall. I remembered the first time Lena had shown up for class, carrying her own broken-in copy.

"Boo Radley's dead, Mrs. English. Stake through the heart." I don't know who said it, one of the girls sitting in the back with Emily, but we all knew she was talking about Macon. The comment was meant for Lena, just like old times. I tensed up as the ripple of laughter died down. I was waiting for the windows to shatter or something, but there wasn't even a crack. Lena didn't react. Maybe she wasn't listening, or she didn't care what they said anymore.

"I bet Old Man Ravenwood isn't even in the town graveyard. That coffin's probably empty. If there is one." The voice was loud enough for Mrs. English to direct her eye toward the back of the room.

"Shut up, Emily," I hissed.

This time, Lena turned around and looked right at Emily. That's all it took—one look. Emily opened her test, like she had any idea what *Jekyll and Hyde* was about. No one wanted to take on Lena. They just wanted to talk about her. Lena was the new Boo Radley. I wondered what Macon would have had to say about that.

I was still wondering, when I heard a scream from the back of the room.

"Fire! Someone help!" Emily was holding her test, and it was burning up in her hand. She dropped the test on the linoleum floor and kept screaming. Mrs. English picked up her sweater off the back of her chair, walked to the back of the room, and swiveled so she could use her good eye. Three good slaps and the fire was out, leaving a charred and smoking test in the charred and smoking spot on the floor.

"I swear, it was some kinda spot-aneous combustion. It just started burnin' while I was writin'."

Mrs. English picked up a shiny black lighter from the center of Emily's desk. "Really? pack up your things. You can explain it all to Principal Harper."

Emily stormed out the door while Mrs. English marched to the front of the classroom. As she passed me, I noticed the lighter was emblazoned with a silver crescent moon.

Lena turned back to her own test and started writing. I stared at the baggy white undershirt, her necklace jingling beneath it. Her hair was up, twisted into a weird knot, another new preference she never bothered to explain. I poked her with my pencil. She stopped writing and looked up at me, curving her mouth into a crooked half-smile, which was about the best she could do these days.

I smiled back at her, but she looked down at her test, as if she would rather consider assonance and consonance than look at me. Like it actually hurt to look at me—or, worse, she just didn't want to.

When the bell rang, Jackson High turned into Mardi Gras. Girls peeled off their tank tops and went running through the parking lot in their bikini tops. Lockers were emptied, notebooks dumped into the trash. Talking turned into shouting, then screaming, as sophomores turned into juniors and juniors into seniors. Everyone finally had what they'd been waiting for all year—freedom, and a fresh start.

Everyone but me.

Lena and I walked to the parking lot. Her bag swung as she walked, and we brushed against each other. I felt the electricity from months ago, but it was still cold. She stepped to the side, avoiding me.

"So, how'd you do?" I was trying to make conversation, as if we were total strangers.

"What?"

"The English final."

"I probably failed it. I didn't really do any of the reading." It was hard to imagine Lena not doing the reading for class, considering she had answered every question for months when we read *To Kill a Mockingbird*.

"Yeah? I aced it. I stole a copy of the test off Mrs. English's desk last week." It was a lie. I would have failed before I cheated in the House of Amma. But Lena wasn't listening anyway. I waved my hand in front of her eyes. "L? Are you listening to me?" I wanted to talk to her about the dream, but first I had to get her to notice I was here.

"Sorry. I have a lot on my mind." She looked away. It wasn't much, but it was more than I'd gotten out of her in weeks.

"Like what?"

She hesitated. "Nothing."

Nothing good? Or nothing you can talk about here?

She stopped walking and turned to face me, refusing to let me in. "We're leaving Gatlin. All of us."

"What?" I hadn't seen this coming. Which must have been what she wanted. She was shutting me out so I couldn't see inside, where things were happening, where she hid the feelings she didn't want to share. I kept thinking she just needed time. I didn't realize it was time away from me.

"I didn't want to tell you. It's only for a few months."

"Does it have anything to do with—" The familiar panic in my stomach dropped like a stone.

"It has nothing to do with her." Lena looked down. "Gramma and Aunt Del think if I get away from Ravenwood, I might think about it less. About him less."

If I get away from you. That's what I heard.

"It doesn't work like that, Lena."

"What?"

"You aren't going to forget Macon by running away."

She tensed at the mention of his name. "Yeah? Is that what your books say? Where am I? Stage five? Six, tops?"

"Is that what you think?"

"Here's a stage for you. Leave it all behind and get away while you still can. When do I get to that one?"

I stopped walking and looked at her. "Is that what you want?"

She twisted her charm necklace on the long silver chain, touching the littlest bits of us, the things we had done and seen together. She twisted it so tight, I thought for a minute it would snap. "I don't know. Part of me wants to leave and never come back, and part of me can't bear to go because he loved Ravenwood and left it to me."

Is that the only reason?

I waited for her to finish—to say she didn't want to leave me. But she didn't.

I changed the subject. "Maybe that's why we're dreaming about that night."

"What are you talking about?" I had her attention.

"The dream we had last night, about your birthday. I mean, it seemed like your birthday except for the part when Sarafine killed me. It seemed so real. I even woke up with this." I held up my shirt.

Lena stared at the raised pink scar, creating a jagged line across my abdomen. She looked like she was going to pass out. Her face went pale, her expression panicked. It was the first time I had seen any kind of emotion in her eyes in weeks. "I don't know what you're talking about. I didn't have a dream last night." There was something about the way she said it, and the look on her face. She was serious.

"That's weird. Usually we both do." I tried to sound calm, but I could feel my heart starting to pound. We had been having the same dreams since before we met. They were the reason for Macon's midnight visits to my room—to take the pieces of my dreams he didn't want Lena to see. Macon had said our connection was so strong that Lena dreamed my dreams. What did it say about our connection if she couldn't anymore?

"It was the night of your birthday, and I heard you calling me. But when I got to the top of the crypt, Sarafine was there and she had a knife."

Lena looked like she was going to be sick. I probably should have stopped there, but I couldn't. I had to keep pushing, and I didn't even know why. "What happened that night, L? You never really told me. Maybe that's why I'm dreaming about it now."

Ethan, I can't. Don't make me.

I couldn't believe it. There she was back in my mind, Kelting again. I tried to crack open the door, an inch further, and get back into hers.

We can talk about this. You have to talk to me.

Whatever Lena was feeling, she shook it off. I felt the door

84

between our minds slam shut. "You know what happened. You fell, trying to climb onto the crypt, and you were knocked out."

"But what happened to Sarafine?"

She tugged on the strap of her bag. "I don't know. There was fire everywhere, remember?"

"And she just disappeared?"

"I don't know. I couldn't see anything, and by the time the fire died down, she was gone." Lena sounded defensive, as if I was accusing her of something. "Why are you making such a big deal about this? You had a dream, and I didn't. So what? It's not like the others. It doesn't mean anything." She started to walk away.

I stepped in front of her and lifted my shirt again. "Then how do you explain this?"

The jagged outline of the scar was still pink and newly healed. Lena's eyes were wide, catching the sunlight of the first day of summer. In the sun, her hazel eyes seemed to glint with gold. She didn't say a word.

"And the song—it's changing. I know you hear it, too. Time is high? Are we going to talk about that?" She started backing away from me, which I guess was her answer. But I didn't care and it didn't matter, because I couldn't stop myself. "Something's happening, isn't it?"

She shook her head.

"What is it? Lena—"

Before I could say anything else, Link caught up to us, snapping me with his towel. "Looks like nobody's goin' to the lake today, except maybe you two."

"What do you mean?"

"Look at the tires, oh Whipped One. They're all slashed, every car in the lot, even the Beater."

"Every car?" Fatty, Jackson's truant officer, would be all over this. I calculated the number of cars in the lot. Enough to get the whole mess kicked up to Summerville, maybe even the sheriff's office. This was out of Fatty's league.

"Every car except Lena's." Link pointed at the Fastback in the parking lot. I still had trouble getting my head around the idea that it was Lena's car. The lot was in total chaos. Savannah was on her cell phone. Emily was screaming at Eden Westerly. The basketball team was going nowhere.

Link bumped his shoulder against Lena's. "I don't really blame you for the rest a them, but did you have to get the Beater? I'm a little short on cash for new tires."

I looked at her. She was transfixed.

Lena, did you?

"It wasn't me." Something was wrong. The old Lena would have bitten our heads off for even asking.

"You think it was Ridley or—" I looked over at Link. I didn't want to say Sarafine's name.

Lena shook her head. "It wasn't Ridley." She didn't sound like herself, or sure of herself. "She's not the only one who hates Mortals, believe it or not."

I looked at her, but it was Link who said the one thing we were both thinking. "How do you know?"

"I just do."

Over the chaos of the parking lot, a motorcycle gunned its engine. A guy in a black T-shirt swerved through the parked cars, blowing exhaust into the faces of angry cheerleaders, and disappeared out onto the road. He was wearing a helmet, so you couldn't see his face. Just his Harley.

But my stomach balled itself up, because the motorcycle

looked familiar. Where had I seen it before? Nobody at Jackson had a motorcycle. The closest thing was Hank Porter's ATV, which hadn't worked since he rolled it after Savannah's last party. Or so I'd heard, now that I no longer made the guest list.

Lena stared after the motorcycle as if she had seen a ghost. "Let's get out of here." She headed for her car, practically running down the stairs.

"Where to?" I tried to catch up to her, Link jogging behind me.

"Anywhere but here."

⇥ 6.12 ⇤

The Lake

If it wasn't Ridley, why weren't your tires slashed?" I pushed again. What happened in the parking lot didn't make sense, and I couldn't stop thinking about it. Or the motorcycle. Why did I recognize it?

Lena ignored me, looking out at the water. "It's probably a coincidence." Neither of us believed in coincidences.

"Yeah?" I grabbed a handful of sand, brown and gritty. Except for Link, we had the lake to ourselves. Everyone else was probably lined up at the BP trying to buy new tires before Ed ran out.

In another town, you might have put your shoes back on and called the sand dirt and this part of our lake a swamp, but the murky water of Lake Moultrie was the closest thing Gatlin had to a swimming pool. Everyone hung out on the northern shore because it was on the edge of the woods and a hike from the cars, so you never ran into anyone who wasn't in high school—especially not your parents.

I didn't know why we were here. It was weird to have the lake to ourselves, since the whole school had planned to be here today. I hadn't believed Lena when she told me she wanted to come. But she did, and we had, and now Link was thrashing around in the water, and we were sharing a dirty towel Link had grabbed out of the back of the Beater before we left.

Lena turned over next to me. For a minute, it seemed like everything was back to normal and she wanted to be there on my towel. But that only lasted until the silence set in. I could see her pale skin glistening under the thin white undershirt, which was sticking to her in the suffocating heat and humidity of a June South Carolina day. The sound of the cicadas chirping almost drowned out the awkward silence. Almost. Lena's black skirt was riding low on her hips. I wished we had our bathing suits for the hundredth time. I'd never seen Lena in one. I tried not to think about it.

Did you forget I can hear you?

I raised an eyebrow. There she was again. Back in my mind, twice in one day, as if she'd never left. One minute she was barely speaking to me, and the next she acted like nothing had changed between us at all. I knew we should talk about it, but I didn't want to fight anymore.

Not like there'd be anything forgettable about you in a bikini, L.

She leaned closer, pulling my faded shirt over my head. I could feel a few stray curls of her hair brushing against my shoulders. She slid her arm around my neck and pulled me closer. Face to face, I could see the sun glinting gold in her eyes. I didn't remember them looking so gold.

She tossed my shirt in my face and took off running for the water, laughing like a little kid as she jumped into the lake, still wearing her clothes. I hadn't seen her laugh or joke around in months. It was like I had her back for an afternoon, even if I didn't know why. I pushed it out of my mind and chased her, running into the water and across the shallow edge of the lake.

"Stop it!" Lena splashed me, and I splashed her back. Her clothes were dripping, and my shorts were dripping, but it felt good to be out in the sun. In the distance, Link was swimming out to the dock. We were really alone.

"L, wait up." She smiled over her shoulder and dove under the water.

"You're not getting away that easy." I grabbed her leg before it disappeared and yanked her toward me. She laughed and kicked, twisting until I fell into the water next to her.

"I think I felt a fish," she squealed.

I pulled her waist into mine. We were face to face, nothing but sun, and water, and the two of us. There was no avoiding each other now.

"I don't want you to leave. I want things to be like they were. Can't we go back, you know, to how it used to—"

Lena reached out and touched my lips with her hand. "Shh." Warmth spread from the tip of her finger down across my shoulders and into my body. I had almost forgotten that feeling, the heat and the electricity. She moved her hands down my arms and clenched them behind my back, laying her head against my chest. It felt like steam was rising off my skin, prickling where she touched me. I hadn't been this close to her in weeks. I inhaled deeply. Lemons and rosemary... and something else. Something different.

I love you, L.

I know.

Lena lifted her face to mine, and I kissed her. Within seconds, she disappeared into my arms, in a way she hadn't in months. The kiss began to move us involuntarily, as if we were under some kind of Cast all our own. I picked her up and lifted her out of the water, her legs dangling over my arms, the water pouring off us. I carried her back to the towel, and we were rolling in the dirty sand. Our warmth turned into fire. I knew we were out of control, and we had to stop.

L.

Lena gasped under the weight of my body, and we rolled again. I tried to catch my breath. She threw her head back and laughed, and a chill ran up my back. I remembered that laugh, straight out of my dream. It was Sarafine's laugh. Lena sounded exactly like her.

Lena.

Was I imagining it? Before I could make sense of it, she was on top of me and I couldn't think about anything else. I was lost in seconds, tangled up in her. My chest tightened, and I felt my breath growing short. I knew if we didn't stop soon, I'd end up in the emergency room, or worse.

Lena!

I felt a searing pain cut through my lip. I pushed her off and rolled over, stunned. Lena slid away from me in the dirt, backing onto her heels. Her eyes were glowing, gold and huge. Barely a trace of green. She was breathing hard. I doubled over, trying to catch my breath. Every raw nerve in my body had been lit on fire, one match at a time. Lena raised her head, and I could hardly see her face through the wild mess of dirt and hair. Just the strange golden glow.

"Get away from me." She spoke slowly, as if each word was coming from a deep, untouchable place within her.

Link was out of the water, rubbing a towel on his spiky hair. He looked ridiculous in the same plastic goggles his mom made him wear when we were little. "Did I miss somethin'?"

I touched my lip, wincing, and looked at my fingers. Blood.

Lena rose to her feet, backing away from us.

I could have killed you.

She turned and bolted into the trees.

"Lena!" I took off after her.

Running through the South Carolina woods barefoot is not something I recommend. We'd been in a drought, and the shoreline around the lake was littered with dry cypress needles, which bit into my feet like a thousand tiny knives. But I kept running. I could hear Lena more than see her, as she crashed through the trees in front of me.

Get away from me!

A heavy pine branch splintered and cracked without warning, smashing across the trail a few feet in front of me. I could already hear another branch groaning ahead.

L, are you crazy?

Branches were falling around me, missing me by inches. Far enough away so they didn't hit me, but close enough to make a point.

Stop it!

Don't follow me, Ethan! Leave me alone!

As the gap between us widened, I sped up. Tree trunks and scrub brush flashed past me. Lena was swerving around the trees, not following any distinct path. She was heading for the highway.

Another tree fell in front of me, catching horizontally on the trunks of the trees on either side of me. I was momentarily trapped. There was an osprey nest upside down in the broken tree. Something Lena, in her right mind, would never have dreamed of hurting. I touched the twigs, checking for broken eggs.

I heard the sound of a motorcycle, and my stomach caved in on itself. I shoved my way under the branches. My face was scratched and bloody, but I made it out to the highway in time to see Lena climb on the back of a Harley.

What are you doing, L?

She looked back at me for a second. Then she disappeared down the highway, black hair flying behind her.

Getting away from here.

Her pale arms were clinging to the biker from the Jackson High parking lot, the tire slasher.

The motorcycle. I finally remembered. It had been in one of Lena's graveyard pictures, the one that vanished from her wall right after I asked about it.

She wouldn't jump on the back of some random guy's bike.

Not unless she knew him.

Right then, I didn't know which was worse.

⊰ 6.12 ⊱

Caster Boy

Link and I didn't talk much on the way back from the lake. We had to take Lena's car, but I was in no shape to drive. My feet were cut up, and I had messed up my ankle trying to climb over that last tree.

Link didn't mind. He was enjoying his turn behind the wheel of the Fastback. "Man, this thing can haul. Pony power, Baby." Link's usual worship of the Fastback was annoying today. My head was spinning and I didn't want to hear about Lena's car for the hundredth time.

"Then speed it up, man. We have to find her. She's hitchhiking on the back of some guy's motorcycle." I couldn't tell him the odds were she knew the guy. When had she taken that picture of the Harley in the graveyard? I punched the door in frustration.

Link didn't state the obvious. Lena ran away from me. It was pretty clear she didn't want to be found. He just drove, and I stared out the window of the passenger's seat as the hot wind stung the hundreds of tiny cuts on my face.

Something had been wrong for a while now. I just didn't want to face it. I wasn't sure if it was something that had been done to us, I had done to her, or she had done to me. Maybe it was something she was doing to herself. Her birthday was when it all started, her birthday and Macon's death. I wondered if it was Sarafine.

All this time, I'd been thinking this was about those stupid stages of grief. I thought about the gold in her eyes and the laugh from the dream. What if this was about different kinds of stages, stages of something else? Something supernatural? Something Dark?

What if this was what we'd been afraid of all along?

I hit the door again.

"I'm sure Lena's okay. She probably needs some space. Girls are always talkin' about needin' space." Link turned on the radio, then turned it off again. "Killer stereo."

"Whatever."

"Hey, we should go by the Dar-ee Keen and see if Charlotte's workin'. Maybe she can hook us up. Especially if we show up in this sweet ride." Link was trying to distract me, but it wasn't going to happen.

"Like there's a person in town who doesn't know whose car this is? We should drop it off, anyway. Aunt Del will be worried." It would also give me an excuse to see if the Harley was at Lena's house.

Link persisted. "You're goin' to show up with Lena's car without Lena? Like that won't worry Aunt Del? Let's stop and get a freeze and figure this out. Who knows, maybe Lena's at the Dar-ee Keen. It's right off the highway."

He was right, but it didn't make me feel any better. It made me feel worse. "If you like the Dar-ee Keen so much, you should have gotten a job there. Oh wait, you couldn't, because you'll be in summer school dissecting frogs with the other Lifers who failed bio." Lifers were the super seniors, the ones who always seemed to be at school and yet somehow never graduated. The guys who wore their letterman jackets years later, when they were working at the Stop & Steal.

"You should talk. Could you have a lamer summer job? The library?"

"I could hook you up with a book, but you'd have to learn to read."

Link was baffled by my summer plans to work at the library with Marian, but I didn't mind. I was still full of questions about Lena, her family, and Light and Dark Casters. Why didn't Lena have to Claim herself on her sixteenth birthday? It didn't seem like the kind of thing you could get out of. Could she really choose to be Light or Dark? Was it that easy? Since *The Book of Moons* was destroyed in the fire, the *Lunae Libri* was the only place that might have the answers.

Then there were the other questions. I tried not to think about my mother. I tried not to think about strangers on motorcycles and nightmares and bloody lips and golden eyes. Instead, I stared out the window and watched the trees pass by in a blur.

The Dar-ee Keen was packed. Not a big surprise, since it was one of the only places within walking distance of Jackson High. In the summer, you could pretty much follow the trail of flies and you would eventually find your way here. Formerly the Dairy King, the place had gotten a new name after the Gentrys bought it but didn't want to fork up the money to pay to put all new letters on the sign. Today everyone looked even sweatier and more pissed off than usual. Walking a mile in the South Carolina heat and missing the first day of hooking up and drinking warm beer at the lake wasn't anyone's idea of a good time. It was like canceling a national holiday.

Emily, Savannah, and Eden were hanging out at the good table in the corner with the basketball team. They were barefoot, in their bikini tops and supershort jean skirts—the kind with one button left open, offering up a powerful flash of bikini bottoms without ever completely falling off. Nobody was in a very good mood. There wasn't a tire left in Gatlin, so half the cars were still sitting in the school parking lot. All the same, there was plenty of loud giggling and hair flipping. Emily was spilling out of her string bikini top, and Emory, her latest victim, was loving it.

Link shook his head. "Man, those two wanna be the bride at the weddin' and the corpse at the funeral."

"Just so long as I'm not invited to either."

"Dude. You need some sugar. I'm gonna get in line. You want somethin'?"

"No, thanks. You need some money?" Link never had any money.

"Naw, I'm gonna get Charlotte to hook me up."

Link could talk his way into and out of almost anything. I pushed my way through the crowd, as far away from Emily and Savannah as I could get. I slumped down at the bad corner table, beneath the shelves of soda cans and bottles from around the country. Some of the sodas had been there since my dad was little, and you could see the different levels of brown and orange and red syrup, disappearing to the bottom of the bottles from years of evaporation. It was pretty disgusting, I guess, that and the fifties soda bottle wallpaper and the flies. After a while, you didn't even notice it anymore.

I sat down and looked at the disappearing dark syrup, my mood in a bottle. What happened to Lena back at the lake? One minute we were kissing, the next she was running away from me. All that gold in her eyes. I wasn't stupid. I knew what it meant. Light Casters had green eyes. Dark Casters had gold. Lena's weren't completely gold, but what I'd seen at the lake was enough to make me wonder.

A fly landed on the shiny red table, and I stared at it. I recognized the familiar churning in my stomach. Dread and panic, all turning into a dull anger. I was so mad at Lena, I wanted to kick out the glass window next to our booth. But at the same time, I wanted to know what was going on and who that guy on the Harley was. Then I'd have to kick his ass.

Link slid into the booth across from me with the biggest freeze I'd ever seen. The ice cream rose about four inches above where the plastic cup ended. "Charlotte has some real potential." Link licked the straw.

Even the sugary smell of the freeze was making me sick. I felt like the sweat and the grease and the flies and the Emorys and Emilys were closing in on me.

"Lena's not here. We should go." I couldn't sit around like everything was normal. Link, on the other hand, could. Rain or shine.

"Chillax. I'll suck it down in five."

Eden walked by on her way to refill her Diet Coke. She smiled down at us, as fake as ever. "What a cute couple. See, Ethan, you didn't need to be wastin' time with that lil' tire slasher window basher. You and Link, y'all lovebirds were meant for each other."

"She didn't slash your tires, Eden." I knew how this was going to look for Lena. I had to shut them down before their mothers got involved.

"Yeah. I did," Link said, his mouth full of ice cream. "Lena's just bummed she didn't think of it first." He could never resist the chance to harass the cheer squad. To them, Lena was an old joke that wasn't funny anymore but nobody could drop. That was the thing about small towns. No one ever changed their opinion of you, even if you changed. As far as they were concerned, even when Lena was a great-grandmother, she would still be the crazy girl who busted out the window in English class. Considering most of our English class would still be living in Gatlin.

Not me. Not if things were going to stay like this. It was the first time I had really thought about leaving since Lena came to Gatlin. The box of college brochures under my bed had stayed under my bed until now. As long as I had Lena, I wasn't counting the days until I could get out of Gatlin.

"Hell-o. Who is that?" Eden's voice was a little too loud.

I heard the bell on the door of the Dar-ee Keen chime as it closed. It was like some kind of Clint Eastwood movie, where the hero steps into the saloon after he's just shot up the whole town. The neck of every girl sitting near us snapped toward the door, greasy blond ponytails flying.

"I don't know, but I'd sure like to find out," Emily purred, coming up behind Eden.

"I've never seen him before. Have you?" I could see Savannah filing through the yearbook in her mind.

"No way. I'd remember *him*." Poor guy. Emily had him in her crosshairs, target locked and loaded. He didn't stand a chance, whoever he was. I turned around to get a look at the guy Earl and Emory would be kicking the crap out of when they realized their girlfriends were drooling over him.

He was standing in the doorway in a faded black T-shirt, jeans, and scuffed black army boots. I couldn't see the scuffs from where I was sitting, but I knew they were there. Because he was wearing exactly the same thing the last time I saw him, when he ripped out of Macon's funeral.

It was the stranger, the Incubus who wasn't an Incubus. The sunlight Incubus. I remembered the silver sparrow in Lena's hand when she was sleeping in my bed.

What was he doing here?

A black tattoo wound around his arm, sort of tribal-looking, like something I'd seen before. I felt a knife in my gut, and touched my scar. It was throbbing.

Savannah and Emily walked up to the counter, trying to act like they were going to order something, as if they touched anything here other than Diet Coke.

"Who is that?" Link wasn't one for competition, not that he was in the running these days.

"I don't know, but he showed up at Macon's funeral."

Link was staring at him. "Is he one of Lena's weird relatives?"

"I don't know what he is, but he isn't related to Lena." Then again, he did come to the funeral to pay his respects to Macon. Still, there was something wrong about him. I'd sensed it since the first time I saw him.

I heard the bell chime again as the door closed.

"Hey, Angel Face, wait up."

I froze. I would have known that voice anywhere. Link was staring at the door, too. He looked like he'd seen a ghost, or worse....

Ridley.

Lena's Dark Caster of a cousin was as dangerous and hot and barely dressed as always, except now it was summer, so she had on even less than usual. She was wearing a skin-tight, lacy black tank and a black skirt so small it was probably made for a ten-year-old. Ridley's legs looked longer than ever, balancing on some kind of high, spiky sandals that could stake a vampire. Now the girls weren't the only ones with their mouths hanging open. Most of the school had been at the winter formal, when Ridley brought down the house and still managed to look hotter than any girl there except one.

Ridley leaned back and stretched her arms over her head, as if we'd woken her from a long nap. She laced her fingers together, stretching even higher, revealing even more skin and the black tattoo encircling her navel. Her tattoo looked a lot like the one on her friend's arm. Ridley whispered something in his ear.

"Holy crap, she's here." Link was slowly absorbing it. He hadn't seen Ridley since the night of Lena's birthday, when he had talked Ridley out of killing my dad. But he didn't need to see her to think about her. It was pretty clear he'd been thinking about her a lot, based on every song he'd written since she left. "She's with that guy? Do you think he's, you know, like her?" A Dark Caster. He couldn't say it.

"Doubt it. His eyes aren't yellow." But he was something. I just didn't know what.

"They're comin' over here." Link looked down at his freeze, and Ridley was on us.

"Well, if it isn't two of my favorite people. Fancy meeting you here. John and I were dying for a drink." Ridley tossed her blond and pink strands over her shoulder. She slid into the booth across from us and motioned for the guy to sit down. He didn't.

"John Breed." He said it like it was one name, looking right at me. His eyes were as green as Lena's used to be. What would a Light Caster be doing with Ridley?

Ridley smiled at him. "This is Lena's, you know, the one I was telling you about." She dismissed me with a wave of her purple-polished fingers.

"I'm Lena's boyfriend, Ethan."

John looked confused, but only for a second. He was the kind of guy who looked relaxed, as if he knew everything would go his way eventually. "Lena never told me she had a boyfriend."

Every muscle in my body tightened. He knew Lena, but I didn't know him. He had seen her since the funeral, at least talked to her. When had that happened, and why hadn't she told me?

"How exactly do you know my girlfriend?" My voice was too loud, and I could feel the eyes on us.

"Relax, Short Straw. We were in the neighborhood." Ridley looked across at Link. "How ya been, Hot Rod?"

Link cleared his throat awkwardly. "Good." His voice came out kind of squeaky. "I've been real good. Thought you left town." Ridley didn't answer.

I was still looking at John, and he was staring right back, sizing me up. Probably figuring out a thousand ways to get rid of me. Because he was after something—or someone—and I was in his way. Ridley wouldn't just show up here with this guy now, not after four months.

I kept my eyes on him. "Ridley, you shouldn't be here."

"Don't get your panties in a twist, Boyfriend. We're just passin' through, on our way back from Ravenwood." She said it casually, like it wasn't a big deal.

I laughed. "Ravenwood? They wouldn't let you in the door. Lena would burn the house down first." Ridley and Lena had grown up together, like sisters, until Ridley went Dark. Ridley had helped Sarafine find Lena on her birthday, which almost got us all, including my father, killed. There was no way Lena would hang out with her.

She smiled. "Times have changed, Short Straw. I'm not on the best terms with the rest of my family, but Lena and I have worked things out. Why don't you ask her?"

"You're lying."

Ridley unwrapped a cherry lollipop, which looked innocent enough but was the ultimate weapon in her hands. "You clearly have trust issues. I'd love to help you with that, but we've gotta get going. Have to fill up John's bike before that hick gas station of yours runs out of gas." I was holding the side of the table, and my knuckles went white.

His bike.

It was sitting out front right now, and I bet it was a Harley. The same bike I had seen in the photograph on the wall of Lena's room. John Breed had picked up Lena from Lake Moultrie. And before he said another word, I knew John Breed wasn't about to disappear. He'd be waiting on the corner the next time Lena needed a ride.

I stood up. I wasn't sure what I was going to do, but Link was. He slid out of the booth and shoved me toward the door. "Let's get outta here, man."

Ridley called after us. "I really did miss you, Shrinky Dink." She tried to make it sound sarcastic, like one of her jokes. But the sarcasm stuck in her throat, and it came out sounding more like the truth. I slammed my palm against the door, sending it flying open.

But before it swung shut, I heard John's voice. "Nice to meet you, Ethan. Say hi to Lena for me." My hands were shaking, and I heard Ridley laugh. She didn't have to lie to hurt me today. She had the truth.

We didn't talk on the way to Ravenwood. Neither one of us knew what to say. Girls can do that to you, especially Caster girls. When we reached the top of the long drive leading to Ravenwood Manor, the gates were closed, something I'd never seen before. The ivy had grown over the twisting metal, as if it had always been there. I got out of the car and shook the gate to see if it would swing open, knowing it wouldn't. I looked up at the house behind it. The windows were dark, and the sky over the house looked even darker.

What had happened? I could've handled Lena's freak-out at the lake and feeling like she had to take off. But why him? Why the Caster boy with the Harley? How long had she been hanging out with him without telling me? And what did Ridley have to do with it?

I had never been this mad at her before. It was one thing to be attacked by someone you hated, but this was something else. This was the kind of hurt that could only be inflicted by someone you loved, who you thought loved you. It was sort of like being stabbed from the inside out.

"You okay, man?" Link slammed the driver's side door.

"No." I looked down the long driveway ahead of us.

"Me neither." Link tossed the key through the Fastback's open window, and we headed down the hill.

We hitched back to town, Link turning every few minutes to check the stretch of road behind us for a Harley. But I didn't think we'd see it. That particular Harley wouldn't be headed into town. For all I knew, it could be inside those gates already.

I didn't come down for dinner, which was my first mistake. My second was opening the black Converse shoe box. I shook it open, the contents spilling across my bed. A note Lena had written me on the back of a wrinkled Snickers wrapper, a ticket stub from the movie we saw on our first date, a faded receipt from the Dar-ee Keen, and a highlighted page ripped out of a book that had reminded me of her. It was the box where I stashed all our memories—my version of Lena's necklace. It didn't seem like the kind of thing a guy should do, so I didn't let on that I did it, not even to her.

I picked up the crumpled photo from the winter formal, taken the second before we were doused with liquid snow by my so-called friends. The picture was blurry, but we were captured in a kiss, so happy it was hard to look at now. Remembering that night, even though I knew the next moment was going to be awful, it felt like part of me was still back there kissing her.

"Ethan Wate, is that you?"

I tried to shove everything back into the box when I heard my door opening, and the box fell, scattering everything onto the floor.

"You feelin' all right?" Amma came into my room and sat at the foot of my bed. She hadn't done that since I'd had stomach flu in sixth grade. Not that she didn't love me. We just had things worked out in a way that didn't include sitting on beds.

"I'm tired, that's all."

She looked at the mess on the floor. "You look lower than a catfish at the bottom a the river. And a perfectly good pork chop's lookin' as sorry as you are, down in my kitchen. That's two kinds a sorry." She leaned forward and brushed my brown hair out of my eyes. She was always after me to cut my hair.

"I know, I know. The eyes are the window to the soul, and I need a haircut."

"You need a good sight more than a haircut." She looked sad and grabbed my chin as if she could lift me up by it. Given the right circumstances, I bet she could. "You're not right."

"I'm not?"

"You're not, and you're my boy, and it's my fault."

"What do you mean?" I didn't understand and she didn't elaborate, which was generally how our conversations went.

"She's not right either, you know." Amma spoke softly, looking out my window. "Not bein' right isn't always somebody's fault. Sometimes it's just a fact, like the cards you pull." With Amma, everything came down to fate, the cards in her tarot deck, the bones in the graveyard, the universe she could read.

"Yes, ma'am."

She looked into my eyes, and I could see hers shining. "Sometimes things aren't what they seem, and even a Seer can't tell what's comin'." She took my hand and dropped something into it. A red string with tiny beads knotted into it, one of her charms. "Tie it 'round your wrist."

"Amma, guys don't wear bracelets."

"Since when do I make jewelry? That's for women with too much time and not enough sense." She yanked on her apron, straightening it. "A red string's a tie to the Otherworld, offers the kinda protection I can't. Go on, put it on."

I knew better than to argue when Amma had that look on her face. It was a mixture of fear and sadness, and she wore it like a burden too heavy for her to carry. I held out my arm and let her tie the string around my wrist. Before I could say anything else, she was at my window, pouring a handful of salt from her apron pocket all along the sill.

"Everything's gonna be okay, Amma. Don't worry."

Amma stopped in the doorway and looked back at me, rubbing the shine out of her eyes. "Been choppin' onions all afternoon."

Something wasn't right, like Amma said. But I had a feeling it wasn't me. "You know anything about a guy named John Breed?"

She stiffened. "Ethan Wate, don't you make me give that pork chop to Lucille."

"No, ma'am."

Amma knew something, and it wasn't good, and she wasn't talking. I knew it as sure as I knew her pork chop recipe, which didn't have a single onion in it.

⚞ 6.14 ⚟

Bookworm

If it was good enough for Melvil Dewey, it's good enough for me." Marian winked at me as she pulled a stack of new books out of a cardboard box, sniffing deeply. There were books everywhere, in a circle around her almost up to her head.

Lucille was weaving through the towers of books, prowling for a lost cicada. Marian made an exception to the Gatlin County Library's no-pets rule since the place was full of books but empty of people. Only an idiot would be in the library on the first day of summer, or someone who needed a distraction. Someone who wasn't speaking to his girlfriend, or wasn't being spoken to by his girlfriend, or didn't know if he even still had one—all in the space of the two longest days of his life.

I still hadn't talked to Lena. I told myself it was because I was too angry, but that was one of those lies you tell when you're trying to convince yourself that you're doing the right thing.

The truth was, I didn't know what to say. I didn't want to ask the questions, and I was scared to hear the answers. Besides, I wasn't the one who ran off with some guy on a motorcycle.

"It's chaos. Dewey decimal is mocking you. I can't even find one almanac on the history of the moon's orbital pattern." The voice from the stacks startled me.

"Now, Olivia..." Marian smiled to herself as she examined the bindings of the books in her hands. It was hard to believe she was old enough to be my mother. With not a streak of gray in her short hair, and not a wrinkle in her golden-brown skin, she didn't look more than thirty.

"Professor Ashcroft, this isn't 1876. Times do change." It was a girl's voice. She had an accent—British, I think. I'd only heard people talk that way in James Bond movies.

"So has the Dewey decimal system. Twenty-two times, to be exact." Marian shelved a stray book.

"What about the Library of Congress?" The voice sounded exasperated.

"Give me a hundred more years."

"The Universal Decimal Classification?" Now irritated.

"This is South Carolina, not Belgium."

"Perhaps the Harvard-Yenching system?"

"Nobody in this county speaks Chinese, Olivia."

A blond, lanky girl poked her head out from behind the stacks. "Not true, Professor Ashcroft. At least, not for the summer holidays."

"You speak Chinese?" I couldn't help myself. When Marian had mentioned her summer research assistant, she hadn't told me the girl would be a teenage version of herself. Except for the streaky, honey-colored hair, the pale skin, and the accent, they could have been mother and daughter. Even at first glance, the girl had a vague degree of Marian-ness that was hard to describe and that you wouldn't find in anyone else in town.

The girl looked at me. "You don't?" She poked me in the ribs. "That was a joke. In my opinion, people in this country barely speak English." She smiled and held out her hand. She was tall, but I was taller, and she looked up at me as if she was already confident we were great friends. "Olivia Durand. Liv, to my friends. You must be Ethan Wate, which I find hard to believe, actually. The way Professor Ashcroft talks about you, I was expecting more of a swashbuckler, with a bayonet."

Marian laughed, and I turned red. "What has she been telling you?"

"Only that you're incredibly brilliant and brave and virtuous, quite the save-the-day sort. Every bit the son you would expect of the beloved Lila Evers Wate. And that you'll be my lowly assistant this summer, so I can boss you around all I like." She smiled at me, and I blanked.

She was nothing like Lena, but nothing like the girls in Gatlin either. Which was in itself more than confusing. Everything she was wearing had a weathered look, from her faded jeans and the random bits of string and beads around her wrists, to her holey silver high-tops, held together with duct tape, and her ratty Pink Floyd T-shirt. She had a big, black plastic watch with crazy-looking dials on the face, caught between the bits of string. I was too embarrassed to say anything.

Marian swooped in to rescue me. "Don't mind Liv. She's teasing. 'Even the gods love jokes,' Ethan."

"Plato. And stop showing off." Liv laughed.

"I will." Marian smiled, impressed.

"He's not laughing." Liv pointed at me, suddenly serious. "'Hollow laughter in marble halls.'"

"Shakespeare?" I looked at her.

Liv winked and yanked on her T-shirt. "Pink Floyd. I can see you've got a lot to learn." A teenage Marian, and not at all what I expected when I signed on for a summer job in the library.

"Now, children." Marian held out her hand, and I pulled her up from the floor. Even on a hot day like today, she still managed to look cool. Not a hair was out of place. Her patterned blouse rustled as she walked in front of me. "I'll leave the stacks to you, Olivia. I have a special project for Ethan in the archive."

"Right, of course. The highly trained history student sorts out the stacks, while the unschooled slacker is promoted to the archive. How very American." She rolled her eyes and picked up a box of books.

The archive hadn't changed since last month, when I came to ask Marian about a summer job but stayed to talk about Lena and my dad and Macon. She had been sympathetic, the way she always was. There were piles of old Civil War registries on the shelf above my mother's desk, and her collection of antique glass paperweights. A glistening, black sphere sat next to the misshapen clay apple I made for her in first grade. My mom's and Marian's books and notes were still stacked across the desk, over yellowed maps of Ravenwood and Greenbrier spread open on the tables. Every scribbled scrap of paper I saw made it feel like she was here. Even though everything in my life seemed to be going wrong, I always felt better in this place. It was like I was with my mom, and she was the one person who always knew how to fix things, or at least make me believe there was a way to fix them.

But something else was on my mind. "*That*'s your summer intern?"

"Of course."

"You didn't tell me she'd be like that."

"Like what, Ethan?"

"Like you."

"Is that what's bothering you? The brains, or is it perhaps the long blond hair? Is there a certain way a librarian should look? Big glasses and hair in a graying bun? I would have thought between your mother and me, we would have disabused you of at least that notion." She was right. My mom and Marian had always been two of the most beautiful women in Gatlin. "Liv won't be here very long, and she's not much older than you are. I was thinking the least you could do would be to show her around town, introduce her to some people your age."

"Like who? Link? To improve his vocabulary and kill off a few thousand of her brain cells?" I didn't mention that Link would spend most of his time trying to hook up with her, which I didn't see happening.

"I was thinking of Lena." The silence in the room was embarrassing, even to me. Of course she had been thinking of Lena. The question was, why hadn't I? Marian looked at me evenly. "Why don't you tell me what's really on your mind today?"

"What is it you need me to do in here, Aunt Marian?" I didn't feel like talking about it.

She sighed and turned back to the archive. "I thought maybe you could help me sort through some of this. Obviously a great deal of the material in here relates to the locket and Ethan and Genevieve. Now that we know the end of that story, we might want to make some room for the next one."

"What's the next one?" I picked up the old photo of Genevieve wearing the locket. I remembered the first time I looked at it with Lena. It felt like years since then, instead of months.

"It would seem to me that it's yours and Lena's. The events on her birthday raised a number of questions, most of which I can't answer. I've never heard of an incident when a Caster didn't have to choose Light or Dark on the night of their Claiming—except in the case of Lena's family, when the choice is made for them. Now that we don't have Macon to help us, I'm afraid we're going to have to search out the answers ourselves." Lucille jumped up onto my mother's chair, her ears perking up.

"I wouldn't know where to start."

"'He who chooses the beginning of the road chooses the place it leads to.'"

"Thoreau?"

"Harry Emerson Fosdick. A bit older and more obscure, but still quite relevant, I think." She smiled and put her hand on the edge of the door.

"Aren't you going to help me?"

"I can't leave Olivia alone for long, or she'll reshelve the entire collection, and then we'll all have to learn Chinese." She paused for a moment, watching me, looking so much like my mom. "I think you can handle this one on your own. At least the beginning."

"I don't have a choice, do I? You can't really help me since you're a Keeper." I was still bitter about Marian's revelation that she had known my mother was involved with the Caster world, but she would never explain why or how. There were so many things about my mother and her death that Marian had never told me. It always came back to the endless rules that Bound Marian to her job as a Keeper.

"I can only help you help yourself. I can't determine the course of events, the unraveling of Darkness and Light, the Order of Things."

"That's such a load of crap."

"What?"

"It's like the prime directive on *Star Trek*. You have to let the planet evolve at its own pace. You can't introduce hyperspace or warp speed until they discover it for themselves. But Captain Kirk and the crew of the *Enterprise* always end up breaking the rule."

"Unlike Captain Kirk, there is no choice in my case. A Keeper is powerfully Bound to act neither for the Dark nor the Light. I couldn't change my destiny, even if I wanted to. I have my own place in the natural order of the Caster world, in the Order of Things."

"Whatever."

"It's not a choice. I don't have the authority to change the way things work. If I so much as tried, I might destroy not only myself but the very people I was trying to help."

"But my mom still ended up dead." I don't know why I said it, but I couldn't understand the logic. Marian had to remain uninvolved to protect the people she cared about, but the person she cared about most died anyway.

"Are you asking me if I could've prevented your mother's death?" She knew I was. I looked down at my sneakers. I wasn't sure I was ready to hear the answer.

Marian put her hand under my chin and pulled my face up to meet hers. "I didn't know your mother was in danger, Ethan. But she knew the risks." Her voice was uneven, and I knew I had gone too far, but I couldn't help it. I'd been trying to get up the courage to have this conversation for months now. "I would have gladly taken her place in that car. Don't you think I have wondered a thousand times if there was something I knew or could have done that might have saved Lila..." Her voice trailed off.

I feel the same way. You're just holding on to a different edge of the same jagged hole. We're both lost. That's what I wanted to say. Instead, I let her put her arm around my shoulder and pull me into a rough hug. I barely felt it when the arm slipped away and the door closed behind her.

I stared at the stacks of paper. Lucille jumped down from the chair and onto the table. "Be careful. These are a lot older than you." She tilted her head and looked at me with her blue eyes. Then she froze.

She was staring at my mother's chair, eyes wide, fixated. There was nothing there, but I remembered what Amma told me. "Cats can see the dead. That's why they stare at things the way they do for so long, like they're just lookin' into thin air. But they're not. They're lookin' through it."

I stepped closer to the chair. "Mom?" She didn't answer, or maybe she did, because there was a book lying on the chair that wasn't there a minute ago. *Darkness and Light: The Origins of Magic.* It was one of Macon's books. I had seen it in his library at Ravenwood. I lifted it up, and a gum wrapper fell out—one of my mother's bookmarks, no doubt. I bent down to pick up the wrapper, and the room began to sway, the lights and colors swirling around me. I tried to focus on something, anything, to keep from falling, but I was too dizzy. The wood floor rushed up to meet me, and as I hit the ground the smoke burned my eyes—

By the time Abraham returned to Ravenwood, the ash had already made its way inside the house. The charred remnants of Gatlin's great houses wafted down from the open windows on the second floor like black snowflakes. As he ascended the staircase, Abraham's footsteps left impressions in the thin black layer already coating the floor. He secured the upstairs windows, without putting The Book of Moons down for a second. But he couldn't have put it down even if he had wanted to. Ivy, the old cook from Greenbrier, was right; the Book was calling him, a whisper only he could hear.

When he reached the study, Abraham rested the Book on the polished mahogany desk. He knew exactly which page to turn to, as if the Book was flipping the pages itself. As if it knew what he wanted. Even though he had never seen the Book before, Abraham knew the answer was in those pages, an answer that would guarantee Ravenwood's survival.

The Book was offering him the one thing he wanted above all else. But it wanted something in return.

Abraham stared down at the Latin script. He recognized it immediately. It was a Cast he had read about in other books. One he had always considered more of a myth. But he had been wrong, because it was staring back at him.

Abraham heard Jonah's voice before he saw him. "Abraham, we have to get out of the house. The Federals are coming. They've burned everything, and they aren't planning to stop until they reach Savannah. We have to get into the Tunnels."

Abraham's voice was resolute, and it sounded different somehow, even to him. "I'm not going anywhere, Jonah."

"What are you talking about? We have to save what we can and get out of here." Jonah grabbed his brother's arm, noticing the open page beneath them. He stared at the script, unsure he could trust what he was seeing.

"The Daemonis Pactum? The Demon's Trade?" Jonah stepped back. "Is this what I think it is? The Book of Moons?"

"I'm surprised you recognize it. You never paid much attention during our studies."

Jonah was used to Abraham's insults, but there was something different about his tone tonight. "Abraham, you can't."

"Don't tell me what I can't do. You would watch this house burn to the ground before you thought to act. You have never been capable of doing what was required. You are weak, like Mother."

Jonah flinched, as if someone had struck him. "Where did you get it?"

"You don't need to worry about that."

"Abraham, be sensible. The Demon's Trade is too powerful. It cannot be controlled. You are making a bargain, without knowing what you will have to sacrifice. We have other houses."

Abraham pushed his brother aside. Though Abraham barely touched him, Jonah flew across the room. "Other houses? Ravenwood is the seat of our family's power in the Mortal world, and you think I intend to allow a few soldiers to burn it to the ground? I can use this to save Ravenwood."

Abraham's voice rose. "Exscinde, neca, odium incende; mors portam patefacit. *Destroy, kill, hate; death opens the gate.*"

"Abraham, stop!"

But it was too late. The words rolled off Abraham's tongue as if he had known them his entire life. Jonah looked around, panicked, waiting for the Cast to take effect. But he had no idea what his brother had asked for. He only knew that whatever it was, it would be done. That was the power of the Cast, but there was also a price. It was never the same. Jonah rushed toward his brother, and a small, perfectly round orb, the size of an egg, slipped from his pocket and rolled across the floor.

Abraham picked up the sphere, glowing at his feet, and rolled it between his fingers. "What are you doing with an Arclight, Jonah? Is there a particular Incubus you're planning to imprison in this archaic device?"

Jonah backed away as Abraham advanced, matching him step for step, but Abraham was too fast. In the blink of an eye, he pinned Jonah against the wall, his iron grip closing around his brother's throat.

"No. Of course not. I—"

Abraham tightened his hold. "What would an Incubus be doing with the only vessel capable of imprisoning his kind? Do you think I'm that stupid?"

"I am only trying to protect you from yourself."

In one fluid motion, Abraham lunged forward and

plunged his teeth into his brother's shoulder. Then he did the unthinkable.

He drank.

The bargain was made. He would no longer be sustained by the memories and dreams of Mortals. From this day forward, he would crave blood.

When he had his fill, Abraham dropped his brother's limp body and licked the ash from his hand, the taste of flesh still lingering in the black residue. "You should have been more concerned about protecting yourself."

Abraham turned away from his brother's body. "Ethan."

"Ethan!"

I opened my eyes. I was lying on the floor of the archive. Marian was hovering over me in an un-Marian state of panic. "What happened?"

"I don't know." I sat up, rubbing my head, wincing. There was a knot growing underneath my hair. "I must have hit the table on my way down."

Macon's book was lying on the floor, open next to me. Marian looked at me with her uncanny ESP—or not so uncanny, if you stopped to consider that she had followed me into visions herself only months ago. Within seconds, she had a cold pack in her hand and was holding it against my throbbing head. "You're having visions again, aren't you?"

I nodded. My mind was swimming with images, but I couldn't focus on any one of them. "It's the second time. I had one the other night when I was holding Macon's journal."

"What did you see?"

"It was the night of the fires, like in the locket visions. Ethan Carter Wate was already dead. Ivy had *The Book of Moons*, and she gave it to Abraham Ravenwood. He was in both of the visions." His name sounded thick and fuzzy on my tongue. Abraham Ravenwood was the original boogeyman of Gatlin County.

I gripped the edge of the table, steadying myself. Who wanted me to see the visions? More important, why?

Marian paused, still holding the book. "Oh?" She looked at me carefully.

"And someone else. His name began with a J. Judas? Joseph? Jonah. That was it. I think they were brothers. They were Incubuses."

"Not just Incubuses." Marian snapped the book shut. "Abraham Ravenwood was a powerful Blood Incubus, the father of the Ravenwood Blood Incubus line."

"What do you mean?" So, the story folks had been telling for years was true? I had cleared another layer of fog from the supernatural map of Gatlin.

"Although all Incubuses are Dark by nature, not all of them choose to feed on blood. But once one does, the instinct appears to be inherited."

I leaned against the table as the vision sharpened in my mind. "Abraham—he's the reason Ravenwood Manor never burned, right? He didn't make a deal with the Devil. He made it with *The Book of Moons*."

"Abraham was dangerous, maybe more dangerous than any Caster. I can't imagine why you're seeing him now. Fortunately, he died young, before Macon was born."

I tried to do the math. "That's young? How long do Incubuses usually live?"

"A hundred and fifty to two hundred years." She replaced the book on her worktable. "I don't know what any of this has to do with you or Macon's journal, but I never should have given it to you. I interfered. We should leave this book locked up here."

"Aunt Marian—"

"Ethan! Don't pursue this, and don't tell anyone else about it, not even Amma. I can't imagine how she would react if you said the name Abraham Ravenwood in her presence." She put her arm around me and gave me a halfhearted squeeze. "Now, let's go finish up in the stacks before Olivia calls the police." She turned to the door and stuck her key in the lock.

There was one more thing. I had to say it. "He could see me, Aunt Marian. Abraham looked right at me and said my name. That's never happened in the visions before."

Marian stopped, staring at the door as if she could see right through it. It was more than a few seconds before she turned the key in the lock and swung the door open. "Olivia? Do you think Melvil Dewey could spare you for a cup of tea?"

Our conversation was over. Marian was a Keeper and the Head Librarian of the Caster Library, the *Lunae Libri*. She could only tell me so much without violating her obligations. She couldn't take sides or change the course of events once they were set in motion. She couldn't be Macon for me, and she wasn't my mom. I was on my own.

⇥ 6.14 ⇤

Beneath the Paper

A ll of those?" There were three stacks of brown paper pack- ages on the checkout desk. Marian marked the last one with the familiar GATLIN COUNTY LIBRARY stamp, always twice and always tied with the same white string.

"No, take that pile, too." She pointed to a second pile, on the nearest trolley.

"I thought nobody in this town reads."

"Oh, they read. They just don't own up to what they read, which is why we make not only library-to-library deliveries but library-to-home ones as well. Circulating books only. Allowing two to three days for the processing of requests, of course."

Great. I was afraid to ask what was in these brown paper packages, and I was pretty sure I didn't want to know. I picked up a stack of books and groaned. "What are these, encyclopedias?"

Liv pulled the receipt from the top bundle. "Yes. *The Encyclopedia of Ammunition*, actually."

Marian waved us out the door. "Go with Ethan, Liv. You haven't had an opportunity to see our beautiful little town yet."

"I can handle it."

Liv sighed and pushed the trolley toward the door. "Come on, Hercules. I'll help you load up. Can't keep the ladies of Gatlin waiting on their..." She consulted another receipt. "...*Carolin-er Cake Doctor Cookbook*, now can we?"

"Carolina," I said, automatically.

"That's what I said. Carolin-er."

Two hours later, we had delivered most of the books and driven by both Jackson High and the Stop & Steal. As we circled the General's Green, I realized why Marian had been so eager to hire me at a library that was always empty and didn't need summer employees. She had planned for me to be Liv's teenage tour guide all along. It was my job to show her the lake and the Dar-ee Keen and fill in the gaps between what folks around here said and what they meant. My job was to be her friend.

I wondered how Lena was going to feel about that. If she noticed.

"I still don't understand why there's a statue of a general from a war the South didn't win, and one which was generally embarrassing for your country, in the middle of town." Of course she didn't.

"Folks honor the fallen around here. There's a whole museum dedicated to them." I didn't mention the Fallen Soldiers was also the scene of my dad's Ridley-induced suicide attempt a few months ago.

I looked over at Liv from behind the wheel of the Volvo. I couldn't remember the last time there had been any girl except Lena in the passenger's seat.

"You're a terrible tour guide."

"This is Gatlin. There isn't all that much to see." I glanced in the rearview mirror. "Or just not that much I want you to see."

"What do you mean by that?"

"A good tour guide knows what to show and what to hide."

"I stand corrected. You're a terribly misguided tour guide." She pulled a rubber band out of her pocket.

"So I'm more of a mis-guide?" It was a stupid joke, my trademark.

"And I take issue with both your punning and your tour-guiding philosophy, generally speaking." She was working her blond hair into two braids, her cheeks pink from the heat. She wasn't used to the South Carolina humidity.

"What do you want to see? You want me to take you to shoot cans behind the old cotton mill off Route 9? Flatten pennies on the train tracks? Follow the trail of flies into the eat-at-your-own-risk grease pit we call the Dar-ee Keen?"

"Yes. All of the above, particularly the last bit. I'm starving."

Liv dropped the last library receipt into one of two piles. "...seven, eight, nine. Which means I win, you lose, and get your hands off those chips. They belong to me now." She pulled my chili fries over to her side of the red plastic table.

"You mean fries."

"I mean business." Her side of the table was already covered with onion rings, a cheeseburger, ketchup, mayonnaise, and my sweet tea. I knew whose side was whose because she had made a line between us, laying french fries end to end, like the Great Wall of China.

"'Good fences make good neighbors.'"

I remembered the poem from English class. "Walt Whitman."

She shook her head. "Robert Frost. Now keep your hands off my onion rings."

I should've known that one. How many times had Lena quoted Frost's poems or twisted them into one of her own?

We had stopped for lunch at the Dar-ee Keen, which was down the road from the last two deliveries we'd made —Mrs. Ipswich (*Guide to Colon Cleanliness*) and Mr. Harlow (*Classic Pinups of World War II*), which we had given to his wife because he wasn't home. For the first time, I understood the reason for the brown paper.

"I can't believe it." I wadded up my napkin. "Who would have figured Gatlin was so romantic?" I had bet on church books. Liv had bet on romance novels. I lost, eight to nine.

"Not only romantic, but romantic *and* righteous. It's a wonderful combination, so—"

"Hypocritical?"

"Not at all. I was going to say American. Did you notice we delivered *It Takes a Bible* and *Divinely Delicious Delilah* to the very same house?"

"I thought that was a cookbook."

"Not unless Delilah's cooking up something quite a bit hotter than these chili chips." She waved a fry in the air.

"Fries."

"Exactly."

I turned bright red, thinking about how flustered Mrs. Lincoln had looked when we dropped those books off at her door. I didn't point out to Liv that Delilah's devotee was the mother of my best friend, and the most ruthlessly righteous woman in town.

"So, you like the Dar-ee Keen?" I changed the subject.

"I'm mad about it." Liv took a bite of her cheeseburger, big enough to put Link to shame. I'd already seen her wolf down more than the average varsity basketball player at lunch. She didn't seem to care what I thought about her one way or another, which was a relief. Especially since everything I did around Lena lately was wrong.

"So what would we find in your brown paper package? Church books, romance novels, or both?"

"I don't know." I had more secrets than I knew what to do with, but I wasn't about to share any of them.

"Come on. Everyone has secrets."

"Not everyone," I lied.

"There's nothing at all beneath your paper?"

"Nope. Just more paper, I guess." In a way, I wished it was true.

"So you're rather like an onion?"

"More like a regular old potato."

She picked up a fry and examined it. "Ethan Wate is no regular old potato. You, sir, are a french fry." She popped it into her mouth, smiling.

I laughed and conceded. "Fine. I'm a french fry. But no brown paper, nothing to tell."

Liv stirred her sweet tea with her straw. "That confirms it.

126

You are definitely on the waiting list for *Divinely Delicious Delilah*."

"You caught me."

"I can't promise anything, but I will tell you that I know the librarian. Rather well, it turns out."

"So you'll hook me up?"

"I will hook you up, dude." Liv started laughing, and I did, too. She was easy to be around, like I'd known her forever. I was having fun, which, by the time we stopped laughing, turned into feeling guilty. Explain that to me.

She returned to her fries. "I find all the secrecy sort of romantic, don't you?" I didn't know how to answer that, considering how deep the secrets went around here.

"In my town, the pub is on the same street as the church, and the congregation moves directly from one to the other. Sometimes we even eat Sunday dinner there."

I smiled. "Is it divinely delicious?"

"Nearly. Maybe not quite so hot. But the drinks are not quite so cold." She pointed at her sweet tea with a fry. "Ice, my friend, is something you find on the ground more often than in your glass."

"You have a problem with Gatlin County's famous sweet tea?"

"Tea is meant to be hot, sir. From a kettle."

I stole a fry and pointed it back at her sweet tea. "Well, ma'am, to a strict Southern Baptist, that is the Devil's drink."

"You mean because it's cold?"

"I mean because it's tea. No caffeine allowed."

Liv looked shocked. "No tea? I'll never understand this country."

I stole another fry. "You want to talk about blasphemy? You weren't there when Millie's Breakfast 'n' Biscuits over on Main started serving premade freezer biscuits. My great-aunts, the Sisters, pitched a fit that nearly took down the place. I mean, chairs were flying."

"Are they nuns?" Liv stuck an onion ring inside her cheeseburger.

"Who?"

"The Sisters." Another onion ring.

"No. They're actual sisters."

"I see." She slapped the bun back down.

"You don't, not really."

She picked up the burger and took a bite. "Not at all." We both started laughing again. I didn't hear Mr. Gentry walk up behind us.

"Y'all get enough to eat?" he asked, wiping his hands with a rag.

I nodded. "Yes, sir."

"How's that girlfriend a yours?" He asked as if he was hoping I had come to my senses and dumped Lena by now.

"Um, fine, sir."

He nodded, disappointed, and walked back toward the counter. "Say hello to Miss Amma for me."

"I take it he doesn't like your girlfriend?" She said it like a question, but I didn't know what to say. Was a girl still technically your girlfriend if she drove off with another guy? "I think Professor Ashcroft may have mentioned her."

"Lena. My—her name is Lena." I hoped I didn't look as uncomfortable as I felt. Liv didn't seem to notice.

She took another sip of her tea. "I'll probably meet her at the library."

"I don't know if she'll be coming by the library. Things have been weird lately." I don't know why I said it. I barely knew Liv. But it felt good to say it out loud, and my insides untwisted a little.

"I'm sure you'll work it out. Back home, I fought with my boyfriend all the time." Her voice was light. She was trying to make me feel better.

"How long have you guys been together?"

Liv waved her hand in the air, the weird watch sliding down her wrist. "Oh, we broke up. He was a bit of a prat. I don't think he liked having a girlfriend who was smarter than he was."

I wanted to get off the subject of girlfriends, and ex-girlfriends. "So what's that thing, anyway?" I nodded at the watch, or whatever it was.

"This?" She held her wrist over the table so I could see the clunky black watch. It had three dials and a little silver needle that rested on a rectangle with zigzags all over it, sort of like one of those machines that track the strength of earthquakes. "It's a selenometer."

I looked at her blankly.

"Selene, the Greek goddess of the moon. *Metron*, or 'measure' in Greek." She smiled. "A little rusty on your Greek etymology?"

"A little."

"It measures the moon's gravitational pull." She turned one of the dials, thoughtfully. Numbers appeared under the pointer.

"Why do you care about the moon's gravitational pull?"

"I'm an amateur astronomer. I'm interested in the moon, mostly. It has a tremendous impact on the Earth. You know, the tides and everything. That's why I made this."

I almost spit out my Coke. "You made it? Seriously?"

"Don't be so impressed. It wasn't that difficult." Liv's cheeks

129

flushed again. I was embarrassing her. She reached for another fry. "These chips really are brilliant."

I tried to imagine Liv sitting in the English version of the Dar-ee Keen, measuring the gravitational pull of the moon over a mountain of fries. It was better than picturing Lena on the back of John Breed's Harley. "So let's hear about your Gatlin. The one where they call fries by the wrong name." I had never been any farther than Savannah. I couldn't imagine what life would be like in another country.

"My Gatlin?" The pink spots on her cheeks faded.

"Where you're from."

"I'm from a town north of London, called Kings Langley."

"What?"

"In Hertfordshire."

"Doesn't ring a bell."

She took another bite of her burger. "Maybe this will help. It's where they invented Ovaltine. You know, the drink?" She sighed. "You stir it in milk, and it makes the milk into a chocolate malted?"

My eyes widened. "You mean chocolate milk? Kind of like Nesquik?"

"Exactly. It's amazing stuff, really. You should try it sometime."

I laughed into my Coke, which spilled on my faded Atari T-shirt. Ovaltine girl meets Quik boy. I wanted to tell Link, but he would get the wrong idea.

Even though it had only been a few hours, I had the feeling she was a friend.

"What do you do when you're not drinking Ovaltine and making scientific devices, Olivia Durand of Kings Langley?"

She crumpled the paper from her cheeseburger. "Let's see.

130

Mostly I read books and go to school. I study at a place called Harrow. Not the boys' school."

"Is it?"

"What?" She scrunched up her nose.

"Harrowing?" H. A. R. R. O. W. I. N. G. Nine across, as in, gettin' on in years and can't take much more a these harrowin' times, Ethan Wate.

"You can't resist a terrible pun, can you?" Liv smiled.

"And you didn't answer the question."

"No. Not especially harrowing. Not for me."

"Why not?"

"Well, for starters, I'm a genius." She was matter-of-fact, as if she'd just said she was blond, or British.

"So why did you come to Gatlin? We're not exactly a genius magnet."

"Well, I'm part of the AGE, Academically Gifted Exchange, between Duke University and my school. Will you pass the mayo-nnaise?"

"Mann-aise." I tried to say it slowly.

"That's what I said."

"Why would Duke bother to send you to Gatlin? So you could take classes at Summerville Community College?"

"No, silly. So I could study with my thesis adviser, the re-nowned Dr. Marian Ashcroft, truly the only one of her kind."

"What is your thesis about?"

"Folklore and mythology, as it relates to community building after the American Civil War."

"Around here most people still call it the War Between the States," I said.

She laughed, delighted. I was glad someone thought it was

funny. To me, it was just embarrassing. "Is it true people in the South sometimes dress up in old Civil War costumes and fight all the battles over again, for fun?"

I stood up. It was one thing for me to say it, but I didn't want to hear it from Liv, too. "I think it's time to get going. We've got more books to deliver."

Liv nodded, grabbing her fries. "We can't leave these. We should save them for Lucille."

I didn't mention that Lucille was used to Amma feeding her fried chicken and plates of leftover casserole on her own china plate, as the Sisters had instructed. I couldn't see Lucille eating greasy fries. Lucille was partic-u-lar, as the Sisters would say. She liked Lena, though.

As we headed for the door, a car caught my eye through the grease-coated windows. The Fastback was making a three-point turn at the end of the gravel parking lot. Lena made a point of not driving past us.

Great.

I stood and watched the car skid onto Dove Street.

That night, I lay in my bed and stared up at the blue ceiling, my hands folded behind my head. A few months ago, this would've been when Lena and I went to bed in our separate rooms together — reading, laughing, talking through our days. I had nearly forgotten how to fall asleep without her.

I rolled over and checked my old, cracked cell. It hadn't really been working since Lena's birthday, but still, it would ring when someone called me. If someone had.

Not like she'd use the phone.

Right then, I was back to being the same seven-year-old who had dumped every puzzle in my room into one giant, miserable mess. When I was a kid, my mom sat on the floor and helped me turn the mess into a picture. But I wasn't a kid anymore, and my mom was gone. I turned the pieces over and over in my mind, but I couldn't seem to get them sorted out. The girl I was madly in love with was still the girl I was madly in love with. That hadn't changed. Only now the girl I was madly in love with was keeping secrets from me and barely speaking to me.

Then there were the visions.

Abraham Ravenwood, a Blood Incubus who had killed his own brother, knew my name and could see me. I had to figure out how the pieces fit together until I could see something—some kind of pattern. I couldn't get the puzzle back into the box. It was too late for that. I wished someone could tell me where to put even one piece. Without thinking, I got up and pushed open my bedroom window.

I leaned out and breathed in the darkness, when I heard Lucille's distinctive meow. Amma must have forgotten to let her back inside. I was about to call out to tell her I was coming, when I noticed them. Under my window, at the edge of the porch, Lucille Ball and Boo Radley sat side by side in the moonlight.

Boo thumped his tail, and Lucille meowed in response. They sat like that at the top of the porch steps, thumping and meowing, as if they were carrying on as civilized a conversation as any two townsfolk on a summer night. I don't know what they were gossiping about, but it must have been big news. As I lay in bed listening to the quiet conversation of Macon's dog and the Sisters' cat, I drifted off before they did.

⤙ 6.15 ⤚

Southern Crusty

D on't you lay a finger on a single one a my pies until I ask you to, Ethan Wate."

I backed away from Amma, hands in the air. "Just trying to help."

She glared at me while she wrapped a sweet potato pie, a two-time winner, in a clean dish towel. The sour cream and raisin pie sat on the kitchen table next to the buttermilk pie, ready for the icebox. The fruit pies were still cooling on the racks, and a dusting of white flour coated every surface in the kitchen.

"Only two days into summer and you're already under my feet? You'll wish you were over at the high school takin' summer classes if you drop one a my prizewinnin' pies. You want to help? Stop mopin' and go pull the car around."

Tempers were running about as high as temperatures, and we didn't say much as we bumped our way out toward the highway in the Volvo. I wasn't talking, but I can't say anybody noticed. Today was the single biggest day of Amma's year. She had won first place in Baked and Fried Fruit Pies and second place in Cream Pies every year at the Gatlin County Fair for as long as I could remember. The only year she didn't get a ribbon was last year, when we didn't go because it was only two months after my mom's accident. Gatlin couldn't boast the biggest or the oldest fair in the state. The Hampton County Watermelon Festival had us beat by maybe two miles and twenty years, and the prestige of winning the Gatlin Peach Prince and Princess Promenade could hardly compare to the honor of placing in Hampton's Melon Miss and Master Pageant.

But as we pulled into the dusty parking lot, Amma's poker face didn't fool my dad or me. Today was all about pageants and pies, and if you weren't balancing a pie wrapped as snugly as someone's firstborn, you were pushing a kid in curlers holding a baton toward the pavilion. Savannah's mom was Gatlin's Peach Pageant organizer, and Savannah was the defending Peach Princess. Mrs. Snow would be overseeing pageants all day. There was no such thing as too young for a crown in our county. The fair's Best Babies event, where rosy cheeks and diaper dispositions were compared like competing cobblers, drew more spectators than the Demolition Derby did. Last year, the Skipetts' baby was disqualified for cheating when her rosy cheeks came off on the judges' hands. The county fair had strict guidelines—no formal wear until two years old, no makeup until six years old, and then only "age-appropriate makeup" until twelve.

Back when my mom was around, she was always ready to take on Mrs. Snow, and the Peach Pageants were one of her favorite targets. I could still hear her saying, "Age-appropriate makeup? Who are you people? What makeup is age-appropriate for a seven-year-old?" But even my family never missed a county fair, except last year. Now here we were again, carrying pies through the crowds and into the fairgrounds, same as ever.

"Don't jostle me, Mitchell. Ethan Wate, keep up. I'm not gonna let Martha Lincoln or any a those women beat me out a that ribbon on account a you two boys." In Amma's shorthand, *those women* were always the same women—Mrs. Lincoln, Mrs. Asher, Mrs. Snow, and the rest of the DAR.

By the time my hand was stamped, it looked like three or four counties had already beaten us there. Nobody missed the opening day at the fair, which meant a trip to the fairgrounds halfway between Gatlin and Peaksville. And a trip to the fairgrounds meant a disastrous amount of funnel cake, a day so hot and sticky you could pass out just from standing, and if you were lucky, some making out behind the Future Farmers of America poultry barns. My shot at anything but heat and funnel cake wasn't looking too good this year.

My dad and I dutifully followed Amma to the judging tables under an enormous Southern Crusty banner. Pies had a different sponsor every year, and when it couldn't be Pillsbury or Sara Lee, you ended up with Southern Crusty. Pageants were crowd-pleasers, but Pies was the granddaddy of them all. The same families had been making the same recipes for generations, and every ribbon won was the pride of one great Southern house and the shame of another. Word had it that a few women from town had their sights set on keeping Amma from winning first place this year. Judging by the muttering I'd heard in the kitchen all week long, that would happen when hell froze over and *those women* were skating on it.

136

By the time we had unloaded her precious cargo, Amma was already harassing the judges about table placement. "You can't put a vinegar after a cherry, and you can't put a rhubarb between my creams. It'll take the taste right out a them, unless that's what you boys are lookin' to do."

"Here it comes," said my dad, under his breath. As the words came out of his mouth, Amma gave the judges the Look, and they squirmed in their folding chairs.

My dad glanced over at the exit, and we slunk outside before Amma had a chance to put us to work terrorizing innocent volunteers and intimidating judges. The moment we hit the crowds, we instinctively turned in opposite directions.

"You going to walk around the fair with that cat?" My dad looked down at Lucille sitting in the dirt next to me.

"Guess so."

He laughed. I still wasn't used to hearing it again. "Well, don't get into trouble."

"Never do."

My dad nodded at me, like he was the dad and I was the son. I nodded back, trying not to think about the last year, when I was the grown-up and he was out of his mind. He walked his way, I walked mine, and we both disappeared into the hot and sweaty masses.

The fair was packed, and it took me a while to track down Link. But true to form, he was hanging out by the games, trying to flirt with any girl who would look at him, today being a prime opportunity to meet a few who weren't from Gatlin. He was standing in front of one of those scales you hit with a giant rubber mallet to prove how strong you are, the mallet resting on his shoulder. He was in full drummer mode, in his faded Social Distortion T-shirt, with his drumsticks stuck in the back pocket of his jeans, and his wallet chain hanging below the sticks.

"Lemme show ya how it's done, ladies. Stand back. You don't wanna get hurt."

The girls giggled as Link gave it his best shot. The little meter climbed up, measuring Link's strength and his chances of hooking up at the same time. It passed A REAL WUSS and WIMPY and headed toward the bell at the top, A REAL STUD. But it didn't quite make it, stopping about halfway, at CHICKEN LITTLE. The girls rolled their eyes and headed for the Ring Toss.

"This thing's rigged. Everyone knows that," Link shouted after them, dropping the mallet in the dirt. He was probably right, but it didn't matter. Everything in Gatlin was rigged. Why would the carnival games be any different?

"Hey, you got any money?" Link pretended to dig around in his pockets, like he might actually have more than a dime.

I handed him a five, shaking my head. "You need a job, man."

"I've got a job. I'm a drummer."

"That's not a job. It's not called a job unless you get paid."

Link scanned the crowd, looking for girls or funnel cake. It was hard to tell which, since he responded equally to both. "We're tryin' to line up a gig."

"Are the Holy Rollers playing at the fair?"

"This lame scene? Nah." He kicked the ground.

"They wouldn't book you?"

"They said we sucked. But people thought Led Zeppelin sucked, too."

As we walked through the fair, it was hard not to notice that the rides seemed to get a little smaller and the games a little shabbier every year. A pathetic-looking clown dragged a cluster of balloons past us.

Link stopped, hitting me on the arm. "Check it out. Six o'clock. Third Degree Burns." As far as Link was concerned, a girl couldn't get hotter than that.

He was pointing at a blond who was headed in our direction, smiling. It was Liv.

"Link—" I tried to tell him, but he was on a mission.

"As my mom would say, the Good Lord has good taste, hallelujah amen."

"Ethan!" She waved at us.

Link looked at me. "Are you kiddin' me? You've already got Lena. That's just wrong."

"I don't have Liv, and these days I don't even know if I have Lena. Be cool." I smiled at Liv, until I noticed she was wearing a faded Led Zeppelin T-shirt.

Link saw it at the same time I did. "The perfect girl."

"Hey, Liv. This is Link." I elbowed him, hoping he'd close his mouth. "Liv is Marian's summer research assistant. She works with me at the library." Liv held out her hand.

Link stood there gawking. "Wow." The thing about Link was, he never embarrassed himself, just me.

"She's an exchange student from England."

"Holy wow."

I looked at Liv and shrugged. "I told you."

Link broke out his biggest smile for Liv. "Ethan didn't tell me he was workin' with a hot babe a cosmic proportions."

Liv looked at me, pretending to be surprised. "You didn't? I find that rather tragic." She laughed and linked her arms through

139

ours. "Come on, boys. Explain to me exactly how it is you make this strange cotton into candy."

"I can't give away national secrets, ma'am."

"I can." Link squeezed her arm with his.

"Tell me everything."

"Tunnel of Love or the Kissing Booth?" Link grinned even wider.

Liv tilted her head. "Hmm. That's a tough one. I'm going to go with...the Ferris Wheel."

That's when I caught sight of the familiar black hair and the scent of lemons and rosemary in the breeze.

Nothing else was familiar. Lena was a few yards away, standing behind the ticket booth in what had to be Ridley's clothes. Her black tank rode up on her stomach, and her black skirt was about five inches too short. There was a long streak of blue in her hair, twisting down from where it parted around her face, and down her back. But that wasn't what shocked me most. Lena, the girl who never put anything on her face but sunscreen, was covered in makeup. Some guys liked girls with crap all over their faces, but I wasn't one of them. Lena's black-rimmed eyes were especially disturbing.

Surrounded by cutoff denim and dust and straw and sweat and red and white plastic checkered tablecloths, she looked even more out of place. Her old boots were the only thing I recognized. And her charm necklace, dangling like a lifeline back to the real Lena. She wasn't the kind of girl who wore stuff like that. At least, she didn't used to be.

The lowlifes were checking her out, three guys deep. I had to resist the urge to punch all of them in the face.

I dropped Liv's arm. "I'll meet you guys over there."

Link couldn't believe his luck. "No problem, man."

"We can wait," Liv offered.

"Don't worry about it. I'll catch up with you." I hadn't expected to see Lena here, and I didn't know what to say without sounding even more whipped than Link already thought I was. As if there's something you can say to sound cool after your girlfriend takes off with another guy.

"Ethan, I've been looking for you." Lena walked toward me, and she sounded like herself, her old self—the Lena I remembered from a few months ago. The one I was desperately in love with, the one who loved me back. Even if she looked like Ridley. She stood on her tiptoes to push my hair out of my face, her fingers dragging slowly down my jawline.

"That's funny, because the last time I saw you, you were ditching me." I tried to sound casual, but I just sounded angry.

"I wasn't ditching you, exactly." She was defensive.

"No, you were throwing trees at me and jumping on the back of a bike with some other guy."

"I wasn't throwing trees."

I raised an eyebrow. "Yeah?"

She shrugged. "More like branches."

But I could tell I had gotten to her. She twisted the tiny paper-clip star I had given her, until I thought it was going to snap off of her necklace. "I'm sorry, Ethan. I don't know what's going on with me." Her voice was soft, honest. "Sometimes I feel like everything is closing in, and I can't take it. I wasn't ditching you at the lake. I was ditching me."

"You sure about that?"

She looked back up at me, a tear sliding down her cheek. She wiped it away, her fingers balled in frustration. She opened her fist and put her hand on my chest, resting it over my heart.

It's not you. I love you.

"I love you." She said it out loud this time and the words hung in the air between us, so much more public than when we Kelted. My chest tightened when she said it, and my breath caught in my throat. I tried to think of something sarcastic to say, but I couldn't think about anything except how beautiful she was and how much I loved her, too.

But I wasn't letting her off that easy this time. I broke the truce. "What's going on, L? If you love me so much, what's the deal with John Breed?"

She looked away without saying a word.

Answer me.

"It's not like that, Ethan. John's just a friend of Ridley's. There's nothing going on between us."

"How long has nothing been going on? Since you took that picture of him in the graveyard?"

"It wasn't a picture of him. It was his bike. I was meeting Ridley, and he happened to be there." I noticed she ignored the question.

"Since when have you been hanging out with Ridley? Did you forget the part where she separated us so your mother could get you alone and try to convince you to go over to the Dark side? Or when Ridley almost killed my father?"

Lena pulled her arm away from me, and I could feel her withdrawing again, moving back into that place I couldn't reach. "Ridley warned me you wouldn't understand. You're a Mortal. You don't know anything about me, not the real me. That's why I didn't tell you." I felt a sudden breeze as the storm clouds rolled in like a warning.

"How do you know whether I would understand or not? You haven't told me anything. Maybe if you gave me the chance instead of sneaking around behind my back—"

"What do you want me to tell you? That I have no idea what's going on with me? That something's changing, something I don't understand? That I feel like a freak, and Ridley's the only one who can help me figure it out?"

I could hear everything she was saying, but she was right. I didn't understand. "Are you listening to yourself? You think Ridley's trying to help you, that you can trust her? She's a Dark Caster, L. Look at yourself! You think this is you? The things you're feeling, she's probably causing them."

I waited for the downpour, but instead the clouds parted. Lena moved closer and put her hands on my chest again, staring up at me, pleading. "Ethan, she's changed. She doesn't want to be Dark. It ruined her life when she Turned. She lost everyone, including herself. Ridley says going Dark changes the way you feel about people. You can sense the feelings you had, the things you loved, but Rid says the feelings are distant. Almost like they belong to someone else."

"But you said it wasn't something she could control."

"I was wrong. Look at Uncle Macon. He knew how to control it, and Ridley's learning, too."

"Ridley is not Macon."

Heat lightning flashed across the sky. "You don't know anything."

"That's right. I'm a stupid Mortal. I don't know anything about your supersecret Caster world and skanky Caster cousin, or Caster Boy and his Harley."

Lena snapped. "Ridley and I were like sisters, and I can't

turn my back on her. I told you, I need her right now. And she needs me."

I didn't say anything. Lena was so frustrated, I was surprised the Ferris Wheel hadn't come loose and rolled away. I could see the lights from the Tilt-A-Whirl, spinning in the corner of my eye, churning and dizzying. It was the way I felt when I let myself get lost in Lena's eyes. Sometimes love feels that way, and you find your way to a truce when you don't really want to.

Sometimes the truce finds you.

She reached up and laced her fingers behind my neck, pulling me into her. I found her lips, and we were all over each other as if we were afraid we might never have the chance to touch again. This time, when her mouth tugged at my bottom lip, biting gently into my skin, there was no blood. Just urgency. I turned, pushing her against the rough wooden wall behind the ticket booth. Her breath was ragged, echoing in my ear even louder than my own. I raked my hands through her curls, guiding her mouth to mine. The pressure in my chest started to build, the shortness of breath, the sound of the air as I tried to fill my lungs. The fire.

Lena felt it, too. She pushed away from me, and I bent over trying to catch my breath.

"Are you okay?"

I took a deep breath and stood up again. "Yeah, I'm all right. For a Mortal."

She smiled a real smile and reached for my hand. I noticed she had drawn crazy-looking designs on her palm in Sharpie. The black curls and spirals swirled from her palm around her wrist and up the base of her arm. The pattern looked like the henna the fortune-teller wore, in the tent that smelled like bad incense at the other edge of the fairgrounds.

"What is that?" I held her wrist, but she pulled it away. Remembering Ridley and her tattoo, I hoped it was Sharpie.

It is.

"Maybe we should get you something to drink." She led me around the side of the booth, and I let her. I couldn't stay mad, not if there was a possibility the wall between us was finally coming down. When we kissed a minute ago, that's what I felt. It was the opposite of the kiss on the lake, a kiss that had taken my breath away for different reasons. I might never know what that kiss was. But I knew this kiss, and I knew it was all I had—a chance.

Which lasted two seconds.

Because then I saw Liv, carrying two cotton candies in one hand and waving at me with the other, and I knew the wall was about to go back up, maybe for good. "Ethan, come on. I have your cotton candy. We're going to miss the Ferris Wheel!"

Lena dropped my hand. I knew how it must have looked—a tall blond, with long legs and two cotton candies and an expectant smile. I was doomed before Liv even got to the word *we*.

That's Liv, Marian's research assistant. She works with me at the library.

Do you work at the Dar-ee Keen together, too? And the fair?

Another flash of heat lightning tore across the sky.

It isn't like that, L.

Liv handed me the cotton candy and smiled at Lena, holding out her hand.

A blond? Lena looked at me. *Seriously?*

"Lena, right? I'm Liv."

Ah, the accent. That explains everything.

"Hi, *Liv.*" Lena pronounced her nàme like it was an inside joke between us. She didn't touch Liv's hand.

145

If Liv noticed the slight, she ignored it, letting her hand drop. "Finally! I've been trying to get Ethan to introduce us properly, since it seems he and I are chained together for the summer."

Clearly.

Lena wouldn't look at me, and Liv wouldn't stop looking at her.

"Liv, this really isn't a good—" I couldn't stop it. They were two trains colliding in painfully slow motion.

"Don't be silly," Lena interrupted, looking at Liv carefully, as if she was the Sybil in her family and she could read Liv's face. "So nice to meet you."

He's all yours. Take the whole town while you're at it.

It took Liv about two seconds to realize she'd walked into something, but she tried to fill the silence all the same. "Ethan and I talk about you all the time. He says you play the viola."

Lena stiffened.

Ethan and I. There was nothing mean about the way Liv said it, but the words themselves were enough. I knew what they meant to Lena. Ethan and the Mortal girl, the girl who was everything Lena couldn't be.

"I've gotta go." Lena turned around before I could catch her arm.

Lena—

Ridley was right. It was only a matter of time before another new girl came to town.

I wondered what else Ridley had been telling her.

What are you talking about? We're just friends, L.

We were just friends once, too.

Lena took off, pushing her way through the sweaty crowd, causing a chain reaction of chaos as she went. Her ripple effect seemed endless. I couldn't see it perfectly, but somewhere between us a clown fumbled as the balloon character in his hands popped, a child cried as a snow cone dropped, and a woman screamed as a popcorn machine began to smoke and catch fire. Even in the slippery blur of heat and arms and noise, Lena affected everything in her wake, a pull as powerful as the moon to the tides, or the planets to the sun. I was caught in her orbit, even as she pulled away from mine.

I took a step, and Liv put her hand on my arm. Her eyes narrowed as if she was analyzing the situation, or registering it for the first time. "I'm sorry, Ethan. I didn't mean to interrupt. I mean, if I was interrupting, you know. Something." I knew she wanted me to tell her what happened without having to ask. I didn't say anything, which I guess was my answer.

The thing is, I didn't take another step. I let Lena go.

Link walked toward us, fighting his way through the crowd, carrying three Cokes and his own cotton candy. "Man, the line at the drink booth is brutal." Link handed Liv a Coke. "What'd I miss? Was that Lena?"

"She left," Liv said quickly, as if things were that simple.

I wished they were.

"Whatever. Forget the Ferris Wheel. We'd better get over to the main tent. They're gonna announce the winners a the pie-bakin' contest any minute, and Amma will tan your hide if you aren't there to watch her moment a glory."

"Apple pie?" Liv brightened.

"Yep. And you eat it wearin' Levi's, with a napkin tucked into your shirt up here. Drinkin' a Coke and drivin' a Chevy, while singing 'American Pie.'" I listened to Link ramble and

Liv's easy laugh as they walked ahead of me. They didn't have nightmares. They weren't haunted. They weren't even worried.

Link was right. We couldn't miss Amma's moment of glory. I sure wasn't winning any ribbons today. The truth was, I didn't need to bring the mallet down on the old, rigged carnival scale to know what it would say. Link might be CHICKEN LITTLE, but I felt lower than A REAL WUSS. I could pound away all I wanted, but the answer would always be the same. No matter what I did lately, I was caught somewhere between LOSER and ZERO, and it was starting to feel like Lena was holding the hammer. I finally understood why Link wrote all those songs about getting dumped.

Tunnel of Love

If it gets any hotter in here, people are goin' to start droppin' like flies. Flies are gonna start droppin' like flies." Link wiped his sweaty forehead with his sweaty hand, which sprayed liquid Link on those of us lucky to be standing next to him.

"Thanks for that." Liv wiped her face with one hand and pulled her damp shirt away from her body with the other. She looked miserable. The Southern Crusty tent was packed, and the finalists were already standing on the makeshift wooden stage. I tried to see over the row of enormous women in front of us, but it was like standing in the Jackson cafeteria line on cookie day.

"I can barely see the stage." Liv stood on her toes. "Is something supposed to be happening? Did we miss it?"

"Hold on." Link tried to edge between the smaller of the two enormous women in front of us. "Yeah, we can't get any closer. I give up."

"There's Amma." I pointed. "She's won first place almost every year."

"Amma Treadeau," Liv said.

"That's right. How did you know?"

"Professor Ashcroft must have mentioned her."

Carlton Eaton's voice blared over the loudspeaker as he fussed with the portable mic. He always announced the winners because the only thing he loved more than opening everyone's mail was the spotlight. "If y'all will bear with me, folks, we got some technical difficulties...hold on now...can someone call Red? How am I supposed to know how to fix a darn microphone? Shoot, it's hotter than Hades in here." He mopped his forehead with his handkerchief. Carlton Eaton never managed to remember when the microphone was on.

Amma stood proudly to his right, in her best dress, with the tiny violets all over it, holding her prizewinning sweet potato pie. Mrs. Snow and Mrs. Asher were next to her, holding their own creations. They were already dressed for the Mother-Daughter Peach Pageant that started right after Pies. They were equally frightening in their respective aqua and pink pageant mother gowns, which made them look like aging prom dates from the eighties. Thankfully, Mrs. Lincoln was not in the pageant, so she stood next to Mrs. Asher in one of her standard church dresses, holding her famous chess pie. It was still hard to look at Link's mom without remembering the insanity of Lena's last birthday. You don't see your girlfriend's mother stepping out of your best friend's mom's body too many nights of the year. When I saw Mrs. Lincoln now, that's what I thought of — the moment Sarafine emerged like a snake shedding its skin. I shuddered.

Link elbowed me. "Dude, look at Savannah. She's got the crown on and everything. She sure knows how to milk it."

Savannah, Emily, and Eden were sitting in the front row with the rest of the Peach Pageant contestants, sweating away in their tackiest pageant evening wear. Savannah was in yards of glittery Gatlin peach, with her rhinestone Peach Princess crown balanced perfectly on her head, even though the train of her dress kept snagging on the bottom of her cheap metal folding chair. Little Miss, the local dress shop, probably had to special-order it for her all the way from Orlando.

Liv edged her way closer to me, eyeing the cultural phenomenon that was Savannah Snow. "Is she the queen of Southern Crusty, then?" Liv's eyes twinkled, and I tried to imagine how strange this all must look to an outsider.

I almost smiled. "Just about."

"I didn't realize baking was so important to Americans. Anthropologically speaking."

"I don't know about other places, but in the South, women take their baking seriously. And this is the biggest pie-baking contest in Gatlin County."

"Ethan, over here!" Aunt Mercy was waving her handkerchief in one hand and carrying her infamous coconut pie in the other. Thelma was walking behind her, shoving people aside with Aunt Mercy's wheelchair. Every year Aunt Mercy entered the contest, and every year she got an honorable mention for her coconut pie, even though she'd forgotten how to make it about twenty years ago, and none of the judges were brave enough to taste it.

Aunt Grace and Aunt Prue were arm in arm, dragging Aunt Prue's Yorkshire terrier, Harlon James, behind them.

"Well, fancy seein' you here, Ethan. Did you come ta see Mercy win her ribbon?"

"Of course he did, Grace. What else would he be doin' in a tent fulla old ladies?"

I wanted to introduce Liv, but the Sisters didn't give me a chance. They kept talking over one another. I should've known Aunt Prue would take care of that for me. "Who's this, Ethan? Your new girlfriend?"

Aunt Mercy adjusted her spectacles. "What happened ta the other one? The Duchannes girl, with the dark hair?"

Aunt Prue looked at her suspiciously. "Well, Mercy, that's jus' none a our concern. You shouldn't be askin' anything about it. She mighta up and left him."

"Why would she do that? Ethan, you didn't ask that girl ta get nekkid, did ya?"

Aunt Prue gasped. "Mercy Lynne! If the Good Lord doesn't strike us all down on account a that talk…"

Liv looked dizzy. She obviously wasn't used to following the banter of three hundred-year-old women with thick Upcountry accents and fractured grammar.

"Nobody tried—nobody left anyone. Everything is fine between Lena and me," I lied. Even though they'd find out the truth the next time they went to church, if their hearing aids were turned up high enough to hear the gossip. "This is Liv, Marian's summer research assistant. We work together at the library. Liv, this is Aunt Grace, Aunt Mercy, and Aunt Prudence, my great-great-aunts."

"Don't you be addin' any extra *great*s in there." Aunt Prue pulled herself up a little straighter.

"That's her name. Lena! It was on the tip a my tongue." Aunt Mercy smiled at Liv.

Liv smiled back. "Of course. It's a pleasure to meet you all."

Carlton Eaton tapped on the mic just in time. "All right, y'all, I think we can get started."

"Girls, we need ta get up ta the front. They'll be callin' my name in no time." Aunt Mercy was already working her way through the aisles, rolling forward like an army tank. "We'll see you in two shakes of a rabbit's tail, Sweet Meat."

People filed into the tent from all three entrances, and Lacy Beecham and Elsie Wilks, the winners of Casseroles and Barbeque, took their places next to the stage, holding their blue ribbons. Barbeque was a big category, even bigger than Chili, so Mrs. Wilks was about as puffed up as I'd ever seen her.

I watched Amma's face, so proud, not glancing at one of *those women* even once. Then I watched it darken, and she looked off toward one side of the tent.

Link ribbed me again. "Hey, lookit. I mean, you know, the Look." We followed Amma's stinkeye to the far corner of the tent. When I saw who she was looking at, I tensed.

Lena was slouching against one of the tent poles, eyes on the stage. I knew she couldn't have cared less about a pie-baking contest, unless she was here to root for Amma. And from the looks of it, Amma didn't think that's why Lena was here.

Amma shook her head at Lena, ever so slightly.

Lena looked away.

Maybe she was looking for me, though I was probably the last person she wanted to see right now. So what was she doing here?

Link grabbed my arm. "It's—she's—"

Lena glanced across to the pole opposite her. Ridley leaned against the pole in a pink miniskirt, unwrapping a lollipop. Her eyes were fixed on the stage, like she actually cared about who was going to win. I knew she didn't, because the only thing she cared about was causing trouble. Since there were about two hundred people too many in the tent, this seemed about as good a place for trouble as any.

Carlton Eaton's voice echoed over the crowd. "Testin', testin'. Can y'all hear me? All right, then, on to Cream Pies. We have ourselves a close one this year, folks. Had myself the pleasure a tastin' a few a these pies, and I'm here to tell you every single one a 'em's a winner in my O-pinion. But I reckon we can only have one first-place winner here tonight, so let's see who it's gonna be." Carlton fumbled with the first envelope, ripping the paper loudly. "Here it is, folks, our third-place winner is... Tricia Asher's Creamsicle Pie." Mrs. Asher scowled for a millisecond, then flashed her phony smile.

I kept my eyes locked on Ridley. She had to be up to something. Ridley didn't give a crap about pie, or anything that happened in Gatlin. Ridley turned and nodded toward the back of the tent. I looked behind me.

Caster Boy was watching with a smile. He was standing by the rear entrance, his eyes on the finalists. Ridley turned her attention back to the stage and slowly, deliberately, began sucking on her lollipop. Never a good sign.

Lena!

Lena didn't even blink. Her hair began to twist in the stagnant air, blowing in what I knew was the Casting Breeze. I don't know if it was the heat or the close quarters or the grim look on Amma's face, but I was starting to worry. What were Ridley and

154

John up to, and why was Lena Casting here? Whatever they were trying to do, Lena must be trying to counteract it.

Then I figured it out. Amma wasn't the only one dealing out the Look like a bad spread of cards. Ridley and John were staring down Amma, too. Was Ridley stupid enough to mess with Amma? Was anyone?

Ridley held up the lollipop as if to answer.

"Uh-oh." Link stared. "We should probably get outta here."

"Why don't you take Liv to the Ferris Wheel?" I said, trying to catch Link's eye. "I think things are going to be pretty boring for a while."

"Now we've reached the most excitin' part a the judgin'," said Carlton Eaton, as if on cue. "All right, y'all, this is it. Let's see which one a these here ladies is gonna be takin' home a second-place ribbon and five hundred dollars' worth a brand new bakeware, or a first-place ribbon and seven hundred fifty dollars, compliments a Southern Crusty. *'Cause if it ain't Southern Crusty, it ain't the South, and it ain't Crusty—*" Carlton Eaton never finished, because before he could say the words, something else came out—

Of the pies.

The pie tins began to move, and it took people a few seconds to realize what was happening, before they started screaming. Grubs and maggots and palmetto bugs, Carolina cockroaches, started crawling out of the pies. It was as if all the hate and lies and hypocrisy of the whole town—of Mrs. Lincoln and Mrs. Asher and Mrs. Snow, the principal of Jackson High, and the DAR and the PTA and every church auxiliary, all rolled into one—had been baked into those pies, and now it was coming to life. Bugs were pouring out of every pie onstage, more bugs than the pie tins could possibly hold.

Every pie except Amma's. She shook her head, her eyes narrowing into slits like some kind of challenge. Hordes of cream-covered grubs and roaches hit the floor around the contestants' feet. But the trail of scurrying insects diverged in a neatly forking path around Amma.

Mrs. Snow reacted first. She hurled her pie, sticky fruit-covered bugs rocketing into the air and landing all over the front row. Mrs. Lincoln and Mrs. Asher followed suit, maggots raining down on the Peach Pageant contestants' satin dresses. Savannah started screaming, not fake screaming but real, bloodcurdling screams. Everywhere you looked, there were pie-covered worms and people trying not to puke at the sight of them. Some were more successful than others. I saw Principal Harper doubled over a trash can by the exit, getting rid of a whole day's worth of funnel cake. If Ridley was looking to stir up trouble, she had succeeded.

Liv looked ill. Link tried to push forward into the crowd, most likely to rescue his mom. He had been doing that a lot lately, and considering how unrescuable his mother was, I had to give him credit.

Liv grabbed my arm as the crowd surged forward toward the exits.

"Liv, get out of here. Go out that way. Everyone's heading for the sides." I pointed to the back exit of the tent. John Breed was still standing there, smiling at his handiwork, his green eyes fixed on the stage. Green eyes or not, he wasn't one of the good guys.

Link was on the stage brushing worms and bugs off his mother, who was completely hysterical. I worked my way closer to the front.

"Somebody help me!" Mrs. Snow looked like someone in a horror movie, terrified and screaming, her dress alive with squirming bugs. Even I didn't hate her enough to wish this on her.

I caught a glimpse of Ridley, sucking away on her lollipop, bringing bugs to life with every lick. I didn't know she could pull off something this big by herself, but then again she had Caster Boy to help her.

Lena, what's happening?

Amma was still standing on the stage, looking like she could bring down the whole tent with a single look. Bugs and worms were crawling over each other at her feet, but not one was brave enough to touch Amma. Even the bugs knew better. She was staring down at Lena, her eyes narrow and her jaw tight, as she had been from the moment the first grub crawled its way out of Mrs. Lincoln's chess pie. "You fixin' to make me do this now?"

Lena stood at the edge of the tent, her hair still twisting in the Casting Breeze, the corners of her mouth upturned into the smallest shadow of a smile. I recognized it for what it was. Satisfaction.

Now everyone knows what's really in their pies.

Lena hadn't been trying to stop them. She was part of it.

Lena! Stop!

But there was no stopping now. This was payback for the Guardian Angels and the Disciplinary Committee meeting, for every token casserole left at the gates of Ravenwood and every pitying look, for every insincere sentiment offered by the folks of Gatlin. Lena was handing it right back as if she'd saved every bit, storing it all up until it exploded in their faces. I guess this was her way of saying good-bye.

Amma spoke to Lena as if they were the only people in the tent. "Enough, child. You can't get what you want from these folks. Sorry from a sorry town is nothin' but a whole lot more a the same. A pie tin fulla nothin'."

Aunt Prue's voice pierced the din. "Good Lord, help! Grace is havin' a heart attack!" Aunt Grace was lying on the ground, unconscious. Grayson Petty was kneeling over her, taking her pulse while Aunt Prue and Aunt Mercy batted palmetto bugs away from their sister.

"I said enough!" Amma roared from the stage, and as I ran for Aunt Grace, I could've sworn the tent was going to come down on top of us.

As I bent down to help, I saw Amma pull something out of her pocketbook and hold it high above her head. The One-Eyed Menace, our old wooden spoon, in its full glory. Amma brought it down on the table in front of her with a crack.

"Oww!" Across the room, Ridley winced and the lollipop dropped right out of her hand, rolling across the dirt as if Amma had smashed it with the Menace itself.

In that second, everything stopped.

I looked over to Lena, but she was gone. The spell, or whatever it was, was broken. The palmetto bugs scampered out of the tent, leaving only the grubs and worms behind.

And me, leaning over Aunt Grace to make sure she was breathing.

Lena, what have you done?

Link followed me out of the tent, confused as usual. "I don't get it. Why would Lena help Ridley and Caster Boy pull a stunt like that? Someone coulda really gotten hurt."

I scanned the rides closest to us to see if there was any sign of Lena or Ridley. But I didn't see them, just the 4-H volunteers fanning old women and handing out plastic cups of water to the victims of the pie-baking contest from hell.

"You mean, like my Aunt Grace?"

Link yanked on his shorts to make sure they were grub-free. "I thought she was a goner. Lucky she just fainted. Probably the heat."

"Yeah. Lucky." But I didn't feel lucky. I was too angry. I had to find Lena, even if she didn't want to be found. She was going to have to tell me why she would terrorize everyone in that tent to get even with—who? A few aging beauty queens? Link's mom, who was just aging? It was something Ridley would do, not Lena.

It was getting dark, and Link scanned the crowd through the flashing lights and hysterical church ladies. "Where'd Liv go? Wasn't she with you?"

"I don't know. I told her to go out the back when the bugfest started."

Link cringed at the word *bug*. "Should we look for her?"

There was a group of people in line at the Fun House, so I headed that way. "I get the impression Liv knows how to take care of herself. I think this is something we have to do on our own."

"Right on."

We turned the corner a few yards from the entrance to the Tunnel of Love. Ridley, Lena, and John were standing in front of the dingy plastic cars painted to look like gondolas. Lena was standing in the middle, a leather jacket slung over her shoulders. Only she didn't have a leather jacket. John did.

I called her name, without even thinking. "Lena!"

Leave me alone, Ethan.

No. What were you thinking?

I wasn't thinking. I was finally doing something.

Yeah. Something stupid.

Don't tell me you're on their side now.

I was walking fast. Link struggled to keep up with me. "You're gonna start a fight, aren't you? Man, I hope Caster Boy doesn't set us on fire or turn us into statues or somethin'." Link was usually up for a fight. Even though he was skinny, he was almost as tall as me, and twice as crazy. But the prospect of fighting a Supernatural didn't have the same appeal. We'd been burned on that one before.

I wanted to let him off the hook. "I've got this. Go find Liv."

"No way, dude. I've got your back."

When we got to the gondolas, John stepped forward protectively, in front of the girls, as if we were the ones they needed to be protected from.

Ethan, get out of here.

I could hear the fear in her voice, but this time I was the one who didn't answer.

"Hey, Boyfriend, how's it goin'?" Ridley smiled and unwrapped a blue lollipop.

"Screw you, Ridley."

She noticed Link behind me, and her smile changed. "Hiya, Hot Rod. You wanna take a ride through the Tunnel of Love?" Ridley tried to sound playful, but she sounded nervous instead.

Link grabbed her by the arm and pulled her toward him, almost like he really was her boyfriend. "What did you think you were doin' back there? You coulda gotten someone killed.

Ethan's four-hundred-year-old aunt almost had a heart attack."

Ridley snatched her arm back. "It was only a few bugs. Don't be so melodramatic. I think I liked you better when you were a little more compliant."

"Yeah, I bet."

Lena stepped out from behind John. "What happened? Is your aunt okay?" She seemed like my Lena again, kind and concerned, but I didn't trust her anymore. A few minutes ago, she was taking down the women she hated and everyone else in the tent with them, and now she was the girl I kissed behind the ticket booth. It didn't add up.

"What were you doing back there? How could you help them?" I didn't realize how mad I was until I heard myself yelling. But John did.

He slammed his palm against my chest, and I stumbled back.

"Ethan!" Lena was scared, I could tell that much.

Stop! You don't know what you're doing.

Like you said. At least I'm finally doing something.

Do something else. Get out of here!

"You can't talk to her like that. Why don't you leave before you get hurt." What had I missed? Lena had walked away from me barely an hour ago, and now John Breed was defending her like she was already his girlfriend?

"Yeah? You should be careful who you push around, Caster Boy."

"Caster Boy?" He took a step closer to me, curling his hands into fists. Big fists. "Don't call me that."

"What should I call you? Dirtbag?" I wanted him to hit me.

He lunged at me, but I threw the first punch. I'm stupid that way. I released all the frustration and anger I'd been holding inside the second my soft human fist made contact with his steel supernatural jaw. It was like hitting cement.

John blinked, his green eyes turning as black as coal. He hadn't felt a thing. "I'm not a Caster."

I had been in my share of fights, but none of them could have prepared me for what it felt like to be hit by John Breed. I remembered watching Macon and his brother Hunting fighting, their incredible strength and speed. John barely moved, and my back hit the ground. I thought I was going to pass out.

"Ethan! John, stop!" Lena was screaming, black makeup running down her face.

I heard John slam Link into the dirt. To his credit, Link got up faster than I did. Only he was back down again faster, too. I picked myself up off the ground. I wasn't that banged up, but I was going to have a hard time hiding the bruises from Amma.

"That's enough, John." Ridley tried to sound cool, but her voice had an edge and she looked scared—as scared as Ridley could look. She grabbed John's arm. "Let's go. We've got somewhere to be."

Link looked her right in the eye, which took some effort, considering he was lying in the dirt. "Don't do me any favors, Rid. I can take care of myself."

"I can see that. You're a real Golden Glove." Link winced at the dig, or maybe it was the pain.

Either way, he wasn't used to being the one on the ground in a fight. He pushed himself to his feet and held up his fists, ready to go again. "They're the fists a fury, Baby, and they're just gettin' started."

Ridley stepped between John and Link. "No. They're finished."

Link dropped his hands, kicking the dust. "Yeah, well, I could take him if he wasn't a—what the hell are you, man?"

I didn't give John a chance to answer, because I was pretty sure I already knew. "He's some kind of Incubus." I looked at Lena. She was still crying, her arms hugging her waist, but I didn't try to talk to her. I wasn't even sure who she was anymore.

"You think I'm an Incubus? A Demon Soldier?" John laughed.

Ridley rolled her eyes. "Don't be such a show-off. No one calls Incubuses Demon Soldiers anymore."

John cracked his knuckles. "I'm old school."

Link looked confused. "I thought all you vampire dudes had to stay inside durin' the day."

"And I thought all you hillbillies drove Trans Ams with Confederate flags painted on the hoods." John laughed, but it wasn't funny. Ridley stayed between them.

"What does it matter to you, Shrinky Dink? John's not really a rules kinda guy. He's sort of...unique. I like to think of him as the best of both worlds." I had no idea what Ridley was talking about. But whatever John Breed was, she wasn't saying.

"Yeah? I like to think about him as crawlin' back to his own world and stayin' outta ours." Link talked tough, but when John looked at him, all the color drained out of Link's face.

Ridley turned to John. "Let's go." They turned back to the Tunnel of Love, the cars still making the loop under the old wooden arch painted to look like some bridge in Venice. Lena hesitated.

"Lena, don't go with them."

She stood there for a second, like she was thinking about running back into my arms. But something was stopping her. John whispered to her, and she climbed into the plastic gondola. I looked at the only girl I'd ever loved. Black hair and golden eyes, instead of green.

I couldn't pretend the gold didn't mean anything, not anymore.

I watched the car disappear, leaving Link and me behind. As banged up and bruised as the day we had taken on Emory and his brother on the playground in fifth grade.

"Come on. Let's get outta here." Link was already walking away. It was dark now, and the lights from the Ferris Wheel flashed as it turned. "Why'd you think he was an Incubus?" Link was taking comfort in the fact he had gotten his ass kicked by a Demon, not some regular guy.

"His eyes went black, and it felt like I was hit by a two-by-four."

"Yeah, but he was walkin' around durin' the day. And he's got those green eyes, like Lena's..." He stopped, but I knew what he was about to say.

"Used to be? I know. It doesn't make sense." Nothing about tonight did. I couldn't shake the way Lena had looked at me. For a second, I was sure she wasn't going to follow them. I was thinking about Lena, but Link was still talking about John.

"And what was all that crap about the best a both worlds? What worlds? Creep and creepier?"

"I don't know. I was sure he was an Incubus."

Link rotated his shoulder, assessing the damage. "Whatever he is, that dude's got some serious superpowers. I wonder what else he can do."

We turned the corner, near the exit of the Tunnel of Love. I stopped walking. *The best of both worlds.* What if John could do a lot more than rip like an Incubus and beat the two of us to a pulp? He had green eyes. What if he was some kind of Caster, with his own version of Ridley's Power of Persuasion? I didn't think Ridley could influence Lena by herself, but what if John was helping her?

It would explain why Lena was acting so crazy—why she'd looked like she wanted to come with me, until John whispered in her ear. How long had he been whispering to her?

Link hit my arm with the back of his hand. "Hey. You know what's weird?"

"What?"

"They haven't come out."

"What do you mean?"

He pointed to the exit of the Tunnel of Love. "They didn't get off the ride." Link was right. There was no way they could have come out before we turned the corner. We watched as the gondolas kept coming out empty.

"Then where are they?"

Link shook his head, all tapped out of insight for now. "I don't know. Maybe the three of them are doin' somethin' kinky in there." We both winced. "Let's check it out. There's no one around." Link was already halfway to the exit.

He was right. The cars kept coming out empty. Link hopped over the gate around the ride and ducked into the tunnel. Inside, there was a little space on either side of the track, but it was tricky to walk by the moving cars without getting hit.

One of the cars caught Link in the shin. "There's no one in here. Where could they have gone?"

"They couldn't have disappeared." I remembered the way

John Breed ripped out of Macon's funeral. Maybe he could, but Ridley and Lena couldn't Travel.

Link ran his hands along the walls. "You think there's some kinda secret Caster door in here, or somethin'?"

The only Caster doors I knew about led to the Tunnels, the underground labyrinth of passageways that slept quietly under Gatlin and the rest of the Mortal world. It was a world within a world, so different from ours that it altered both time and distance. But, as far as I knew, all the entrances to the Tunnels were inside buildings—Ravenwood, the *Lunae Libri*, the crypt at Greenbrier. A few sheets of painted plywood didn't qualify as a building, and there was nothing under the Tunnel of Love except dirt. "A door leading where? This thing is sitting in the middle of the fair. They just set it up a couple of days ago."

Link inched his way back out of the tunnel. "Where else could they have gone?"

If John and Ridley were using their powers to control Lena, I had to find out. It wouldn't explain away the last few months or her golden eyes, but maybe it would explain what she was doing with John. "I've gotta get down there."

Link had already pulled the keys out of his back pocket. "How'd I know you were gonna say that?"

He followed me to the Beater, the gravel crunching under his sneakers as he jogged to keep up. He yanked the rusty door open and slid behind the wheel. "Where are we goin'? Or am I better off—" He was still talking when I heard it, the tiny words tugging at the bottom of my heart.

Good-bye, Ethan.

They were gone, the voice and the girl. Like a soap bubble, or cotton candy, or the last silvery sliver of a dream.

Unmistakable

The Beater skidded to a stop in front of the Historical Society, the front tires halfway up the curb, the engine dying out on the empty street.

"Can you take it down a notch? Someone's gonna hear us." Not that Link ever drove any differently. Still, we were parked only a few feet from the building that served as the DAR head-quarters. I noticed the roof had finally been rebuilt—it had blown off in Hurricane Lena, a few days before her birthday. Though Jackson High had been hit by the same storm, I guess those repairs could wait. We had our priorities around here.

Almost everyone in South Carolina was related to a Confed-erate, so joining the Daughters of the Confederacy was easy. But to join the DAR, you needed a bloodline going back to someone who fought in the war for American independence. The prob-lem was the proof. Unless you were an actual signer of the

Declaration of Independence, you had to establish a paper trail a mile long. Even then you had to be invited, which required sucking up to Link's mom and signing whatever petition she happened to be passing around. Maybe it was a bigger deal down here than up North, like we needed to prove we had all fought for the same side in a war once. The Mortal part of our town was just as confusing as the Caster one.

Tonight the building looked empty.

"It's not like there's anyone around to hear us. Until the Demolition Derby ends, everyone we know is at the fairgrounds." Link was right. Gatlin may as well have been a ghost town. Most folks were still at the fair, or at home on the phone reporting the details of a certain Southern Crusty bake-off that would go down in history for decades to come. I was pretty sure Mrs. Lincoln wouldn't have let any of the DAR members miss watching her try to beat Amma out of first place in Pies. Although, right about now, I bet Link's mom was wishing she had stuck to pickled okra this year.

"Not everyone." I was out of ideas and explanations, but I knew where we could get some of both.

"You sure this is a good idea? What if Marian's not here?" Link was jumpy. The sight of Ridley hanging out with some kind of mutant Incubus wasn't bringing out the best in him. Not that he had anything to worry about. It was pretty clear who John Breed was after, and it wasn't Ridley.

I checked my cell. It was almost eleven. "It's a bank holiday in Gatlin. You know what that means. Marian should be in the *Lunae Libri* by now." That's how it worked around here. Marian was the Gatlin County Head Librarian from nine in the morning until six at night every weekday. But on bank holidays, she was the Head Caster Librarian from nine at night until six in the morning. The Gatlin Library was closed, which meant the Caster Library was open. And the *Lunae Libri* had a door leading into the Tunnels.

I slammed the door of the Beater as Link pulled a Maglite out of his glove box. "I know, I know. The Gatlin Library's closed and the Caster Library's open all night long, on account a most a Marian's clients don't come around durin' the day." Link waved the flashlight across the building in front of us. A brass placard read DAUGHTERS OF THE AMERICAN REVOLUTION. "Still, if my mom or Mrs. Asher or Mrs. Snow found out what was in the basement a their buildin'..." He was holding the heavy metal flashlight like he was brandishing a weapon.

"You planning to take someone out with that thing?"

Link shrugged. "Never know what we're gonna find down there."

I knew what he was thinking. Neither one of us had been back to the *Lunae Libri* since Lena's birthday. Our last visit had been more about danger than dictionaries.

Danger and death. We did something wrong that night, and some of it had happened right here. If I had gotten to Ravenwood earlier, if I had found *The Book of Moons*, if I could have helped Lena fight Sarafine—if we had done one thing differently, would Macon be alive right now?

We made our way around to the back of the old red brick building, in the moonlight. Link shined his flashlight on the grating near the ground, and I crouched down next to it. "Ready, man?"

The light was shaking in his hand. "Whenever you are."

I reached through the familiar grating built into the back of the building. My hand disappeared, as always, into the illusionary entrance of the *Lunae Libri*. Nothing much in Gatlin was what it first appeared to be—at least not where Casters were concerned.

"I'm surprised that spell still works." Link watched as I pulled my hand back out of the grate, as good as new.

"Lena told me it's not a hard one. Some kind of hiding spell Larkin Cast."

"Ever wonder if it could be a trap?" The flashlight was shaking so badly, the light was barely shining on the grating.

"Only one way to find out." I shut my eyes and stepped through. One minute I was standing in the overgrown bushes behind the DAR, and the next I was inside the stone stairwell leading down into the heart of the *Lunae Libri*. I shivered when I crossed the Charmed threshold into the library, but not because I felt anything supernatural. The shiver, the wrongness, came from not feeling anything different at all. Air was air on either side of the grate, even if it was pitch-black. I didn't feel magical right now, not anywhere in Gatlin or beneath it. I felt bruised and angry but hopeful. I had been convinced Lena had feelings for John. But if there was a possibility I was wrong—that John and Ridley were influencing her—it was worth being on the wrong side of the grate again.

Link stumbled through the doorway after me and dropped his flashlight. It clattered down the stairwell in front of us, and we stood in the dark, until the torches lining the steep passageway lit themselves one by one. "Sorry. That thing always throws me off."

"Link, if you don't want to do this—" I couldn't see his face in the shadows.

It took a second before I heard his voice in the dark. "Of

course I don't wanna do this, but I gotta do it. I mean, I'm not sayin' Rid's the love a my life. She's not. That would be crazy. But what if Lena was tellin' the truth, and Rid wants to change? What if Vampire Boy is doin' somethin' to her, too?" I doubted Ridley was under anyone's influence except her own. But I didn't say anything.

This wasn't just about Lena and me. Ridley was still under Link's skin, in a bad way. You don't want to fall in love with a Siren. Falling for a Caster was rough enough.

I followed him down into the flickering, torch-lit darkness of the world beneath our town. We left Gatlin for the Caster world, a place where anything could happen. I tried not to think back to a time when that was all I wanted.

Whenever I stepped through the stone archway bearing the carved words DOMUS LUNAE LIBRI, I was entering another world, a parallel universe. By now, some parts of the world were familiar—the smell of the mossy stone, the musky scent of parchment dating back to the Civil War and beyond, the smoke drifting up from the torches hovering near the carved ceilings. I could smell the damp walls, hear the occasional drip of underground water making its way down to the patterns in the stone floor. But there were other parts that would never be familiar. The darkness at the edges of the stacks, the sections of the library no Mortal had ever seen. I wondered how much my mother had seen.

We reached the base of the stairs.

"What now?" Link found his flashlight and aimed it at the column next to him. A menacing stone griffin's head snarled back. He pulled the flashlight away, and it flickered on a fanged gargoyle. "If this is a library, I'd hate to see a Caster prison."

I heard the sound of the flames erupting into light. "Wait for it."

One by one, the torches surrounding the rotunda burst into flame, and we could see the carved colonnade, with rows of fierce mythological creatures, some Caster, some Mortal, snaking around every pedestal.

Link cringed. "This place is messed up. Just sayin'."

I touched a woman's face twisted into carved agony in stone flames. Link ran his hand over another face, revealing massive rows of canines. "Check out the dog. It looks like Boo." He looked again and realized the fangs were growing out of a man's head. He yanked his hand away.

There was a swirl of carved rock that appeared to be made of both stone and smoke. A face emerged from the twists and folds of the column, and it looked familiar. It was hard to tell because there was so much rock around it. The face seemed to be fighting the stone, trying to push its way out toward me. For a second, I thought I saw the lips on the face move, as if it was trying to speak.

I backed away. "What the hell is that?"

"What's what?" Link stood next to me, staring at the column, which was just a column swirled with curving waves and spirals again. The face had been swallowed back into the pattern, like a head disappearing under the sea's waves. "The ocean, maybe? Smoke from a fire? Why do you care?"

"Forget it." I couldn't, even if I didn't understand it. I knew that face in the stone. I had seen it somewhere before. This room was eerie, warning that the Caster world was a Dark place, no matter whose side you were on.

Another torch ignited, and the stacks of old books,

manuscripts, and Caster Scrolls revealed themselves. They radiated out from the rotunda in all directions, like spokes on a wheel, and disappeared into the darkness beyond. The last torch burst into flame, and I could see the curving mahogany desk where Marian should have been sitting.

It was empty. Though Marian always said the *Lunae Libri* was a place of old magic, neither Dark nor Light, without her the whole library felt pretty Dark.

"No one's here." Link sounded defeated.

I grabbed a torch off the wall and handed it to him, taking another for myself. "They're down here."

"How do you know?"

"I just do."

I plowed ahead into the stacks as if I knew where I was going. The air was thick with the smell of the bent and crumbling spines of old books and ancient scrolls, the dusty oak shelves straining under the weight of hundreds of years and centuries of words. I held my torch up to the nearest shelf. "*Toes: to Caste Hair on Your Maiden's. Tongues for Binding and Casting. Toffee: Casts Hidden Inside.* We must be in the T's."

"*Destruction of Mortal Life, Total.* That should be in the D's." Link reached for the book.

"Don't touch that. It'll burn your hand." I had learned the hard way, from *The Book of Moons.*

"Shouldn't we at least hide it or something? Behind the *Toffee* one?" Link had a point.

We hadn't gone ten feet when I heard a laugh. A girl's laugh, unmistakable, echoing off the carved ceilings. "You hear that?"

"What?" Link waved his torch, almost setting the nearest pile of scrolls on fire.

"Watch it. There's no fire escape down here."

We reached a crossroads in the stacks. I heard it again, the almost musical laughter. It was beautiful and familiar, and the sound of it made me feel safe, the world I was standing in a little less foreign. "I think it's a girl laughing."

"Maybe it's Marian. She's a girl." I looked at him like he was insane, and he shrugged. "Sort of."

"It's not Marian." I motioned for him to listen, but the sound was gone. We walked in the direction of the laughter, and the passageway turned until we reached another rotunda, similar to the first.

"You think it's Lena and Ridley?"

"I don't know. This way." I could barely follow the sound, but I knew who it was. Part of me always suspected I could find Lena no matter where she was. I couldn't explain it, I just knew.

It made sense. If our connection was so strong we could dream the same dreams and speak without speaking, why wouldn't I be able to sense where she was? It's like when you drive home from school, or some place you go every day, and you remember leaving the parking lot, then the next thing you know you're pulling into your driveway and you don't remember how you got there.

She was my destination. I was always on the way to Lena, even when I wasn't. Even when she wasn't on her way to me.

"A little farther."

The next twist in the passage revealed a corridor covered with ivy. I held up my torch, and a brass lantern lit itself in the middle of the leaves. "Look." The light from the lantern illuminated the outline of a doorway hidden beneath the vines. I felt along the wall until I found the cold, round iron of the latch. It was in the shape of a crescent. A Caster moon.

I heard it again, laughter. It had to be Lena. There are some things a guy just knows. I knew L. And I knew my heart wouldn't lead me astray.

My chest was pounding. I pushed open the door, heavy and groaning. It opened into a magnificent study. Along the far wall of the study, a girl was lying on an enormous four-poster bed, scribbling in a tiny red notebook.

"L!"

She looked up, surprised.

Only it wasn't Lena.

It was Liv.

Wayward Soul

The first moment hung in the air, silent and awkward. The second erupted into noisy confusion. Link yelled at Liv, who yelled at me, and I yelled at Marian, who waited for us to stop.

"What are you doin' here?"

"Why did you leave me at the fair?"

"What is she doing here, Aunt Marian?"

"Come in." Marian pulled the paneled door open and stepped back to let us pass. The door banged shut behind me, and I heard her bolt the lock. I felt a surge of panic, or claustrophobia, which didn't make any sense because the room wasn't small. But it felt close. The air was heavy, and I had the feeling that I was standing someplace very private, like a bedroom. Like the laughter, it felt familiar, even if it wasn't. Like the face in the stone.

"Where are we?"

"One question at a time, EW. I'll answer one of yours, and you'll answer one of mine."

"What's Liv doing here?" I don't know why I was angry, but I was. Could anybody in my life be a normal person? Did everyone have to have a secret life?

"Sit. Please." Marian gestured to the circular table in the center of the room.

Liv looked irritated, and got up from her spot on the bed in front of an impossibly lit fireplace, the smoldering fire white and bright instead of orange and burning.

"Olivia is here because she is my summer research assistant. Now I have a question for you."

"Wait. That's not a real answer. I already knew that." I was every bit as stubborn as Marian was. My voice echoed across the chamber, and I noticed an intricate chandelier hanging from the high, vaulted ceiling. It was made of some kind of smooth, white polished horn, or was it bone? The ironwork held long tapered candles that lit the room with a delicate flickering light, illuminating some corners while leaving others dark and unexposed. In the shadows of the far corner, I noticed the spindles of a tall, ebony four-poster bed. I had seen a bed exactly like it somewhere before. Everything about today was one monster déjà vu, and it was driving me crazy.

Marian sat back in her chair, undeterred. "Ethan, how did you find this place?"

What could I say with Liv standing next to me? I thought I heard Lena, sensed her? But my instincts led me to Liv instead? I didn't understand it myself.

I looked away. Black wooden bookcases ran from floor to ceiling, crammed with books and objects of curiosity that were obviously the personal collection of someone who had been around the world and back more times than I had been to the Stop & Steal. A collection of antique bottles and vials lined one of the shelves, like in an old apothecary. Another was stacked with books. It reminded me of Amma's room, without the stacks of old newspapers and jars of graveyard dirt. But one book stood out from the others: *Darkness and Light: The Origins of Magic.*

I recognized it—and the bed, and the library, and the immaculate arrangement of beautiful things. This room could only belong to one person, who wasn't even a person. "This was Macon's room, wasn't it?"

"Possibly."

Link dropped a strange ceremonial dagger he had been playing with. It clattered to the floor, and he tried to put it back on the shelf, flustered. Dead or not, Macon Ravenwood still scared Link plenty.

"I'm guessing a Caster Tunnel connects it directly to his bedroom at Ravenwood." This room was almost a mirror image of his bedroom in Ravenwood, with the exception of the heavy drapes that blocked out the sunlight.

"It may."

"You brought that book down here because you didn't want me to see it after I had the vision in the archive."

Marian answered carefully. "Let's say you're right, and this is Macon's private study, the place where he collected his thoughts. Even so, how did you find us tonight?"

I kicked the thick Indian rug under my feet. It was black and white, stitched in a complicated pattern. I didn't want to explain how I found this place. It was confusing. And if I said it, it might be true. But how could it be? How could my instincts lead me to anyone but Lena?

Then again, if I didn't tell Marian, I'd probably never get out of this room. So I settled for half of the truth. "I was looking for Lena. She's down here with Ridley, and her friend John, and I think she's in trouble. Lena did something today, at the fair—"

"Let's just say, Ridley was bein' Ridley. But Lena was bein' Ridley, too. The lollipops might be workin' overtime." Link was unwrapping a Slim Jim, so he didn't notice me staring him down. I hadn't planned on telling Marian or Liv the details.

"We were in the stacks, and I heard a girl laughing. She sounded—I don't know—happy, I guess. I followed her here. I mean, her voice. I can't really explain it." I stole a glance at Liv. I saw the pink flush in her pale skin. She was staring at a particular spot of nothing on the wall.

Marian clapped her hands together, the sign of a great discovery. "I'm guessing the laughter was familiar."

"Yeah."

"And you followed it without a thought. More of an instinct."

"You could say that." I wasn't sure where this was going, but Marian had that mad scientist look in her eye.

"When you're with Lena, can you sometimes speak to her without words?"

I nodded. "You mean, Kelting?"

Liv looked up at me, shocked. "How could a regular Mortal possibly know about Kelting?"

"That is an excellent question, Olivia." The way the two of them were looking at each other irritated me. "One that deserves

179

an answer." Marian walked to the shelves, rummaging through Macon's library like she was looking for car keys in her purse. Watching her flip through his books bothered me, even though he wasn't here to see it.

"It just happened. We sort of found each other in our heads."

"You can read minds, and you didn't tell me?" Link stared at me like he just found out I was the Silver Surfer. He rubbed his head nervously. "Hey, man, all that stuff about Lena? I was yankin' your chain." He looked away. "Are you doin' it now? You're doin' it, aren't you? Dude, get out of my head." He backed away from me and into the bookshelf.

"I can't read your mind, you idiot. Lena and I can hear each other's thoughts sometimes." Link look relieved, but he wasn't getting off that easy. "What were you thinking about Lena?"

"Nothin'. I was messin' with you." He pulled a book off the shelf and pretended to look through it.

Marian took the book out of Link's hands. "There it is. Exactly the book I was looking for." She opened the tattered leather volume, flipping through the crackling pages so quickly it was obvious she was looking for something specific. It looked like an old textbook or reference manual.

"There." She held the book out to Liv. "Does any of this sound familiar?" Liv leaned closer, and they started to turn the pages together, nodding. Marian straightened and took the book from Liv. "Now. How can a regular Mortal Kelt, Olivia?"

"He can't. Unless he's not a regular Mortal, Professor Ashcroft." They were smiling at me like I was a kid who had taken his first steps, or like someone was about to tell me I had a terminal illness, and the combined effect made me want to bolt.

"You mind letting me in on the joke?"

"It's no joke. Why don't you see for yourself?" Marian handed me the book.

I looked at the page. I was right about the textbook part. It was some kind of Caster encyclopedia, with drawings and languages I didn't understand on every page. But some of it was in English. "The Wayward." I looked up at Marian. "Is that what you think I am?"

"Keep going."

"The Wayward: the one who knows the way. Synonyms: *dux, speculator, gubernator*. General. Scout. Navigator. The one who marks the path." I looked up, confused.

For once, Link wasn't. "So he's like a human compass? As far as superpowers go, that's pretty lame. You're like the Caster equivalent of Aquaman."

"Aquaman?" Marian didn't read a lot of comics.

"He talks to fish." Link shook his head. "Not exactly X-ray vision."

"I don't have any superpowers." Did I?

"Keep reading." Marian pointed to the page.

"Since before the Crusades, we have served. We have had many names, and none. Like the whisper in the ear of China's first emperor as he contemplated the Great Wall, or the loyal companion at the side of Scotland's most valiant knight as he toiled for his country's independence, Mortals with great purpose have always had those who guided them. As the lost vessels of Columbus and Vasco da Gama had those who guided them to New Worlds, we exist to guide Casters whose paths hold great meaning. We are—" I couldn't make sense of the words.

Then I heard Liv's voice next to me, as if she had committed the words to memory. "The one who finds what is lost. The one who knows the way."

"Finish it." Marian was suddenly serious, as if the words were some kind of prophecy.

"We are given to the great, for great purpose, to great ends. We are given to the grave, for grave purpose, to grave ends." I closed the book and handed it back to Marian. I didn't want to know any more.

Marian's expression was difficult to read. She turned the book over and over in her hands and looked at Liv. "Do you think?"

"It's possible. There have been others."

"Not for a Ravenwood. Or a Duchannes, for that matter."

"But you said it yourself, Professor Ashcroft. Lena's decision carries consequences. If she chooses to go Light, all the Dark Casters in her family will die, and if she choose to go Dark..." Liv didn't finish. We all knew the rest. All the Light Casters in her family would die. "Wouldn't you say her path holds great meaning?"

I didn't like the way this conversation was going, even though I wasn't completely sure where it was headed. "Hello? I'm sitting right here. Want to clue me in?"

Liv spoke slowly, as if I was a kid at the library for a read aloud. "Ethan, in the Caster world, only those with great purpose have a Wayward. Waywards don't come along often, maybe once in a century, and never by accident. If you are a Wayward, you're here for a reason — a great or terrible purpose, all your own. You're a bridge between worlds for Casters and Mortals, and whatever you do, you have to be very careful."

I sat down on the bed, and Marian sat next to me. "You have

a destiny of your own, like Lena. Which means things could become very complicated."

"You think these past few months haven't been complicated?"

"You have no idea of the things I've seen. The things your mother saw." Marian looked away.

"So you think I'm one of those Waywards? I'm a human compass or something, like Link said?"

"It's more than that. Waywards don't just know the way. They *are* the way. They guide Casters along the path they are destined to take, a path they might not otherwise find on their own. You might be the Wayward for a Ravenwood or a Duchannes. It's not clear which at the moment." Liv seemed to know what she was talking about, which didn't make sense. That's what my mind kept going back to as I stumbled over what they were saying.

"Aunt Marian, tell her. I can't be one of these Waywards. My parents are regular Mortals." Nobody said the obvious, that my mom had been a part of the Caster world, like Marian, only in a way no one would ever talk about, at least not to me.

"Waywards are Mortals, a bridge between the Caster world and ours." Liv reached for another book. "Of course, your mother was hardly what you could call a regular Mortal, any more than I am, or Professor Ashcroft."

"Olivia!" Marian froze.

"You don't mean—"

"His mother didn't want him to know. I promised, if anything were to happen—"

"Stop!" I slammed the book down on the table. "I'm not in the mood for your rules. Not tonight."

Liv fidgeted with her science experiment of a watch, nervously. "I'm such an idiot."

"What do you know about my mother?" I turned on Liv. "Tell me right now."

Marian crumpled into the chair next to me. The pink spots on Liv's cheeks flushed. "I'm so sorry." She shook her head, looking from Marian to me, helplessly.

Marian held up her hand. "Olivia knows all about your mother, Ethan."

I turned to Liv. I knew what she was going to tell me, before she said it. The truth had been pushing its way into my mind. Liv knew too much about Casters and Waywards, and she was here, in the Tunnels, standing in Macon's study. If I hadn't been so confused about what they thought I was, I would've realized what Liv was. I don't know why it had taken me this long to see it.

"Ethan."

"You're one of them, like Aunt Marian and my mom."

"Them?" Liv asked.

"You're a Keeper." The words made it real, and I was feeling everything and nothing at the same time—my mom, down here in the Tunnels with Marian's massive ring of Caster keys. My mom with her secret life, in this secret world my father and I had never been, and could never be, part of.

"I'm not a Keeper." Liv looked embarrassed. "Not yet. One day, maybe. I'm training."

"Training to be more than the Gatlin County librarian, which is why you're here, in the middle of nowhere with your fancy scholarship. If there is one. Or was that a lie, too?"

"I'm a terrible liar. I do have a scholarship, but it's paid by a

184

society of scholars that far predates Duke University."

"Or the Harrow School."

She nodded. "Or Harrow."

"What about the Ovaltine? Was that even true?"

Liv smiled ruefully. "I'm from Kings Langley, and I do love Ovaltine, but if I'm to be perfectly honest, I've come to prefer Quik since arriving in Gatlin."

Link sat down on the bed, speechless. "I don't understand a word she's sayin'."

Liv turned the pages of the book until a timeline of Keepers appeared. My mom's name stared back at me. "Professor Ashcroft is right. I studied Lila Evers Wate. Your mother was a brilliant Keeper, a tremendous writer. It's part of my coursework to read the notes left by the Keepers who have come before me."

Notes? My mom had notes Liv had seen, and I hadn't? I resisted the urge to punch a hole through the wall. "Why? So you don't make the mistakes they made? So you don't end up dead in an accident nobody saw and no one can explain? So you don't leave your family behind, wondering about your secret life and why you never told them about it?"

The two pink spots appeared on Liv's cheeks again. I was getting used to them. "So I can continue their work and keep their voices alive. So one day, when I become a Keeper, I'll know how to safeguard the Caster archive—the *Lunae Libri*, the scrolls, the records of the Casters themselves. That isn't possible without the voices of the Keepers who came before me."

"Why not?"

"Because they're my teachers. I learn from their experiences, the knowledge they gathered while they were Keepers.

Everything is connected, and without their records, I can't make sense of the things I discover myself."

I shook my head. "I don't understand."

"You don't understand? What the hell are we even talkin' about?" Link spoke up from the bed.

Marian put her hand on my shoulder. "The voice you heard, the laughter from the hall, I imagine it was your mother. Lila led you here, most likely because she wanted us to have this conversation. So you would understand your purpose, and Lena's or Macon's. Because you're Bound to one of their Houses and one of their destinies. I just don't know whose yet."

I thought about the face in the column, the laughter, and the feeling of déjà vu in Macon's room. Was it my mom? I'd been waiting months for a sign from her, since the afternoon in the study when Lena and I found the message in the books.

Was she finally trying to contact me now?

What if she wasn't?

I realized something else. "If I am one of these Waywards — and I'm not saying I'm buying any of this — then I can find Lena, right? I'm supposed to take care of her because I'm her compass, or whatever."

"We don't know that for sure. You're Bound to someone, but we don't know who."

I pushed back the chair and walked over to the bookcase. Macon's book sat on the edge of the shelf. "I bet I know someone who does." I reached for it.

"Ethan, stop!" Marian shouted. My fingers had barely scraped the cover when I felt the floor give way into the nothingness of another world.

At the last second, a hand grabbed mine. "Take me with you, Ethan."

"Liv, no—"

A girl with long brown hair clung desperately to a tall boy, her face buried in his chest. The branches of a huge oak reached down around them, creating the impression they were alone instead of a few yards away from clusters of Duke University's ivy-covered buildings.

He cradled her tear-stained face gently in his hands. "Do you think this is easy for me? I love you, Jane, and I know I'll never feel this way about anyone again. But we don't have a choice. You knew there would come a time when we would have to say good-bye."

Jane lifted her chin, resolute. "There are always choices, Macon."

"Not in this situation. Not a choice that wouldn't put you in danger."

"But your mother said there might be a way. What about the prophecy?"

Macon slammed his palm against the tree, frustrated. "Damn it, Jane. That's an old wives' tale. There's no way it doesn't end with you dead."

"So we can't be together physically—I don't care about that. We can still be together. That's all that matters."

Macon pulled away, his face twisted in pain. "Once I change, I'll be dangerous, a Blood Incubus. They thirst for blood, and my father says I will be one of them like he is, and his father before him. Like all the men in my family, as far back as my great-great-great-grandfather Abraham."

"Grandfather Abraham, the one who believed the greatest sin imaginable was for a Supernatural to fall in love with a Mortal—to taint the supernatural bloodlines? And you can't trust your father. He feels the same way. He wants to keep us apart so you'll return to Gatlin, that god-awful town, and creep around underground like your brother. Like a monster."

"It's too late. I can already feel the Transformation. I stay up all night listening to the thoughts of Mortals, hungering. Soon I'll be hungering for more than their thoughts. Already, it feels like my body can't hold what's inside me, as if the beast might literally burst free."

Jane turned away, her eyes welling up with tears again. But Macon wasn't going to let her ignore him this time. He loved her. And because he loved her, he had to make her understand why they couldn't be together. "Even standing here, the light is beginning to burn through my skin. I can feel the heat of the sun with such intensity, all the time now. I'm changing already, and it will only get worse."

Jane buried her face in her hands, sobbing. "You're saying this to scare me, because you don't want to find a way."

Macon grabbed Jane's shoulders, forcing her to look at him. "You're right. I am trying to scare you. Do you know what my brother did to his Mortal girlfriend after the Transformation?" Macon paused. "He ripped her apart."

188

Without warning, Macon's head jerked back, his golden-yellow eyes shining around strange black pupils, like the eclipse of twin suns. He turned his head away from Jane. "Don't ever forget, Ethan. Things are never as they seem."

I opened my eyes, but I couldn't see anything until the fog lifted. The vaulted ceiling of the study came into focus.

"That was creepy, man. Like *The Exorcist* creepy." Link was shaking his head. I held out my arm, and he pulled me up. My heart was still pounding, and I tried not to look at Liv. I had never shared a vision with anyone except Lena and Marian, and I wasn't too comfortable doing it now. Every time I looked at her, all I could think about was the moment I walked into this room. The moment I thought she was Lena.

Liv sat up, groggy. "You told me about the visions, Professor Ashcroft. But I had no idea they were so physical."

"You shouldn't have done that." It felt like I was betraying Macon by bringing Liv into his private life.

"Why not?" She rubbed her eyes, trying to readjust.

"Maybe you weren't supposed to see it."

"What I see in a vision is totally different from what you see. You're not a Keeper. No offense, but you have no training."

"Why do you say 'no offense' when you're planning to offend me?"

"Enough." Marian looked at us expectantly. "What happened?"

But Liv was right. I didn't understand what the vision meant, except that Incubuses couldn't be with Mortals any more than Casters could. "Macon was there with a girl, and he was talking about becoming a Blood Incubus."

Liv looked smug. "Macon was going through the Transformation. He appeared to be in a very vulnerable state. I don't know why the vision showed us that particular moment, but it must be significant."

"Are you sure you weren't seeing Hunting, not Macon?" Marian asked.

"No," we said, our voices overlapping. I looked at Liv. "Macon wasn't like Hunting."

Liv thought for a moment, then reached for the notebook on the bed. She scribbled something and snapped it shut.

Great. Another girl with a notebook.

"You know what? You're the experts. I'm going to let you two figure this one out. I'm going to find Lena before Ridley and her friend convince her to do something she'll regret."

"Are you suggesting Lena is under Ridley's influence? That's not possible, Ethan. Lena's a Natural. A Siren can't control her." Marian dismissed the idea.

But she didn't know about John Breed. "What if Ridley had help?"

"What sort of help?"

"An Incubus who can walk around in the daylight, or a Caster with Macon's strength and the ability to Travel. I'm not sure which." It wasn't the best explanation, but I didn't know what John Breed really was.

"Ethan, you must be mistaken. There's no record of an Incubus or a Caster with those abilities." Marian was already pulling a book from the shelves.

"There is now. His name is John Breed." If Marian didn't know what John was, we weren't going to find the answer in one of those books.

"If what you're describing is accurate, and I find it hard to believe that it could be, I'm not sure what he might be capable of."

I looked at Link. He was twisting the chain on his wallet. We were thinking the same thing. "I have to find Lena." I didn't wait for a response.

Link unlocked the door.

Marian stood up. "You can't go after her. It's too dangerous. There are Casters and creatures of unfathomable power in those Tunnels. You've only been down here once before, and the sections you've seen are passageways compared to the larger Tunnels. They're like another world."

I didn't need permission. My mom may have led me here, but she was still gone. "You can't stop me because you can't get involved, right? All you can do is sit there and watch me screw things up and write about it so someone like Liv can study it later."

"You don't know what you'll find, and when you find it, I won't be able to help you."

It didn't matter. I was at the door by the time Marian finished. Liv was following me. "I'm going, Professor Ashcroft. I'll make sure nothing happens to them."

Marian moved to the doorway. "Olivia. This isn't your place."

"I know. But they'll need me."

"You cannot change what is to be. You have to stay out of it. No matter how much it pains you. A Keeper's role is only to record and bear witness, not to change what unfolds."

"You're like a hall cop." Link grinned. "Like Fatty."

Liv's eyes narrowed. They must have truant officers in England, too. "You don't need to explain the Order of Things to me, Professor Ashcroft. I've studied it since my K levels. But how can I witness what I'm never allowed to see?"

"You can read about it in the Caster Scrolls, like the rest of us."

"I can? The Sixteenth Moon? The Claiming that could've broken the Duchannes curse? Could you have read about any of that in a scroll?" Liv glanced at her moon watch. "There's something happening. This Supernatural with unprecedented power, Ethan's visions—and there are scientific anomalies. Subtle changes I've picked up on my selenometer."

Subtle, as in nonexistent. I recognized a scam when I saw one. Olivia Durand was as trapped as the rest of us, and we were her ticket out. She wasn't worried about Link and me in the Tunnels. She wanted to have a life. Like another girl I knew, not too long ago.

"Remember—"

The door closed before Marian could finish, and we were gone.

Exile

The door slammed behind us. Liv straightened her worn leather knapsack, and Link grabbed a torch from the wall of the tunnel. They were ready to follow me into the great unknown, but instead we stood there, staring at each other.

"Well?" Liv looked at me expectantly. "It's not rocket science. You either know the way, or you—"

"Shh. Give him a second." Link clamped his hand over Liv's mouth. "Use the force, young Skywalker." This Wayward thing apparently carried some weight. They actually thought I knew where to go, which only left one problem. I didn't.

"This way." I was going to have to make it up as I went along.

Marian said the Caster Tunnels were endless, a world beneath our own, but I never really understood what she meant until now. As we turned the first corner, the passage changed, narrowing into damper and darker circular walls that felt more like a tube than a tunnel. I pressed against the walls to push myself forward, and my torch fell in the mud.

"Crap." I gripped the torch's wooden handle between my teeth and kept going.

"This sucks." Link was muttering behind me as his torch burned out.

Liv was behind him. "Mine's out, too." We were in complete darkness. The ceiling was so low, we had to duck beneath the muddy rock.

"This is really freakin' me out." Link had never liked the dark.

Liv called out from behind us. "Eventually you're going to reach the..."

I hit my head against something hard and splintery in the darkness. "Ouch!"

"...Doorwell."

Link must have pulled his flashlight out of his pocket, because a flickering circle of light hit the round door in front of me. It was some kind of cold metal, not the splintering wood or crumbling stone of the other doors we'd seen. It looked more like a manhole cover in the wall. I pushed my shoulder against it, but it didn't budge.

"What now?" I called back to Liv, my stand-in for Marian on all Caster-related issues. I heard her flipping pages in her notebook.

"I don't know. Maybe push harder?"

"You had to check your little book for that?" I was annoyed.

"You want me to crawl up there and do it for you?" Liv wasn't happy either.

"Come on, kids. I'll push Ethan, you push me, Ethan pushes the door."

"Brilliant," Liv said.

"Shoulder to shoulder, MJ."

"Excuse me?"

"Marian Junior. You're the one who wanted an adventure. You got a better idea?"

The door had no handle or valve. It fit into a perfect seam, a circle of metal in a circular doorway. Not even a slit of light escaped through the cracks. "Link's right. We don't have a choice, and we're not going back now." I wedged my shoulder against the door. "One, two, three. Push!"

When the tips of my fingers touched the door, it swung open as if my skin was somehow the genetic recognition, the key that opened the door. Link smashed into me, and Liv tumbled on top of both of us. I cracked my head against what seemed like stone as I hit the ground. I felt so dizzy, I couldn't see anything. When I opened my eyes, I was staring up at a streetlamp.

"What happened?" Link sounded as disoriented as I was.

I felt around the edge of the stones with my fingertips. Cobblestones. "I just touched the door, and it opened."

"Amazing." Liv stood up, taking it all in.

I was lying in a city street that looked like London or an old town right out of a history book. Behind me, I could see the round doorway, at the road's end. There was a brass street sign next to it that said WESTERN DOORWELL, CENTRAL LIBRARY.

Link sat up next to me, rubbing his head. "Holy crap. This is like one of those alleys where people got hacked up by Jack the

195

Ripper." He was right. We could have been standing in the mouth of an alley in nineteenth-century London. The street was dark, lit by only the dim glow of a few lampposts. The alley was framed on both sides by the backs of tall brick row houses.

Liv stood up and made her way down the deserted cobblestone street, looking up at an old iron street sign: THE KEEP. "That must be the name of this particular tunnel. Unbelievable. Professor Ashcroft told me, but I never imagined. I suppose books couldn't really do it justice, could they?"

"Yeah, it looks nothin' like the postcards." Link pulled himself to his feet. "All I wanna know is, where'd the ceilin' go?" The curved arch of the tunnel's ceiling was gone, and in its place was a dark evening sky, as big and real and full of stars as any sky I'd ever seen.

Liv pulled out her notebook and started writing. "Don't you get it? These are Caster Tunnels. They're not some supernatural subway system, so Casters can creep around under Gatlin borrowing library books."

"Then what are they?" I ran my hand along the rough brick on the side of the nearest building.

"More like roads to another world. Or, in a way, a whole world all to themselves."

I heard something, and my heart jumped. I thought Lena was Kelting, reconnecting with me. But I was wrong.

It was music.

"Do you hear that?" Link asked. I was relieved. For once, the music wasn't coming from inside my head. It was coming from the end of the alley. It sounded like the Caster music from the party at Ravenwood last Halloween, the night I saved Lena from Sarafine's psychic attack.

I listened for Lena, felt for her, remembering that night. Nothing.

Liv checked her selenometer and wrote something else in her notebook. "*Carmen*. I was transcribing one yesterday."

"English, please." Link was still staring up at the sky, trying to figure it all out.

"Sorry. It means 'Charmed Song.' It's Caster music."

I took off, following the sound down the alley. "Whatever it is, it's coming from down here."

Marian had been right. It was one thing to wander through the damp tunnels of the *Lunae Libri*, but this was something entirely different. We had no idea what we had gotten ourselves into. I already knew that much.

As I walked down the alley, the music grew louder, the cobblestones smoothed their way into asphalt beneath my feet, and the street changed from Old World London to modern-day slum. It was a street you could find in any big city, in some forgotten run-down neighborhood. The buildings looked like abandoned warehouses, iron grating covered the shattered windows, and the remnants of broken signs blinked fluorescent light into the darkness. There were cigarette butts and trash all over the street, and a strange sort of Caster graffiti—symbols I couldn't begin to understand—on the sides of the buildings. I pointed it out to Liv. "Do you know what any of that means?"

She shook her head. "No, I've never seen anything like it. But it means something. Every symbol in the Caster world has significance."

"This place is even freakier than the *Lunae Libri*." Link was trying to play it cool in front of Liv, but he was having a hard time pulling it off.

"Do you wanna go back?" I wanted to give him an out, but I knew he had as much of a reason to be down here as I did. His reason was just blonder.

"Are you callin' me a wuss?"

"Shh, shut up—" I heard it.

The Caster music drifted through the air, the seductive melody replaced by something else. This time, I was the only one who could hear the words.

> *Seventeen moons, seventeen fears,*
> *Pain of death and shame of tears,*
> *Find the marker, walk the mile,*
> *Seventeen knows just exile...*

"I hear it. We must be close." I followed the song as it looped over and over in my head.

Link looked at me like I was crazy. "Hear what?"

"Nothing. Just follow me."

The huge metal doors lining the filthy street were all the same, dented and scratched, as if they'd been attacked by an enormous animal or something worse. Except for the last door, the one with *Seventeen Moons* playing inside. It was painted black and covered with more Caster graffiti. But one of the symbols looked different, and it wasn't spray-painted on the door. It was carved into it. I ran my fingers over the cuts in the wood. "This one looks different, almost Celtic."

Liv's voice was a whisper. "Not Celtic. Niadic. It's an ancient Caster language. A lot of the older scrolls in the *Lunae Libri* are written in it."

"What does it say?"

She examined the symbol carefully. "Niadic doesn't translate directly into words. I mean, you can't think about the words as words, not exactly. This symbol means place, or moment, either in physical space or time." She ran her finger over a slash in the wood. "But this line cuts through it, see? So now the place becomes a lack of place, a no place."

"How can a place be a no place? You're either in a place, or you're not." But as I said it, I knew it wasn't true. I had been in a no place for months now, and so had Lena.

She looked up at me. "I think it says something like 'Exile.'"

Seventeen knows just exile.

"That's exactly what it says."

Liv gave me a strange look. "You can't know that, or do you suddenly speak Niadic?" She had a gleam in her eye, as if this was further proof I might be a Wayward.

"I heard it in a song." I reached for the door, but Liv grabbed my arm. "Ethan, this isn't a game. This isn't the pie-baking contest at the county fair. You're not in Gatlin anymore. There are dangerous things down here, creatures far more deadly than Ridley and her lollipops."

I knew she was trying to scare me, but it wasn't working. Since the night of Lena's birthday, I knew more about the dangers of the Caster world than any librarian could, Keeper or not. I didn't blame her for being afraid. You would have to be stupid not to be—like me.

"You're right. It's not the library. I'll understand if you guys don't want to go in there, but I have to. Lena's here, somewhere."

Link pushed open the door and walked in like it was the

Jackson High locker room. "Whatever. I'm into dangerous creatures."

I shrugged and followed him. Liv tightened her hand around the strap of her knapsack, ready to swing it at someone's head if necessary. She took a tentative step, and the door closed behind her.

Inside it was even darker than on the street. Huge crystal chandeliers, completely out of place among the exposed pipes overhead, provided the only light. The rest of the room was pure industrial rave. It was one gigantic space, with circular booths covered in dark red velvet scattered around the perimeter. Some were surrounded by heavy drapes attached to tracks in the ceiling so they could be closed around the booth, the way the curtains close around hospital beds. There was a bar in the back, in front of a round chrome door with a handle.

Link spotted it, too. "Is that what I think it is?"

I nodded. "A vault."

The weird chandeliers, the bar that looked more like a counter, the huge windows covered haphazardly with black tape, the vault. This place could have been a bank once, if Casters had banks. I wondered what they had kept behind that door — or maybe I didn't want to know.

But nothing was weirder than the people, or whatever they were. The crowd surged and receded like at one of Macon's parties, where time seemed to fade in and out, depending on where you looked. From turn-of-the-century suited gentlemen who looked like Mark Twain, with stiff white-winged collars and striped silk ties, to Goth-looking leather-clad punks, they were all drinking, dancing, and mingling.

200

"Dude, tell me those creepy-lookin' see-through people aren't ghosts." Link backed away from one hazy figure, nearly stepping into another. I didn't want to tell him that's exactly what they were. They looked like Genevieve in the graveyard, partially materialized, only here there were at least a dozen of them. But we had never seen Genevieve move. These ghosts weren't floating around like the ones in cartoons. They were walking, dancing, moving like normal people, except they were doing it above the ground—the same pace and even strides, but their feet weren't touching the floor. One glanced our way and raised an empty glass from the table as if offering a toast.

"Am I seein' things, or did that ghost pick up a glass?" Link elbowed Liv.

She stepped between us, her hair brushing against my neck. Her voice was so quiet we had to lean in to hear her. "Technically, they aren't called ghosts. They're Sheers—souls who haven't been able to cross over to the Otherworld because they have unfinished business in the Caster or Mortal world. I have no idea why there are so many out tonight. They usually keep to themselves. Something's off."

"Everything about this place is off." Link was still watching the Sheer with the glass. "And you didn't answer the question."

"Yes, they can pick up anything they want. How do you think they slam doors and move furniture in haunted houses?"

I wasn't interested in haunted houses. "What kind of unfinished business?" I knew enough dead people with unfinished business. I didn't want to meet any more tonight.

"Something they left unresolved when they died—a

powerful curse, a lost love, a shattered destiny. Use your imagination."

I thought about Genevieve and the locket and wondered how many lost secrets, how much unfinished business there was in the graveyards and cemeteries of Gatlin.

Link stared at a beautiful girl with elaborate markings around her neck. They looked similar to the ones inked on Ridley and John. "I'd like to have some unfinished business with her."

"She'd like it, too. She would have you jumping off a cliff in no time." I scanned the room.

There was no sign of Lena. The more I looked around, the more I was grateful for the darkness. The booths were filling up with couples, drinking and making out, while the dance floor was packed with girls, spinning and turning like they were weaving some kind of web. *Seventeen Moons* wasn't playing anymore, if it was ever playing at all. Now the music was harder, more intense, a Caster version of Nine Inch Nails. The girls were all dressed differently, one in a medieval gown, another in skintight leather. Then there were the Ridleys—girls in miniskirts and black tank tops, with red, blue, or violet streaks in their hair, sliding around one another, spinning a different kind of web. Maybe they were all Sirens. I couldn't tell. But they were all beautiful, and they all had some version of Ridley's dark tattoo.

"Let's check in the back." I let Link go ahead so Liv could walk between us. Even though she was checking out every corner of the club as if she wanted to remember it all, I knew she was nervous. This was no place for a Mortal girl, or a Mortal guy, and I felt responsible for dragging Link and Liv into this.

We kept close to the wall, circling the perimeter. But it was crowded, and I felt my shoulder bump against someone. Someone with a body.

"Sorry." I said instinctively.

"No problem." The guy stopped, noticing Liv. "Quite the opposite." He winked at her. "You lost?" He smiled, his shiny black eyes gleaming in the darkness. She froze. The red liquid swirled in his glass as he leaned closer.

Liv cleared her throat. "No. I'm fine, thanks. Just looking for a friend."

"I'll be your friend." He smiled. His white teeth were unnaturally bright in the dim light of the club.

"A...different sort of friend, I'm afraid." I could see Liv's hand shaking where it held the strap of her knapsack.

"If you find her, I'll be over here." He turned back to the bar, where Incubuses were lined up to refill their glasses with red liquid from a strange glass tap. I tried not to think about it.

Link pulled us against one of the velvet curtains on the wall. "I'm startin' to get the feelin' this was a bad idea."

"When did you come to this brilliant conclusion?" Liv's sarcasm was lost on Link.

"I don't know, right about the time I saw that dude's drink. Which I'm guessin' wasn't punch." Link glanced around the room. "How do we even know if they're here, man?"

"They're here." Lena had to be here. I was about to tell Link about how I'd heard the song and could sense she was here, when a stripe of pink and blond hair spun onto the dance floor.

Ridley.

When she saw us, she stopped spinning, and I could see

across the dance floor behind her. John Breed was dancing with a girl, her arms wrapped around his neck, and his hands resting on her hips. Their bodies were pressed against each other, and they seemed to be in their own world. At least, that's how it felt when my hands were resting on those hips. My hands balled into fists, and my stomach lurched. I knew it was her even before I saw the black curls.

Lena—

Ethan?

⊰ 6.15 ⊱

Vexed

*I*t's *not what you think.*

What do I think?

She pushed John away as I crossed the dance floor. He turned around, his eyes black and menacing. Then he smiled to let me know I wasn't a threat. He knew I was no match for him physically, and after seeing him and Lena on the dance floor together, I bet he didn't consider me any other kind of threat anymore.

What did I think?

I knew I was in the moment before the thing happens—the thing that changes your life forever. It was like time stopped, even though everything around me was still moving. The thing I had dreaded for months was actually happening. Lena was slipping through my fingers. And it wasn't because of her birthday, or her mother and Hunting, or any curse or Cast or attack.

It was another guy.

Ethan! You have to go.

I'm not going anywhere.

Ridley stepped in front of me, the dancers swelling around us. "Slow down, Boyfriend. I knew you had guts, but this is crazy." She sounded concerned, like she actually gave a crap about what happened to me. It was a lie, like everything else about her.

"Get out of my way, Ridley."

"You're done here, Short Straw."

"Sorry, the lollipops don't work on me, or whatever you and John are using to manipulate Lena."

She grabbed my arm, her icy fingers cutting into my skin. I had forgotten how strong she was, and how cold. She lowered her voice. "Don't be stupid. You're way out of your league and way out of your mind."

"You should know."

She tightened her grip on my arm. "You don't wanna do this. You shouldn't be in here. Go home before—"

"Before what? Before you cause even more trouble than usual?" Link caught up to me. Ridley locked eyes with him. For a second, I thought there was a flutter, the slightest spark in her eye, like the sight of Link called up something almost human in her. Something that made her as vulnerable as he was. It disappeared as quickly as it had surfaced.

Ridley was rattled and starting to panic. I could tell by the way she was unwrapping a lollipop before she could even get the words out of her mouth. "What the hell are you doing here? Get out of here now, and take him with you." The playful tone was gone. "Go!" She shoved us both as hard as she could.

I stood my ground. "I'm not going until I talk to Lena."

"She doesn't want you here."

"She'll have to tell me that herself."

Say it to my face, L.

Lena was winding her way through the crowd. John Breed hung back, his eyes fixed on us. I didn't want to imagine what she must have said to him to keep him there. That she would handle this? It was nothing, just a guy who couldn't get over her? Some desperate Mortal who couldn't compete with everything she had now?

Like him.

She had John, and he had me beat in the only way that counted. He was part of her world.

I'm not leaving unless you say it.

Ridley dropped her voice, more serious than I'd ever seen her. "We don't have time to screw around. I know you're bent outta shape, but you don't understand. He'll kill you, and if you're lucky, the rest of them won't join in for fun."

"Who, Vampire Boy? We can take him." Link was lying, but there was no way he wouldn't go down swinging, either for me or for her.

Ridley shook her head, pushing him farther back. "You can't, you idiot. This is no place for a couple of Boy Scouts. Get out of here." She reached for Link's cheek, but he grabbed her wrist before she could touch him. Ridley was like a beautiful snake — you couldn't let her get close without the risk of being bitten.

Lena was only a few feet away.

If you don't want me here, tell me yourself.

A part of me believed if we were close enough, I could break whatever hold Ridley and John had over her.

Lena stopped behind Ridley. Her expression was unreadable, but I could see the silvery streak where a single tear had fallen.

Say it, L. Say it, or come with me.

Lena's eyes flickered, and she looked past me to where Liv was standing at the edge of the dance floor.

"Lena, you shouldn't be here. I don't know what Ridley and John are doing to you—"

"No one is *doing* anything to me, and I'm not the one in danger here. I'm not a Mortal." Lena looked over at Liv.

Like her.

Lena's face darkened, and I could see her stray curls beginning to twist.

"You're not like them either, L."

The lights in the bar flickered, and the bulbs shattered over the dance floor, sending sparks and tiny pieces of glass over both of us. The crowd, even that crowd, started moving away from us. "You're wrong. I am like them. This is where I belong."

"Lena, we can figure this out."

"No, we can't, Ethan. Not this."

"Haven't we made it through everything else together?"

"No. Not together. You don't know anything about me anymore." For a second, something passed across her face. Sadness, maybe? Regret?

I wish things could be different, but they can't.

She started to walk away.

I can't go where you're going, Lena.

I know.

You'll be all alone.

She didn't turn around.

I'm already alone, Ethan.

Then tell me to go. If that's what you really want.

She stopped walking and turned slowly to look at me.

"I don't want you here, Ethan." Lena disappeared across the dance floor, away from me. Before I could take a step, I heard the rip—

John Breed materialized in front of me, black leather jacket and all. "Me neither."

We were only a few feet apart. "I'm going, but it's not because of you." He smiled, and his green eyes glowed.

I turned and pushed my way through the crowd. I didn't care if I pissed off someone who could drink my blood or make me jump off a cliff. I kept moving because more than anything else, I wanted to get out of there. The heavy wooden door slammed behind me, shutting out the music, the lights, and the Casters.

But it didn't shut out what I was hoping for. The image of his hands on her hips, swaying to the music, her twisting black hair. Lena in the arms of some other guy.

I barely noticed as the alley turned from modern-day asphalt and filth back to cobblestones. How long had it been going on, and what had happened between them? Casters and Mortals can't be together. That's what the visions were telling me, as if the Caster world didn't think I understood by now.

I heard the sound of footsteps echoing against the cobblestones behind me. "Ethan, are you okay?" Liv put her hand on my shoulder. I hadn't realized she was following me.

I turned around, but I didn't know what to say. I was standing on a street out of the past, in an underground Caster Tunnel, thinking about Lena with some guy who was my polar opposite. A guy who could take whatever I had, whenever he wanted. Tonight had proven it.

"I don't know what to do. This isn't Lena. Ridley and John have some kind of hold on her."

Liv bit her bottom lip nervously. "I know it's not what you want to hear, but Lena's making her own decisions."

Liv didn't understand. She had never seen what Lena was really like before Macon died and John Breed showed up. "There's no way you can be sure. You heard Aunt Marian. We don't know what kind of powers John has."

"I can't imagine how hard this is for you." Liv was speaking in absolutes, and there was nothing absolute about what was happening to Lena and to me.

"You don't know her—"

Liv's voice dropped to a whisper. "Ethan, her eyes are gold."

The words echoed in my head, like I was underwater. My emotions sank like a stone as logic and reason fought their way to the surface.

Her eyes are gold.

It was such a small detail, but it meant everything. No one could force her to go Dark, or make her eyes turn gold.

Lena wasn't being controlled. No one was using the Power of Persuasion to manipulate her into jumping onto the back of John's bike. No one was forcing her to be with him. She was making her own choices, and she was choosing him. *I don't want you here, Ethan.* I heard the words over and over. Which wasn't even the worst part. She meant them.

Everything felt hazy and slow, like none of this could really be happening.

Liv's face was full of concern as she stared up at me with her blue eyes. There was something soothing about their blueness—not the green of a Light Caster, or the black of an Incubus, or the gold of a Dark Caster. She was different from Lena in the most important way. She was a Mortal. Liv wasn't going to go Light or Dark or run off with a guy with superhuman strength who could suck your blood or steal your dreams while you slept. Liv was training to be a Keeper, but even then she would still be an observer. Like me, she would never really be part of the Caster world. Right then, there was nothing I wanted more than to be as far away from that world as I could get.

"Ethan?"

But I didn't answer her. I pushed her shiny blond hair away from her face and leaned down, our faces only inches apart. She inhaled softly, our lips so close I could feel her breath and the scent of her skin, like honeysuckle in the springtime. She smelled like sweet tea and old books, like she had always been here.

I pulled my fingers through her hair and held it at the back of her neck. Her skin was soft and warm, like a Mortal girl's. There was no electric current, no shocks. We could kiss for as long as we wanted. If we had a fight, there wouldn't be a flood or a hurricane, or even a storm. I wouldn't find her on the ceiling of her bedroom. No windows would shatter. No exams would catch fire.

Liv held up her face to be kissed.

She wanted me. *Not lemons and rosemary, not green eyes and black hair. Blue eyes and blond hair...*

I didn't realize I was Kelting, reaching out for someone who wasn't there. I pulled away so fast, Liv didn't have time to react. "I'm sorry. I shouldn't have done that."

Liv's voice was shaky, and she put her hand on her neck, where my hands had been a moment before. "It's okay."

It wasn't. I watched the emotions play out in her eyes— disappointment, embarrassment, regret. "It's no big deal." She was lying. Her cheeks were flushed, and she was staring at the ground. "You're upset about Lena. I get it."

"Liv, I'm—"

Link's voice interrupted my lame attempt at an apology. "Hey, man, nice exit. Thanks for ditchin' me." He pretended he was joking, but his voice was edgy. "At least your cat waited for me." Lucille was trotting casually behind him.

"How did she get here?" I bent down to scratch her head, and she purred. Liv didn't look at either of us.

"Who knows? That cat's as crazy as your great-aunts. It was probably followin' you."

We started walking, and even Link could feel the weight of the silence. "So what happened back there? Was Lena with Vampire Boy, or what?" I didn't want to think about it, but I could tell he was trying not to think about someone, too. Ridley wasn't just under his skin. She was crawling around in there.

Liv was walking a foot or so ahead of us, but she was listening.

"I don't know. That's how it looked." There was no point in trying to deny it.

"The Doorwell should be straight ahead." Liv held her head high and almost tripped over a cobblestone. I could see how awkward things were going to be between us. How many things

212

could a guy screw up in one day? I had probably set some kind of record.

Link put his hand on my shoulder. "I'm sorry, dude. That's real—" Liv stopped so fast neither of us noticed, until Link bumped right into her. "Hey, what's up, MJ?" Link nudged Liv with his elbow playfully.

But she didn't move or make a sound. Lucille froze, the hair on her back standing on end, her eyes transfixed. I followed her gaze to see what she was staring at, but I had no idea what it was. There was a shadow across the street, lurking just inside a stone archway. It was formless, a dense fog, constantly shifting in a way that gave it shape. It was wrapped in some kind of material, like a shroud or a cloak. It had no eyes, but I could tell it was watching us.

Link took a step backward. "What the—"

"Shh." Liv hissed. "Don't attract its attention." The color drained from her face.

"I think it's too late for that," I whispered. The thing, whatever it was, shifted slightly, moving closer to the street and to us.

I took her hand without thinking. It was buzzing, and I realized it wasn't her hand but the contraption on her wrist. Every dial was spinning. Liv stared at its face, unbuckling the black plastic strap to get a better look.

"I'm getting insane readings," she whispered.

"I thought you made that up."

"I did," she whispered again. "At first."

"Then what? What does it mean?"

"I have no idea." She couldn't take her eyes off the device, but the black shadow shifted closer to us.

"I hate to bother you when you're having so much fun with your watch, but what is that thing? A Sheer?"

She looked up from the spinning dials, her hand shaking in mine. "I wish. It's a Vex. I've only read about them. I've never seen one, and I bloody well hoped I never would."

"Fascinatin'. Why don't we bolt and talk about this later?" The Doorwell was in sight, but Link was already turning around, willing to take his chances with the Dark Casters and creatures at Exile.

"Don't run." Liv put her hand on Link's arm. "They can Travel, disappear and materialize anywhere faster than you can blink."

"Like an Incubus."

She nodded. "This could explain why we saw so many Sheers at Exile. It's possible they were responding to some kind of disturbance in the natural order. The Vex is most likely that disturbance."

"Speak English, real English." Link was panicking.

"Vexes are part of the Demon world, the Underground. They're the closest things to pure evil in the Caster or Mortal world." Liv's voice was shaky.

The Vex continued to move slightly, as if it was being blown by the wind. But it didn't come any closer. It seemed to be waiting for something.

"They aren't Sheers, ghosts as you call them. Vexes don't have a physical being, unless they possess the living. They have to be summoned from the Underground by someone very powerful, for only the Darkest tasks."

"Hello. We're already underground." Link didn't take his eyes off the Vex.

"Not the kind of Underground I'm talking about."

"What does it want with us?" Link risked a glance down the street, mentally calculating the distance to Exile.

The Vex began to move, dissolving into mist and back into shadow again.

"I think we're about to find out." I squeezed Liv's hand, trembling in my own.

The black fog, the Vex itself, thrust forward like angry open jaws. And a sound, loud and shrill, erupted from deep within. It was impossible to describe—fierce and menacing like a roar, but terrifying like a scream. Lucille hissed, her ears flattening against her head. The sound intensified, and the Vex reared back, rising above us as if it was planning to attack. I pushed Liv to the ground and tried to shield her body with mine. I covered my neck, like I was about to be devoured by a grizzly bear instead of a body-snatching Demon.

I thought about my mom. Was this how she felt when she knew she was about to die?

I thought about Lena.

The scream reached a crescendo, and I heard another sound rising above it, a familiar voice. But it wasn't my mother's, or Lena's.

"Dark Demon a the Devil, bend to Our will and leave this place!" I looked up and saw them standing behind us under the lamplight. She was holding a string of beads and bone in front of her like a crucifix, and they were gathered around her, glowing and luminous, with purpose in their eyes.

Amma and the Greats.

I can't explain what it was like to see Amma and four generations of the spirits of her ancestors towering above her, like the

215

faces from old black and white pictures. I recognized Ivy from the visions, her dark skin gleaming, dressed in a high-necked blouse and calico skirt. But she looked more intimidating than she had in the visions, and the only one who looked fiercer stood to her right, her hand on Ivy's shoulder. She had a ring on every finger, and she was wearing a long dress that looked like it had been stitched from silk scarves, with a tiny bird embroidered on the shoulder. I was staring at Sulla the Prophet, and she made Amma look about as harmless as a Sunday school teacher.

There were two other women, most likely Aunt Delilah and Sister, and an old man, his face punished by the sun, standing in the back with a beard that would've put Moses to shame. Uncle Abner. I wished I had some Wild Turkey for him.

The Greats tightened their circle around Amma, chanting the same verse again and again, in Gullah, the original language of her family. Amma repeated the same verse in English, shaking the beads and bone, shouting to the heavens.

"Of Vengeance and Wrath, Bind the Suspended, Hasten his path."

The Vex rose even higher, the fog and shadow circling and swirling above Amma and the Greats. Its scream was deafening, but Amma didn't even flinch. She closed her eyes and raised her voice to meet the demonic cry.

"Of Vengeance and Wrath, Bind the Suspended, Hasten his path."

Sulla raised her bracelet-laden arm, spinning a long stick with dozens of tiny charms dangling from it, back and forth between her fingers. She took her hand from Ivy's shoulder and rested it on Amma's, her glowing, translucent skin glimmering in the darkness. The second her hand touched Amma's shoulder, the Vex let out a final gnarled cry and was sucked into the void of the night sky.

Amma turned to the Greats. "I'm much obliged."

The Greats disappeared, as if they had never been there at all.

It probably would've been better if I had disappeared with the Greats, because one look at Amma's face made it clear that she had only saved us so she could kill us herself. We would've had better odds against the Vex.

Amma was seething, her eyes narrow and focused on her main targets, Link and me.

"V. E. X. A. T. I. O. N." She grabbed us by our collars at the same time, as if she could have thrown us up the Doorwell behind her with a single toss. "As in, trouble. Worry. Agitation. Botheration. Need me to go on?"

We shook our heads.

"Ethan Lawson Wate. Wesley Jefferson Lincoln. I don't know what business the two a you think you have down in these Tunnels." She was shaking her bony finger as she pointed at us. "You don't have a lick a sense between you, but you think you're ready to be battlin' Dark forces."

Link tried to explain. Big mistake. "Amma, we weren't tryin' to battle any Dark forces. Honest. We were just—"

Amma advanced, that finger barely an inch from Link's eyes. "Don't you tell me. When I get through with you, you're gonna wish I'd told your mamma about what you were doin' in my basement when you were nine years old." He backed up until he hit the wall behind him, next to the Doorwell. Amma matched him step for step. "That story's as sad as the day is long."

Amma turned to Liv. "And you're studyin' to be a Keeper. But you don't have any more sense than they do. Knowin' what you do and still lettin' these boys drag you into this dangerous business. You're in a world a trouble with Marian." Liv slunk down a few inches.

Amma whipped around to face me. "And you." She was so angry she was talking with her jaw clenched. "You think I don't know what you're up to? You think because I'm an old woman, you can fool me? It'll take you three lifetimes before you can sell me a raft that doesn't float. Soon as Marian told me you were down here, I found you straightaway." I didn't ask her how she'd found us. Whether it was chicken bones or tarot cards or the Greats, she had her ways. Amma was the closest thing I'd ever seen to a Supernatural without actually being one.

I didn't look her in the eye. It was like avoiding a dog attack. Don't make eye contact. Keep your head down and your mouth shut. Instead, I kept walking, with Link looking back at Amma every few steps. Liv wandered behind us, confused. I knew she hadn't counted on a run-in with a Vex, but Amma was more than she could handle.

Amma shuffled along behind us, muttering to herself or the Greats. Who knew? "Think you're the only one who can find somethin'? Don't need to be a Caster to see what you fools are up to." I could hear the bones rattling against the beads. "Why do you think they call me a Seer? Because I can see the mess you're into just as soon as you're into it."

She was still shaking her head as she disappeared up the Doorwell, not a speck of mud on her sleeves or a rumple in her dress. What had felt like a rabbit hole on the way down was a broad stairwell on the way up, as if it had expanded out of respect for Miss Amma herself.

"Takin' on a Vex, as if a day with this child wasn't trouble enough..." She sniffed with every step. It went on like that the whole way back. We dropped Liv off on our way through the Tunnels, but Link and I kept walking. We didn't want to be too close to that finger, or those beads. ·

⇥ 6.16 ⇤

Revelations

By the time I crawled into my bed, it was nearly sunrise. There would be even more hell to pay in the morning when Amma saw me, but I had a feeling Marian wasn't expecting me to be on time for work. She was as scared of Amma as anyone. I kicked off my shoes and fell asleep before I hit the pillow.

Blinding light.

I was overwhelmed by the light. Or was it the dark?

I felt my eyes ache, as if I had been staring at the sun too long, creating spots of darkness. All I could make out was a silhouette, blocking out the light. I wasn't scared. I knew this particular shadow intimately, the slight waist, the delicate hands and fingers. Every strand of hair, twisting in the Casting Breeze.

Lena stepped forward, reaching out for me. I watched, frozen, as her hands moved out of the darkness and into the light where I was standing. The light crept up her arms, until it hit her waist, her shoulders, her chest.

Ethan.

Her face was still shrouded in shadow, but now her fingers were touching me, moving along my shoulders, my neck, and finally my face. I held her hand against my cheek, and it burned me, though not with heat but cold.

I'm here, L.

I loved you, Ethan. But I have to go.

I know.

In the darkness, I could see her eyelids lift and the golden glow — the eyes of the curse. The eyes of a Dark Caster.

I loved you, too, L.

I reached out my hand and gently closed her eyes. The chill of her hand disappeared from my face. I looked away and forced myself to wake up.

I was prepared to face Amma's wrath when I got downstairs. My dad had gone to the Stop & Steal to get a newspaper, and it was just the two of us. The three of us if you counted Lucille, who was staring at the dry cat food in her bowl, something she'd probably never seen before. I guess Amma was mad at her, too.

Amma was at the stove, pulling out a pie. The table was set, but breakfast wasn't cooking. There were no grits or eggs, not even a piece of toast. It was worse than I thought. The last time she baked in the morning instead of making breakfast was the day after Lena's birthday, and before that, the day after my mom died. Amma kneaded dough like a prizefighter. Her fury could generate enough cookies to feed the Baptists and the Methodists combined. I hoped the dough had taken the brunt of it this morning.

"I'm sorry, Amma. I don't know what that thing wanted with us."

She slammed the oven door shut, her back to me. "Of course you don't. There's a lot you don't know, but that didn't stop you from wanderin' around where you didn't have any business. Now did it?" She picked up her mixing bowl, stirring the contents with the One-Eyed Menace, as if she hadn't used it to scare Ridley into submission the day before.

"I went down there looking for Lena. She's been hanging out with Ridley, and I think she's in trouble."

Amma spun around. "You think she's in trouble? You have any idea what that thing was? The one that was about to take you outta this world and into the next?" She stirred madly.

"Liv said it was called a Vex, and it was summoned by someone powerful."

"And Dark. Someone who doesn't want you and your friends pokin' around in those Tunnels."

"Who would want to keep us out of the Tunnels? Sarafine and Hunting? Why?"

Amma slammed the bowl on the counter. "Why? Why are you always askin' so many questions about things that are none a your concern? I reckon it's my fault. I let you run me ragged with those questions when you weren't tall enough to see over this counter." She shook her head. "But this is a fool's game. There can't be a winner."

Great. More riddles. "Amma, what are you talking about?"

She pointed her finger at me again, the same way she had last night. "You've got no business in the Tunnels, you hear me? Lena's havin' a hard time and I'm ten kinds a sorry, but she's got to figure all this out for herself. There's nothin' you can do. So you stay out a those Tunnels. There are worse things down there than Vexes." Amma turned back to her pie, pouring the filling from the bowl into a pie shell. The conversation was over. "You go on to work now, and keep your feet aboveground."

"Yes, ma'am."

I didn't like lying to Amma, but technically I wasn't. At least, that's what I told myself. I was going to work. Right after I stopped by Ravenwood. After last night, there was nothing left to say, and everything.

I needed answers. How long had she been lying to me and sneaking around behind my back? Since the funeral, the first time I saw them together? Or the day she took the picture of his motorcycle in the graveyard? Were we talking about months or weeks or days? To a guy, those distinctions mattered. Until I knew, it would gnaw away at me and what little pride I had left.

Because here's the thing: I heard her, inside and out. She'd said the words, and I saw her with John. *I don't want you here, Ethan.* It was over. The one thing I never thought we'd be.

I pulled up in front of Ravenwood's twisted iron gates and turned off the engine. I sat in the car with the windows rolled up, even though it was already sweltering outside. The heat would be suffocating in a minute or two, but I couldn't move. I closed my eyes, listening to the cicadas. If I didn't get out of the car, I wouldn't have to know. I didn't have to drive through those gates at all. The key was still in the ignition. I could turn it and drive back to the library.

Then none of this would be happening.

I turned the key, and the radio came on. It wasn't on when I turned the car off. The Volvo's reception wasn't much better than the Beater's, but I heard something buried in the static.

> *Seventeen moons, seventeen spheres,*
> *The moon before her time appears,*
> *Hearts will go and stars will follow,*
> *One is broken, One is hollow...*

The engine died, and the music with it. I didn't understand the part about the moon, except that it was coming, which I already knew. And I didn't need the song to tell me which one of us was gone.

When I finally opened the car door, the stifling Carolina heat seemed cool by comparison. The gates creaked as I slipped inside. The closer I got to the house, the sorrier it looked now that Macon was gone. It was worse than the last time I was here.

I walked up the steps of the veranda, listening to each board creak under my feet. The house probably looked as bad as the garden, but I couldn't see it. Everywhere I looked, the only thing I saw was Lena. Trying to convince me to go home the first night I met Macon, sitting on the steps in her orange prison jumpsuit the week before her birthday. Part of me wanted to walk the path out to Greenbrier, to Genevieve's grave, so I could remember Lena huddled up next to me with an old Latin dictionary while we tried to make sense of *The Book of Moons*.

But those were all ghosts now.

I studied the carvings above the doorway and found the familiar Caster moon. I fingered the splintery wood on the lintel and hesitated. I wasn't sure how welcome I would be, but I pressed it anyway. The door swung open, and Aunt Del smiled up at me. "Ethan! I was hoping you would come by before we left." She pulled me in for a quick hug.

Inside it was dark. I noticed a mountain of suitcases by the stairs. Sheets covered most of the furniture, and the shades were drawn. It was true. They were really leaving. Lena hadn't said a word about the trip since the last day of school, and with everything else that had happened, I'd almost forgotten. At least, I wanted to. Lena hadn't even mentioned they were packing. There were a lot of things she didn't tell me anymore.

"That's why you're here, isn't it?" Aunt Del squinted, confused. "To say good-bye?" As a Palimpsest, she couldn't separate layers of time, so she was always a little lost. She could see everything that had happened or would happen in a room the minute she walked in, but she saw it all at once. Sometimes I wondered what she saw when I walked into this room. Maybe I didn't want to know.

"Yeah, I wanted to say good-bye. When are you leaving?"

Reece was sorting through books in the dining room, but I could still see her scowl. I looked away, out of habit. The last thing I needed was Reece reading everything that had happened last night in my face. "Not until Sunday, but Lena hasn't even packed. Don't distract her," Reece called out.

Two days. She was leaving in two days, and I didn't know. Was she even planning to say good-bye?

I ducked my head and stepped into the parlor to say hi to Gramma. She was an immovable force sitting in her rocking chair, with a cup of tea and the paper, as if the bustle of the morning didn't apply to her. She smiled, folding the paper in half. I had assumed it was *The Stars and Stripes*, but it was written in a language I didn't recognize.

"Ethan. I wish you could come with us. I will miss you, and I'm sure Lena will be counting the days until we get back." She rose from the chair and hugged me.

Lena might be counting the days, but not for the reason Gramma thought. Her family had no idea what was going on with us anymore, or with Lena, for that matter. I had a feeling they didn't know she was hanging out in underground Caster clubs like Exile, or hitching rides on the back of John's Harley. Maybe they didn't know about John Breed at all.

I remembered when I first met Lena, the long list of the places she'd lived, the friends she had never made, the schools she'd never been able to go to. I wondered if she was going back to a life like that.

Gramma was staring at me curiously. She put her hand on my cheek. It was soft, like the gloves the Sisters wore to church. "You've changed, Ethan."

"Ma'am?"

"I can't quite put my finger on it, but something's different."

I looked away. There was no point in pretending. She would sense that Lena and I were no longer connected, if she hadn't already. Gramma was like Amma. She was usually the strongest person in the room, by sheer force of will alone. "I'm not the one who changed, ma'am."

She sat down again, picking her newspaper back up. "Nonsense. Everyone changes, Ethan. That's life. Now go tell my granddaughter to get packing. We need to go before the tides change and we're marooned here forever." She smiled as if I was in on the joke. Only I wasn't.

Lena's door was open just a crack. The walls, the ceiling, the furniture—everything was black. Her walls weren't covered in Sharpie anymore. Now her poetry was scrawled in white chalk. Her closet doors were covered with the same phrase over and over: *runningtostandstillrunningtostandstillrunningto standstill.* I stared at the words, separating them the way I often had to when it came to Lena's writing. Once I did, I recognized them from an old U2 song and realized how true they really were.

It's what Lena had been doing all this time, every second since Macon died.

Her little cousin, Ryan, was sitting on the bed, holding Lena's face in her hands. Ryan was a Thaumaturge and only used her healing powers when someone was in great pain. Usually it was me, but today it was Lena.

I barely recognized her. She looked like she hadn't slept last night. She was wearing an oversize, faded black T-shirt as a nightgown. Her hair was tangled, her eyes red and swollen.

"Ethan!" The minute Ryan saw me, she was a regular kid again. She jumped into my arms, and I picked her up, swinging her legs from side to side. "Why aren't you coming with us? It's

227

going to be so boring. Reece is going to boss me around the whole summer, and Lena isn't any fun either."

"I have to stick around here and take care of Amma and my dad, Chicken Little." I put Ryan down gently.

Lena looked annoyed. She sat down on her unmade bed, with her legs folded under her, and waved Ryan out of the room. "Out now. Please."

Ryan made a face. "If you two do anything disgusting and you need me, I'll be downstairs." Ryan had saved my life on more than one occasion when Lena and I had gone too far and the electrical current between us had nearly stopped my heart.

Lena would never have that problem with John Breed. I wondered if it was his shirt she was wearing.

"What are you doing here, Ethan?" Lena stared up at the ceiling, and I followed her eyes to the words on the walls. I couldn't look at her. *When you look up / Do you see the blue sky of what might be / Or the darkness of what will never be? / Do you see me?*

"I want to talk about last night."

"You mean about why you were following me?" Her voice was harsh, which pissed me off.

"I wasn't following you. I was looking for you because I was worried. But I can see how that would be inconvenient when you were busy hooking up with John."

Lena's jaw tightened, and she stood up, the T-shirt grazing her knees. "John and I are just friends. We weren't hooking up."

"Do you hang all over all your friends like that?"

Lena stepped closer to me, the ends of her ratty curls beginning to lift gently off her shoulders. The chandelier hanging from the center of her ceiling began to sway. "Do you try to kiss all of yours?" She looked me right in the eye.

There was a flash of light and sparks, then darkness. The lightbulbs on the chandelier exploded, tiny shards raining down on her bed. I heard the patter of rain on the roof.

"What are you—?"

"Don't bother lying, Ethan. I know what you and your library partner were doing outside Exile." The voice in my head was sharp and bitter.

I heard you. You were Kelting. "Blue eyes and blond hair"? Sound familiar?

She was right. I was Kelting, and she'd heard every word.

Nothing happened.

The chandelier crashed onto her bed, missing me by inches. The floor seemed to drop out from under me. She'd heard me.

Nothing happened? Did you think I wouldn't know? Did you think I wouldn't feel it?

It was worse than looking Reece in the eye. Lena could see everything, and she didn't need her powers to do it.

"I lost it when I saw you with that guy John, and I wasn't thinking."

"You can tell yourself that, but everything happens for a reason. You almost kissed her, and you did it because you wanted to."

Maybe I just wanted to piss you off, because I saw you with another guy.

Be careful what you wish for.

I searched her face, the dark circles around her eyes, the sadness.

The green eyes I loved so much were gone—changed into the golden eyes of a Dark Caster.

What are you doing with me, Ethan?

I don't know anymore.

Lena's face fell for a second, but she caught herself. "You've been dying to get that out, haven't you? Now you can run off with your little Mortal girlfriend guilt-free." She said *Mortal* as if she could hardly stand to say the word. "I bet you can't wait to hang out at the lake with her." Lena was seething. Whole sections of ceiling were beginning to cave, where the chandelier had fallen.

Whatever pain she might have been feeling was totally eclipsed by her anger. "You'll be back on the basketball team by the time school starts, and she can join the cheer squad. Emily and Savannah will love her."

I heard a cracking sound, and another stretch of drywall smashed to the ground next to me.

My chest tightened. Lena was wrong, but I couldn't help but think about how easy it would be to date a regular girl, a Mortal girl.

I always knew that's what you wanted. Now you can have it.

Another crash. Now I was covered with the fine white dust of her fallen ceiling, broken chunks scattered on the floor around me.

She was fighting back tears.

That's not what I meant, and you know it.

Do I? All I know is that it shouldn't be so hard. Loving someone shouldn't be so hard.

I never cared about that.

I felt her fading away, pushing me out of her mind and out of her heart. "You belong with someone like you, and I belong with someone like me, someone who understands what I'm going through. I'm not the same person I was a few months ago, but I guess we both know that."

Why can't you stop punishing yourself, Lena? It wasn't your fault. You couldn't have saved him.

You don't know what you're talking about.

I know you think it's your fault your uncle's dead, and that torturing yourself is some kind of penance.

There's no penance for what I did.

She started to turn away.

Don't run away.

I'm not running. I'm already gone.

I could barely hear her voice in my head. I moved closer to her. It didn't matter what she'd done or if things between us were over. I couldn't watch her destroy herself.

I pulled her to my chest and wrapped my arms around her, like she was drowning and I just wanted to get her out of the water. I could feel every inch of her burning cold against me. Her fingertips brushed mine. My chest was numb where her face pressed into it.

It doesn't matter if we're together or not. You're not one of them, L.

I'm not one of you either.

Her last words were a whisper. I tangled my hands into her hair. There was no part of me that could let go. I think she was crying, but I couldn't tell for sure. As I watched the ceiling, the last bits of plaster around the hole began to splinter into a thousand fissures, as if the rest of the roof might fall in on us any minute.

So this is it?

It was, but I didn't want her to answer. I wanted to stay in this moment for a little while longer. I wanted to hold on to her and pretend she was still mine to hold.

"My family leaves in two days. By the time they wake up tomorrow, I'll be gone."

"L, you can't—"

She touched my mouth. "If you ever loved me, and I know you did, leave it alone. I'm not going to let any more people I care about die because of me."

"Lena."

"This is my curse. It's mine. Let me have it."

"What if I say no?"

She looked at me, her whole face darkening into a single shadow. "You don't have a choice. If you come by Ravenwood tomorrow, I can guarantee you won't feel like talking. And you won't be able to either."

"Are you saying you're going to put a Cast on me?" It was an unspoken line between us she had never crossed.

She smiled and put her finger over my lips. "*Silentium*. Latin for 'silence,' which is what you'll hear if you try to tell anyone I'm leaving before I go."

"You wouldn't."

"I just did."

Finally. Here we were. The only thing left between us was the unimaginable power she had never used against me. Her eyes flared gold and bright. There wasn't a trace of green. I knew she meant every word.

"Swear you won't come back here." Lena slipped out of my arms and turned away from me. She didn't want to show me her eyes anymore, and I couldn't stand to see them.

"I swear."

She didn't say a word. She nodded and wiped the tears running down her face. By the time I walked away, it was raining plaster.

—☙

I walked through the halls of Ravenwood one last time. The house grew darker and darker the farther I went. Lena was going. Macon was gone. Everyone was leaving, and the house felt dead. I dragged my fingers along the polished mahogany banister. I wanted to remember the smell of the varnish, the smooth feel of the old wood, maybe the faintest smell of Macon's imported cigars, Confederate jasmine, blood oranges, and books.

I stopped in front of Macon's bedroom door. Painted a flat black, it could have been any door in the house. But it wasn't any door, and Boo was sleeping in front of it, waiting for a master who was never coming home. He didn't look like a wolf anymore, just a regular dog. Without Macon, he was as lost as Lena. Boo looked up at me, barely moving his head.

I put my hand on the doorknob and pushed the door open. Macon's room was exactly as I remembered. No one had dared to put a sheet over anything in here. The ebony four-poster bed in the center of the room shined, as if it had been lacquered a thousand times by House or Kitchen, Ravenwood's invisible staff. Black plantation shutters kept the room completely dark, so it was impossible to tell day from night. Tall candlesticks held black candles, and a black wrought iron chandelier hung from the ceiling. I recognized the Caster pattern burned into the iron. At first I couldn't place it, but then I remembered.

I had seen it on Ridley and John Breed, and at Exile. The mark of a Dark Caster. The tattoo they all shared. Each one looked different yet unmistakably similar. More like a brand than a tattoo, as if it had been burned into them rather than inked.

I shuddered and picked up a small object from the top of a black dresser. It was a framed photograph of Macon and a woman. I could see Macon standing next to her, but it was dark and I could only make out the outline of her silhouette, a shadow caught on film. I wondered if it was Jane.

How many secrets had Macon carried to his grave? I tried to put the frame back, but it was so dark I misjudged the distance and the picture fell. When I bent to pick it up, I noticed the corner of the rug was flipped back. It looked exactly like the rug I had seen in Macon's room in the Tunnels.

I lifted up the rug, and underneath there was a perfect rectangle cut into the floorboards, big enough for a man. It was another door into the Tunnels. I yanked on the floorboard, and it came loose. I could see down into Macon's study, but there were no stairs, and the stone floor looked too far down to jump without risking serious head trauma.

I remembered the cloaked door to the *Lunae Libri*. There was no way to find out, except to try. I held on to the edge of the bed and stepped down carefully. I stumbled for a second, then felt something solid under my foot. A step. Though I couldn't see it, I could feel the splintery wooden stair under my feet. Seconds later, I was standing on the stone floor of Macon's study.

He didn't spend all of his days sleeping. He spent them in the Tunnels, probably with Marian. I could picture the two of them looking up obscure old Caster legends, debating antebellum garden formations, having tea. She had probably spent more time with Macon than anyone, except Lena.

I wondered if Marian was the woman in the picture and her name was really Jane. I hadn't considered it before, but it would explain a lot of things. Why the countless brown library packages were kept neatly piled in Macon's study. Why a Duke professor would be hiding out as a librarian, even as a Keeper, in a town like Gatlin. Why Marian and Macon were inseparable so much of the time, at least for a reclusive Incubus who didn't go anywhere.

Maybe they had loved each other all these years.

I looked around the room until I saw it, the wooden box that held Macon's thoughts and secrets. It was on the shelf where Marian had left it.

I closed my eyes and reached for it —

It was the thing Macon wanted least and most — to see Jane one last time. It had been weeks since he'd seen her, unless you counted the nights he had followed her home from the library, watching her from a distance, wishing he could touch her.

Not now, not when the Transformation was so close. But she was here, even though he'd told her to stay away. "Jane, you have to get out of here. It's not safe."

She walked slowly across the room to where he was standing. "Don't you understand? I can't stay away."

"I know." He drew her to him and kissed her, one last time.

Macon took something out of a small box in the back of his closet. He put the object in Jane's hand, closing her fingers around it. It was round and smooth, a perfect sphere. He closed his hand around hers, his voice grave. "I can't protect you after the Transformation, not from the one thing that poses the greatest threat to your safety. Me." Macon looked down at their hands, gently cradling the object he had hidden so carefully. "If something happens, and you're in danger...use this."

Jane opened her hand. The sphere was black and opalescent, like a pearl. But as she watched, the sphere began to change and glow. She could feel the buzz of tiny vibrations emanating from it. "What is it?"

Macon stepped back, as if he didn't want to touch the orb now that it had come to life. "It's an Arclight."

"What is it for?"

"If the time comes when I become a danger to you, you'll be defenseless. There's no way you will be able to kill me or hurt me. Only another Incubus can do that."

Jane's eyes clouded over. Her voice was a whisper. "I could never hurt you."

Macon reached out and touched her face tenderly. "I know, but even if you wanted to, it would be impossible. A Mortal cannot kill an Incubus. That's why you need the Arclight. It's the only thing that can contain my kind. The only way you would be able to stop me if —"

"What do you mean, contain?"

Macon turned away. "It's like a cage, Jane. The only cage that can hold us."

Jane looked down at the dark orb glowing in her palm. Now that she knew what it was, it felt as if it was burning a hole in her hand and her heart. She dropped it on his desk, and it rolled across the tabletop, its glow

*fading to black. "You think I'm going to imprison you
in that thing, like an animal?"*

"I'll be worse than an animal."

*Tears ran down Jane's face and over her lips. She
grabbed Macon's arm, forcing him to face her. "How
long would you be in there?"*

"Most likely, forever."

*She shook her head. "I won't do it. I would never
condemn you to that."*

*It looked as if tears were welling up in Macon's eyes,
even though Jane knew it was impossible. He had no tears
to shed, yet she swore she could see them glistening. "If
something happened to you, if I hurt you, you would be
condemning me to a fate, an eternity, far worse than anything I would find in here." Macon picked up the Arclight
and held it up between them. "If the time comes and you
have to use it, you have to promise me you will."*

*Jane choked back her tears, her voice shaking. "I
don't know if I—"*

*Macon rested his forehead against hers. "Promise
me, Janie. If you love me, promise me."*

*Jane buried her face in his cool neck. She took a deep
breath. "I promise."*

*Macon raised his head and looked over her shoulder.
"A promise is a promise, Ethan."*

I woke up lying on a bed. There was light streaming in a window, so I knew I wasn't in Macon's study anymore. I stared at

the ceiling, but there was no crazy black chandelier, so I wasn't in his room at Ravenwood either.

I sat up, groggy and confused. I was in my own bed, in my room. The window was open, and the morning light was shining into my eyes. How could I have passed out there and ended up here, hours later? What had happened to space and time and all the physics in between? What Caster or Incubus was powerful enough to do that?

The visions had never affected me like this before. Both Abraham and Macon had seen me. How was that possible? What was Macon trying to tell me? Why did he want me to see these visions? I couldn't put it together, except for one thing. Either the visions were changing, or I was. Lena had made sure of that.

Inheritance

I stayed away from Ravenwood, like I promised. By morning, I didn't know where Lena was or where she was headed. I wondered if John and Ridley were with her.

The only thing I knew was Lena had waited all her life to take charge of her own destiny—to find a way to Claim herself, in spite of the curse. I wasn't going to be the person to stand in her way now. And, as she pointed out, she wasn't going to let me.

Which left me with my own immediate destiny: to stay in bed all day feeling sorry for myself. Me and some comic books, anything but *Aquaman*.

Gatlin had planned otherwise.

The county fair meant a day of pageants and pies and a night of hooking up, if you were lucky. All Souls meant something else entirely. It was a tradition in Gatlin. Instead of spending the day in shorts and flip-flops at the fair, everyone in town spent all day at the graveyard in their Sunday best, paying their respects to their dead relatives and everyone else's. Forget the fact that All Souls Day was actually a Catholic holiday that took place in November. In Gatlin, we had our own way of doing things. So we turned it into our own day of remembrance, guilt, and general competition over who could pile the most plastic flowers and angels on our ancestors' graves.

Everyone turned out on All Souls: the Baptists, the Methodists, even the Evangelicals and the Pentecostals. It used to be that the only two people in town who didn't show up at the cemetery were Amma, who spent All Souls at her own family plot in Wader's Creek, and Macon Ravenwood. I wondered if those two had ever spent All Souls together, in the swamp with the Greats. I doubted it. I couldn't imagine Macon or the Greats appreciating plastic flowers.

I wondered if the Casters had their own version of All Souls, if Lena was somewhere feeling the same way I was feeling now. Like she wanted to crawl back into bed and hide until the day was over. Last year, I didn't make it to All Souls. It was too soon. The years before that, I spent the day standing over the graves of Wates I never knew or barely remembered.

But today I would be standing over the grave of someone I thought about every day. My mother.

Amma was in the kitchen in her good white blouse, the one with the lace collar, and her long blue skirt. She was clutching one of those tiny old-lady pocketbooks. "You best get on over to your aunts'." She pulled on the knot of my tie to straighten it. "You know how they get all worked up if you're late."

"Yes, ma'am." I grabbed the keys to my dad's car off the

counter. I had dropped him off at the gates of His Garden of Perpetual Peace an hour ago. He wanted to spend some time alone with my mom.

"Wait a second."

I froze. I didn't want Amma to look into my eyes. I couldn't talk about Lena right now, and I didn't want her to try to get it out of me.

Amma rifled through her bag, pulling out something I couldn't see. She opened my hand, and the chain dropped into my palm. It was thin and gold, with a tiny bird hanging from the center. It was much smaller than the ones from Macon's funeral, but I recognized it right away. "It's a sparrow for your mamma." Amma's eyes were shiny, like the road after the rain. "To Casters, sparrows mean freedom, but to a Seer, they mean a safe journey. Sparrows are clever. They can travel a long ways, but they always find their way back home."

The knot was building in my throat. "I don't think my mom will be making any more journeys."

Amma wiped her eyes and snapped her purse shut. "Well, you're mighty sure a everythin', aren't you, Ethan Wate?"

When I pulled up the Sisters' gravel driveway and opened the car door, Lucille sat on the passenger's seat instead of jumping out. She knew where we were, and she knew she'd been exiled. I coaxed her out of the car, but she sat on the sidewalk where the cement and the grass met.

Thelma opened the door before I knocked. She looked right past me to the cat, crossing her arms. "Hey there, Lucille."

Lucille licked her paw lazily, then busied herself with sniffing her tail. She might as well have flipped Thelma off. "You comin' by to say you like Amma's biscuits better 'n mine?" Lucille was the only cat I knew who ate biscuits and gravy instead of cat food. She meowed, as if she had a few choice words on the subject.

Thelma turned to me. "Hey there, Sweet Meat. I heard ya pull up." She kissed me on the cheek, which always left bright pink lip prints no amount of sweaty palm could wipe off. "Ya all right?"

Everyone knew today wasn't going to be easy for me. "Yeah, I'm okay. Are the Sisters ready?"

Thelma put her hand on her hip. "Have those girls ever been ready for anything in their lives?" Thelma always called the Sisters girls, even though they were older than her, twice over.

A voice called from the living room. "Ethan? Is that you? Come on in here. We need ya ta take a look at somethin'."

There was no telling what that meant. They could be making casts out of *The Stars and Stripes* for a family of raccoons or planning Aunt Prue's fourth—or was it fifth?—wedding. Of course, there was a third possibility I hadn't considered, and it involved me.

"Come on in." Aunt Grace waved me in. "Mercy, give him some a them blue stickers." She was fanning herself with an old church program, most likely from one of their respective husbands' funerals. Since the Sisters never let anyone actually keep one at the service, they had plenty of them lying around the house.

"I'd get 'em for you myself, but I hafta be careful on account a my accident. I've got complications." It was the only thing she talked about since the county fair. Half the town knew she had fainted, but to hear Aunt Grace tell it, she had suffered a near-fatal complication that would keep Thelma, Aunt Prue, and Aunt Mercy scurrying to do her bidding until the end of her days.

"No, no. Ethan's color's red, I told ya. Give him the red ones." Aunt Prue was scribbling madly on a yellow legal pad.

Aunt Mercy handed me a sheet of stickers with red dots on them. "Now Ethan, go 'round the livin' room and put one a these stickers underneath a the things you want. Go on now." She stared at me expectantly, as if she would be offended if I didn't slap one of them on her forehead.

"What are you talking about, Aunt Mercy?"

Aunt Grace pulled a framed photo of an old guy in a Confederate uniform off the wall. "This here's Gen'ral Robert Charles Tyler, last Rebel gen'ral killed in the War Between the States. Give me one a them stickers. This here'll be worth somethin'."

I had no idea what they were into and was afraid to ask. "We have to get going. Did you forget it was All Souls?"

Aunt Prue frowned. "'Course we didn't forget. That's why we're gettin' our affairs in order."

"That's what the stickers are for. Everyone's got a color. Thelma's yella, you're red, your daddy's blue." Aunt Mercy paused, as if she had lost her train of thought.

Aunt Prue silenced her with a look. She didn't like being interrupted. "You put those little stickers on the bottom a the things you want. That way when we die, Thelma'll know exactly who gets what."

"It was on account a All Souls that we got ta thinkin' about it." Aunt Grace smiled proudly.

"I don't want anything, and none of you are dying." I dropped the sheet of stickers on the table.

"Ethan, Wade'll be here next month, and he's jus' as greedy as a fox in a henhouse. You need ta do your choosin' first." Wade was my Uncle Landis' illegitimate son, another person in my family who would never make it onto the Wate Family Tree.

There was really no point in arguing with the Sisters when they got like this. So I spent the next half hour putting little red stickers underneath unmatched dining room chairs and Civil War memorabilia, but I still had time to kill while I waited for the Sisters to pick out their hats for All Souls. Choosing the right hat was serious business, and most of the ladies in town had already been down to Charleston to do their shopping weeks ago. To see them walking up the hill, wearing everything from peacock feathers to freshly cut roses on their heads, you would think the ladies of Gatlin were going to a garden party instead of a graveyard.

The place was a mess. Aunt Prue must have made Thelma drag down every box from the attic, full of old clothes, quilts, and photo albums. I flipped through the pages of the album on top. Old pictures were taped onto the brown pages: Aunt Prue and her husbands, Aunt Mercy standing in front of her old house on Dove Street, my house, Wate's Landing, back when my granddad was a kid. I turned the last page, and another house stared back at me.

Ravenwood Manor.

But not the Ravenwood I knew. This was a Ravenwood fit for the Historical Society Registry. Cypress trees lined the walk leading up to the crisp white veranda. Every pillar, every shutter was freshly painted. There were no traces of the strangling overgrowth, the crooked stairs of Macon's Ravenwood. Underneath the photo, there was an inscription, carefully added in delicate handwriting.

Ravenwood Manor, 1865

I was staring at Abraham's Ravenwood.

"Whatcha got there?" Aunt Mercy shuffled in wearing the biggest, pinkest flamingo of a hat I'd ever seen. There was some kind of weird netting on the front, like a veil, topped with a very unrealistic bird perched in a pink nest. When she moved the slightest bit, the whole thing kind of flapped, as if it could fly right off her head. No, this wouldn't give Savannah and the cheer squad any ammo.

I tried not to look at the flapping bird. "It's an old photo album. It was sitting on the top of this box." I handed the album to her.

"Prudence Jane, bring me my spectacles!"

There was some banging around in the hall, and Aunt Prue appeared in the doorway in an equally large and disturbing hat. This one was black, with a wraparound veil that made Aunt Prue look like the mother of a mob boss at his funeral. "If you wore them 'round your neck, like I told ya..."

Either Aunt Mercy had her hearing aid turned down or she was ignoring Aunt Prue. "Look what Ethan found." The book was still open to the same page. The Ravenwood of the past stared back at us.

"Lord 'ave mercy, look at that. The Devil's workshop if I ever saw it." The Sisters, and most of the old folks in Gatlin, were convinced Abraham Ravenwood made some kind of deal with the Devil to save Ravenwood Plantation from General Sherman's

burning campaign of 1865, which had left every other plantation along the river in ashes. If the Sisters only knew how close
it was to the truth.

"Ain't the only evil Abraham Ravenwood done." Aunt Prue
backed away from the book.

"What do you mean?" Ninety percent of what the Sisters
said was nonsense, but the other ten percent was worth hearing.
The Sisters were the ones who had told me about my mysterious
ancestor, Ethan Carter Wate, who died during the Civil War.
Maybe they knew something about Abraham Ravenwood.

Aunt Prue shook her head. "No good can come from talkin'
'bout him."

But Aunt Mercy could never resist an opportunity to defy her
older sister. "Our granddaddy used ta say Abraham Ravenwood
played on the wrong side a right and wrong—tempted fate. He
was in league with the Devil all right, practicin' witchcraft,
communin' with evil spirits."

"Mercy! You stop all that talk!"

"Stop what? Speakin' the truth?"

"Don't you drag the truth inta this house!" Aunt Prue was
flustered.

Aunt Mercy looked me straight in the eye. "But the Devil
turned on him after Abraham had done his biddin', and when
the Devil was done with him, Abraham wasn't even a man anymore. He was somethin' else."

As far as the Sisters were concerned, every evil deed, decep-
tion, or criminal act was the work of the Devil, and I wasn't
going to try to convince them otherwise. Because after what I'd
seen Abraham Ravenwood do, I knew he was more than evil. I
also knew it had nothing to do with the Devil.

"Now you're tellin' tales, Mercy Lynne, and you best quit before the Good Lord strikes you down here in this house, on All Souls, a all days. And I don't want ta get hit by a stray bolt." Aunt Prue whacked Aunt Mercy's chair with her cane.

"You don't think this boy knows 'bout the strange goin's on in Gatlin?" Aunt Grace appeared in the doorway in her own nightmarishly lavender hat. Before I was born, someone made the mistake of telling Aunt Grace lavender was her color, and nearly everything she wore had been disproving it ever since. "No use in tryin' ta put the milk back in the jug after it's spilt."

Aunt Prue banged her cane on the floor. They were speaking in riddles, like Amma, which meant they knew something. Maybe they didn't know there were Casters wandering around in the Tunnels below their house, but they knew something.

"Some messes can be cleaned up easier than others. I don't want any part a this one." Aunt Prue pushed past Aunt Grace as she left the room. "This ain't a day ta be speakin' ill a the dead."

Aunt Grace shuffled over toward us. I took her elbow and guided her to the couch. Aunt Mercy waited for the tapping of Aunt Prue's cane to echo down the hall. "Is she gone? I don't have my hearin' aid turned up."

Aunt Grace nodded. "I think so."

The two of them leaned in as if they were about to give me launch codes for nuclear missiles. "If I tell ya somethin', you promise not ta tell your daddy? 'Cause if you do, we're bound ta end up in the Home for sure." She was referring to the Summerville Assisted Seniors House — the seventh circle of hell, as far as the Sisters were concerned.

Aunt Grace nodded in agreement.

"What is it? I won't say anything to my dad. I promise."

"Prudence Jane's wrong." Aunt Mercy dropped her voice to a whisper. "Abraham Ravenwood's still around, sure as I'm sittin' here today."

I wanted to say they were crazy. Two ancient, senile old ladies claiming to see a man, or what most people thought was a man, no one had seen for a hundred years. "What do you mean, still around?"

"I saw him with my own eyes, last year. Behind the church, a all places!" Aunt Mercy fanned herself with her handkerchief, as if she might faint from the thought of it. "After church on Tuesdays, we wait for Thelma out in front, on account a she has ta teach Bible study down the way at First Methodist. Anyhow, I let Harlon James out from inside my pocketbook so he could stretch his little legs—you know Prudence Jane makes me carry him. But soon as I set him down, he ran 'round the back a the church."

"You know that dog can't mind ta save his life." Aunt Grace shook her head.

Aunt Mercy glanced at the door before continuing. "Well, I had ta follow him because you know how Prudence Jane is 'bout that dog. So I went 'round back and jus' when I turned the corner ta holler for Harlon James, I saw it. Abraham Ravenwood's ghost. Out in the cemet'ry behind the church. Those progressives at the Round Church in Charleston got one thing right." Folks in Charleston said the Round Church was built that way so the Devil couldn't hide in the corners. I never pointed out the obvious, that the Devil usually had no problem marching right down the middle aisle, as far as some of our local congregations were concerned.

"I saw him, too," Aunt Grace whispered. "And I know it was him, 'cause his picture's on the wall down at the Historical

Society, where I play rummy with the girls. Right up there in the Founders Circle, on account a the Ravenwoods bein' the first ones in Gatlin. Abraham Ravenwood, plain as day."

Aunt Mercy shushed her sister. With Aunt Prue out of the room, it was her turn to call the shots. "It was him, all right. He was out there with Silas Ravenwood's boy. Not Macon — the other one, Phinehas." I remembered the name from the Ravenwood Family Tree. Hunting Phinehas Ravenwood.

"You mean Hunting?"

"Nobody called that boy by his given name. They all called him Phinehas. It's from the Bible. You know what it means?" She paused dramatically. "Serpent's tongue."

For a second, I held my breath.

"There was no mistakin' that man's ghost. As the Good Lord as my witness, we cleared outta there faster than a cat with its tail on fire. Now, Lord knows I couldn't move like that these days. Not since my complications..."

The Sisters were crazy, but their brand was usually based in crazy history. There was no way of knowing what version of the truth they were telling, but it was usually a version. Any version of this story was dangerous. I couldn't figure it out, but if I had learned anything this year, it was that sooner or later I was going to have to.

Lucille meowed, scratching at the screen door. Guess she'd heard enough. Harlon James growled from under the couch. For the first time, I wondered what the two of them had seen, hanging around this house for so long.

But not every dog was Boo Radley. Sometimes a dog was just a dog. Sometimes a cat was just a cat. Still, I opened the screen door and stuck a red sticker on Lucille's head.

⊰ 6.17 ⊱

Keeping

If there was one reliable source of information around here, it was the folks in Gatlin. On a day like today, you didn't have to look too hard to see most everyone from the town in the same half mile. The cemetery was packed by the time we got there, late as usual thanks to the Sisters. Lucille wouldn't get in the Cadillac, then we had to stop at Gardens of Eden because Aunt Prue wanted to get flowers for all her late husbands, only none of the flowers looked good enough, and when we were finally back in the car, Aunt Mercy wouldn't let me drive over twenty miles an hour. I had been dreading today for months. Now it was here.

I trudged up the sloping gravel path of His Garden of Perpetual Peace, pushing Aunt Mercy's wheelchair. Thelma was behind me, with Aunt Prue on one arm and Aunt Grace on the other. Lucille was trailing after them, picking her way through the pebbles, careful to keep her distance. Aunt Mercy's patent-leather purse swung on the handle of her wheelchair, jabbing me in the gut every second step. I was already sweating, thinking about that wheelchair getting caught in the thick summer grass. There was a strong possibility Link and I would be doing the fireman's carry.

We made it up the rise in time to see Emily preening in her new white halter dress. Every girl got a new dress for All Souls. There were no flip-flops or tank tops, only your scrubbed Sunday best. It was like an extended family reunion, only ten times over because pretty much the whole town, and for the most part the whole county, was in one way or another related to you, your neighbor, or your neighbor's neighbor.

Emily was giggling and hanging all over Emory. "Did you bring any beer?"

Emory opened his jacket, revealing a silver flask. "Better than that."

Eden, Charlotte, and Savannah were holding court near the Snow family plot, which enjoyed a prime location in the center of the rows of headstones. It was covered with bright plastic flowers and cherubs. There was even a little plastic fawn nibbling grass next to the tallest headstone. Decorating graves was another one of Gatlin's contests—a way to prove that you and your family members, even the dead ones, were better than your neighbors and theirs. People went all out. Plastic wreaths wrapped in green nylon vines, shiny rabbits and squirrels, even birdbaths, so hot from the sun they could burn the skin right off your fingers. There was no overdoing it. The tackier, the better.

My mom used to laugh about her favorites. "They're still

lifes, works of art like the ones painted by the Dutch and Flemish masters, only these are made of plastic. The sentiment's the same." My mom could laugh at the worst of Gatlin's traditions and respect the best of them. Maybe that's how she survived around here.

She was particularly partial to the glow-in-the-dark crosses that lit up at night. Some summer evenings, the two of us would lie on the hill in the cemetery and watch them light up at dusk, as if they were stars. Once I asked her why she liked to lie out there. "This is history, Ethan. The history of families, the people they loved, the ones they lost. Those crosses, those silly plastic flowers and animals, they were put there to remind us of someone who is missed. Which is a beautiful thing to see, and it's our job to see it." We never told my dad about those nights in the cemetery. It was one of those things we did alone.

I would have to walk past most of Jackson High and step over a plastic rabbit or two to get to the Wate family plot on the outskirts of the lawn. That was the other thing about All Souls. There wasn't actually much remembering involved. In another hour, everyone over twenty-one would be standing around gossiping about the living, right after they finished gossiping about the dead, and everyone under thirty would be getting wasted behind the mausoleums. Everyone but me. I'd be too busy remembering.

"Hey, man." Link jogged up alongside me and smiled at the Sisters. "Afternoon, ma'ams."

"How are you today, Wesley? You're growin' like a weed, aren't ya?" Aunt Prue was huffing and sweating.

"Yes, ma'am." Rosalie Watkins was standing behind Link, waving at Aunt Prue.

"Ethan, why don't you go on with Wesley? I see Rosalie, and I need to ask her what kinda flour she uses in her hummingbird cake." Aunt Prue dug her cane into the grass, and Thelma helped Aunt Mercy out of her wheelchair.

"You sure you'll be all right?"

Aunt Prue scowled at me. " 'Course we'll be all right. We've been lookin' after ourselves since before you were born."

"Since before your daddy was born," Aunt Grace corrected.

"I almost forgot." Aunt Prue opened her pocketbook and fished something out. "Found that darned cat's tag." She looked down at Lucille disapprovingly. "Not that it helped us any. Not like *some* people care about years a loyalty and all those walks on your very own clothesline. I reckon it doesn't buy you a drop a gratitude, when it comes ta some people." The cat wandered away without so much as a look back.

I looked at the metal tag with Lucille's name etched into it, and slipped it in my pocket. "The ring is missing."

"Best put it in your wallet, in case you have ta prove she doesn't have rabies. She's a biter. Thelma'll see 'bout fetchin' another one."

"Thanks."

The Sisters linked arms, and those three gargantuan hats knocked up against each other as they shuffled toward their friends. Even the Sisters had friends. My life sucked.

"Shawn and Earl brought some beer and Jim Beam. Everyone's meetin' behind the Honeycutt crypt." At least I had Link.

We both knew I wouldn't be getting drunk anywhere. In a few minutes, I would be standing over my dead mother's grave. I'd be thinking about the way she always laughed when I told her about Mr. Lee and his twisted version of U.S. History, or

U.S. Hysteria, as she called it. How she and my dad danced to James Taylor in our kitchen in bare feet. How she knew exactly what to say when everything was going wrong, like when my ex-girlfriend would rather be with some kind of mutant Supernatural than with me.

Link put his hand on my shoulder. "You okay?"

"Yeah, I'm fine. Let's walk around." I would be standing over her grave today, but I wasn't ready. Not yet.

L, where are —

I caught myself and tried to pull my mind away. I don't know why I still reached for her. Habit, I guess. But instead of Lena's voice, I heard Savannah's. She stood in front of me, wearing way too much makeup but somehow still managing to look pretty. She was all glossy hair and gloppy eyelashes and tied-up little straps on her sundress that were probably only there to make a guy think about untying them. I mean, if you didn't know what a bitch she was, or didn't care.

"I'm real sorry about your mamma, Ethan." She cleared her throat awkwardly. Her mother probably made her come over here, pillar of the community that Mrs. Snow was. Tonight, though it was barely over a year since my mom died, I'd find more than one casserole on our doorstep, just like the day after her funeral. Time passed slowly in Gatlin, kind of like dog years, only in reverse. And like the day after the funeral, Amma would leave every one of them out there for the possums.

Seems possums never get tired of ham 'n' apple casserole.

It was still the nicest thing Savannah had said to me since September. Even though I didn't care what she thought of me, today it was nice to have one less thing to feel like crap about. "Thanks."

Savannah smiled her fake smile and walked off, her high heels jerking as they got stuck in the grass. Link loosened his tie, which was crooked and too short. I recognized it from sixth-grade graduation. Underneath it, he had snuck out of the house wearing a T-shirt that said I'M WITH STUPID, with arrows pointing in all different directions. It pretty much summed up how I was feeling today, too. Surrounded by stupid.

The hits kept on coming. Maybe folks were feeling guilty because I had a crazy father and a dead mother. More likely, they were scared of Amma. Anyway, I must have surpassed Loretta West, a three-time widow whose last husband died after a gator bit a hole in his stomach, as the most pathetic person at All Souls. If they gave out prizes, I would've won the blue ribbon. I could tell by the way folks shook their heads when I walked by. *What a pity, Ethan Wate doesn't have a mamma anymore.*

It was the same way Mrs. Lincoln was shaking her head right now, as she headed my way, with *You Poor Misguided Motherless Boy* written on her face. Link ducked out before she hit her target. "Ethan, I wanted to say how much we *all* miss your mamma." I wasn't sure who she was talking about—her friends in the DAR, who couldn't stand my mom, or the women who sat around the Snip 'n' Curl talking about how my mother read too many books and no good could come from that. Mrs. Lincoln blotted a nonexistent tear from her eye. "She was a good woman. You know, I remember how much she loved to garden. Always outside tendin' her roses with her tender heart."

"Yes, ma'am."

The closest my mom ever came to gardening was when she sprinkled cayenne pepper all over the tomatoes so my dad

255

wouldn't kill the rabbit that kept eating them. The roses were Amma's. Everyone knew that. I wished Mrs. Lincoln would try that "tender heart" comment to Amma's face. "I like to think she's right up there with the angels, tendin' that old, sweet Garden a Eden now. Prunin' and trimmin' the Tree a Knowledge, with the cherubs and the—"

Snakes?

"I've gotta go find my dad, ma'am." I had to get away from Link's mom before lightning struck her—or me, for wanting it to.

Her voice trailed after me. "Tell your daddy I'm gonna drop him off one a my famous ham 'n' apple casseroles!" That sealed the deal. I was getting the blue ribbon for sure. I couldn't get away from her fast enough. But at All Souls, there was no escape. As soon as you made it past one creepy relative or neighbor, there was another one right around the corner. Or, in Link's case, another creepy parent.

Link's dad slung his arm around Tom Watkins' neck. "Earl was the best of us. He had the best uniform, the best battle formations—" Link's dad choked back a drunken sob. "And he made the best ammunition." Coincidently, Big Earl was killed making some of that ammo, and Mr. Lincoln had replaced him as the leader of the Cavalry, in the Reenactment of the Battle of Honey Hill. Some of that guilt was here today in the form of whiskey.

"I wanted to bring my gun and give Earl a proper salute, but Dammit Doreen hid it from me." Ronnie Weeks' wife was generally known as Dammit Doreen, sometimes shortened to DD, on account of that's all he ever said to her. He took another swig of whiskey.

256

"To Earl!" They grabbed each other around the neck, raising their cans and bottles over Earl's grave. Beer and Wild Turkey sloshed all over the headstone, Gatlin's tribute to the fallen.

"Jeez, I hope we don't end up like that one day." Link slunk away, and I followed. His parents never failed to embarrass him. "Why couldn't my parents be like yours?"

"You mean mental? Or gone? No offense, but I think you've got the mental part covered."

"Your dad's not mental anymore, at least not more than anyone else around here. No one cares if you walk around in your pajamas when your wife just died. My folks don't have an excuse. They're a few pistons short of an engine."

"We won't end up like that. Because you'll be a famous drummer in New York, and I'll be doing—I don't know, something that doesn't involve a Confederate uniform and Wild Turkey." I tried to sound convincing, but I didn't know which was more unlikely—Link becoming a famous musician or me getting out of Gatlin.

I still had the map on my bedroom wall, the one with the thin green line connecting all the places I'd read about, the places I wanted to go. I'd spent my whole life thinking about roads leading anywhere but Gatlin. Then I met Lena, and it was like the map never existed. I think I would've been able to deal with getting stuck anywhere, even here, as long as we were together. Funny how the map seemed to have lost its appeal when I needed it the most.

"I'd better get over to see my mom." I said it like I was going by the library to see her in the archive. "You know what I mean."

Link tapped his knuckles against mine. "I'll catch you later.

I'm gonna walk around for a while." Walk around? Link didn't walk around. He tried to get drunk and hit on girls who wouldn't hook up with him.

"What's up? You're not going looking for the next Mrs. Wesley Jefferson Lincoln, are you?"

Link ran his hand over his spiky blond hair. "I wish. I know I'm an idiot, but there's only one girl in my head right now." The one girl who shouldn't be. What could I say? I knew how it felt to be in love with a girl who didn't want anything to do with you.

"Sorry, man. I guess Ridley's not that easy to forget."

"Yeah, and seein' her last night didn't help." He shook his head, frustrated. "I know she's supposed to be Dark and all, but I can't shake the feelin' what we had was more than just an act."

"I know what you mean."

We were a couple of pathetic losers. Though I didn't think Ridley was capable of anything real, I didn't want to make him feel worse. Link wasn't looking for an answer, anyway.

"You know all that stuff you told me about Casters and Mortals not bein' able to be together 'cause it'll kill the Mortal?"

I nodded. It was only about eighty percent of what I thought about. "What about it?"

"We came close more than once." He kicked the grass, making a brown spot on the perfectly manicured lawn.

"Too much information."

"I'm makin' a point here. I wasn't the one who put on the brakes. It was Rid. I figured she was slummin' with me, like I was good enough to mess around with, and that's it." Link was pacing. "But now, when I think back on it, maybe I was wrong.

Maybe she didn't want to hurt me." Link had clearly put a lot of thought into this.

"I don't know. She's still a Dark Caster."

Link shrugged. "Yeah, I know, but a guy's gotta have a dream."

I wanted to tell Link what was going on, that Ridley and Lena might already have taken off. I opened my mouth, then shut it without making a single sound. If Lena had put a Cast on me, I didn't want to know.

I had only visited my mom's grave once since the funeral, but it wasn't on All Souls. I couldn't face it that soon. I didn't feel like she was actually here, hanging around the graveyard like Genevieve or the Greats. The only place I sensed her was in the archive or the study at our house. Those were the places she loved, the places I could imagine her spending her days wherever she was now.

But not here, not under the ground, where my dad was kneeling with his face in his hands. He'd been here for hours and it showed.

I cleared my throat so my dad would know I was there. It felt like I was eavesdropping on a private moment between them. He wiped his face and stood up. "How are you holding up?"

"I'm okay, I guess." I didn't know what I was feeling, but it wasn't okay.

He shoved his hands in his pockets, staring down at the headstone. A delicate white flower lay on the grass beneath it.

Confederate jasmine. I read the curving letters carved into the stone.

LILA EVERS WATE

BELOVED WIFE AND MOTHER

SCIENTIAE CUSTOS

I repeated the last line. I'd noticed it the last time I was here, in the middle of July, a few weeks before my birthday. But I had come alone, and by the time I got home I was so numb from staring at my mother's grave, I'd forgotten all about it. *"Scientiae Custos."*

"It's Latin. It means 'Keeper of Knowledge.' Marian suggested it. It's fitting, don't you think?" If he only knew.

I forced a smile. "Yeah. It sounds like her."

My dad put his arm around my shoulder and gave it a squeeze, the way he used to after my Little League team lost a game. "I really miss her. I still can't believe she's gone."

I couldn't say anything. My breath was caught in my throat, my chest so tight I thought I was going to pass out. My mom was dead. I would never see her again, no matter how many pages she flipped open in her books or how many messages she sent me.

"I know this has been really hard for you, Ethan. I wanted to say I'm sorry I wasn't there for you this year the way I should've been. I just—"

"Dad." I could feel my eyes watering, but I didn't want to cry. I wouldn't give the town casserole factory that kind of satisfaction. So I cut him off. "It's okay."

He gave my shoulder one last squeeze. "I'll give you some time alone with her. I'm going to take a walk."

I kept staring at the headstone, with the tiny Celtic symbol of Awen etched into the stone. It was a symbol I knew, one my mother had always loved. Three lines representing rays of light, converging at the top.

I heard Marian's voice behind me. "*Awen*. It's a Gaelic word that means 'poetic inspiration' or 'spiritual illumination.' Two things your mother respected." I thought about the symbols in the lintel at Ravenwood, the symbols on *The Book of Moons*, and the one on the door of Exile. Symbols meant something. In some cases, more than words. My mom had known that. I wondered if it was the reason she became a Keeper, or if she learned it from the Keepers before her. There was so much about her I would never know.

"Ethan, I'm sorry. Would you like to be alone?"

I let Marian hug me. "No. I don't really feel like she's here. You know what I mean?"

"I do." She kissed my forehead and smiled, pulling a green tomato out of her pocket. She balanced it on the top of the tombstone.

I leaned back and smiled. "Now if you were a real friend, you would have fried it."

Marian put her arm around me. She was in her best dress, like everyone else, but her best dress was somehow better. It was soft and yellow, the color of butter, with a loose bow near the neck. The skirt folded into about a thousand crinkly pleats, like a dress from an old-fashioned movie. It looked like something Lena would have worn.

"Lila knows I would do no such thing." She squeezed me tighter. "I really only came out here to see you."

"Thanks, Aunt Marian. It's been a rough couple of days."

"Olivia told me. A Caster bar, an Incubus, and a Vex, all in the same night. I'm afraid Amma will never let you visit me again." She didn't mention the trouble I imagined Liv was in today.

"There's something else." Lena. I couldn't bring myself to say her name. Marian pushed my hair out of my eyes. "I heard, and I'm sorry. But I brought you something." She opened her bag and took out a small wooden box with a worn design carved into its surface. "As I said, I really came here to see you and give you this." She held out the box. "It was your mother's, one of her most valuable possessions. It's older than the rest of her collection. I think she would want you to have it."

I took it. The box was heavier than it looked.

"Be careful. It's delicate."

I lifted the lid gently, expecting to find another one of my mother's treasured Civil War relics—a scrap of a flag, a bullet, a piece of lace. Something marked by history and time. But when I opened the box, it was something else, marked by a different kind of history and time. I knew what it was, the second I saw it.

The Arclight, from the visions.

The Arclight Macon Ravenwood gave to the girl he loved.

Lila Jane Evers.

I had seen it stitched on an old pillow once that belonged to my mom when she was little. *Jane.* My Aunt Caroline said only my grandmother called her that, but my grandmother died before I was born, so I'd never heard it myself. Aunt Caroline was wrong. My grandmother wasn't the only one who had called her Jane.

Which meant—

My mom was the girl in the visions.

And Macon Ravenwood was the love of my mother's life.

262

⪥ 6.17 ⪥

The Arclight

My mom and Macon Ravenwood. I dropped the Arclight as if it had stung me. The box fell, and the ball rolled harmlessly across the grass, like a child's toy instead of some kind of supernatural prison.

"Ethan? What is it?" It was obvious Marian had no idea I recognized the Arclight. I had never mentioned it when I told her about the visions. I hadn't thought much about it. It was another little detail about the Caster world I didn't understand.

But this one little detail mattered.

If this was the Arclight from the vision, then my mother had loved Macon the way I loved Lena. The way my father had loved her.

I needed to know if Marian knew where my mother had gotten it, or who had given it to her. "Did you know?"

She bent down and picked up the sphere, its dark surface

gleaming in the sunlight. She slid it back into the box. "Did I know what? Ethan, you aren't making any sense."

The questions were coming faster than my mind could process them. How did my mother meet Macon Ravenwood? How long were they together? Who else knew? And the biggest one...

What about my dad?

"Did you know my mom was in love with Macon Ravenwood?"

Marian's face crumbled, which told me everything. She had only meant to give away a gift from my mom, not my mother's deepest secret. "Who told you that?"

"You did. When you handed me the Arclight Macon gave to the girl he loved. My mother."

Marian's eyes filled with tears, but they didn't fall. "The visions. They were about Macon and your mother." She was figuring it out, piecing it together.

I remembered the night when I first met Macon. *Lila Evers*, he had said. *Lila Evers Wate*, I had corrected.

Macon had mentioned my mother's work, but claimed he didn't know her. Another lie. My head was spinning.

"So you knew." It wasn't a question. I shook my head, wishing I could shake everything I'd just learned back out again. "Does my dad know?"

"No. And you can't tell him, Ethan. He wouldn't understand." Her voice was desperate.

"He wouldn't understand? I don't understand!" More than a few people stopped gossiping and looked over at us.

"I'm so sorry. I never thought it would be a story I would have to tell. It was your mother's story, not mine."

"In case you haven't noticed, my mom is dead. She's not exactly taking questions." My voice was harsh and unforgiving, which pretty much summed up how I felt.

Marian looked down at my mother's headstone. "You're right. You need to know."

"I want the truth."

"That's what I intend to give you." Her voice was shaking. "If you know about the Arclight, I assume you know why Macon gave it to your mother."

"So she could protect herself from him." I'd felt sorry for Macon before. Now I felt sick. My mom was Juliet in some kind of twisted play where Romeo was an Incubus, even if it was Macon.

"That's right. Macon and Lila struggled with the same reality as you and Lena. It has been hard to watch you these past few months without drawing certain...comparisons. I can't think how difficult it must have been for Macon."

"Please. Stop."

"Ethan, I understand this is hard for you, but it doesn't change what happened. I'm a Keeper, and these are the facts. Your mother was a Mortal. Macon was an Incubus. They couldn't be together, not after Macon changed and became the Dark creature he was born to be. Macon didn't trust himself. He was afraid he might hurt your mother, so he gave her the Arclight."

"Facts. Lies. Whatever." I was so tired of it all.

"Fact. He loved her more than his own life." Why was Marian defending him?

"Fact. Not killing the love of your life doesn't make you a hero." I was furious.

"It nearly killed him, Ethan."

"Yeah? Well, look around. My mom's dead. They both are. So Macon's plan didn't really help much, did it?"

Marian took a deep breath. I knew the look, and a lecture was coming. She pulled me by the arm, and we walked away from the graveyard, away from everyone above and below the ground. "They met at Duke. They were both studying American history. They fell in love, like any two people."

"You mean, like any unsuspecting undergraduate and an evolving Demon. If we're sticking to the facts."

"'In Light there is Dark, and in Dark there is Light.' Your mother used to say that."

I wasn't interested in philosophical ideas about the nature of the Caster world. "When did he give her the Arclight?"

"Eventually, Macon told Lila what he was and what he would become—that a future between the two of them was impossible." Marian spoke slowly and carefully. I wondered if it was as hard to say as it was to hear, and I felt sorry for both of us.

"It broke her heart, and his. He gave her the Arclight, which thankfully she never had to use. He left the university and came back home to Gatlin."

She waited for me to say something cruel. I tried to come up with something, but in spite of everything, I was curious. "What happened after Macon came back? Did they see each other again?"

"Sadly, no."

I gave her an incredulous look. "Sadly?"

Marian shook her head at me. "It was sad, Ethan. It was the saddest I'd ever seen your mother. I was so worried, and I didn't know what to do. I thought she was going to die from a broken heart, from how broken every part of her was."

We had been walking the loop that circled Perpetual Peace. Now we were surrounded by trees and out of sight from most of Gatlin.

"But." I had to know the end, even if it hurt to hear.

"But your mother followed Macon to Gatlin, through the Tunnels. She couldn't bear to be away from him, and she swore to find a way they could be together. A way Casters and Mortals could spend their lives together. She was obsessed with the idea."

I understood. I didn't like it, but I understood.

"The answer to that question did not lie in the Mortal world but in the Caster world. So your mother found a way to become part of it, even if she couldn't be with Macon."

We started walking again. "You're talking about her job as a Keeper, right?"

Marian nodded. "Lila found a calling that allowed her to study the Caster world and its laws, its Light and its Darkness. A way to look for the answer."

"How did she get the job?" I didn't think there was a Caster Yellow Pages, but since Carlton Eaton delivered our Yellow Pages aboveground and the Caster mail below, who knew?

"At the time, there was no Keeper in Gatlin." Marian paused, uncomfortable. "But a powerful Caster requested one, since the *Lunae Libri* resides here and, at one time, *The Book of Moons*."

Now it all made sense.

"Macon. He asked for her, didn't he? He couldn't stay away, after all that."

Marian wiped her face with a handkerchief. "No. It was Arelia Valentin, Macon's mother."

267

"Why would Macon's mother want my mom to be a Keeper? Even if she felt sorry for her son, she knew they couldn't be together."

"Arelia is a powerful Diviner, capable of seeing fragments of the future."

"Like a Caster version of Amma?"

Marian wiped her face. "I guess you could think of it that way. Arelia recognized something in your mother, her ability to find the truth—to see what is hidden. I think she was hoping your mother would find the answer, a way Casters and Mortals could be together. Light Casters have always hoped for that possibility. Genevieve wasn't the first Caster to fall in love with a Mortal." Marian looked off into the distance, where families were beginning to lay out their picnics on the sloping grass. "Or maybe she did it for her son."

Marian stopped walking. We had made another circle and were standing at Macon's grave. I could see the angel weeping in the distance. Only the grave looked nothing like it had at his funeral. Where there had only been dirt, now there was a wild garden shaded by two impossibly tall lemon trees, flanking either side of the headstone. In the shade, a bed of spreading jasmine and tangles of rosemary grew over his grave. I wondered if anyone had visited him today to notice.

I pressed my hands against my temples, trying to keep my head from exploding. Marian laid her hand gently on my back. "I know it's a lot to take in, but it doesn't change anything. Your mother loved you."

I shrugged Marian's hand away. "Yeah, she just didn't love my dad."

Marian jerked my arm, forcing me to face her. My mother

may have been my mom, but she was also Marian's best friend, and I wasn't going to get away with questioning her integrity in front of Marian. Not today, or any day. "Don't you say that, EW. Your mother loved your father."

"But she didn't move to Gatlin for my dad. She moved here for Macon."

"Your parents met at Duke when we were working on our dissertation. As the Keeper, your mother was living in the Tunnels underneath Gatlin, traveling between the *Lunae Libri* and the university to work with me. She wasn't living in the town, in the world of the DAR and Mrs. Lincoln. So she did move to Gatlin for your father. She moved out of the darkness and into the light, and believe me, it was a big move for your mom. Your father saved her from herself when none of us could. Not me. Not Macon."

I stared at the lemon trees shading Macon's grave, and past them, to my mom's gravesite. I thought about my dad kneeling there. I thought of Macon, braving the Garden of Perpetual Peace, if only so he could rest one tree over from my mom.

"She moved into a town where no one accepted her, because your father wouldn't leave, and she loved him." Marian held my chin between her thumb and her fingers. "She just didn't love him first."

I took a deep breath. At least my whole life wasn't a total lie. She loved my dad, even if she loved Macon Ravenwood, too. I took the Arclight from Marian's hand. I wanted to hold it, to have a piece of both of them. "She never found the answer, the way Mortals and Casters can be together."

"I don't know if there is a way." Marian put her arm around me, and I leaned my head on her shoulder. "You're the one who might be a Wayward, EW. You tell me."

For the first time since I saw Lena standing in the rain, almost a year ago, I didn't know. Like my mom, I hadn't found any answers. All I had found was trouble. Was that what she found, too?

I looked at the box in Marian's hands. "Is that why my mom died? Trying to find the answer?"

Marian took my hand and pressed the box into it, wrapping my fingers around it with hers. "I've told you what I know. Draw your own conclusions, but I can't interfere. Those are the rules. In the great Order of Things, I don't matter. Keepers never do."

"That's not true." Marian mattered to me, but I couldn't say it. My mom mattered. That part I didn't have to say.

Marian smiled as she lifted her hand, leaving the box in mine. "I'm not complaining. I chose this path, Ethan. Not everyone gets to choose their place in the Order of Things."

"You mean not Lena? Or not me?"

"You matter, whether you like it or not, and so does Lena. That's not a choice." She pushed the hair out of my eyes, the way my mom used to. "The truth is the truth. 'Rarely pure and never simple,' as Oscar Wilde would say."

"I don't understand."

"'All truths are easy to understand once they are discovered; the point is to discover them.'"

"More Oscar Wilde?"

"Galileo, the father of modern astronomy. Another man who rejected his place in the Order of Things—the idea that the sun didn't revolve around the Earth. He knew, perhaps better than anyone, that we don't get to choose what is true. We only get to choose what we do about it."

270

I took the box, because deep down I knew what she was say-ing, even if I didn't know anything about Galileo and knew even less about Oscar Wilde. I was part of all this, whether I wanted to be or not. I couldn't run from it, any more than I could stop the visions.

Now I had to decide what to do about it.

Jump

When I crawled into bed that night, I was dreading my dreams. They say you dream about the last thing you were thinking about before you fell asleep, but the more I tried to not think about Macon and my mom, the more I thought about them. Exhausted from all that thinking about not thinking, it was only a matter of time before I sunk through the mattress into the blackness, and my bed became a boat....

The willows were waving over my head.

I could feel myself rocking back and forth. The sky was blue, cloudless, surreal. I turned my head and looked to the side. Splintery wood, painted a peeling shade of blue that looked a lot like the ceiling in my bedroom. I was in a dinghy or a rowboat, floating along the river.

I sat up and the boat rocked. A small white hand fell to the side, dragging a slender finger through the water. I stared at the ripples disturbing the reflection of the perfect sky, otherwise cool and calm as glass.

Lena was lying across from me at the end of the boat. She wore a white dress, the kind you saw in old movies, where everything is shot in black and white. Lace and ribbon and tiny pearl buttons. She was holding a black parasol, and her hair, her nails, even her lips, were black. She lay curled on her side, slumped against the dinghy, her hand dragging along behind us as we floated.

"Lena?"

She didn't open her eyes, but she smiled. "I'm cold, Ethan."

I looked at her hand, which was now up to her wrist in the water. "It's summer. The water's warm." I tried to crawl over to her, but the boat rocked, and she slumped farther over the edge, exposing the black Chucks beneath her dress.

I couldn't move.

Now the water was up to her arm, and I could see strands of her hair beginning to float on the surface.

"Sit up, L! You're going to fall in!"

She laughed and dropped the parasol. It floated, spinning, in the ripples of water behind us. I lurched toward her, and the boat rocked violently.

"Didn't they tell you? I've already fallen."

I lunged for her. This couldn't be happening, but it was. I knew because I was waiting for the sound of the splash.

When I hit the edge of the boat, I opened my eyes. The world was rocking, and she was gone. I looked down, and all I could see was the murky greenish-brown water of the Santee and her dark hair. I reached into the water. I couldn't think.

Jump or stay in the boat.

The hair floated downward, unruly, quiet, breathtaking, like some kind of mythical sea creature. There was a white face, blurred by the depths of the river. Trapped beneath the glass.

"Mom?"

I sat up in bed, drenched and coughing. Moonlight was streaming into my window. It was open again. I walked to the bathroom and drank water out of my hand until the coughing subsided. I stared into the mirror. It was dark, and I could barely make out my features. I tried to find my eyes within the shadows. But instead I saw something else . . . a light in the distance.

I couldn't see the mirror anymore, or the shadows of my face. Just the light, and bits of images as they flashed by.

I tried to focus and make sense of what I was seeing, but everything was coming too fast, rushing by me, jerking up and down, like I was on a ride. I saw the street—wet, shiny, and dark. It was only inches away from me, which made it seem as if I was crawling on the ground. But that was impossible because everything was moving so fast. Tall, straight corners jutting out into my field of vision, the street rising up to meet me.

All I could see was the light and the street that was so awkwardly close. I felt the cold porcelain as I gripped the sides of the sink, trying not to fall. I was dizzy, and the flashes kept coming at me, the light getting closer. My view shifted sharply, as if I had turned the corner in a maze, and everything started to slow.

Two people were leaning against the side of a dirty brick

building, under a streetlight. It was the light that had been jerking in and out of focus. I was looking up at them from below, like I was lying on the ground. I stared up at the silhouettes in front of me.

"I should've left a note. My gramma will be worried." It was Lena's voice. She was right in front of me. This wasn't a vision, not like the ones from the locket or Macon's journal.

"*Lena!*" I called out her name, but she didn't move.

The other person stepped closer. I knew it was John before I saw his face. "If you had left a note, they could've used it to find us with a simple Locator Cast. Especially your grandma. She has crazy power." He touched her shoulder. "Guess it runs in the family."

"I don't feel powerful. I don't know what I feel."

"You aren't having second thoughts, are you?" John reached out and took her hand, holding it open so he could see her palm. He reached into his pocket and pulled out a marker, and started writing on her hand absentmindedly.

Lena shook her head, watching as he wrote. "No. I don't belong there anymore. I would've ended up hurting them. I hurt everyone who loves me."

"*Lena—*" It was pointless. She couldn't hear me.

"It won't be like that when we get to the Great Barrier. There's no Light or Dark, no Naturals or Cataclysts, only magic in its purest form. Which means no labels or judgments."

They were staring at her hand as John moved the marker around her wrist. The way their heads were bent, they were almost touching. Lena rotated her wrist slowly in his hand. "I'm scared."

"I would never let anything happen to you." He tucked a

strand of hair back behind her ear, the way I used to. I wondered if she remembered.

"It's hard to imagine a place like that really exists. People have been judging me my whole life." Lena laughed, but I could hear the edge in her voice.

"That's why we're going. So you can finally be yourself." His shoulder twitched awkwardly, and he grabbed it, wincing. He shook it off before Lena noticed. But not before I did.

"Myself? I don't even know who that is." Lena stepped away from the wall and looked out into the night. The streetlight outlined her profile, and I could see her necklace shining.

"I'd like to know," John leaned into Lena. He was speaking so softly, I could barely hear the words.

Lena looked tired, but I recognized her crooked half-smile. "I'll introduce you if I ever meet her."

"You cats ready to go?" Ridley walked out of the building, sucking on a cherry-red lollipop.

Lena turned around, and as she did, the light caught her hand—the one John had been writing on. But there were no words. It was inked in black designs. They were the same designs I had seen on her hands at the fair, and along the edges of her notebook. Before I could see anything else, my point of view shifted away from them, and all I could see was a wide street and the wet cobblestones in front of me. Then nothing.

I don't know how long I stood there, holding on to the sink. It felt like I would pass out if I let go. My hands were shaking, my legs buckling underneath me. What just happened? It wasn't a vision. They were so close, I could've reached out and touched her. Why couldn't she hear me?

It didn't matter. She had really done it—run away, just like she said she would. I didn't know where she was, but I had seen enough of the Tunnels to recognize them.

She was gone, headed for the Great Barrier, wherever it was. It didn't have anything to do with me anymore. I didn't want to dream it or see it or hear about it.

Forget about it. Go back to sleep. That's what I needed to do. *Jump or stay in the boat.*

What a screwed-up dream. As if it was up to me. This boat was sinking, with or without me.

I let go of the sink long enough to heave into the toilet and stumble back to my room. I walked over to the stacks of shoe boxes along the wall, the boxes that held everything important to me, or anything I wanted to hide. For a second, I stood there. I knew what I was looking for, but I didn't know which box it was in.

Water like glass. I thought of it when I remembered the dream.

I tried to remember where to find it. Which was ridiculous, because I knew what was in every single one of those boxes. At least, I knew yesterday. I tried to think, but all I could see were the seventy or eighty boxes stacked around me. Black Adidas, green New Balance...I couldn't remember.

I had opened about twelve boxes before I found the black Converse one. The carved wooden box was still inside. I lifted the smooth, delicate sphere from its velvet lining. The impression of the sphere remained in the velvet, dark and crushed, as if it had been there a thousand years.

The Arclight.

It had been my mother's most valuable possession, and Marian had given it to me. Why now?

In my hand, the pale orb began to reflect the room around me until the curved surface was alive and swirling with colors. It was glowing, a pale green. I could see Lena again in my mind, and hear her. *I hurt everyone I love.*

The glow began to fade, and once again the Arclight was black and opaque, cold and lifeless in my hand. But I could still feel Lena. I could sense where she was, as if the Arclight was some kind of compass leading me to her. Maybe there was something to this Wayward thing, after all.

Which made no sense, because the last place I wanted to be was wherever Lena and John were. So why was I seeing them?

My mind was racing. *The Great Barrier?* A place where there was no Light and no Dark? Was that possible?

There was no point trying to sleep now.

I pulled on a crumpled Atari T-shirt. I knew what I had to do.

Together or not, this was bigger than Lena and me. Maybe it was as big as the Order of Things, or Galileo realizing the Earth revolved around the sun. It didn't matter if I didn't want to see it. There were no coincidences. I was seeing Lena and John and Ridley for a reason.

But I had no idea what it was.

Which is why I had to go talk to Galileo herself.

As I stepped out into the darkness, I could hear Mr. Mackey's fancy roosters starting to crow. It was 4:45, and the sun wasn't close to coming up, but I was walking around town like it was the middle of the afternoon. I listened to the sound of my feet as

I walked across the cracked sidewalk and the sticky asphalt.

Where were they going? Why was I seeing them? Why did it matter?

I heard a noise. When I turned around, Lucille cocked her head and sat down on the pavement behind me. I shook my head and kept walking. That crazy cat was going to follow me, but I didn't mind. We were probably the only ones awake in the whole town.

But we weren't. Gatlin's very own Galileo was awake, too. When I turned the corner onto Marian's street, I could see the light on in her spare room. As I got closer, I saw a second light flicker from the front porch.

"Liv." I jogged up the steps and heard a clatter in the darkness.

"Bloody hell!" The lens of an enormous telescope swung toward my head, and I ducked. Liv grabbed the end of the lens, her messy braids swinging behind her. "Don't sneak up on me like that!" She twisted a knob, and the telescope locked back into place on the tall aluminum tripod.

"It's not exactly sneaking when you walk up the front steps." I tried not to stare at her pajamas—some kind of girly boxers under a T-shirt with a picture of Pluto and the caption DWARF PLANET SAYS: PICK ON SOMEONE YOUR OWN SIZE.

"I didn't see you." Liv adjusted the eyepiece and stared into the telescope. "What are you doing up, anyway? Are you mental?"

"That's what I'm trying to figure out."

"Let me save you some time. The answer is yes."

"I'm not joking."

She studied me, then picked up her red notebook and started

scribbling. "I'm listening. I just have to write down a few things."

I looked over her shoulder. "What are you looking at?"

"The sky." She looked back into the scope and then at her selenometer. She wrote another set of numbers.

"I know that."

"Here." She stepped aside, motioning me closer. I looked through the lens. The sky exploded into light and stars and the dust of a galaxy that didn't remotely resemble the Gatlin sky. "What do you see?"

"The sky. Stars. The moon. It's pretty amazing."

"Now look." She pulled me away from the lens, and I looked up at the sky. Though it was still dark, I couldn't make out nearly half the stars I had seen through the telescope.

"The lights aren't as bright." I looked back to the telescope. Once again, the sky burst into sparkling stars. I pulled back from the lens and stared out into the night. The real sky was darker, dimmer, like lost, lonely space. "It's weird. The stars look so different through your telescope."

"That's because they're not all there."

"What are you talking about? The sky's the sky."

Liv looked up at the moon. "Except when it's not."

"What does that mean?"

"Nobody really knows. There are Caster constellations, and there are Mortal constellations. They aren't the same. At least, they don't look the same to the Mortal eye. Which unfortunately is all you and I have." She smiled and switched one of the settings. "And I've been told the Mortal constellations can't be seen by Casters."

"How is that possible?"

280

"How is anything possible?"

"Is our sky real? Or does it only look real?" I felt like a carpenter bee the moment he found out he'd been tricked into thinking a coat of blue paint on the ceiling was the sky.

"Is there a difference?" She pointed up at the dark sky. "See that? The Big Dipper. You know that one, right?" I nodded.

"If you look straight down, two stars from the handle, you see that bright star?"

"It's the North Star." Any former Boy Scout in Gatlin could tell you that.

"Exactly. Polaris. Now see where the bottom of the cup ends, the lowest point? Do you see anything there?" I shook my head.

She looked into her scope, turning first one dial, then a second. "Now look." She stepped back.

Through the lens, I could see the Big Dipper, exactly as it looked in the regular sky, only shining more brightly. "It's the same. Mostly."

"Now look at the bottom of the cup. Same place. What do you see?"

I looked. "Nothing."

Liv sounded annoyed. "Look again."

"Why? There's nothing there."

"What do you mean?" Liv leaned down and looked through the lens. "That's not possible. There's supposed to be a seven-pointed star, what Mortals call a faery star."

A seven-pointed star. Lena had one on her necklace.

"It's the Caster equivalent of the North Star. It marks due south, not north, which has a mystical importance in the Caster world. They call it the Southern Star. Hold on. I'll find it for you." She bent over the scope again. "But keep talking. I'm sure you aren't here for a lecture on faery stars. What's going on?"

There was no point in putting it off any longer. "Lena ran away with John and Ridley. They're down in the Tunnels somewhere."

Now I had her attention. "What? How do you know?"

"It's hard to explain. I saw them in this weird vision that wasn't a vision."

"Like when you touched the journal in Macon's study?"

I shook my head. "I didn't touch anything. One minute I was staring at my reflection in the mirror, and a second later all I could see was stuff flying past me like I was running. When I stopped, they were standing in an alley a few feet away, but they couldn't see or hear me." I was rambling.

"What were they doing?" Liv asked.

"Talking about some place called the Great Barrier. Where everything will be perfect and they can live happily ever after, according to John." I tried not to sound bitter.

"They actually said they were going to the Great Barrier? Are you sure?"

"Yeah. Why?" I could feel the Arclight, suddenly warm in my pocket.

"The Great Barrier is one of the most ancient Caster myths. A place of powerful old magic, long before there was Light or Dark—a sort of Nirvana. No logical person believes it really exists."

"John Breed does."

Liv looked up at the sky. "Or so he says. It's rubbish, but it's powerful rubbish. Like thinking the Earth is flat. Or that the sun orbits the Earth." Like Galileo. Of course.

I had come here looking for a reason to go back to bed, back to Jackson and my life. An explanation for why I could see Lena in my bathroom mirror that didn't mean I was crazy. An answer that didn't lead back to Lena. But I found the opposite.

Liv kept talking, oblivious to the sinking stone in my stomach, and the one burning in my pocket. "The legends say if you follow the Southern Star, you'll eventually find the Great Barrier."

"What if the star isn't there?" With that one thought, another began to stir, and then another, all coming loose in my mind.

Liv didn't answer because she was frantically adjusting her telescope. "It has to be there. There must be something wrong with my telescope."

"What if it's gone? The galaxy changes all the time, right?"

"Of course. By the year three thousand, Polaris won't be the North Star anymore, Alrai will be. It means 'the shepherd' in Arabic, since you asked."

"By the year three thousand?"

"Exactly. In a thousand years. A star can't suddenly disappear, not without a serious cosmic bang. It's not a subtle thing."

"'This is the way the world ends, not with a bang but a whimper.'" I remembered the line from a T. S. Eliot poem. Lena couldn't get it out of her head, before her birthday.

"Yes, well, I love the poem, but the science is a bit off."

Not with a bang but a whimper. Or was it not with a whimper but a bang? I couldn't remember the exact words, but Lena had written it into a poem on the wall of her bedroom when Macon died.

Had she known where this was going all along? I had a sick feeling in my stomach. The Arclight was so hot, it was singeing my skin.

"There's nothing wrong with your telescope."

Liv studied her selenometer. "I'm afraid something is off. It's not just the scope. Even the numbers don't follow."

"Hearts will go and Stars will follow." I said it without thinking, as if it was any old song stuck in my head.

"What?"

"*Seventeen Moons.* It's nothing. just a song I keep hearing. It has something to do with Lena's Claiming."

"A Shadowing Song?" She looked at me in disbelief.

"Is that what it is?" I should've known it would have a name.

"It foreshadows what's to come. You've had a Shadowing Song this whole time? Why didn't you tell me?"

I shrugged. Because I was an idiot. Because I didn't like to talk about Lena with Liv. Because horrible things came out of that song. Take your pick.

"Tell me the whole verse."

"There's something about spheres, and a moon before her time appears. Then it says the part about the stars following where the hearts go.... I can't remember the rest."

Liv sank down onto the top step of the porch. "A moon before her time appears. Is that exactly what the song said?"

I nodded. "First the moon. Then the star follows. I'm sure."

The sky was now streaked with light. "Calling a Claiming Moon out of time. That would explain it."

"What? The missing star?"

Liv closed her eyes. "It's more than the star. Calling a moon out of time could change the whole Order of Things, from every magnetic field to every magical one. It would explain any shift in the Caster sky. The natural order in the Caster world is as delicately balanced as our own."

"What could do that?"

"You mean *who*." Liv hugged her knees.

She could only be talking about one person. "Sarafine?"

"There are no records of a Caster powerful enough to call out the moon. But if someone is pulling a moon out of time, there's no way to know when the next Claiming will come. Or where." A Claiming. Which meant Lena.

I remembered what Marian said in the archive. *We don't get to choose what is true. We only get to choose what we do about it.*

"If we're talking about a Claiming Moon, this is about Lena. We should wake up Marian. She can help us." But even as I said it, I knew the truth. She might be able to help us, but that didn't mean she would. As a Keeper, she couldn't get involved.

Liv was thinking the same thing. "Do you really think Professor Ashcroft is going to let us chase after Lena in the Tunnels, after what happened the last time we were down there? She'll have us locked up in the rare-books collection for the rest of the summer."

Worse, she'd call Amma, and I would be carting the Sisters to church every day in Aunt Grace's ancient Cadillac.

Jump or stay in the boat.

It wasn't really a decision, not anymore. I'd made it a long time ago, when I first got out of my car on Route 9, one night in the rain. I had jumped. There was no staying in the boat, not for me, whether Lena and I were together or not. I wasn't going to

285

let John Breed or Sarafine or a missing star or the wrong kind of moon or some crazy Caster skies stop me now. I owed the girl on Route 9 that much.

"Liv, I can find Lena. I don't know how, but I can. You can track the moon with your selenometer, right?"

"I can measure variances in the magnetic pull of the moon, if that's what you're asking."

"So you can find the Claiming Moon?"

"If my calculations are correct, if the weather holds, if the typical corollaries between the Caster and Mortal constellations stay true..."

"It was more of a yes or no question."

Liv tugged on one of her braids, thinking. "Yes."

"If we're going to do this, we have to go before Amma and Marian wake up."

Liv hesitated. As a Keeper-in-Training, she wasn't supposed to get involved. But every time we were together, we found our way to trouble. "Lena could be in a lot of danger."

"Liv, if you don't want to come—"

"Of course I want to come. I've been studying the stars and the Caster world since I was five. All I've ever wanted was to be part of it. Up until a few weeks ago, the only thing I'd done was read about it and watch it through my telescope. I'm tired of watching. But Professor Ashcroft..."

I had been wrong about Liv. She wasn't like Marian. She wouldn't be content shelving Caster Scrolls. She wanted to prove the world wasn't flat.

"Jump or stay in the boat, Keeper. Are you coming?" The sun was rising, and we were running out of time.

"Are you sure you want me to?" She didn't look at me, and I

didn't look at her. The memory of the kiss that never happened hung between us.

"You know anyone else with a spare selenometer and a mental map of missing Caster stars?"

I wasn't sure her variances or corollaries or calculations were going to help me. But I knew the song was never wrong, and the things I saw tonight proved it. I needed help, and so did Lena, even if what we had was over. I needed a Keeper, even a runaway Keeper with a crazy watch, looking for action everywhere but inside a book.

"Jump," Liv said softly. "I don't want to stay in the boat anymore." She turned the handle on the screen door quietly, without making so much as a click. Which meant she was going inside to get her stuff. Which meant she was going with me.

"You sure?" I didn't want to be the reason she was going, at least not the only reason. That's what I told myself, but I was full of crap.

"You know anyone else dumb enough to search for a mythical place where a rogue Supernatural is trying to call a Claiming Moon?" She smiled, opening the door.

"As a matter of fact, I do."

❧ 6.18 ☙

Outer Doors

Summer school: never stop learnin' if you want to start earnin'.

That's what the letter board said, where it usually read GO WILDCATZ. Liv and I stared up at it, from the bushes lining the front steps of Jackson High.

"I'm reasonably sure there are G's in learning and earning."

"They probably ran out of G's. You know, graduation, GED, Get Outta Gatlin." This was going to be tricky. Summer or not, Miss Hester would still be sitting in the attendance office, keeping watch on the front door. If you failed a class, you had to enroll in summer school. But that didn't mean you couldn't ditch — if you could get by Miss Hester. Even though Mr. Lee never made good on his threat to fail us for not showing up at the Reenactment of the Battle of Honey Hill, Link had failed biology, which meant I had to find a way to get inside.

288

"Are we going to hang out in the bushes all morning?" Liv was getting cranky.

"Give me a second. I've spent all my time thinking up ways to get out of Jackson. I never put much thought into how to get in. But we can't leave without Link."

Liv smiled at me. "Never underestimate the power of the British accent. Watch and learn."

Miss Hester looked over her glasses at Liv, who had twisted her blond hair into a bun. It was summer, which meant Miss Hester was wearing one of her sleeveless blouses and knee-length polyester shorts, with her white slip-on Keds. From where I was hiding under the counter next to Liv, I had a clear view of the bottom of Miss Hester's green shorts and her buniony feet.

"I'm sorry. Who did you say you were with?"

"The BEC." Liv kicked me, and I edged toward the hall.

"Of course. And that would be?"

Liv sighed impatiently. "The British Educational Consulate. As I said, we're looking for high-functioning schools in the United States to use as models for educational reform."

"High functionin'?" Miss Hester sounded confused. I made my way around the corner on my hands and knees.

"I can't believe no one informed you of my visit. May I speak with your headmaster, please?"

"Headmaster?" By the time Miss Hester figured out what a headmaster was, I was halfway up the stairs. Beyond the blond, even beyond the brains, Liv was a girl with a lot of hidden talents.

"All right, enough a the *Charlotte's Web* jokes. Grab your specimen firmly with one hand, and make your incision down the belly, top to bottom, with your scissors." I could hear Mrs. Wilson through the door. I knew what was going on in biology today, from the smell alone. Not to mention the commotion.

"I think I'm going to pass out—"

"Wilbur, no!"

"Ewww!"

I looked through the window in the door. Pink fetal pigs were lined up in a row on the lab tables. They were small, pinned to black, waxy boards inside metal trays. Except Link's.

Link's pig was massive. He raised his hand. "Um, Mrs. Wilson? I can't crack the sternum with scissors. Tank's too big for that."

"Tank?"

"Tank, my pig."

"You can use the garden shears in the back a the room."

I knocked on the window. Link walked right by, but he didn't hear me. Eden was sitting at the long black lab table next to Link's, holding her nose with one hand and poking around inside her pig with tweezers. I was surprised she was in there with the rest of the flunkies—not because she was a rocket scientist or anything, but because I would've expected her mom and the DAR mafia to find a way to get her out of it.

Eden pulled a long yellow rope out of her pig. "What is all this yellow stuff?" She looked like she was going to hurl.

Mrs. Wilson smiled. This was her favorite moment of the year. "Miss Westerly, how many times did you go to the Dar-ee Keen this week? Did you have a shake with your fries and your burger? Onion rings? A side a pie?"

"What?"

"It's fat. Now let's look for the bladder."

I knocked again, as Link walked by with a pair of enormous

shears. He saw me and opened the door. "Mrs. Wilson, I gotta use the bathroom."

We took off down the hall, shears and all. When we banged our way around the corner in front of the attendance office, Liv smiled at Miss Hester and closed her notebook. "Thanks ever so much. I'll be in touch."

She disappeared out the front door behind us, her blond hair falling out of her bun. You would have to be brain-damaged to not realize Liv was a teenager, in her ripped jeans.

Miss Hester watched in bewilderment, shaking her head. "Redcoats."

The thing about Link was, he never asked for details. He just went with it. He went with it when we tried to cut a real tire to make a tire swing. He went with it when I made him help me build a gator trap in my backyard, and every time I stole the Beater to chase a girl the rest of the school thought was a freak. It was a great quality in a best friend, and sometimes I wondered if I would do the same for him if things were reversed. Because I was always the one who asked, and he was always the one who was game.

Within five minutes, we were rolling down Jackson Street. We made it all the way to Dove Street, when we pulled over at the Dar-ee Keen. I checked my watch. Amma would know I was gone by now. Marian would be waiting for Liv at the library, if she hadn't missed her at breakfast. And Mrs. Wilson would've sent someone to drag Link out of the bathroom. We were running out of time.

The actual plan didn't come together until we sat down with

greasy food on greasy yellow trays at our greasy red table.

"Can't believe she ran off with Vampire Boy."

"How many times do I have to tell you? He's an Incubus," Liv corrected.

"Whatever. If he's a Blood Incubus, he can suck your blood. Same difference." Link shoved a biscuit into his mouth while he rolled another one around in the pool of gravy on his plate.

"A Blood Incubus is a Demon. A vampire is something in a movie."

I didn't want to do it, but there was something I had to get out on the table. "Ridley's with them, too."

Link sighed and crumpled up the biscuit paper. His expression didn't change, but I knew he was feeling the same knot in his stomach I had in mine. "Well, that blows." He tossed the paper at the trash can. It hit the rim and fell onto the floor. "You're sure they're in the Tunnels?"

"That's what it looked like." On the way to the Dar-ee Keen, I told Link about the vision, but I left out the part about how I saw it in my bathroom mirror. "They're headed for some place called the Great Barrier."

"A place that doesn't exist." Liv was shaking her head, checking the rotating dials on her wrist.

Link pushed away his plate, still covered with food. "So let me get this straight. We're gonna go down into the Tunnels and find this moon outta time with Liv's fancy watch?"

"Selenometer." Liv didn't look up from copying numbers from the dials into her red notebook.

"Whatever. Why don't we tell Lena's family what's goin' on? Maybe they can make us invisible or lend us some crazy Caster weapons."

A weapon. Like the one I had with me right now.

I could feel the curve of the Arclight in my pocket. I had no idea how it worked, but maybe Liv did. She knew how to read the Caster sky.

"It won't make us invisible, but I have this." I held the sphere above the shiny plastic table.

"Dude. A ball? Seriously?" Link wasn't impressed.

Liv was stunned. She reached out tentatively, her hand hovering. "Is that what I think it is?"

"It's an Arclight. Marian gave it to me on All Souls. It belonged to my mom."

Liv tried to hide her irritation. "Professor Ashcroft had an Arclight all this time, and she never showed it to me?"

"Here you go. Knock yourself out." I dropped the sphere into Liv's hands. She held it carefully, as if it was an egg.

"Careful! Do you have any idea how rare these are?" Liv couldn't take her eyes away from its glossy surface.

Link sucked down the rest of his Coke until he hit ice. "Anyone gonna clue me in here? What's it do?"

Liv was mesmerized. "This is one of the most powerful weapons in the Caster world. It's a metaphysical prison for an Incubus, if you know how to use it." I looked at her hopefully. "Which, unfortunately, I don't."

Link poked at the Arclight. "Like Incubus kryptonite?"

Liv nodded. "Something like that."

There was no doubt the Arclight was powerful, but it wasn't going to help us with the problem at hand. I was out of ideas. "If this thing can't help us, how do we get into the Tunnels?"

"It's not a holiday." Liv handed me the Arclight reluctantly. "If we're going to get into the Caster Tunnels, it has to be through one of the Outer Doors. We can't go through the *Lunae Libri*."

"So there are other ways in? Through these Outer Door things?" Link asked.

Liv nodded. "Yes. But only Casters and a few Mortals, like Professor Ashcroft, know where they are. And she's not going to tell us. I'm sure she's packing my things right now."

I had expected Liv to have the answer, but it was Link who came up with it. "You know what that means?" He grinned and put his arm around Liv. "You're finally gonna get your chance. Time for the Tunnel of Love."

Fairgrounds after the fair were just grounds. I kicked a clump of dirt and weeds.

"Look, you can still see the indentations where the rides were." Liv pointed, Lucille trailing behind her.

"Yeah, but how do you know which rides the marks are from?" It seemed like a good idea at the Dar-ee Keen, but now we were standing in an empty field.

Link shouted and waved from a few yards away. "I think this is where the Ferris Wheel was. I can tell by all the cigarette butts. That old carny was chain-smoking all day."

We caught up with him. Liv pointed to a black patch in the distance. "Isn't that where Lena saw us?"

"What?" I stumbled over the word *us*.

"I mean, saw me." She blushed. "I think that's where the popcorn machine blew up when she walked by. Before she popped the clown's balloon and made the little children cry." How could I forget?

It was hard to find the impressions in the ground under the tall grass. I bent down and pushed the weeds out of the way, but there was nothing. Just a few paper snow cone cups and tickets. As I stood up, I felt the Arclight heating up in my pocket again, and a dull buzzing. I took it out of my pocket, and it was glowing a clear blue.

I waved Liv over. "What do you think this means?"

She studied the sphere, watching the color intensify. "I have no idea. I've never read about them changing color."

"What's up, kids?" Link wiped the sweat off his forehead with his ratty Black Sabbath T-shirt. "Whoa. When did it start with the mood ring action?"

"A second ago." I don't know why, but I started walking slowly, a few steps at a time. As I walked, the glow of the Arclight grew stronger.

"Ethan, what are you doing?" Liv was right behind me.

"I'm not sure." I switched directions, and the color began to fade. Why was it changing?

I turned around and headed back the other way. Sure enough, with every step the Arclight grew warmer in my hand, the vibrations stronger. "Look." I opened my hand so Liv could see the deep blue color radiating from it.

"What's happening?"

I shrugged. "It's like the closer we get, the crazier it goes."

"You don't think..." She stared down at her dusty silver high-tops, thinking. We were thinking the same thing.

I turned it over in my hand. "Could it be some kind of compass?"

Liv watched as the sphere glowed so brightly that Lucille was leaping along beside us, like she was trying to catch fireflies.

When we reached a bleached patch of grass, Liv stopped.

The Arclight was swirling a dark, inky blue. I looked at the ground carefully. "There's nothing here."

Liv bent down, pushing the grass aside. "I'm not so sure about that." A shape emerged as Liv brushed away the dirt.

"Look at the lines. It's a door." Link was right. It was like the trapdoor under the rug in Macon's room.

I knelt next to them and ran my hand along the edges of the door, clearing away the remaining dirt. I looked at Liv. "How did you know?"

"You mean, aside from the fact the Arclight is going crazy?" She looked smug. "The Outer Doors aren't that difficult to find if you know what you're looking for."

"I hope they aren't too difficult to open either." Link pointed at the center of the door. There was a keyhole.

Liv sighed. "It's locked. We need a Caster key. We can't get in without one."

Link pulled the massive garden shears he stole from the bio lab out of his belt. Far be it from Link to put anything back in its rightful place. "Caster key, my ass."

"It's not going to work." Liv squatted next to Link in the grass. "It's a Caster lock, not something on your locker door."

Link huffed as he worked the gardening shears into the crack. "You're not from around here. Isn't a door in this whole county that can't be opened with a set of pliers or a sharp toothbrush."

I looked at Liv. "You realize he makes this stuff up."

"Yeah?" Link grinned up at us as the door opened with a resentful creak. He held up his fist to me. "Pound it."

Liv was shocked. "Well, that's not in the books."

Link leaned over and looked inside. "It's dark, and there're no stairs. Looks like a pretty big drop."

"Take a step." I knew what was coming.

"Are you nuts?"

"Trust me."

Link felt around with his foot, and a second later he was standing in the air. "Man, where do Casters get this stuff? Are there, like, Caster carpenters? A supernatural construction union?" He disappeared out of sight. A second later his voice echoed up from the hole. "It's not that far down. You two comin', or what?"

Lucille stared into the darkness and leaped into the hole. That cat must have picked up more than a little crazy, living with my aunts all these years. I looked over the edge, and I could see the flickering light of a torch. Link was standing below us, Lucille sitting at his feet. "Ladies first."

"Why is it men only say that when it's something horrible or dangerous?" Liv put one foot into the hole, uncertain. "No offense."

I smiled at her. "None taken."

Her silver sneakers dangled for a minute and she wobbled, off balance. I grabbed her hand. "You know, if we find Lena, she may be completely—"

"I know." I looked into Liv's calm blue eyes, which would never be gold or green. The sun lit her hair, as blond as honey. She smiled at me, and I let go of her hand.

I realized she was the one steadying me.

As I disappeared into the darkness behind her, the door banged shut after me, blocking out the sky.

The entrance to the tunnel was dank and mossy, like the one that led from the *Lunae Libri* to Ravenwood. The ceiling over the stairs was low, and the stone walls were old and weathered like some kind of dungeon. Every drop of water and every sound echoed off the walls.

At the bottom of the stairs, we found ourselves at a cross-roads. Not a proverbial one but a real one.

"So which way do we go?" Link looked down two very different tunnels. This trip was more complicated than the one to Exile. That had been a straight shot, but this time it was different, and there were choices to be made.

Choices I had to make.

The tunnel to the left looked more like a meadow than a tunnel. As it widened, there were weeping willows hanging over a dusty footpath, framed by tangles of wildflowers and tall grass. Rolling hills spread out under a cloudless blue sky. You could almost imagine the birds chirping and see the rabbits nibbling grass, if it wasn't a Caster tunnel, where nothing was ever as it seemed.

The tunnel to the right wasn't a tunnel at all but a curving city street underneath its own Caster sky. The dark street was a sharp contrast to the sunny countryside scene of the first tunnel. Liv was scribbling notes in her book. I looked over her shoulder. *Asynchronous time zones in adjacent tunnels.*

The only light came from a blinking motel sign at the end of the street. Tall apartment buildings with small iron balconies and fire escape ladders lined either side. Long wires crisscrossed the street from building to building, forming an intricate web with a few pieces of clothing caught in it. An abandoned trolley track was embedded in the asphalt.

"Which way do we go?" Link was anxious. Wandering around creepy Caster Tunnels wasn't agreeing with him. "I vote for the *Wizard of Oz* path." He headed for the sunshine.

"I don't think we'll need to vote." I took the Arclight out of my pocket, its heat warming my hand before I noticed the light. Its ebony surface began to glow a pale green.

Liv's eyes were wide. "Amazing."

I took a few steps down the dark street, and the light intensified.

Link came up behind us. "Hello? I was walkin' away over there? You're not gonna stop me?"

"Watch this." I held the Arclight high enough for him to see and kept walking.

"Killer flashlight."

Liv checked her selenometer. "You were right. It's guiding us like a compass. My readings confirm it. The moon's magnetic pull is stronger in this direction, which is completely wrong for this time of year."

Link shook his head. "I should've known we'd have to go down the creepy street. We're probably gonna get killed by another one a those Vexes."

Every time I took a step closer to the street, the Arclight glowed a brighter and deeper shade of green. "We're going this way."

"Of course we are."

After Link convinced himself we were headed for certain death, the dark street was nothing but a dark street. The short walk to where the motel sign was still blinking was uneventful. The street was a dead end, leading right up to a doorway under the sign. There was another street running perpendicular to it, lined with unlit doorways. Between the motel sign and the building next to it, there was a steep set of stone stairs. Another Doorwell.

"Should we go left or right?" Liv asked, stepping back onto the street.

I looked at the Arclight's incandescent light, now emerald green. "Neither. We're going up."

I pushed open the heavy door at the top of the stairs. We stepped out from behind an enormous stone arch, stumbling into sunlight that reached through the branches of a gargantuan oak. A woman with white shorts and white hair pedaled a white bike with a white poodle riding in her white bike basket. A giant golden retriever chased the bike. The dog was pulling a man holding its leash. Lucille took one look at the retriever and took off into the bushes.

"Lucille!" I bent down between the bushes, but she was gone. "Great. I lost my aunt's cat again."

"Technically, she's your cat. She lives with you." Link thrashed around in the azaleas. "Don't worry. She'll come back. Cats have a good sense a direction."

"How would you know that?" Liv looked amused.

"Cat Week. Like Shark Week, but with cats." I shot him a look.

Link turned red. "What? My mom watches a lot a weird stuff on TV."

"Come on."

As we stepped out from behind the trees, a girl with purple hair bumped into Link, almost dropping her giant sketch pad. We were surrounded by dogs and people and bikes and skaters, in a park lined with azalea bushes and shaded by huge oaks. There was an ornate stone fountain in the center, with carved naked mermen spitting water on each other. Walking paths radiated in every direction.

"What happened to the Tunnels? Where are we?" Link was more confused than usual.

"We're in some sort of park," Liv said.

I knew exactly where we were, and I smiled. "Not some park. Forsyth Park. We're in Savannah."

"What?" Liv was digging through her bag.

"Savannah, Georgia. I've been coming here with my mom since I was little."

Liv unfolded a map of what looked like the Caster sky. I recognized the Southern Star, the seven-pointed one that was missing from the real Caster sky. "It doesn't make sense. If the Great Barrier exists, which I'm not saying I believe, it's definitely not in the middle of a Mortal city."

I shrugged. "This is where it led us. What can I say?"

"We walked, like, five miles. How can we be in Savannah?" Link still hadn't grasped the idea that things were different in the Tunnels.

Liv clicked open her pen, muttering to herself. "Place and time not subject to Mortal physics."

Two little old ladies were pushing two tiny dogs in strollers. We were definitely in Savannah. Liv closed her red book. "Time, space, distance—they're all different down here. The Tunnels are part of the Caster world, not the Mortal one."

As if on cue, the glow of the Arclight faded to a glossy black. I slipped it back into my pocket.

"What the—? How do we know where to go from here?" Link panicked, but I didn't.

"We don't need it. I think I know where we're supposed to go."

Liv crinkled her brow. "How?"

"There's only one person I know in Savannah."

Through the Looking Glass

My Aunt Caroline lived on East Liberty Street near the Cathedral of St. John the Baptist. I hadn't been to her house in a few years, but I knew to keep heading up Bull Street, because her house was on the Historic Savannah Trolley Tour, which ran up and down Bull. Besides, the streets ran from the park to the river, and there was a public square about every other block to mark your way. It was hard to get lost in Savannah, whether you were a Wayward or not.

Between Savannah and Charleston, you could find a historic tour for just about anything. Plantation tours, Southern cooking tours, Daughters of the Confederacy tours, ghost tours (my personal favorite), and the classic—historic-home tours. Aunt Caroline's house had been part of that one for as long as I could remember. Her attention to detail was legendary, not only in our family but in all of Savannah. She was the curator of the Savannah History Museum, and she knew as much about the history of every building, landmark, and scandal in the City of Oaks as my mom had known about the Civil War. It was no small feat, considering scandals were as common as tours around here.

"Are you sure you know where you're goin', man? I think we should take a break and get somethin' to eat. I'd kill for a burger." Link had more faith in the Arclight's ability to navigate than mine. Lucille, who had reappeared, sat down at his feet and cocked her head to the side. She wasn't so sure either.

"Keep heading up toward the river. We'll hit East Liberty sooner or later. Look." I pointed to the steeple of the cathedral a few blocks away. "That's St. John's Cathedral. We're almost there."

Twenty minutes later, we were still wandering in circles near the cathedral. Link and Liv were losing their patience, and I didn't blame them. I looked down East Liberty for something familiar. "It's a yellow house."

"Yellow must be a popular color. Every other house on this street is yellow." Even Liv was annoyed with me. I'd taken us around the same block three times now.

"I thought it was off Lafayette Square."

"I think we should find a phone book and look up her number." Liv wiped the sweat from her forehead.

I squinted at a figure in the distance. "We don't need a phone book. That's the house at the end of the block."

Liv rolled her eyes. "How do you know?"

"Because Aunt Del is standing out front."

There was nothing weirder than ending up in Savannah after walking only a few hours in the Caster Tunnels, in some sort of altered time. Except getting to Aunt Caroline's and finding Lena's Aunt Del standing by the curb, waving. She was expecting us.

"Ethan! I'm so glad I finally found you. I've been everywhere—Athens, Dublin, Cairo."

"You were looking for us in Egypt and Ireland?" Liv looked as confused as I felt, but this was something I could clear up for her.

"Georgia. Athens, Dublin, and Cairo are cities in Georgia." Liv blushed. Sometimes I forgot she was as far away from Gatlin as Lena, only in a different way.

Aunt Del took my hand and patted it affectionately. "Arelia tried to Divine your location, but Georgia was all she could come up with. Unfortunately, Divination is more of an art than a science. Thank the stars I've found you."

"What are you doing here, Aunt Del?"

"Lena's missing. We were hoping she was with you." She sighed, realizing she was wrong.

"She's not, but I think I can find her."

Aunt Del smoothed her rumpled skirt. "Then I can help you."

Link scratched his head. He had met Aunt Del, but he'd never seen a demonstration of her gifts as a Palimpsest. It was clear he couldn't see how a scattered old woman was going to help us. After spending a dark night with her at Genevieve Duchannes' grave, I knew better.

I struck the heavy iron knocker against the door. Aunt Caroline opened the door, wiping her hands on her G.R.I.T.S. apron. Girls Raised in the South. She smiled, her eyes crinkling at the corners.

"Ethan, whateva are you doin' here? I didn't know you were goin' to be in Savannah."

I hadn't thought far enough ahead to come up with a good lie, so I had to settle for a bad one. "I'm in town visiting...a friend."

"Where's Lena?"

"She couldn't make it." I stepped away from the door so I could distract her with introductions. "You know Link, and this is Liv and Lena's Aunt Delphine." I was sure the first thing Aunt Caroline would do after I left was call my dad to say how nice it had been to see me. So much for keeping my whereabouts a secret from Amma and living to see my seventeenth birthday.

"Nice to see you again, ma'am." I could always count on Link to be a good old boy when I needed him to be. I tried to think of someone in Savannah my aunt wouldn't know, as if that was possible. Savannah was bigger than Gatlin, but all Southern towns are the same. Everyone knows each other.

Aunt Caroline ushered us all inside. In a matter of seconds, she disappeared and reappeared with sweet tea and a plate of Benne Babies, maple cookies that were even sweeter than the tea. "Today has been the strangest day."

"What do you mean?" I reached for a cookie.

"This mornin' when I was at the museum, someone broke into the house, but that's not even the oddest part. They didn't take a thing. Ransacked the entire attic and didn't even touch the rest of the house."

I glanced at Liv. There were no coincidences. Aunt Del might have been thinking the same thing, too, but it was hard to tell. She was looking a little woozy, like she was having trouble sorting through all the different things that had happened in this room since the house was built in 1820. She was probably flashing through two hundred years all at once while we sat here eating cookies. I remembered what she said about her gift the night in the graveyard with Genevieve. Palimpsestry was a great honor and an even greater burden.

I wondered what Aunt Caroline could possibly have that was worth stealing. "What's in the attic?"

"Nothing, really. Christmas ornaments, some architectural plans for the house, some of your mother's old papers." Liv nudged my foot underneath the table. I was thinking the same thing. Why weren't they in the archive?

"What sort of papers?"

Aunt Caroline put out some more cookies. Link was eating them faster than she could serve them. "I'm not really sure. A month or so before she died, your mother asked me if she could store a few boxes here. You know your mother with her files."

"Do you mind if I take a look? I'm working at the library this summer with Aunt Marian, and she may be interested in some of them." I tried to sound casual.

"Be my guest, but it's a mess up there." She picked up the empty plate. "I have a few calls to make, and I still have to finish filin' the police report. But I'll be down here if you need me."

Aunt Caroline was right; the attic was a mess. Clothes and papers were strewn everywhere. Someone must have dumped the contents of every box up there into one gigantic pile. Liv picked up a few stray papers.

"How the—" Link looked at Aunt Del, embarrassed. "I mean, how the heck are we gonna find anything in here? What are we even lookin' for?" He kicked an empty box across the floor.

"Anything that could've been my mom's. Someone was

looking for something up here." Everyone dove into a different part of the pile.

Aunt Del found a hatbox full of Civil War shell casings and round balls. "There used to be a lovely hat in here."

I picked up my mom's old high school yearbook and a field guide to the battlefield at Gettysburg. I noticed how worn the field guide was, compared to her yearbook. That was my mom.

Liv knelt over a stack of papers. "I think I found something. I mean, it seems these belonged to your mother, but they're nothing, really—old sketches of Ravenwood Manor and some notes on Gatlin's history."

Anything that had to do with Ravenwood was something. She handed me the notes and I flipped through the pages. Gatlin Civil War registries, yellowed sketches of Ravenwood Manor and the older buildings in town—the Historical Society, the old firehouse, even our house, Wate's Landing. But none of it seemed to amount to anything.

"Here, kitty kitty. Hey, I found a friend for..." Link lifted up a cat preserved by the Southern art of taxidermy, then dropped it when he realized it was a stuffed dead cat with mangy black fur. "Lucille."

"There has to be something else. Whoever was here wasn't looking for Civil War registries."

"Maybe they found what they came for." Liv shrugged.

I looked at Aunt Del. "There's only one way to find out."

A few minutes later, we were all sitting cross-legged on the floor, like we were in a campfire circle. Or a séance. "I'm really not sure this is a good idea."

"It's the only way to find out who broke in here, and why."

Aunt Del nodded, barely convinced. "All right. Remember, if you feel sick, put your head between your knees. Now join hands."

Link looked at me. "What's she talkin' about? Why would we feel sick?"

I grabbed Liv's hand, completing the circle. It was soft and warm in mine. But before I could think about the fact that we were holding hands, images started to flash before my eyes —

One after the next, opening and closing like doors. Each image cued the next, like dominoes, or one of those flip-books I read as a kid.

Lena, Ridley, and John dumping out boxes in the attic...

"It has to be here. Keep looking." John tosses old books onto the floor.

"How can you be so sure?" Lena reaches inside another box, her hand covered in black designs.

"She knew how to find it, without the star."

Another door opened. Aunt Caroline, dragging boxes across the attic floor. She kneels in front of a box, holding an old photo of my mother, and runs her hand over the picture, sobbing.

And another. My mother, her hair hanging over her shoulder, held back by her red reading glasses. I could see her as clearly as if she was standing right in front of me. She scribbles madly in a weathered leather journal, then rips out the page, folds it, and slides it into an envelope. She scrawls something across the front of the envelope and slips it into the back of the journal. Then she pushes an old trunk away from the wall. Behind the trunk, she pulls a loose board free from the wainscoting. She looks around, as if she senses someone might be watching, and slides the journal into the narrow opening.

Aunt Del let go of my hand.

"Holy crap!" Link was way beyond remembering his manners in front of a lady. He was green, and stuck his head between his knees immediately, like he was coming in for a crash landing. I hadn't seen him like that since the day after Savannah Snow dared him to drink an old bottle of peppermint schnapps.

"I'm so sorry. I know it's difficult to acclimate after a trip." Aunt Del patted Link's back. "You're doing fine for your first time."

I didn't have time to think about everything I'd seen. So I focused on one thing: *She knew how to find it, without the star.* John was talking about the Great Barrier. He thought my mom knew something about it, something she may have written in her journal. Liv and I must have been thinking the same thing, because we touched the old trunk at the same time.

"It's heavy. Be careful." I started to pull it away from the wall. It felt like someone had filled it with bricks.

Liv reached for the wall, working the board free. But she didn't reach into the opening. I put my hand inside and immediately touched the battered leather. I pulled out the journal, feeling the weight of it in my hand. It was a piece of my mother. I flipped to the back. My mother's delicate handwriting stared back at me from the front of the envelope.

Macon

I ripped it open, unfolding the single sheet.

If you're reading this, it means I wasn't able to get to you in time to tell you myself. Things are much worse

*than any of us could have imagined. It may already
be too late. But if there is a chance, you are the only
one who will know how to prevent our worst fears
from becoming reality.*

*Abraham is alive. He's been in hiding. And he's not
alone. Sarafine is with him, as devoted a disciple as
your father.*

*You have to stop them before we all run out of
time.*

– LJ

My eyes dragged across the bottom of the page. *LJ.* Lila Jane.
I noticed something else — the date. I felt like I'd been kicked in
the stomach. March 21st. A month before my mother's accident.
Before she was murdered.

Liv stepped away, sensing she was witnessing something private
and painful. I flipped through the pages of the journal,
looking for answers. There was another copy of the Ravenwood
Family Tree. I'd seen it before in the archive, but this one looked
different. Some of the names were crossed out.

RAVENWOOD FAMILY TREE

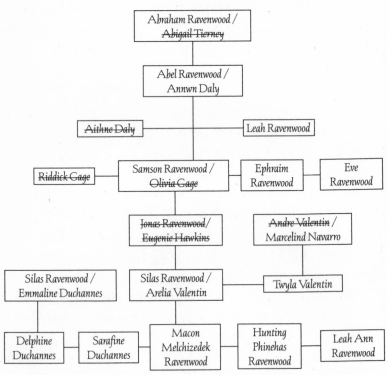

Abraham Ravenwood / ~~Abigail Tierney~~

Abel Ravenwood / Annwn Daly

~~Aithne Daly~~   Leah Ravenwood

~~Riddick Gage~~   Samson Ravenwood / ~~Olivia Gage~~   Ephraim Ravenwood   Eve Ravenwood

~~Jonas Ravenwood/ Eugenie Hawkins~~   ~~Andre Valentin~~ / Marcelind Navarro

Silas Ravenwood / Emmaline Duchannes   Silas Ravenwood / Arelia Valentin   Twyla Valentin

Delphine Duchannes   Sarafine Duchannes   Macon Melchizedek Ravenwood   Hunting Phinehas Ravenwood   Leah Ann Ravenwood

As I turned the pages, a loose paper slipped out and floated to the floor. I picked it up, unfolding the fragile sheet. It was vellum, thin and slightly transparent, like tracing paper. There were strange shapes penned on one side. Misshapen ovals, with dips and rises, as if a child were drawing clouds. I turned to Liv, holding the vellum open so she could see the shapes. She shook her head without a word. Neither one of us knew what it meant.

I folded the delicate paper and replaced it in the journal, skipping ahead to the end. I turned to the last page. There was something else that didn't make any sense, at least not to me.

> *In Luce Caecae Caligines sunt,*
> *Et in Caliginibus, Lux.*
> *In Arcu imperium est,*
> *Et in imperio, Nox.*

Instinctively, I ripped out the page and shoved it in my pocket. My mother was dead because of the letter, and possibly what was written on these pages. They belonged with me now.

"Ethan, are you all right?" Aunt Del's voice was full of concern.

I was so far from right I couldn't remember what it felt like. I had to get out of this room, away from my mom's past, out of my head.

"Be right back." I bolted down the stairs to the guest room and lay on the bed in my dirty clothes. I stared at the ceiling, painted sky blue, just like the one in my bedroom. Stupid bees. The joke was on them, and they didn't even know.

Or maybe on me.

I was numb, the way you get when you try to feel everything

at once. I might as well have been Aunt Del walking into this old house.

Abraham Ravenwood wasn't a piece of the past. He was alive, hiding in the shadows with Sarafine. My mother had known, and Sarafine had killed her because of it.

My eyes were blurry. I wiped them, expecting tears, but there was nothing there. I squeezed my eyes shut, but when I opened them all I could see were colors and lights flashing by me, as if I was running. I saw bits and pieces—a wall, dented silver trash cans, cigarette butts. Whatever I'd experienced when I was staring into my bathroom mirror was happening again. I tried to get up, but I was too dizzy. The pieces kept flying by, finally slowing so my mind could catch up.

I was in a room, a bedroom, maybe. It was hard to tell from where I was standing. The floor was gray concrete, and the white walls were covered in the same black designs I had seen on Lena's hands. As I looked at them, they seemed to move.

I scanned the room. She had to be here somewhere.

"I feel so different from everyone else, even other Casters." It was Lena's voice. I looked up, following the sound.

They were above me, lying on the black-painted ceiling. Lena and John were head to head, talking back and forth without looking at each other. They were staring at the floor the way I stared at my ceiling at night, when I couldn't fall asleep. Lena's hair fell around her shoulders, flat against the ceiling as if she was lying on the floor.

It would seem impossible, if I hadn't already seen it. Only this time, she wasn't the only one on the ceiling. And I wasn't there to pull her back down.

"No one can explain my powers to me, not even my family.

Because they don't know." She sounded miserable and far away. "And every day I wake up, and I can do things I couldn't the day before."

"It's the same for me. One day I woke up and thought about somewhere I wanted to go, and a second later I was there." John was tossing something up in the air and catching it, over and over. Except he was tossing it toward the floor instead of the ceiling.

"Are you saying that you didn't know you could Travel?"

"Not until I did it." He closed his eyes, but he didn't stop tossing the ball.

"What about your parents? Did they know?"

"I never knew my parents. They took off when I was little. Even Supernaturals know a freak when they see one." If he was lying, I couldn't tell. His voice was bitter and hurt, which sounded genuine to me.

Lena rolled onto her side and propped herself up on her elbow so she could see him. "I'm sorry. That must have been awful. At least I had my gramma to take care of me." She looked at the ball and it froze in midair. "Now I don't have anyone."

The ball dropped to the floor. It bounced a few times and rolled under the bed. John turned to look at her. "You have Ridley. And me."

"Trust me, once you get to know me, you won't be able to get away fast enough."

They were only inches apart now. "You're wrong. I know what it's like to feel alone even when you're with other people."

She didn't say anything. Is that what it was like when she was with me? Did she feel alone even when we were together? When she was in my arms?

"L?" I felt sick when he said it. "When we get to the Great Barrier, it's gonna be different, I promise."

"Most people say it doesn't exist."

"That's because they don't know how to find it. You can only get there through the Tunnels. I'm going to take you there." He lifted her chin so she could see into his eyes. "I know you're scared. But you have me, if you want me."

Lena looked away, wiping one of her eyes with the back of her hand. I could see the black designs, which looked darker now. Less like Sharpie and more like Ridley's and John's tattoos. She was staring right at me, but she couldn't see me. "I have to make sure I can't hurt anyone else. It doesn't matter what I want."

"It matters to me." John ran his thumb under her eye, catching her tears, leaning closer to her. "You can trust me. I'd never hurt you." He pulled her to his chest, her head resting on his shoulder.

Can I?

I couldn't hear anything else, and it became harder to see her, like I was zooming out somehow. I blinked hard, trying to stay focused, but when I opened my eyes again, all I could see was the swirling blue ceiling. I turned on my side, facing the wall.

I was back in Aunt Caroline's room, and they were gone. Together, wherever they were.

Lena was moving on. She was opening up to John, and he was reaching a part of her I thought was gone. Maybe I was never meant to reach it.

Macon had lived in the Dark, and my mom in the Light.

Maybe we weren't meant to find a way that Mortals and

316

Casters could be together, because we weren't meant to be.

Someone knocked on the door, even though it was open. "Ethan? Are you okay?" Liv. Her footsteps were quiet, but I could hear them. I didn't move.

The edge of the bed sank a little when she sat down. I felt her hand as she rubbed the back of my head. It was soothing and familiar, as if she'd done it a thousand times. That was the thing about Liv—it was like I'd known her forever. She always seemed to sense what I needed, as if she knew things I didn't even know about myself.

"Ethan, it's going to be okay. We'll figure out what it all means, I promise." I knew she meant it.

I rolled over. The sun had set, and the room was dark. I hadn't bothered to turn on the lights. But I could make out her silhouette as she stared down at me.

"I thought you weren't supposed to get involved."

"I'm not. It's the first thing Professor Ashcroft taught me." She paused. "But I can't help it."

"I know."

We stared at each other in the darkness, her hand resting against my jaw, where it had fallen when I rolled over. But I was really seeing her, the possibility of her, for the first time. I felt something. There was no denying it, and Liv felt it, too. I could tell every time she looked at me.

Liv slid down and curled up against me, leaning her head on my shoulder.

My mom found a way to move on after Macon. She had fallen in love with my dad, which seemed to prove you could lose the love of your life and fall in love all over again.

Didn't it?

I heard a quiet whisper, not from inside my heart but a breath away from my ear. Liv leaned closer. "You'll figure this out, like everything else. Besides, you have something most Waywards don't have."

"Yeah? What's that?"

"An excellent Keeper."

I slid my hand to the back of Liv's neck. Honeysuckle and soap—that's what she smelled like.

"Is that why you came? Because I needed a Keeper?"

She didn't answer right away. I could sense her trying to work it out in her mind. How much she should say, what she should risk. I knew that's what she was doing, because I was doing the same thing.

"It's not the only reason, but it should be."

"Because you aren't supposed to get involved?"

I could feel her heart beating against my chest. She fit under my shoulder perfectly.

"Because I don't want to get hurt." She was scared, but not of Dark Casters or mutant Incubuses or golden eyes. She was afraid of something simpler but equally dangerous. Smaller but infinitely more powerful.

I pulled her closer. "Me neither." Because I was afraid of it, too.

We didn't say anything else. I held her close, and I thought about all the ways a person could get hurt. The ways I could hurt her and hurt myself. Those two things were intertwined somehow. It's hard to explain, but when you were as closed off as I was the past few months, opening up felt about as wrong as stripping naked in church.

Hearts will go and Stars will follow, One is broken, One is hollow.

That had been our song, Lena's and mine. And I had been broken. Did that mean I had to stay hollow? Or was there something different out there for me? Maybe a whole new song?

Some Pink Floyd, for a change? *Hollow laughter in marble halls.*

I smiled in the darkness, listening to the rhythmic sound of her breathing until it softened into sleep. I was exhausted. Even though we were back in the Mortal world, it still felt as if I was part of the Caster world, and Gatlin was unbelievably far away. I couldn't make sense of how I had gotten to this place any more than I could measure the miles I had come or the distance I still had to go.

I drifted into oblivion not knowing what I would do when I got there.

⊰ 6.19 ⊱

Bonaventure

I was running, being chased. Scrambling over hedges and skidding across empty streets and backyards. The one constant was the adrenaline. There was no stopping.

Then I saw the Harley, driving straight at me, the lights getting closer and closer. They weren't yellow but green, flashing in my eyes so bright I had to cover my face with my hands....

I woke up. All I could see was green, flashing on and off.

I didn't know where I was, until I realized the green glow was coming from the Arclight, now lit up like the Fourth of July. It was on the mattress, where it must have rolled out of my pocket. Only the mattress looked different, and the light was flashing out of control.

I remembered slowly—the stars, the Tunnels, the attic, the guest room. Then I realized why the mattress looked different.

Liv was gone.

It didn't take long to figure out where Liv was. "Do you ever sleep?"

"Not as much as you do, apparently." As usual, Liv didn't look up from her telescope, though this one was aluminum and much smaller than the one she kept on Marian's porch.

I sat down next to her on the back step. The yard was as calm as my aunt herself, a quiet patch of green spreading underneath a broad magnolia tree. "What are you doing up?"

"I got a wake-up call." I tried to sound casual, instead of how I actually felt. Awkward. I motioned at the guest room window on the second floor. Even from down here, you could see pulsing green light shining through the glass panes.

"Strange. I suppose I got one as well. Take a look through the celestron." She handed me the miniature scope. It looked like a flashlight except for the large lens fitted to one end.

Our hands touched as I took it. Not so much as a shock.

"Did you make this, too?"

She smiled. "Professor Ashcroft gave it to me. Now stop talking and look. There." She pointed right over the magnolia, which to my Mortal eye looked like a dark expanse of starless sky.

I fitted the scope to my eye. Now the sky over the tree was streaked with light, a kind of ghostly aura trailing toward the ground not far from us. "What is that, a falling star? Do falling stars leave trails like that?"

"It might. If it was a falling star."

"How do you know it's not?"

She tapped the scope. "It might be falling, but it's a Caster

321

star falling in the Caster sky, remember? Otherwise we could see it without the scope."

"Is that what your crazy watch is saying?"

She picked it up from the step next to her. "I'm not sure what it's saying. I thought it was broken until I saw the sky."

The Arclight was still flashing in the window, a constant green strobe light.

I remembered something from my dream. It felt as if the Harley was headed right at me. "We can't stay here. Something's happening." Something here in Savannah.

Liv strapped her selenometer back onto her wrist. "Whatever it is seems to be happening over there." She dropped the scope into her backpack and pointed into the distance. It was time to go.

I held out my hand, but she pulled herself to her feet. "You wake up Link. I'll get my things."

"I still don't see why this couldn't wait until mornin'." Link was grouchy, and his spiky hair was sticking up everywhere.

"Does this thing look like it could wait until morning?" The Arclight was so bright now, it lit up the whole street in front of us.

"Can you put it on a lower setting or somethin'? Switch off the high beams already." Link shielded his eyes.

"I don't think it's working." I shook the Arclight, but the flashing green light didn't stop.

"Man, you broke the Magic 8 Ball."

"I didn't break it. I—" I gave up, jamming it into my pocket. "Yeah, it's pretty much broken." The light was shining through my jeans.

"It's possible some sort of Caster power surge triggered it and shifted the normal balance of how the Arclight functions." Liv was intrigued.

Link wasn't. "Like an alarm? That's not good."

"We don't know that."

"Are you kidding? It's never good when Commissioner Gordon activates the Bat-Signal. When the Fantastic Four see the number four in the sky."

"I get the idea."

"Yeah? Can you get one that gets us where we're tryin' to go, since Ethan broke the 8 Ball?"

Liv consulted her selenometer and started walking. "I can get us to the general area where the star fell." She looked at me. "I mean, if it was a star. But Link might be right. I don't know exactly where we're going, or what we'll find when we get there."

"Almost makes a guy wish he had his own pair of garden shears," I said, following Liv down the street.

"Speakin' a things that aren't normal, look who's here." Link pointed to the curb in front of a house with red shutters. Lucille was sitting on the edge of the sidewalk, staring at us as if we were holding her up. "Told you she'd come back."

Lucille licked her brown paws sulkily, waiting.

"Couldn't live without me, could you, girl? I have that effect on women." Link grinned, scratching her head. She batted his fingers away.

"Come on, now. Aren't you comin'?" Lucille didn't budge.

"Yep. He's got that effect on women," I said to Liv as Lucille stretched out in front of the house.

"She'll come around," Link said. "They always do."

That's when Lucille took off running down the street, in the opposite direction from the way we went.

—⁀☌

It was the middle of the night and pitch-dark by the time we found ourselves heading out of town. It felt like we had been walking for hours. The main road was always busy during the day. Now it was deserted. Which made sense, considering where it had led us.

"You sure about this?"

"Not at all. It's only an approximation based on the available data." Liv had been checking her little telescope about every five blocks. There was no doubting the data.

"I love it when she talks nerdy." Link pulled on her braid and Liv batted him away.

I stared at the tall stone columns flanking the entrance to Savannah's famed Bonaventure Cemetery, on the outskirts of town. It was one of the most famous cemeteries in the South, and one of the most well protected. Which was a problem, since it had closed at dusk.

"Dude, this is a joke, right? Are you guys sure this is where we're supposed to be?" Link didn't look too happy about wandering around the cemetery at night, especially with a guard at the entrance and a patrol car that passed by the front gates every so often.

Liv looked up at a statue of a woman clinging to a cross. "Let's get this over with."

Link pulled out his garden shears. "I don't think these babies will do the job."

"Not through the gates." I pointed at the wall on the other side of the trees. "Over them."

Liv managed to step on every part of my face, kick me in the neck, and wrench her sneakers deep into my shoulder blade before I shoved all six pounds of her over the gate. She lost her balance at the top and landed with a thump.

"I'm fine. No worries," Liv called from the other side of the wall.

Link and I looked at each other, and he bent down. "You first. I'll climb up the hard way."

I stepped on his back, grabbing onto the wall. He pushed himself up until he was standing. "Yeah? How are you gonna do that?"

"Gotta look for a tree that's close enough to the wall. Has to be one somewhere around here. Don't worry. I'll find you."

I was at the top. I clung to the wall with both hands.

"I didn't ditch school all these years for nothin'."

I smiled, and let myself fall.

Five minutes and seven trees later, the Arclight led us deeper into the cemetery, past the crumbling Confederate headstones and the statues guarding the homes of those who had been forgotten. There was a tight cluster of moss-covered oaks, whose crossed branches created an arch over the path, barely wide enough to squeeze through. The Arclight was flashing and pulsing.

"We're here. This is it, right?" I looked over Liv's shoulder at the selenometer.

Link looked around. "Where? I don't see anything." I pointed to space between the trees. "Seriously?"

Liv looked nervous, too. She didn't want to climb through brambles of Spanish moss in a dark graveyard. "I can't get a reading now. It's going crazy."

"It doesn't matter. This is it, I'm sure."

"You think Lena and Ridley and John are back there?" Link looked like he was planning to go back and wait for us out front, or maybe at a rib joint.

"I don't know." I pushed the moss aside and stepped through. On the other side, the trees were even more ominous, hanging over our heads and creating a sky of their own. There was a clearing ahead of us, with a huge statue of a beseeching angel in the center of the graves. The graves were bordered in stone, outlining the breadth of each plot. You could almost see the coffins buried in the earth beneath them.

"Ethan, look." Liv pointed past the statue. I could see silhouettes framed by a tiny slice of moonlight. They were moving.

We had company.

Link shook his head. "This can't be good."

For a second, I couldn't move. What if it was Lena and John? What were they doing in a graveyard at night, alone? I followed the path, flanked by even more statues—kneeling angels staring into the heavens, or the ones looking down at us as they wept.

I had no idea what to expect, but when the two figures came into view, they were the last two people I expected to see.

Amma and Arelia, Macon's mother. The last time I'd seen her was at Macon's funeral. They were sitting between the graves. I was a dead man. I should have known Amma would find me.

There was another woman sitting in the dirt with them. I didn't recognize her. She was a little older than Arelia, with the same golden skin. Her hair was woven in hundreds of tiny braids, and she was wearing twenty or thirty strands of beads—some gemstones and colored glass, others tiny birds and animals. She had at least ten holes winding around each ear, and long earrings hung from each hole.

The three of them were sitting cross-legged in a circle, head-stones dotting the dirt around them. Their hands were joined in the center of the circle. Amma had her back to us, but I had no doubt she knew I was there.

"It took you long enough. We've been waitin', and you know how I hate to wait." Amma's voice was no more agitated than usual, which didn't make any sense, since I had disappeared without even a note.

"Amma, I'm really sorry—"

She waved her hand as if she was swatting a fly. "No time for that now." Amma shook the bone in her hand—a graveyard bone, I was willing to bet.

I looked at Amma. "Did you bring us here?"

"Can't say I did. Somethin' else brought you, somethin' stronger than me. I just knew you were comin'."

"How?"

Amma gave me some of her best stinkeye. "How does a bird know to fly south? How does a catfish know how to swim? I don't know how many times I have to tell you, Ethan Wate. They don't call me a Seer for nothin'."

"I foresaw your arrival, too." Arelia was stating a fact, but it annoyed Amma just the same. I could tell by the look on her face.

Amma raised her chin. "After I mentioned it." Amma was used to being the only Seer in Gatlin, and she didn't like being trumped, even if it was by a Diviner with supernatural gifts.

The other woman, the one I didn't know, turned to Amma. "We bes' get started, Amarie. They're waitin'."

"Come sit down here." Amma motioned to us. "Twyla's ready." Twyla. I recognized the name.

Arelia answered the question before I asked. "This is my

sister, Twyla. She's come a long way to be with us here tonight."
I remembered. Lena had mentioned her Great-Aunt Twyla, the
one who had never left New Orleans. Until now.

"'At's right. Now you come on sit by me, *cher*. Don't be 'fraid.
It's only a Circle a Sight." Twyla patted the space next to her.
Amma was sitting on Twyla's other side, giving me the Look.
Liv stepped back, looking pretty freaked out, even if she was
training to be a Keeper. Link stayed right behind her. Amma
had that effect on people, and from the looks of things, Twyla
and Arelia did, too.

"My sister is a powerful Necromancer." Arelia's voice was
proud.

Link made a face and whispered to Liv. "She gets with dead
people? That's the kinda thing a person should keep to themselves."

Liv rolled her eyes. "Not a necrophiliac, stupid. A Necromancer,
a Caster capable of calling and communicating with the dead."

Arelia nodded. "That's right, and we need help from someone who's already left this world."

I knew right away who she was talking about, or at least I
hoped I did. "Amma, are we trying to call Macon?"

Sadness passed across her face. "I wish I could say we were,
but wherever Melchizedek's gone, we can't go."

"It's time." Twyla pulled something out of her pocket and
looked at Amma and Arelia. You could feel the shift in their
demeanor. The three of them were all business now, even if it
was the business of waking the dead.

Arelia opened her hands in front of her lips and spoke softly
into them. "My power is your power, sisters." She tossed tiny
stones into the center of the circle.

"Moonstones," Liv whispered.

Amma pulled out a sack of chicken bones. I would know that smell anywhere. It was the smell of my kitchen back home. "My power's your power, sisters."

Amma tossed the bones into the circle with the moonstones. Twyla opened her own hand, revealing a tiny carving in the shape of a bird. She spoke the words that gave it power.

"One unto this world, one unto da next.
Open the door to da one who's annexed."

She started to chant, loud and feverish, the unfamiliar words rippling through the air. Her eyes rolled back in her head, but her eyelids remained open. Arelia began to chant as well, shaking long strands of tasseled beads.

Amma grabbed my chin so she could look me in the eye. "I know this isn't goin' to be easy, but there are things you need to know."

The air in the center of the Circle of Sight began to swirl and churn, creating a thin white mist. Twyla, Arelia, and Amma continued to chant, their voices reaching a crescendo. The mist seemed to act on their command, gaining speed and density, swirling upward like a growing tornado.

Without warning, Twyla inhaled sharply, as if she was taking her last breath. The mist seemed to follow, disappearing into her mouth. For a minute, I thought she was going to drop dead. She sat there, her back so straight you would've thought she was tied to a rack, eyes rolled back in her head, mouth still open.

Link retreated to a safe distance while Liv scrambled forward to help, reaching for Twyla. But Amma grabbed her arm in midair. "Wait."

Twyla exhaled. The white mist raced from her lips, rising over the circle. Taking form. The mist swirled upward, creating a body as it moved. The bare feet, peeking out beneath a white dress, the torso filling the dress as if inflating a balloon. It was a Sheer, rising from the haze. I watched as the mist snaked upward, creating a torso, a delicate neck, and finally a face.

It was—

My mother.

Staring back at me with the same luminous, ethereal quality unique to Sheers. But beyond the translucence, she looked exactly like my mother. Her eyelids fluttered, and she looked at me. The Sheer didn't just look like my mother. It was my mother.

She spoke, and her voice was as soft and melodic as I remembered. "Ethan, sweetheart, I've been waiting for you."

I stared at her, speechless. In every dream I'd had of her since the day she died, every photograph, every memory—she was never as real as this.

"There is so much I need to tell you, so much I can't say. I've tried to show you the way, send you the songs...."

She sent me the songs. The songs only Lena and I could hear. I spoke, but my voice sounded far away, as if it wasn't my own. *Seventeen Moons*—the Shadowing Song. "It was you, this whole time."

She smiled. "Yes. You needed me. But now he needs you, and you need him, too."

"Who? Are you talking about Dad?" But I knew she wasn't talking about my father. She was talking about the other man who meant so much to both of us.

Macon.

She didn't know he was gone.

"Are you talking about Macon?" I saw a spark of recognition in her eyes. I had to tell her. If something had happened to Lena, I would want someone to tell me. No matter how much everything changed. "Macon's gone, Mom. He died a few months ago. He can't help me."

I watched her shimmer in the moonlight. She was as beautiful as the last time I saw her, when she hugged me on the rainy porch before I left for school. "Listen to me, Ethan. He'll always be with you. Only you can redeem him." Her image began to fade.

I reached out, desperate to touch her, but my hand only slipped through the air. "Mom?"

"The Claiming Moon has been called." She was disappearing, vanishing into the night. "If Darkness prevails, the Seventeenth Moon will be the last." I almost couldn't see her anymore. The mist was swirling slowly again, above the circle. "Hurry, Ethan. You don't have much time, but you can do this. I have faith." She smiled and I tried to memorize her expression, because I knew she was slipping away.

"What if I'm too late?"

I could hear her distant voice. "I tried to keep you safe. I should have known I couldn't. You were always special."

I stared at the white haze, churning like my stomach.

"My sweet summer boy. I'll be thinking of you. I love—"

The words dwindled into nothing. My mom had been here. For a few minutes, I had seen her smile and heard her voice. Now she was gone.

I had lost her all over again.

"I love you, too, Mom."

⊰ 6.19 ⊱

Scars

There's somethin' I've got to tell you." Amma wrung her hands nervously. "It's about the night a the Sixteenth Moon, Lena's birthday." It took a second to realize she was talking to me. I was still staring into the center of the circle, where my mother had been a moment before.

This time, my mom wasn't sending me messages in books or the verses of a song. I had seen her.

"Tell da boy."

"Hush, Twyla." Arelia put her hand on her sister's arm.

"Lies. Lies are da place where darkness grows. You tell da boy. Tell him now."

"What are you talking about?" I looked from Twyla to Arelia. Amma shot them a look that Twyla answered with a shake of her beaded braids.

"Listen to me, Ethan Wate." Amma's voice was uneven and

shaky. "You didn't fall from the top of the crypt, at least not the way we told you."

"What?" She wasn't making any sense. Why was she talking about Lena's birthday after I had just seen the ghost of my dead mother?

"You didn't fall, see?" she repeated.

"What are you talking about? Of course I fell. I woke up on the ground, flat on my back."

"That's not how you got there." Amma hesitated. "It was Lena's mamma. Sarafine stabbed you with a knife." Amma looked right into my eyes. "She killed you. You were dead, and we brought you back."

She killed you.

I repeated the words to myself, the pieces snapping together so fast I could barely make sense of them. Instead, they made sense of me —

the dream that wasn't a dream, but a memory of not breathing and not feeling and not thinking and not seeing —

the dirt and flames that carried my body away as my life flowed out —

"Ethan! You all right?" I could hear Amma, but she was far away, as far as she was that night when I was on the ground.

I could be in the ground now, like my mom and Macon.

I should be.

"Ethan?" Link was shaking me.

My body filled with sensations I couldn't control and didn't want to remember. Blood in my mouth, blood roaring into my ears —

"He's passing out." Liv was holding my head.

333

There had been pain and noise and something else. Voices. Shapes. People.

I had died.

I reached under my shirt, running my hand over the scar on my stomach. The scar from where Sarafine had stabbed me with a real knife. I barely noticed it anymore, but now it would be a constant reminder of the night I died. I remembered how Lena reacted when she saw it.

"You're still the same person, and Lena still loves you. Her love is the reason you're here now." Arelia's voice was gentle, knowing. I opened my eyes, letting the blur of shapes become people as I settled back into myself again.

My thoughts were so jumbled. Even now, nothing was making any sense. "What do you mean, her love is the reason I'm here now?"

Amma spoke quietly, and I had to strain to hear her. "Lena's the one who brought you back. I helped her, me and your mamma."

The words didn't fit together, so I tried unrolling them out again for myself. Lena and Amma brought me back from the dead, together. And together they had kept it from me until now. I rubbed the scar on my skin. It felt like the truth.

"Since when does Lena know how to raise the dead? If she did, don't you think she would've brought Macon back by now?"

Amma looked at me. I had never seen her so scared. "She didn't do it on her own. She used the Binding Spell from *The Book a Moons*. Binds death to life."

Lena had used *The Book of Moons*.

The Book that had cursed Genevieve and Lena's whole family for generations, Claiming all the children in Lena's family

334

for Light or Dark on their sixteenth birthdays. The Book Genevieve had used to bring Ethan Carter Wate back from the dead for only a second — an act she spent the rest of her life paying for.

I couldn't think. My mind started caving in on itself again, and I couldn't follow my own thoughts. *Genevieve. Lena. The price.*

"How could you?" I pushed myself away from them, out of their Circle of Sight. I'd seen enough.

"I didn't have a choice. She couldn't let you go." Amma looked at me, ashamed. "I couldn't either."

I scrambled to my feet, shaking my head. "It's a lie. She wouldn't do it." But I knew she would. They both would. It was exactly what they would have done. I knew, because I would've done it, too.

It didn't matter now.

In my whole life, I had never been so angry with Amma, or so disappointed. "You knew the Book wouldn't give anything without taking something in return. You told me that yourself."

"I know."

"Lena will have to pay a price for this, because of me. You both will." My head felt like it was going to split in half, or explode.

A renegade tear caught on Amma's cheek. She put two fingers on her forehead and closed her eyes, Amma's version of making the sign of the cross, a silent prayer. "She's payin' it right now."

I couldn't breathe.

Lena's eyes. The stunt at the fair. Running away with John Breed. The words found their way out, even as I tried to hold them in.

"She's going Dark because of me."

"If Lena's going Dark, it's not because a that Book. The Book made a different kinda trade." Amma stopped, as if she couldn't bear to tell me the rest.

"What kind of trade?"

"It gave one life but took another. We knew there'd be consequences." The words caught in her throat. "We just didn't know it would be Melchizedek."

Macon.

It couldn't be true.

It gave one life but took another. A different kind of trade.

My life for Macon's.

It all made sense. The way Lena had been acting the past few months. The way she had been pulling away from me, from everyone. The way she had been blaming herself for Macon's death.

It was true. She had killed him.

To save me.

I thought about her notebook and the Charmed page I'd found. What had the words said? Amma? Sarafine? Macon? The Book? It was the real story of that night. I remembered the poems written on her wall. Nobody the Dead and Nobody the Living. Two sides of the same coin. Macon and me.

Nothing green can stay. Months ago, I believed she'd gotten the Frost poem wrong. But of course, she hadn't. She was talking about herself.

I thought about how it seemed painful for her to look at me. No wonder she felt guilty. No wonder she ran. I wondered if she could ever stand to look at me again. Lena had done it all because of me. It wasn't her fault.

It was mine.

No one said anything. There was no turning back now, not for any of us. What Lena and Amma had done that night couldn't be undone. I shouldn't be here, but I was.

"It's da Order, and you can't stop da Order." Twyla closed her eyes, as if she could hear something I couldn't.

Amma pulled a handkerchief from her pocket and wiped her face. "I'm sorry I didn't tell you, but I'm not sorry we did it. It was the only way."

"You don't understand. Lena thinks she's going Dark. She ran away with some kind of Dark Caster, or Incubus. She's in danger because of me."

"Nonsense. That girl did what she had to do because she loves you."

Arelia collected their offerings from the ground—the bones, the sparrow, the moonstones.

"Nothing can make Lena go Dark, Ethan. She has to choose it."

"But she thinks she's Dark because she killed Macon. She thinks she's already chosen."

"But she hasn't," Liv said. She was standing a few feet away, to give us some privacy.

Link was sitting on an old stone bench, a few steps behind her. "Then we have to find her and tell her." He didn't act like he just found out that I'd died and been brought back to life. He acted like everything was the same. I went over and sat down on the bench next to Link.

Liv looked over at me. "Are you all right?"

Liv. I couldn't look at her. I'd been jealous and hurt, and I had dragged Liv into the middle of my own broken mess of a life. All because I thought Lena didn't love me anymore. But I was stupid, and I was wrong. Lena loved me so much, she was willing to risk everything to save me.

I had given up on Lena, after she had refused to give up on me. I owed her my life. It was as simple as that.

My fingers touched something carved into the edge of the bench. Words.

IN THE COOL, COOL, COOL
OF THE EVENING

It was the song that was playing at Ravenwood the first night I met Macon. The coincidence was too much, especially for a world with no coincidences. It had to be some kind of sign.

Sign of what? What I had done to Macon? I couldn't even think about how Lena must have felt, realizing she had lost him in my place. What if I had lost my mom that way? Would I have been able to look at Lena alive without seeing my mother dead?

"Just a minute." I pushed off the bench and took off down the path through the trees, the way we had come. I breathed the night air deep into my lungs, because I could still breathe. When I finally stopped running, I stared up at the stars and the sky.

Was Lena staring at the same sky, or one I could never see? Were our moons really so different?

I reached into my pocket for the Arclight, so it could show me how to find her, but it didn't. Instead, it showed me something else—

Macon had never been like his father, Silas, and they both knew it. He had always been more like his mother, Arelia. A powerful Light Caster, who his father had fallen deeply in love with while he was away at college in New Orleans. Not unlike the way he and Jane had met and fallen in love when he was studying at Duke. And like Macon, his father had fallen in love with his mother before the Transformation. Before his grandfather had convinced Silas a relationship with a Light Caster was an abomination against their kind.

It had taken Macon's grandfather years to tear his mother and father apart. By that time, he and Hunting and Leah were born. His mother had been forced to use her powers as a Diviner to escape Silas' rage and his uncontrollable urge to feed. She had fled to New Orleans with Leah. His father would never have let her take his sons.

His mother was the only one Macon could turn to now. The only one who would understand that he had fallen in love with a Mortal. The greatest act of sacrilege against his kind, the Blood Incubus.

The Demon Soldier.

Macon hadn't told his mother he was coming, but she would be expecting him. He climbed up from the Tunnels into the sweet heat of a New Orleans summer night. Fireflies blinked in the darkness, and the smell of magnolias was overpowering. She was waiting for him on the porch, tatting lace in an old wooden rocking chair. It had been a long time.

"Mamma, I need your help."

She put down her needle and hoop and rose from the chair. "I know. Everything's ready, cher."

There was only one thing powerful enough to stop an Incubus, aside from one of its own kind.

An Arclight.

They were considered medieval devices, weapons created to control and imprison the most powerful of the Harmers, the Incubus. Macon had never seen one before. There were very few left, and they were almost impossible to find.

But his mother had one, and he needed it.

Macon followed her into the kitchen. She opened a small cabinet that served as an altar to the spirits. She unwrapped a small wooden box with Niadic script, the ancient Caster language, around the perimeter.

THE ONE WHO SEEKS IT SHALL FIND IT
THE HOUSE OF THE UNHOLY
THE KEY TO THE TRUTH

"Your father gave this to me before the Transformation. It was passed down in the Ravenwood family for generations. Your granddaddy claimed it belonged to Abraham himself, and I believe it did. It's marked by his hatred and bigotry."

She opened the box, revealing the ebony sphere. Macon could feel the energy, even without touching it—the grisly possibility of an eternity within its glistening walls.

"Macon, you must understand. Once an Incubus is trapped inside the Arclight, there is no way out from within. You must be released. If you give this to someone, you have to be sure with all certainty that you can trust them, because you will be putting more than your

life in their hands. You will be giving them a thousand lives. That's what an eternity would feel like in there."

She held the box higher so he could see it, as if he could imagine the confines just by looking at it.

"I understand, Mamma. I can trust Jane. She's the most honest and principled person I've ever met, and she loves me. Despite what I am."

Arelia touched Macon's cheek. "There is nothing wrong with who you are, cher. If there were, it would be my fault. I doomed you to this fate."

Macon bent down and kissed her forehead. "I love you, Mamma. None of this is your fault. It's his."

His father.

Silas was possibly a greater threat to Jane than he was. His father was a slave to the doctrine of the first Ravenwood Blood Incubus. Abraham.

"It's not his fault, Macon. You don't know what your grandfather was like. How he bullied your father into believing his twisted brand of superiority — that Mortals were beneath Casters and Incubuses alike, simply a source of blood to satisfy their lust. Your father was indoctrinated, like his father before him."

Macon didn't care. He stopped feeling sorry for his father long ago, stopped wondering what it was about Silas his mother could have loved.

"Tell me how to use it." Macon reached out tentatively. "Can I touch it?"

"Yes. The person who touches you with it must have intent, and even then it's harmless without the Carmen Defixionis."

His mother removed a small pouch, a gris-gris bag, the strongest protection voodoo could offer, from the door of the cellar and disappeared down the dark stairs. When she returned, she was carrying something wrapped in a dusty piece of burlap. She laid it on the table and unwrapped it.

The Responsum.

Literally translated, it meant "the Answer."

It was written in Niadic. It contained all the laws that governed his kind.

It was the oldest of books. There were only a few copies in the world. His mother turned the brittle pages carefully, until she reached the right one.

"Carcer."

The Prison.

The sketch of the Arclight looked exactly like the one resting in the velvet-lined box sitting on his mother's kitchen table, next to her uneaten étouffée.

"How does it work?"

"It's rather simple. A person need only touch the Arclight and the Incubus they wish to imprison and speak the Carmen, at the same moment. The Arclight will do the rest."

"Is the Carmen in the book?"

"No, it's much too powerful to be trusted to the written word. You must learn the Carmen from someone who knows it, and commit it to memory."

She lowered her voice as if she was afraid someone might be listening. Then she whispered the words that could condemn him to an eternity of misery.

"Comprehende, Liga, Cruci Fige.
Capture, Cage, and Crucify."

*Arelia closed the lid of the box and handed it to
Macon. "Be careful. In the Arc there is power, and in
the power there is Night."*

Macon kissed her forehead. "I promise."

*He turned to leave, but his mother's voice called him
back. "You'll need this." She scrawled several lines on a
piece of parchment.*

"What's this?"

*"The only key to that door." She gestured to the box
tucked under his arm. "The only way to get you back out."*

I opened my eyes. I was on my back in the dirt, staring up at the
stars. The Arclight was Macon's, as Marian had said. I didn't know
where he was, the Otherworld or some kind of Caster heaven. I
didn't know why he was showing me all this, but if I had learned
anything tonight, I knew everything happened for a reason.

I had to figure out the reason before it was too late.

We were still standing in Bonaventure Cemetery, although now
we were near the entrance. I didn't bother to tell Amma I wasn't
coming back with her. She seemed to know.

"We better take off." I hugged Amma.

She grabbed my hands and gave them a squeeze, hard. "One
step at a time, Ethan Wate. Your mamma may say this is somethin' you hafta do, but I'll be watchin' every step a the way." I

knew how hard it was for her to let me go, instead of grounding me and sending me straight to my room, for the rest of my life.

Things were as bad as they seemed. This was proof.

Arelia stepped forward and pressed something into my hand, a small doll like the ones Amma made. It was a voodoo charm. "I had faith in your mother, and I have faith in you, Ethan. This is my way of saying good luck, because this isn't going to be easy."

"The right thing and the easy thing are never the same." I repeated the words my mother had said to me a hundred times. I was channeling her, in my own way.

Twyla touched my cheek with her bony finger. "Da truth in both da worlds. Have to lose to gain. We're not here long, *cher*." It was a warning, almost like she knew something I didn't. After what I'd seen tonight, I was sure she did.

Amma threw her skinny arms around me in one last bone-crushing hug. "I'm gonna make you some luck, my way," she whispered, and turned to Link. "Wesley Jefferson Lincoln, you best come back in one piece, or I'll tell your mamma what you were doin' in my basement when you were nine years old, you hear me?"

Link smiled at the familiar threat. "Yes, ma'am."

Amma didn't say anything to Liv—just a quick nod in her direction. It was her way of showing where her loyalties lay. Now that I knew what Lena had done for me, I had no doubt about how Amma felt about her.

Amma cleared her throat. "The guards are gone, but Twyla can't hold them off forever. You'd best get on."

I pushed open the wrought iron gate, with Link and Liv behind me.

I'm coming, L. Whether you want me to or not.

Down Below

Nobody said a word as we walked along the edge of the road toward the park and the Savannah Doorwell. We decided not to risk going back to Aunt Caroline's, since Aunt Del would be there and wasn't likely to let us keep going without her. Beyond that, there didn't seem to be anything worth saying. Link tried to get his hair to stick up without the aid of industrial strength hair gel, and Liv checked her selenometer and scribbled in her tiny red notebook once or twice.

The same old things.

Only the same old things weren't the same this morning, in the gloomy darkness before dawn. My mind was reeling, and I stumbled more than a few times. This night was worse than a nightmare. I couldn't wake up. I didn't even have to shut my eyes to see the dream, Sarafine and the knife—Lena crying out for me.

I had died.

I was dead, for who knows how long.

Minutes?

Hours?

If it wasn't for Lena, I would be lying in the dirt in His Garden of Perpetual Peace right now. The second sealed cedar box in our family plot.

Had I felt things? Seen things? Had it changed me? I touched the hard line of the scar beneath my shirt. Was it really my scar? Or was it the memory of something that happened to the other Ethan Wate, the one who didn't come back?

It was all a confusing blur, like the dreams Lena and I shared, or the difference between the two skies Liv had shown me, the night the Southern Star disappeared. Which part was real? Had I unconsciously known what Lena had done? Had I sensed it somewhere below everything else that had happened between us?

If she had known what she was choosing, would she have chosen differently?

I owed my life to her, but I didn't feel happy. All I felt was brokenness. The fear of dirt and nothingness and being alone. The loss of my mom and Macon and, in a way, Lena. And something else.

The crippling sadness and the incredible guilt of being the one who lived.

Forsyth Park was eerie at dawn. I had never seen it when it wasn't teeming with people. Without them, I almost didn't recognize the door to the Tunnels. No trolley bells, no sightseers. No miniature dogs or gardeners trimming azaleas. I thought of all the living, breathing people who would wander through the park today.

"You didn't see it." Liv pulled on my arm.

"What?"

"The door. You walked right by it."

She was right. We had walked past the archway before I recognized it. I almost forgot how subtly the Caster world worked, always hidden in plain sight. You couldn't have seen the Outer Door in the park unless you were looking for it, and the archway kept it in perpetual shadow, probably a Cast of its own. Link went to work, ratcheting his shears into the crack between the door and the frame as quickly as possible, prying it open with a groan. The dim recesses of the tunnel were even darker than the summer dawn.

"I can't believe that works." I shook my head.

"I've been thinking about it since we left Gatlin," Liv said. "I think it makes loads of sense."

"It makes sense that a crappy pair of garden shears can open a Caster door?"

"That's the beauty of the Order of Things. I told you, there's the magical universe and the material universe." Liv stared up at the sky.

My eyes followed hers. "Like the two skies."

"Exactly. One isn't any more real than the other. They coexist."

"So rusty metal scissors can take on a magic portal?" I don't know why I was surprised.

"Not always. But where the two universes meet, there will always be some sort of seam. Right?" It made perfect sense to Liv.

I nodded.

"I wonder if a strength in one universe corresponds to a weakness in the other." She was talking to herself as much as to me.

"You mean, the door is easy for Link to open because it's impossible for a Caster?" Link had been having a suspiciously easy time with the Doorwells. On the other hand, Liv didn't know Link had been picking locks since his mom gave him his first curfew, in about sixth grade.

"Possibly. It might account for what's happening with the Arclight."

"Or what about this? The Caster doors keep on openin' because I'm a ragin' stud." Link flexed.

"Or the Casters who built these Tunnels hundreds of years ago weren't thinking about garden shears," I said.

"Because they were thinkin' about my extreme studliness, in both universes." He stuck the shears back in his belt. "Ladies first."

Liv climbed down into the tunnel. "As if I should be surprised."

We followed the stairs back down into the still air of the tunnel. It was completely quiet, without even an echo from our footsteps. The silence settled over us, thick and heavy. The air beneath the Mortal world had none of the weightlessness of the air above.

At the bottom of the Doorwell, we found ourselves facing the same dark road that had led us to Savannah. The one that had split into two directions: the forbidding, shadowy street we were on, and the meadow path suffused with light. Directly in front of us, the old neon motel sign was flickering on and off now, but that was the only difference.

That, and Lucille lying rolled up beneath it, the light hitting her fur as it blinked. She yawned to see us, slowly pulling herself up one paw at a time.

"You're gettin' to be a tease, Lucille." Link squatted on his heels to scratch her ears. Lucille meowed, or growled, depending on how you looked at it. "Aw, I forgive you." Everything was a compliment to Link.

"What now?" I faced the crossroads.

"Stairway to hell, or the Yellow Brick Road? Why don't you give your 8 Ball a shake and see if it's ready to play again." Link stood up.

I took the Arclight out of my pocket. It was still glowing, flashing on and off, but the emerald color that led us to Savannah was gone. Now it had turned a deep blue, like one of those satellite photos of the Earth.

Liv touched the sphere, the color deepening under her fingertip. "The blue is so much more intense than the green. I think it's getting stronger."

"Or your superpowers are getting stronger." Link gave me a shove, and I almost dropped the Arclight.

"And you wonder why this thing stopped working?" I pulled it away from him, annoyed.

Link checked me with his shoulder. "Try to read my mind. Wait, no. Try to fly."

"Stop messing around," Liv snapped. "You heard Ethan's mom. We don't have much time. The Arclight will work or it won't. Either way, we need an answer."

Link straightened up. The weight of what we had seen at the graveyard was on all our shoulders now. The strain was beginning to show.

"Shh. Listen—" I took a few steps forward, in the direction

of the tunnel carpeted in tall grass. You could actually hear the birds chirping now.

I raised the Arclight and held my breath. I wouldn't have minded if it went black and sent us down the other path, the one with the shadows, the rusty fire escapes crawling down the sides of dark buildings, the unmarked doors. As long as it gave us an answer.

Not this time.

"Try the other way," Liv said, never taking her eyes off the light. I retraced my steps.

No change.

No Arclight, and no Wayward. Because deep down I knew that without the Arclight, I wouldn't have been able to find my way out of a paper bag, especially not in the Tunnels.

"I guess that's the answer. We're screwed." I pocketed the ball.

"Great." Link started down the sunlit path without another thought.

"Where are you going?"

"No offense, but unless you have some kinda secret Wayward clue about where to go, I'm not goin' down there." He looked back at the darker path. "The way I see it, we're lost no matter what, right?"

"Pretty much."

"Or if you look at it the other way, we've got a fifty-fifty chance of gettin' things right half the time." I didn't try to correct his math. "So I figure we take our chances on Oz and tell ourselves things are finally lookin' up. 'Cause what do we have to lose?" It was hard to argue with Link's twisted logic when he tried to be logical.

"Got a better idea?"

Liv shook her head. "Shockingly, no."

We headed for Oz.

The tunnel really was right out of a page of one of my mom's tattered old L. Frank Baum books. Willows stretched over the dusty path, and the underground sky was open and endless and blue.

The scene was calm, which had the opposite effect on me. I was used to the shadows. This path seemed too idyllic. I expected a Vex to fly down over the hills in the distance any second.

Or a house to drop on my head when I least expected it.

My life had taken a stranger turn than I could've ever imagined. What was I doing on this path? Where was I headed really? Who was I to take on a battle between powers I didn't understand—armed with a runaway cat, a uniquely bad drummer, a pair of garden shears, and an Ovaltine-drinking teen Galileo?

To save a girl who didn't want to be saved?

"Wait up, you stupid cat!" Link scrambled after Lucille, who had become the leader, zigzagging her way in front of us as if she knew exactly where we were going. It was ironic, because I didn't have a clue.

Two hours later, the sun was still shining, and my uneasy feelings were growing. Liv and Link were walking ahead of me, which was Liv's way of avoiding me, or at least the situation. I couldn't blame her. She'd seen my mother and heard everything Amma said. She knew what Lena had done for me, how it explained her Dark and erratic behavior. Nothing had changed, but the reasons for everything had. For the second time this summer, a girl I cared about—who cared about me—couldn't bear to look me in the eye.

Instead, she was passing the time walking up the path with Link, teaching him British insults and pretending to laugh at his jokes.

"Your room is grotty. Your car is skanky, maybe manky," Liv teased, but her heart wasn't in it.

"How do you know?"

"From looking at you." Liv sounded distant. Teasing Link didn't seem to be enough of a distraction.

"What about me?" Link ran his hand over his spiky hair, to make sure it was sticking up just right.

"Let's see. You, you're a git, a prat." Liv tried to force a smile.

"That's all good, right?"

"Of course. The best."

Good old Link. His trademark charmless charm could salvage almost any desperate social situation.

"Do you hear that?" Liv stopped walking. Usually when I heard singing, I was the only one, and it was Lena's song. This time, everyone heard it, and the song was a far cry from the hypnotic voice of *Seventeen Moons*. This was bad singing, dying animal bad. Lucille meowed, her hair standing on end.

Link looked around. "What is that?"

"I don't know. It sounds almost like..." I stopped.

"Someone in trouble?" Liv held her hand near her ear.

"I was going to say 'Leaning on the Everlasting Arms.'" It was an old hymn they sang at the Sisters' church. I was half right.

When we rounded the corner, Aunt Prue was walking toward us holding on to Thelma's arm, singing as if it was Sunday at church. She was wearing her white flowered dress and matching white gloves, shuffling along in her beige orthopedic shoes.

Harlon James was scampering along behind them, nearly as large as Aunt Prue's patent-leather handbag. It looked like the three of them were out for a stroll on a sunny afternoon.

Lucille meowed and sat down on the path in front of us.

Link scratched his head behind her. "Dude, am I seein' things? 'Cause that looks a lot like your crazy aunt and that fleabag dog a hers." At first, I didn't answer him. I was too busy figuring the odds of this being some kind of Caster mind trick. We'd get close enough, then Sarafine would step right out of my aunt's skin and kill all three of us.

"Maybe it's Sarafine." I was thinking out loud, trying to find the logic in something completely illogical.

Liv shook her head. "I don't think so. Cataclysts can project themselves into the bodies of others, but they can't inhabit two people at once. Three, if you count the dog."

"Who would count that dog?" Link made a face.

Part of me, the biggest part of me, wanted to take off and figure it out later. But they saw us. Aunt Prue, or the creature impersonating Aunt Prue, waved her hankie in the air. "Ethan!"

Link looked back at me. "Should we make a run for it?"

"Findin' you was harder than herdin' cats!" Aunt Prue called, shuffling across the grass as fast as she could. Lucille meowed, tossing her head. "Now, Thelma, keep up." Even at a distance, it was impossible to mistake the off-kilter walk and the bossy tone.

"No, that's her." Too late to run.

"How did they get down here?" Link was as stumped as I was. It was one thing to find out Carlton Eaton delivered the mail to the *Lunae Libri*, but seeing my hundred-year-old great-aunt wandering around in the Tunnels in her church dress was something else.

Aunt Prue dug her cane into the grass, working her way up the path. "Wesley Lincoln! Are you gonna stand there and watch an old woman work herself inta a state, or are you gonna get on over here and help me up this hill?"

"Yes, ma'am. I mean, no, ma'am." Link almost tripped as he ran to hook his arm through hers. I caught the other.

The shock of seeing her was starting to wear off a little. "Aunt Prue, how did you get down here?"

"Same way as you, I expect. Came down through one a them doors. There's one right behind Missionary Baptist. I used it ta sneak outta Bible school when I was younger than you."

"But how did you know about the Tunnels?" I couldn't figure it. Had she followed us?

"I've been down in these Tunnels more times than a sinner's swore offa the bottle. You think you're the only one who knows 'bout what goes on in this town?" She knew. She was one of them, like my mom and Marian and Carlton Eaton—Mortals who had somehow become part of the Caster world.

"Do Aunt Grace and Aunt Mercy know?"

"'Course not. Those two can't keep a secret ta save their lives. That's why my daddy only told me. And I never told a soul, 'cept Thelma."

Thelma squeezed Aunt Prue's arm affectionately. "She only told me because she couldn't climb down the stairs on her own anymore."

Aunt Prue swatted at Thelma with her handkerchief. "Now, Thelma, you know that's not true. Don't tell stories."

"Did Professor Ashcroft send you after us?" Liv looked up nervously from her notebook.

Aunt Prue sniffed. "No one sends me anywhere, not hardly.

I'm too old ta be sent. Came on my own." She pointed at me. "But you best hope Amma isn't down here lookin' for you. She's been boilin' bones since you left."

If she only knew.

"Then what are you doing down here, Aunt Prue?" Even if she was in the know, the Tunnels didn't seem like the safest place for an old lady.

"Came ta bring you these." Aunt Prue opened her pocket-book and held it out so we could see inside. Under the sewing scissors and coupons and King James pocket Bible was a thick stack of yellowed papers, folded neatly into a bundle. "Go on, now. Take 'em." She might as well have told me to stab myself with the sewing scissors. There was no way I was going to reach into my aunt's purse. It was the ultimate violation of Southern etiquette.

Liv seemed to understand the problem. "May I?" Maybe British men didn't go through women's purses either.

"That's what I brought 'em for."

Liv lifted the papers gently out of Aunt Prue's purse. "These are really old." She opened them carefully on the soft grass. "They can't be what I think they are."

I bent down and studied them. The papers looked like schematics or architectural plans. They were marked in all different colors and written by many different hands. They were painstakingly drawn across a grid, each line perfectly measured and straight. Liv smoothed the paper flat, and I could see the long rows of lines intersecting one another.

"Depends on what ya think they are, I reckon."

Liv's hands were shaking. "They're maps of the Tunnels." She looked up at Aunt Prue. "Do you mind if I ask where you got these, ma'am? I've never seen anything like them, not even in the *Lunae Libri*."

Aunt Prue unwrapped a red and white striped peppermint from her purse. "My daddy gave 'em ta me, like my granddaddy gave 'em ta him. They're older than dirt."

I was speechless. No matter how normal Lena thought my life would be without her, she was wrong. Curse or no curse, my family tree was all tangled up with Casters.

And their maps, fortunately for us.

"They're not close ta done. I was a real draftswoman in my day, but my bursitis got the best a me."

"I tried to help, but I don't have the knack for it, like your aunt." Thelma looked apologetic. Aunt Prue waved her handkerchief.

"You drew these?"

"I drew my share." She pushed on her cane, straightening with pride.

Liv stared at the maps in awe. "How? The Tunnels are absolutely endless."

"An itty bit at a time. Those maps don't show all a the Tunnels. The Carolinas mostly, and some a Georgia. That's 'bout as far as we got." It was unbelievable. How could my scattered aunt have drafted maps of the Caster Tunnels?

"How did you do this without Aunt Grace and Aunt Mercy finding out?" I couldn't remember a time when the three of them weren't so close, they were bumping into each other.

"We didn't always live together, Ethan." She lowered her voice, as if Aunt Mercy and Aunt Grace might be listening. "And I don't really play bridge on Thursdays." I tried to imagine Aunt Prue charting the Caster Tunnels while the other elderly members of the DAR played cards at the church social hall.

"Take 'em. I reckon you'll need 'em if you're fixin' ta stay down here. Gets real confusin' after a while. Some days I'd get myself so turned around, I could barely get myself back ta South Carolina."

"Thanks, Aunt Prue. But—" I stopped. I didn't know how to explain it all—the Arclight and the visions, Lena and John Breed and the Great Barrier, the moon out of time and the missing star, not to mention the crazy dials spinning on Liv's wrist. Least of all, Sarafine and Abraham. It wasn't a story for one of the oldest citizens in Gatlin.

Aunt Prue cut me off with a wave of her handkerchief in my face. "Y'all are as lost as a hog at a pig pick. Unless you wanna be slapped on a bun with Carolina Gold, you best pay attention."

"Yes, ma'am." I thought I knew right where this particular lecture was headed. But I was as wrong as Savannah Snow wearing a sleeveless dress and chewing gum at youth choir.

"Now you listen up, ya hear?" She pointed her bony finger at me. "Carlton came sniffin' around ta see what I knew 'bout someone breakin' inta the Caster door at the fairgrounds. Next thing I hear, that Duchannes girl is missin', you and Wesley have run off, and that girl stayin' with Marian—you know, the one who puts milk in her tea—is nowhere ta be seen. Seems ta me that's one too many coincidences, even for Gatlin."

Big surprise there. Carlton spreading the news.

"Whatever it is, you need these, and I want you ta take 'em. I don't have time for all this nonsense." I guessed right. She knew what we were doing, whether she let on or not.

"I sure appreciate your concern, Aunt Prue."

"I ain't concerned. Not so long as you take the maps." She patted my hand. "Ya'll are gonna find that gold-eyed Lena Du-channes. Even a blind squirrel sometimes finds himself a nut."

"I hope so, ma'am."

Aunt Prue patted my hand and took hold of her cane. "Then you better stop talkin' ta old ladies and meet that trouble halfway, so there'll only be half as much. Good Lord willin' and the creek don't rise." She steered Thelma away from us.

Lucille ran along behind them for a minute, the bell on her collar jingling. Aunt Prue stopped and smiled. "See you still got that cat. I was waitin' for the right time ta let her offa that clothesline. She knows a trick or two. You'll see. You still got her tag, don't ya?"

"Yes, ma'am. It's in my pocket."

"Needs one a those rings to fix it on her collar. But you hold on ta it, and I'll get ya one." Aunt Prue unwrapped another peppermint and dropped it on the ground for Lucille. "I'm real sorry I called you a deserter, ole girl, but you know Mercy'd never have let me give you up otherwise."

Lucille sniffed the peppermint.

Thelma waved and smiled her big Dolly Parton smile. "Good luck, Sweet Meat."

I watched them walk down the hill behind us, wondering what else I didn't know about the people in my family. Who else seemed senile and clueless, but was actually watching my every move? Who else was protecting Caster Scrolls and secrets in their spare time or mapping a world most of Gatlin didn't know existed?

Lucille licked the peppermint. If she knew, she wasn't talking.

"Okay, so we've got a map. That's gotta be something, right, MJ?" Link's mood improved after Aunt Prue and Thelma disappeared down the path.

358

"Liv?" She didn't hear me. She was flipping pages in her notebook with one hand and tracing a pathway across the map with the other.

"Here's Charleston, and this must be Savannah. So if you assume the Arclight has been helping us find the southern pathway, toward the coast..."

"Why the coast?" I interrupted.

"Due south. As if we were following the Southern Star, remember?" Liv sat back, frustrated. "There are so many branching pathways. We're only a few hours from the Savannah Doorwell, but that could mean anything down here." She was right. If time and physics didn't directly correspond above and below the ground, who was to say we weren't in China by now?

"Even if we knew where we were, it could take days to find it on this map. We don't have time."

"Well, we'd better get started. It's all we've got."

But it was something—something that made it feel like we might actually be able to find Lena. I wasn't sure whether it was because I believed the maps could get us there or because I thought I could.

It didn't matter, as long as I found Lena in time.

Good Lord willin' and the creek don't rise.

⊰ 6.19 ⊱

Bad Girl

My optimism was short-lived. The more I thought about finding Lena, the more I thought about John. What if Liv was right, and Lena would never go back to being the girl I remembered? What if we were already too late? I thought about the swirling black designs on her hands.

I was still thinking about it when the words drifted into my mind. They were faint at first. For a second, I thought it was Lena's voice. But when I heard the familiar melody, I knew I was wrong.

> *Seventeen moons, seventeen years*
> *Know the loss, stay the fears*
> *Wait for him and he appears*
> *Seventeen moons, seventeen tears...*

My Shadowing Song. I tried to figure out what my mother was trying to tell me. *You don't have much time.* Her words rattled around in my mind. *Wait for him and he appears....* Was she talking about Abraham?

If she was, what was I going to do?

I was so absorbed in the verse, I didn't realize Link was talking to me. "Did you hear that?"

"The song?"

"What song?" He signaled us to be quiet. He was talking about something else. It sounded like dry leaves crunching behind us, and the low whipping of the wind. But there wasn't even a breeze.

"I don't—" Liv began, but Link shut her down.

"Shh!"

Liv rolled her eyes. "Are all American guys as brave as the two of you?"

"I heard it, too." I looked around, but there was nothing, not a single living thing. Lucille's ears perked up.

Everything happened so quickly it was impossible to follow. Because it wasn't a living thing I'd heard.

It was Hunting Ravenwood, Macon's brother—and his killer.

Hunting's menacing, inhuman smile was the first thing I saw. He materialized a few feet away from us, so quickly he was almost a blur. Another Incubus appeared, and another. They ripped out of nowhere, one after the next, like links in a chain. The chain tightened, and they formed a circle around us.

They were all Blood Incubuses, with the same black eyes and matching ivory canines, except for one. Larkin, Lena's cousin and Hunting's lackey, had a long brown snake curled around his neck. The snake had the same yellow eyes as Larkin.

He nodded at the snake slithering down his arm. "Copperheads.

Nasty little bitches. You don't want to get bit by one of these. But then there are a lot of ways to get bitten."

"I would have to agree." Hunting laughed, baring his canines. A rabid-looking animal crouched behind him. It had the huge muzzle of a Saint Bernard, but instead of big, droopy eyes, it had sharp, yellow ones. The hair on its back bristled like a wolf's. Hunting had gotten himself a dog—or something.

Liv clung to my arm, her nails digging into my skin. She couldn't take her eyes off Hunting or his pet. I was pretty sure she had only seen a Blood Incubus in one of her Caster volumes. "That's a Packhound. They're trained to go for blood. Stay away from it."

Hunting lit a cigarette. "Ah, Ethan, I see you've found yourself a Mortal girlfriend. It's about time. And I think this one's a real *keeper*." He laughed at his own bad joke, exhaling wide smoke rings into the perfectly blue sky. "Almost makes me want to let you go." The Packhound growled low in its throat. "Almost."

"You—you can let us go," Link stammered. "We won't tell anybody. We swear." One of the Incubuses laughed. Hunting jerked his head around, and the Demon didn't utter another sound. It was obvious who was calling the shots.

"Why would I care if you told anyone? In fact, I enjoy the limelight. I'm a bit of a thespian." He stepped closer to Link, but I was the one he was watching. "Who would you tell, anyway? Now that my niece killed Macon. Didn't see that one coming."

Hunting's Packhound was foaming at the mouth, and so were his other dogs, the Incubuses that only looked human. One of them inched closer to Liv. She jumped, tightening her grip around my arm.

"Why don't you stop trying to scare us?" I tried to sound tough, but I wasn't fooling anyone. This time, they all roared with laughter.

"You think we're trying to scare you? Thought you were smarter than that, Ethan. My boys and I are hungry. We missed breakfast."

Liv's voice was tiny. "You can't mean…"

Hunting winked at Liv. "Don't worry, sweetheart. We may just bite that pretty neck of yours and make you one of us." My breath caught in my throat. It had never occurred to me that Incubuses could transform humans into their kind.

Could they?

Hunting flicked his cigarette into a patch of bluebells. For a second, I was struck by the irony of the situation. A pack of leather-clad, cigarette-smoking Incubuses were standing in a meadow right out of *The Sound of Music*, waiting to kill us while the birds were singing in the trees. "It's been fun chatting with the three of you, but I'm getting bored. I have a rather short attention span."

He whipped his neck around, farther than any human's could possibly turn. Hunting was going to kill me, and his buddies were going to kill Link and Liv. My brain tried to process it while my heart focused on beating.

"Let's do this," Larkin said, flicking a forked tongue that matched his snake's.

Liv buried her face into my shoulder. She didn't want to watch. I tried to think. I was no match for Hunting, but everyone had an Achilles' heel, right?

"On my count," growled Hunting. "No survivors."

My mind raced. The Arclight. I had the ultimate weapon

against an Incubus, but I had no idea how to use it. I moved my hand closer to my pocket.

"No," Liv whispered. "There's no use." She shut her eyes, and I pulled her closer. My last thoughts were about the two girls who meant so much to me. Lena, the one I would never save. And Liv, the one I was about to get killed.

But Hunting never attacked.

Instead, he cocked his head to the side awkwardly, like a wolf listening to another wolf calling. Then he stepped back and the other Incubuses followed, even Larkin and the demonic Saint Bernard. His minions were disoriented, looking around at each other. They stared at Hunting, waiting for direction, but he didn't give them any. Instead, he backed up slowly and the others followed. They were closing in on us, but in reverse. Hunting's expression changed, and he looked more like a man again, rather than the Demon he truly was.

"What's happening?" Liv whispered.

"I don't know." It was clear Hunting and his lackeys were confused, too, because they kept circling and pacing, moving farther and farther away from us. Something was controlling them, but what?

Hunting locked eyes with me. "I'll be seeing you. Sooner than you think." They were leaving. Hunting kept shaking his head, as if he was trying to shake something—or someone—out of it. The pack had a new leader, someone he had no choice but to follow.

Someone very persuasive.

And very pretty.

Ridley was leaning against a tree a couple of yards behind them, licking away at a lollipop. The Incubuses dematerialized, one by one.

"Who is that?" Liv noticed Ridley, oddly not that out of place with her pink and blond streaked hair, weird miniskirt with some sort of suspenders, and spiky sandals. She looked like a Caster Little Red Riding Hood, taking poisoned muffins to her wicked grandmother. Liv may not have gotten a good look at Ridley at Exile, but she was impossible to miss now.

Link's eyes locked on Ridley. "A real bad girl."

Ridley sauntered toward us, overconfident as usual. She tossed the lollipop into the grass. "Damn, that really took it out of me."

"Did you save us?" Liv was still rattled.

"Sure did, Mary Poppins. You can thank me later. We should get outta here. Larkin's an idiot, but Uncle Hunting's powerful. My influence won't last long on him." Her brother and her uncle—a lot of bad apples had fallen off Lena's family tree. Ridley zeroed in on my arm, or rather Liv's arm wrapped around mine. She took off her shades, and her yellow eyes glowed.

Liv barely noticed. "What's with you people? It's always Mary Poppins. Is she the only British character Americans have ever heard of?"

"I don't believe we've been properly introduced, although I keep seeing you everywhere." Ridley looked at me, narrowing her eyes. "I'm Lena's cousin, Ridley."

"I'm Liv. I work at the library with Ethan."

"Well, since I've seen you at a Caster club and now in a Caster Tunnel, I'm assuming we aren't talking about that hayseed library in Gat-dung. Which would make you a Keeper. Am I getting warm?"

Liv let go of my arm. "Actually, I'm a Keeper-in-Training, but my preparation has been quite extensive."

Ridley looked Liv up and down and unwrapped a piece of gum. "Obviously not that extensive if you don't recognize a Siren when you see one." Ridley blew a bubble. It popped in Liv's face. "Let's get going before my uncle starts thinking for himself again."

"We're not going anywhere with you."

She rolled her eyes, twisting her gum around her finger. "If you'd rather be my uncle's lunch, suit yourself. It's a personal choice, but I've gotta tell you, he has disgusting table manners."

"Why did you help us? What's the catch?" I asked.

"No catch." Ridley looked over at Link, who was recovering from the shock of seeing her. "Couldn't let anything happen to my boy toy."

"Because I mean so much to you, right?" Link snapped.

"Don't look so wounded. We had fun while it lasted." Link may have been hurt, but Ridley was the one who looked uncomfortable.

"Whatever you say, Babe."

"Don't call me Babe." Ridley tossed her hair and popped another bubble. "You can follow me, or stay here and try to take on my uncle by yourselves." She stalked off into the trees. "The Blood pack will be tracking you the second I get out of their heads."

The Blood pack. Great. They had a name.

Liv said what we were all thinking. "Ridley's right. If the pack is tracking us, it isn't going to take them long to catch up with us again." She looked at me. "We don't have a choice." Liv disappeared into the forest after Ridley.

As much as I didn't want to follow Ridley anywhere, getting killed by a pack of Blood Incubuses wasn't an appealing alternative. We didn't discuss it, but Link must have agreed, because we fell in line behind them.

Ridley seemed to know exactly where she was going, though I noticed Liv never put away the maps. Ridley cut across the meadow, ignoring the path, and headed for a cluster of trees in the distance. Her sandals didn't seem to slow her down, and the rest of us had trouble keeping up.

Link jogged ahead to catch up with her. "So what're you really doin' here, Rid?"

"It's pathetic to admit, but I'm here to help you and your merry band of fools."

Link stifled a laugh. "Yeah, right. The lollipops don't work anymore. Try again."

The grass was higher as we neared the trees. We were walking so fast the blades cut against my shins, but I didn't slow down. I wanted to know what Ridley was up to as much as Link did.

"I don't have an agenda, Hot Stuff. I'm not here for you. I'm here to help my cousin."

"You don't care about Lena," I snapped.

Ridley stopped and turned to face me. "You know what I don't care about, Short Straw? You. But for whatever reason, you and my cousin have a connection, and you may be the only person who can convince her to turn around before it's too late."

I stopped walking.

Liv looked at her coldly. "You mean before she gets to the Great Barrier? The place *you* told her about?"

Ridley's eyes narrowed, and she glanced at Liv. "Give this girl a prize. Keeper does know a thing or two." Liv didn't smile.

"But I wasn't the one who told her about the Barrier. It was John. He's obsessed with it."

"John? You mean the John you introduced her to? The guy you convinced her to run away with?" I was shouting, and I didn't care if the whole Blood pack heard me.

"Slow down, Short Straw. Lena makes her own decisions, whether you believe it or not." Ridley's voice lost some of its edge. "She wanted to go."

I remembered watching Lena and John, listening to them talk about a place where they could be accepted for who they were. A place where they could be themselves. Of course Lena wanted to go there. It was what she had dreamed about her whole life.

"Why the sudden change of heart, Ridley? Why do you want to stop her now?"

"The Barrier is dangerous. It's not what she thinks."

"You mean Lena doesn't know Sarafine is trying to pull the Seventeenth Moon out of time? But you knew, didn't you?" Ridley looked away. I was right.

Ridley was picking at the purple polish on her nails, a nervous habit Casters and Mortals shared. She nodded. "Sarafine isn't doing it alone."

My mother's letter to Macon flashed through my mind. Abraham. Sarafine was working with Abraham, someone who was powerful enough to help her call the moon.

"Abraham," Liv said quietly. "Well, that's lovely."

Link reacted before I did. "And you didn't tell Lena? Are you really that crazy and screwed up?"

"I—"

I cut her off. "She's a coward."

Ridley straightened, her yellow eyes glowing with rage. "I'm a coward because I don't want to end up dead? Do you know what my aunt and that *monster* would do to me?" Her voice was shaky, but she tried to hide it. "I'd like to see you face those two, Short Straw. Abraham makes Lena's mom look like your little kitty cat."

Lucille hissed.

"It doesn't matter, as long as Lena doesn't get to the Barrier. And if you want to stop her, we need to get moving. I don't know the way there. I just know where I ditched them."

"Then how did you plan to get to the Great Barrier?" It was impossible to tell if she was lying.

"John knows the way."

"Does John know Sarafine and Abraham are there?" Had he been setting Lena up all along?

Ridley shook her head. "I don't know. The guy's hard to read. He's got...issues."

"How are we going to convince her not to go?" I had already tried to talk Lena out of running away, and it hadn't gone well.

"That's your department. Maybe this will help." She tossed me a battered spiral notebook. I would have recognized it anywhere. I had spent enough afternoons watching Lena write in it.

"You stole her notebook?"

Ridley tossed her hair. "*Steal* is such an ugly word. I borrowed it, and you should be thanking me. Maybe there's something useful in all that disgusting, sentimental dribble."

I unzipped my backpack and slid the notebook inside. It felt weird to hold a piece of Lena in my hands again. Now I was carrying Lena's secrets in my backpack and my mother's in my back pocket. I wasn't sure how many more secrets I could handle.

Liv was more interested in Ridley's motives than Lena's notebook. "Hold on. Now we're supposed to believe you're one of the good guys?"

"Hell no. I'm bad to the bone. And I could give a rat's ass what you believe." Ridley shot me a look out of the corner of her eye. "In fact, I'm having a hard time figuring out what you're doing here in the first place."

I stepped in before Ridley used another lollipop to get Liv to offer herself to Hunting as a snack. "So that's it? You want to help us find Lena?"

"That's right, Short Straw. We may not like each other, but we have common interests." She turned toward Liv but spoke to me. "We love the same person, and she's in trouble. So I defected. Now let's get a move on before my uncle catches the three of you."

Link stared at Ridley. "Man, I didn't see this comin'."

"Don't make more of it than it is. I'll be back to my own bad self as soon as we get Lena to turn back."

"You never know, Rid. Maybe the Wizard will give you a heart if we kill the Wicked Witch."

Ridley turned away, digging the spikes of her sandals into the mud. "Like I'd want one."

Consequences

We tried to keep up with Ridley, who was weaving in and out of the trees. Liv was behind her, consulting the map or her selenometer constantly. She didn't trust Ridley any more than the rest of us did.

There was something bothering me. A part of me believed her. Maybe she really cared about Lena. It was unlikely, but if there was a chance Ridley was telling the truth, I had to follow her. I owed Lena a debt I could never repay.

I didn't know if there was a future for us. If Lena would ever again be the girl I fell in love with. But it didn't matter.

The Arclight was heating up inside my pocket. I pulled it out, expecting to see a pool of iridescent color, but the surface was black. Now all I could see was my reflection. The Arclight seemed more than broken. It had become completely random.

Ridley's eyes widened when she saw it, and she stopped

walking for the first time in a long while. "Where'd you get that, Short Straw?"

"Marian gave it to me." I didn't want Ridley to know it had been my mother's, or who had given it to her.

"Well, that might even the odds a little. I don't think you can get my Uncle Hunting in there, but maybe one of the members of his pack."

"I'm not exactly sure how to use it." I almost didn't tell her, but it was true.

Ridley lifted an eyebrow. "Little Miss Know-It-All couldn't tell you?" Liv's cheeks flushed. Ridley took her time unwrapping a stick of pink gum and folded it into her mouth. "You have to touch him with it." She stepped closer to me. "Which means you have to get close."

"Whatever." Link pushed past her. "There are two of us. We can swing it."

Liv tucked her pencil behind her ear. She had been taking notes. "Link might be right. I wouldn't want to get near any of them. But if we had no choice, it would be worth a try."

"Then you have to lay the Cast. You know, speak the incantation and all." Ridley was leaning against a tree, smirking. She knew we didn't know the Cast. Lucille was sitting at Ridley's feet, studying her.

"I'm guessing you aren't going to tell us what it is."

"How should I know? It's not like there are a lot of those things around."

Liv spread the map out in her lap, carefully smoothing it. "We're going the right way. If we keep going east, this path should eventually lead to the shore." She pointed to a dense cluster of trees.

"Where? That forest?" Link looked dubious.

"Don't be scared, Hot Rod. I'll take Hansel, you take Gretel." Ridley winked at Link, like she still had power over him. Which she did, but it had nothing to do with her gifts as a Siren.

"I'll be all right on my own. Why don't you have another piece a gum?" Link pushed past her.

Maybe Ridley was like chicken pox; you could only catch it once.

—⌒⌒

"How long can it take to pee?" Ridley threw a rock in the direction of a clump of bushes, anxious to get going again.

"I can hear you." Link's voice came from the bushes.

"Good to know at least some of your bodily functions are working."

Liv looked at me and rolled her eyes. The longer we walked, the more Link and Ridley went at it.

"You're not makin' it any easier."

"You need me to come back there and help you?"

"You're all talk, Rid," Link called from behind the bushes. She started to get up, and Liv looked shocked. Ridley smiled and sat down again, satisfied.

I studied the sphere in my hands as the color changed from black to an iridescent green. Nothing useful, just colors that seemed on perpetual overload. Maybe Link was right. Maybe I had broken it.

Ridley looked confused, or interested. It was hard to tell. "What's with the light?"

"It's like a compass. It lights up if we're going the right way." At least, it used to.

"Hmm. I didn't know they did that." She was bored again.

"I'm sure there are a lot of things you don't know." Liv smiled innocently.

"Careful, or I might convince you to take a swim in the river."

I watched the Arclight. There was something different about it. The light began to pulse with a brightness and speed I hadn't seen since we left Bonaventure Cemetery. I turned to show Liv. "L, look at this."

Ridley's head whipped toward me, and I froze.

I had called Liv "L."

There was only one L in my life. Even though Liv didn't notice, Ridley did. Her eyes were wild as she sucked on her lollipop. She was staring right at me, and I could feel my will slipping away. I dropped the Arclight, and it rolled across the mossy forest floor.

Liv crouched over the Arclight, sitting on her heels. "That's strange. Why do you suppose it's flashing green again? Another visit from Amma, Arelia, and Twyla?"

"It's probably a bomb." I heard Link's voice, but I couldn't say a word. I dropped to the ground at Ridley's feet. It had been a while since she had flexed her Siren powers on me. I had a fleeting thought before my face hit the mud. Either Link was right, and he was immune to her now, or she was really holding back. If that was true, it was something new for her.

"If you hurt my cousin...if you so much as *think* about hurting my cousin, you'll spend the rest of your miserable life as my slave. Understand, Short Straw?"

My head lifted involuntarily and twisted, which made my neck feel like it was about to snap. My eyes forced themselves open, and I was staring into Ridley's glowing yellow eyes. They were burning so bright, I was getting dizzy.

"Stop that." I heard Liv's voice and felt the weight of my body slam against the ground before I regained control of it. "For goodness sake, Ridley, don't be stupid."

Liv and Ridley were standing face to face. Liv's arms were folded across her chest. Ridley held the lollipop between the two of them. "Settle down, Poppins. Short Straw and I are friends."

"It doesn't look that way to me." Liv's voice was rising. "Don't forget, we're the ones risking our lives to save Lena." Their faces were lit with flashes of colored light. The Arclight was going wild, pulsing color through the trees.

"Don't get your knickers in a twist, Mate." Ridley's eyes were steely.

Liv's were dark. "Don't be a bloody fool. If Ethan doesn't care about Lena, then what are we doing in the middle of these godforsaken woods?"

"Good question, Keeper. I know what I'm doing here. But if you don't care about Boyfriend, what's your excuse?" Ridley was standing inches from Liv, but Liv didn't back down.

"What am I doing here? The Southern Star has vanished, a Cataclyst is calling a moon out of time at the mythical Great Barrier, and you're asking what I'm doing here? Are you serious?"

"So this has nothing to do with Boyfriend?"

"Ethan, who is, in fact, no one's boyfriend, doesn't know anything about the Caster world." Liv wasn't rattled. "He's in over his head. He needs a Keeper."

"Actually, you're a Keeper-in-Training. Asking you for help is like asking a nurse to perform open-heart surgery. And according to your job description, you're not supposed to get involved. So the way I see it, you aren't a very good Keeper." Ridley was right. There were rules, and Liv was breaking them.

"That may be true, but I am an excellent astronomer. And without my readings, we wouldn't be able to use this map at all, or find the Great Barrier, or Lena."

The Arclight went cold in my hand. It was completely black again.

"Did I miss somethin'?" Link stepped out of the bushes, zipping his fly. The girls stared at him as I pulled myself up out of the mud. "Sweet tea in the toilet. I always miss the good stuff."

"What—" Liv tapped on her selenometer. "Something's wrong. The dials are going crazy."

Beyond the trees, a crashing noise echoed through the forest. Hunting must have caught up with us. Then I had another thought, fleeting, but it didn't make me feel any less guilty.

Maybe it was someone else, someone who didn't like us following her. Someone who could control things in the natural world.

"Go!"

The crashing grew louder. Without warning, the trees on either side collapsed in front of me. I backed away. The last time trees had fallen in front of me, it hadn't been an accident.

Lena! Is that you?

A few feet around us, great moss-covered oaks and white pines ripped up out of the mud, roots and all, crashing back to the ground.

Lena, don't!

Link stumbled toward Ridley. "Unwrap a sucker, Babe."

"I told you not to call me Babe."

For the first time in hours, I could see the sky. Only now it was dark. The black clouds of Caster magic had rolled in over us. Then I felt something, from far away.

376

More like, I heard something.

Lena.

Ethan, run!

It was her voice, the voice that had been silent for so long. But if Lena was telling me to run, who was tearing the trees out of the ground?

L, what's happening?

I couldn't hear her answer. There was only darkness, those Caster clouds rushing at us like they were chasing us. Until I saw the clouds for what they were.

"Look out!" I pulled Liv backward and pushed Link toward Ridley just in time. We fell into the brush as a shower of broken pines came falling from the sky like rain. The branches flattened into a great pile exactly where we had been standing. Dust stung my eyes, and I couldn't see anything. The dirt caught in my throat as I coughed.

Lena's voice was gone, but I heard something else. A humming sound, as if we'd stumbled across the hive of a thousand bees, all looking to kill for their queen.

The dust was so thick, I could barely make out the shapes around me. Liv was lying next to me, bleeding above one eye. Ridley was whimpering, huddled around Link, who was pinned by a massive tree branch. "Wake up, Shrinky Dink. Wake up."

As I crawled toward them, Ridley shrank back. The look on her face was pure terror. Only she wasn't looking at me. She was looking at something behind me.

The humming sound grew louder. I felt the burning cold of Caster darkness on the back of my neck. When I turned around, the massive pile of pine needles that had almost buried us had formed some kind of bonfire. The pyramid of needles created a pyre, a giant burning platform pointing up into the black clouds. But the flames weren't red, and they didn't produce heat. They were as yellow as Ridley's eyes, and they emitted only cold, sorrow, and fear.

Ridley's whimpering grew louder. "She's here."

I looked up as a stone slab emerged from the hissing yellow flames of the pyre. A woman lay on top of the rock. She looked almost peaceful, like a dead saint about to be carried through the streets. But she was no saint.

Sarafine.

Her eyes jerked open, and her lips curved into a cold smile. She stretched, like a cat waking from a nap, then rose to stand on the stone. From down below where we stood, she might as well have been fifty feet tall.

"Were you expecting someone else, Ethan? I can understand the confusion. You know what they say. Like mother, like daughter. In this case, more and more every day now."

My heart was pounding. I could see Sarafine's red lips, her long black hair. I turned away. I didn't want to see her face, the face that looked so much like Lena's. "Get away from me, witch."

Ridley was still crying, huddled next to Link, rocking back and forth like a madwoman.

Lena? Can you hear me?

Sarafine's haunting voice rose over the flames, and she was there again, standing at the top of the fire. "I'm not here for you, Ethan. I'll leave you for my darling daughter. She's grown up so much this year, hasn't she? There's nothing like watching your child reach her full potential. Really makes a mother proud."

I watched the flames crawl up her legs. "You're wrong. Lena's not like you."

"I think I've heard that somewhere before—on Lena's birthday, perhaps. Except then you believed it, and now you're lying. You know you've lost her. She can't change what was meant to be."

The flames were at her waist. She had the perfect features of the Duchannes women, but they seemed disfigured on Sarafine. "Maybe Lena can't change it, but I can. I'll do whatever I have to do to protect her."

Sarafine smiled, and I cringed. Her smile was so much like Lena's, or how Lena's smile seemed lately. As the flames moved up her chest, she disappeared.

"So strong and so much like your mother. Her last words were something like that. Or were they?" I heard a whisper in my ear. "You see, I've forgotten, because it didn't matter."

I froze. Sarafine was standing right next to me now, still wreathed in flames. I knew it wasn't an earthly fire, though, because the closer she came, the colder I felt.

"Your mother didn't matter. Her death was neither noble nor important. It was simply something I felt like doing at the time. It meant nothing." The flames rose to her neck and leaped up, consuming her body. "Just like you."

I reached for her throat. I wanted to tear it out. But my hand slipped through her, into the air. There was nothing there. She was an apparition. I wanted to kill her and I couldn't even touch her.

Sarafine laughed. "You think I would waste my time coming here in the flesh, Mortal?" She turned to Ridley, who was still rocking, with her hands clamped over her mouth. "Amusing, don't you think, Ridley?" Sarafine raised her hand and flung open her fingers.

Ridley rose to her feet, her hands clinging to her own throat. I watched as the spikes of Ridley's sandals rose, hovering above the ground as her face turned purple and she choked herself. Her blond hair hung down from her body, like a lifeless doll.

Sarafine's ghostly form dissolved into Ridley's body. Ridley glowed with yellow light—her skin, her hair, her eyes. The light was so bright, she had no pupils at all. Even in the darkness of the forest, I had to shield my face. Ridley's head jerked up, like a marionette's, and she started to speak.

"My power is growing, and soon the Seventeenth Moon will be upon us, called out of time, as only a mother can. I decide when the sun sets. I have moved stars for my child, and she will Claim herself and join me. Only my daughter could block out the Sixteenth Moon, and only I can raise the Seventeenth. There are no others like us, not in either of our worlds. We are the beginning and the end." Ridley's body collapsed back onto the ground, like an empty sack.

The Arclight was burning in my pocket. I hoped Sarafine couldn't sense it. I remembered the flashing—the Arclight tried to warn me. I should have paid attention.

"You betrayed us, Ridley. You're a traitor. The Father is not as forgiving as I am." The Father. Sarafine could only be talking about one person—the father of the Ravenwood line of Blood Incubuses, the father who started it all. Abraham.

Sarafine's voice echoed over the sound of the flames. "You will be judged, but I will not deny him the pleasure. You were my responsibility, and now you're my shame. I think it's only fitting that I leave you with a parting gift." She raised her arms high above her head. "Since you are so intent on helping these Mortals, from this moment forward you will live as a Mortal and die as one. Your powers have been returned to the Dark Fire from which they were born."

Ridley bolted upright and screamed, her pain echoing through the forest. Then it was gone—the fallen trees, the fire, Sarafine—everything. The forest was just as it had been a few minutes before. Green and dark, full of pines and oaks and black mud. Every tree, every branch, was back in place, as if nothing had happened.

Liv was pouring water from a plastic bottle into Ridley's mouth. Liv's face was still muddy and bleeding, but she seemed okay. Ridley, on the other hand, was as white as a ghost.

"That was incredibly powerful magic. An apparition able to possess a Dark Caster." Liv shook her head. I touched the blood above her eye, and she winced. "And Cast at the same time, if what she said about Ridley's powers is true." I looked at Ridley doubtfully. It was hard to imagine Ridley without her Power of Persuasion. "In any event, Ridley won't be quite right, not for some time." Liv doused part of her sweatshirt with water and wiped Ridley's face. "I didn't realize the chance she was taking by coming here. She must really care about all of you."

"Not all of us," I said, trying to help Liv prop Ridley up. Ridley coughed out the water and pulled her hand across her mouth, smearing her pink lipstick. She looked like a cheerleader who had been dunked at the school fair one too many times. She tried to speak. "Link. Is he...?"

I was kneeling next to him. The tree limb that had fallen on him had disappeared, but Link was still moaning in pain. It seemed impossible that he was hurt, that any of us were, since there was no sign of what had happened here—no fallen trees, not a twig out of place. But Link's arm was purple and about twice its normal size, and his pants were ripped.

"Ridley?" Link opened his eyes.

"She's fine. We're all fine." I ripped open his pant leg even more. His knee was bleeding.

Link tried to laugh. "What're you lookin' at?"

"Your ugly face." I leaned over him, watching to see if his eyes could focus. He was going to be okay.

"You're not gonna kiss me, are you?"

Right then, I was so relieved I almost could have.

"Pucker up."

⊰ 6.19 ⊱

No One Special

That night, we slept in the forest between the roots of an enormous tree, the biggest I'd ever seen. Link's knee was bandaged in my spare T-shirt, and his arm was in a sling made from part of my Jackson sweatshirt. Ridley lay on the opposite side of the tree with her eyes wide open, staring up at the sky. I wondered if she was staring at the Mortal sky now. She looked exhausted, but I didn't think she was going to get any sleep.

I wondered what she was thinking, if she regretted helping us. Had Ridley really lost her powers?

How would it feel to be Mortal when you had always been something else, something more? When you had never felt the "powerlessness of human existence," as Mrs. English had said in class last year. She had been talking about H. G. Wells' *The Invisible Man*, but right now Ridley seemed just as invisible.

Could you be happy if you woke up and suddenly you were no one special?

Could Lena? Is that what life with me would feel like? Hadn't Lena suffered enough for me already?

Like Ridley, I couldn't fall asleep, but I didn't want to stare at the sky. I wanted to see what was in Lena's notebook. A part of me knew it was an invasion of her privacy, but I also knew there might be something in those crumpled pages that could help us. After about an hour, I convinced myself reading her notebook was for the greater good, and I opened it.

At first it was hard to read, since my cell phone was my only light source. After my eyes adjusted, Lena's handwriting stared back at me from between the blue lines. I had seen the familiar print often enough in the months since her birthday, but I didn't think I would ever get used to it. It was such a sharp contrast to the girly script she wrote in before that night. It surprised me even more to see actual writing, after so many months of headstone photographs and black designs. Dark Caster designs, like the ones on her hands, were scribbled in the margins. But the first few entries were dated only days after Macon's death, when she was still writing.

emptycrowded daynights / all the same (more or less) fear (less and more) afraid / waiting for truth to strangle me in my sleep / if i ever slept

Fear (less and more) afraid. I understood the words, because that's how she had acted. Fearless and more afraid. Like she had nothing to lose but was afraid to lose it.

I flipped ahead and stopped when a date caught my eye. June 12th. The last day of school.

darkness hides and i think i can hold her / smother her in the palm of my hand / but when i look my hands are empty / quiet as her fingers fold around me

I read it over and over. She was describing the day at the lake, the day she had taken things too far. The day she could have killed me. Who was the "her"? Sarafine?

How long had she been fighting it? When did it start? The night Macon died? When she started wearing his clothes?

I knew I should close the notebook, but I couldn't. Reading her words was almost like hearing her thoughts again. I hadn't known them in such a long time, and I wanted to so badly. I turned each page, looking for the days that haunted me.

Like the day of the fair—

mortal hearts and mortal fears / something they can share i untie him like a sparrow

Freedom—that's what sparrows meant to a Caster.

All along I thought she was trying to be free from me, but really she was trying to set me free. As if loving her was a cage I couldn't escape.

I closed the notebook. It hurt too much to read it, especially when Lena was so far away, in all the ways that mattered.

A few feet away, Ridley was still staring blankly into the Mortal stars. For the first time, we saw the same sky.

Liv was wedged between two roots, with me on one side and

Link on the other. After I found out the truth about what happened on Lena's birthday, I guess I expected my feelings for Liv to disappear. But even now I found myself wondering. If things were different, if I had never met Lena, if I had never met Liv...

I spent the next few hours watching Liv. When she slept, she looked peaceful, beautiful. Not Lena's kind of beautiful, something different. She looked content—like a sunny day, a cold glass of milk, an unopened book before you cracked the binding. There was nothing tortured about her. She looked the way I wanted to feel.

Mortal. Hopeful. Alive.

When I finally drifted off, I felt that way, just for a minute....

Lena was shaking me. "Wake up, Sleepyhead. We have to talk." I smiled and pulled her into my arms. I tried to kiss her, but she laughed and ducked away. "This isn't that kind of a dream."

I sat up and looked around. We were in Macon's bed in the Tunnels. "All my dreams are that kind of dream, L. I'm almost seventeen."

"This is my dream, not yours. And I've only been sixteen for four months."

"Won't Macon be mad if we're here?"

"Macon's dead, don't you remember? You must really be asleep." She was right. I had forgotten everything, and now it all came crashing back. Macon was gone. The trade.

And Lena had left me, only she hadn't. She was here.

"So this is a dream?" I was trying to keep my stomach from twisting with loss, the guilt of everything I'd done, everything I owed her.

Lena nodded.

"Am I dreaming you, or are you dreaming me?"

"Does it ever make a difference, when it comes to us?" She was avoiding the question.

I tried again. "When I wake up, will you be gone?"

"Yes. But I had to see you. This was the only way for us to really talk." She was wearing a white T-shirt, one of my oldest, softest ones. She looked tousled and beautiful, in the way I loved best, when she thought she looked the worst.

I put my hands around her waist and pulled her close. "L, I saw my mom. She told me about Macon. I think she loved him."

"They loved each other. I've seen the visions, too." So our connection was still there. I felt a wave of relief.

"They were like us, Lena."

"And they couldn't be together. Like us."

It was a dream, I was sure of it. Because we could speak these terrible truths with a strange remove, as if they were happening to other people. She rested her head on my chest, picking mud off my shirt with her fingers. How had my shirt gotten so muddy? I tried to remember but couldn't.

"What are we going to do, L?"

"I don't know, Ethan. I'm scared."

"What do you want?"

"You," she whispered.

"So why is it so hard?"

"We're all wrong. Everything's all wrong when I'm with you."

"Does this feel wrong?" I held her tighter.

"No. But how I feel doesn't matter anymore." I felt her sigh against my chest.

"Who told you that?"

"No one had to tell me." I stared into her eyes. They were still gold.

"You can't go to the Great Barrier. You have to come back."

"I can't stop now. I have to see how it ends."

I played with a strand of her curling black hair. "Why didn't you have to see how it ended with us?"

She smiled and touched my face. "Because now I know how it ends with you."

"How does it end?"

"Like this." She bent over and kissed me, and her hair fell around my face like rain. I pulled up the covers, and she climbed beneath them, folding into my arms. As we kissed, I felt the heat of her touch. We tumbled in the bed. I was on top of her, then she was on top of me. The heat intensified to the point where I couldn't breathe. I thought my skin was on fire, and when I broke away from her kiss, it was.

We were both on fire, surrounded by flames that rose higher than we could see, and the bed wasn't a bed at all but a stone slab. It was burning all around us, the yellow flames of Sarafine's fire.

Lena screamed and clung to me. I looked down from where we were, on top of the massive pyramid of splintered trees. There was a strange circle chiseled into the stone we were lying on, some kind of Dark Caster symbol.

"Lena, wake up! This isn't you. You didn't kill Macon. You're not going Dark. It was the Book. Amma told me everything."

The pyre had been for us, not Sarafine. I could hear her laughing—or was it Lena? I couldn't tell the difference anymore. "L, listen to me! You don't have to do this—"

Lena was screaming. She couldn't stop screaming.

By the time I woke up, the flames had consumed us both.

"Ethan? Wake up. We have to get going."

I sat up, breathing hard and dripping with sweat. I held out my hands. Nothing. Not a burn, not so much as a scratch. It was a nightmare. I looked around. Liv and Link were already up. I rubbed my face with my hands. My heart was still pounding, as if the dream was real and I had almost died. I wondered again if it was my dream or Lena's. I wondered if that was really how it ended for us. Fire and death, just as Sarafine would want it.

Ridley was sitting on a rock, sucking on a lollipop, which was sort of pathetic. During the night, she seemed to have moved from a state of shock to one of denial. She was acting as if nothing happened. No one really knew what to say. She was like one of those war vets suffering from post-traumatic stress disorder, who come home and think they're still on the battlefield.

She was staring at Link, tossing her hair and looking at him expectantly. "Why don't you come on over here, Hot Rod?"

Link limped over to my backpack and pulled out a bottle of water. "I'll pass."

Ridley pushed her shades on top of her head and stared at him even more intently, which made it clear her powers were gone. In the light of day, Ridley's eyes were as blue as Liv's.

"I said come over here." Ridley inched her short skirt farther up her bruised thigh. I felt sorry for her. She wasn't a Siren anymore, just a girl who looked like one.

"Why?" Link wasn't catching on.

Ridley's tongue was bright red as she gave her lollipop one last lick. "Don't you want to kiss me?" For a second, I thought Link might play along, but that would only delay the inevitable.

"No, thanks." He turned away, and it was obvious he felt guilty.

Ridley's lip quivered. "Maybe it's temporary, and my powers will come back." She was trying to convince herself more than anyone.

Someone had to tell her. The sooner she faced reality, the sooner she would be able to move on. If she could. "I think they're really gone, Ridley."

She whipped around to face me, her voice shaky. "You don't know that. Just because you went out with a Caster doesn't mean you know anything."

"I know Dark Casters have yellow eyes."

I heard the breath catch in her throat. She grabbed the bottom of her filthy tank top and yanked it up. Her skin was still smooth and golden, but the tattoo that had encircled her navel was gone. She ran her hands across her stomach, and then crumbled.

"It's true. She really took my powers." Ridley opened her fingers, letting the lollipop fall into the dirt. She didn't make a sound, but the tears ran down her face in two silver lines.

Link walked over and held out his hand to pull her up. "That's not true. You're still pretty bad. I mean, hot. For a Mortal."

Ridley jumped to her feet, hysterical. "You think this is funny? That losing my powers is like losing one of your stupid basketball games? They're who I am, you idiot! Without them I'm nothing." Black streaks ran down her cheeks. She was shaking.

Link picked up her lollipop out of the dirt. He opened the water bottle and doused it. "Give it some time, Rid. You'll develop charms all your own. You'll see." He handed it back to her. Ridley stared back at him blankly.

Without looking away, she hurled the lollipop as far as she could.

⊰ 6.20 ⊱

Common Thread

I had barely slept. Link's arm was swollen and purple. None of us were in any shape to trek through the muddy forest, but we didn't have a choice.

"You guys okay? We should go."

Link touched his arm and winced. "I've felt better. Like, I don't know, every other day a my life."

The gash on Liv's face was already beginning to scab over. "I've felt worse, but that's a long story, which involves Wembley Stadium, a bad trip on the tube, and far too many döner kebabs."

I picked up my backpack, caked with mud. "Where's Lucille?"

Link looked around. "Who knows? That cat's always disappearin'. Now I know why your aunts kept her on a leash."

I whistled into the trees, but there was no sign of her. "Lucille! She was here when we got up."

"Don't worry, man. She'll find us. Cats have that sixth sense, you know?"

"She was probably tired of following us around, since we never get anywhere," Ridley said. "That cat's a whole lot smarter than we are."

I lost track of their conversation after that. I was too busy listening to the one in my head. I couldn't stop thinking about Lena and what she'd done for me. Why had it taken me so long to see what was right in front of me?

I knew Lena had been punishing herself all this time. The self-imposed isolation, the morbid pictures of headstones taped to her walls, the Dark symbols in her notebook and all over her body, wearing her dead uncle's clothes, even hanging out with Ridley and John — it was never about me. It was about Macon.

But I never realized I was an accomplice. Lena had a constant reminder of the crime she was trying herself for, over and over again. A constant reminder of what she lost.

Me.

She had to look at me every day and hold my hand and kiss me. No wonder she was so hot and cold, kissing me one minute and running away from me the next. I thought about the song lyrics, written over and over again on her walls.

Running to stand still.

She couldn't get away, and I wouldn't let her. In my last dream, I told her I knew about the trade. I wondered if she had the dream, too — if she knew I shared her secret burden. That she didn't have to carry it alone anymore.

I'm so sorry, L.

I listened for her voice in the corners of my mind, the faintest possibility she was listening. I didn't hear a sound, but I saw something, fleeting images in my peripheral vision. Snapshots rushing past me like cars in the fast lane on the interstate...

I was running, jumping, moving so fast I couldn't focus. Not until my vision adjusted as it had twice before, and I could make out the shapes of trees, leaves, and branches rushing by. At first, all I could hear were the leaves crunching beneath me, the sound of the air as I moved through it. Then I heard voices.

"We have to go back." It was Lena. I followed the sound into the trees.

"We can't. You know that."

Sunlight broke easily through the leaves. All I could see were boots—Lena's thrashed ones and John's heavy black ones. They were standing a few feet away.

Then I saw their faces. Lena's expression was stubborn. I knew that look. "Sarafine found them. They could be dead!"

John walked closer and winced, the same way he had when I saw them in the bedroom. It was an involuntary reflex, a reaction to some kind of pain. He looked down into her golden eyes. "Don't you mean Ethan?"

She avoided his gaze. "I mean all of them. Aren't you at least a little worried about Ridley? She disappeared. You don't think those two things could be connected?"

"What two things?"

Lena's shoulders tensed. "My cousin disappearing and Sarafine showing up out of nowhere?"

He reached out and took her hand, lacing his fingers between hers the way I used to. "She's always been somewhere, Lena. Your mother is probably the most powerful Dark Caster in the world. Why would she want to hurt Ridley, one of her own?"

"I don't know." Lena was shaking her head, her resolve weakening. "It's just…"

"What?"

"Even though we're not together, I don't want to see him get hurt. He tried to protect me."

"From what?"

From myself.

I heard the words, even though she didn't speak them. "From a lot of things. It was different then."

"You were pretending to be someone you weren't, trying to make everyone happy. Did you ever think he wasn't protecting you but holding you back?" I could feel my heart beating faster, my muscles tensing.

I was holding him back.

"You know, I had a Mortal girlfriend once."

Lena looked shocked. "You did?"

John nodded. "Yeah. She was sweet, and I loved her."

"What happened?" Lena was hanging on every word.

"It was too hard. She didn't understand what my life was like. That I don't always get to do whatever I want…" He sounded like he was telling the truth.

"Why couldn't you do what you wanted?"

"My childhood was what you would call strict. Straitjacket strict. Even the rules had rules."

Lena looked confused. "You mean about dating Mortals?"

John winced again, cringing this time. "No, it wasn't like that. The way I was raised was because I was different. The man who raised me was the only father I've ever known, and he didn't want me to hurt anyone."

"I don't want to hurt anyone either."

"You're different. I mean, we are."

John grabbed Lena's hand and pulled her next to him. "Don't worry. We'll find your cousin. She probably ran off with that drummer from Suffer." He was right about the drummer, just not the one he was betting on. Suffer? Lena was hanging out with John's kind, in places called Exile and Suffer. She thought that's what she deserved.

Lena didn't say anything else, but she didn't let go of his hand. I tried to force myself to follow them, but I couldn't. I didn't have control. That much was obvious from this bizarre vantage point, so close to the ground. I was always looking up at them. It didn't make any sense. But it didn't matter, because now I was running again, through a dark tunnel. Or was it a cave? I could smell the sea as the black walls streaked by.

I rubbed my eyes, surprised to be walking behind Liv instead of lying on the ground. It was crazy to think I could be watching Lena in one place and following Liv through the Tunnels at the same time. How was it possible?

The strange visions, with the off-kilter perspective and the flashing images—what was happening? Why was I able to see Lena and John? I had to figure it out.

I looked down at my hands. I wasn't holding anything except the Arclight. I tried to think back to the first time I saw Lena this way. It was in my bathroom, and I didn't have the Arclight then. The only thing I'd been touching was the sink. There had to be a common thread, but I couldn't see it.

Ahead, the tunnel opened up into a stone hall, where the entrances to four tunnels converged.

Link sighed. "Which way?"

I didn't answer. Because when I looked down at the Arclight, I saw something else just beyond it.

Lucille.

Sitting in the mouth of the tunnel opposite us, expectantly. I reached into my back pocket and pulled out the silver tag Aunt Prue had given me, with Lucille's name engraved on it. I could still hear Aunt Prue's voice.

See you still got that cat. I was just waitin' for the right time ta let her offa that clothesline. She knows a trick or two. You'll see.

In a split second, everything fell into place and I knew.

It was Lucille.

The images speeding past me every time I found my way to Lena and John. The ground so close, closer than it could ever be if I was standing. The strange vantage point, as if I was lying on my stomach looking up at them. It all made sense. The way Lucille kept disappearing and reappearing randomly. Only it wasn't random.

I tried to remember the times Lucille had vanished, ticking them off in my head one by one. The first time I saw Lena with John and Ridley, I was staring into my bathroom mirror. I didn't remember Lucille disappearing, but I remembered she was sitting on the front porch the next morning. Which didn't make any sense, because we never left her outside at night.

The second time, Lucille had bolted in Forsyth Park when we got to Savannah, and she didn't show up until after we left Bonaventure—after I had seen Lena and John when I was at Aunt Caroline's. And this time, Link noticed Lucille was gone when we came back down into the Tunnels, but now here she was, sitting in front of us, right after I had just seen Lena.

I wasn't the one seeing Lena.

Lucille was. She was tracking Lena, the same way we were following the maps or the lights or the pull of the moon. I was watching Lena through the cat's eyes, maybe the same way Macon had watched the world through Boo's. How was it possible? Lucille wasn't a Caster cat any more than I was a Caster.

Was she?

"What are you, Lucille?"

The cat looked me in the eye and cocked her head to the side.

"Ethan?" Liv was watching me. "Are you all right?"

"Yeah." I shot Lucille a meaningful look. She ignored me, sniffing the tip of her tail gracefully.

"You realize she's a cat." Liv was still staring at me curiously.

"I know."

"Just checking."

Great. Not only was I talking to a cat, but now I was talking *about* talking to a cat. "We should get going."

Liv took a deep breath. "Yes, about that. I'm afraid we can't."

"Why not?"

Liv motioned me over to where all of Aunt Prue's maps were laid out on the smooth dirt. "You see this mark here? That's the nearest Doorwell. It took me a while, but I've figured out loads of things about this map. Your aunt wasn't kidding. She must have spent years marking it up."

"The Doorwells are marked?"

"Looks that way on the map. See these red D's, with the little circles around them?" They were everywhere. "And these thin red lines? I believe they're closer to the surface. There's a pattern.

It seems the darker the color gets, the deeper underground."

I pointed to a grid of black lines. "You're saying these would be the deepest."

Liv nodded. "Possibly also the Darkest. The concept of Dark and Light territories within the Underground—it's groundbreaking, really. Certainly not widely known."

"So what's the problem?"

"This." She pointed to two words scribbled across the southernmost edge of the largest page. *L O C A   S I L E N T I A.*

I remembered the second word. It sounded like the one Lena said when she laid the Cast to keep me from telling her family she was leaving Gatlin. "You're saying the map is too quiet?"

Liv shook her head. "This is where the map *falls silent*, I'm afraid. Because we're at the end. We've reached the southern shore, which means we're off the map. *Terra incognita.*" She shrugged. "You know what they say. *Hic dracones sunt.*"

"Yeah, I hear that one a lot." I had no idea what she was talking about.

"'Here be dragons.' It's what sailors used to write on maps five hundred years ago, when the map ended but the ocean didn't."

"I'd rather face dragons than Sarafine." I looked at the place where Liv was tapping her finger. The web of Tunnels we had come from was as complex as any highway system. "So what now?"

"I'm out of ideas. I've done nothing but stare at this map since your aunt gave it to us, and I still don't know how to get to the Great Barrier. And I don't even know if I believe it's a real place." We stared at the map together. "I'm sorry. I know I've let you down—everyone, really."

I traced the outline of the coast with my finger until I came to Savannah, where the Arclight had stopped working. The red mark for the Savannah Doorwell lay just beneath the first L in *L O C A S I L E N T I A.* As I stared at the letters and the red marks around them, the missing pattern slowly surfaced. It reminded me of the Bermuda Triangle, some kind of void where everything magically disappeared. "*Loca silentia* doesn't mean 'where the map falls silent.'"

"It doesn't?"

"I think it means something more like radio silence, for a Caster anyway. Think about it. When did the Arclight stop working the first time?"

Liv thought back. "Savannah. Right after we" — she looked at me, blushing — "found everything in the attic."

"Exactly. Once we entered the territory marked *Loca silentia*, the Arclight stopped guiding us. I think we've been in a sort of supernatural no-fly zone, like the Bermuda Triangle, since we moved south of there."

Liv looked slowly from the map to me, working it out in her mind. When she finally spoke, she couldn't keep the excitement out of her voice. "The seam. We're at the seam. That's what the Great Barrier is."

"The seam of what?"

"The place where two universes meet." Liv looked at the dial on her wrist. "The Arclight could've been on some kind of magical overload this whole time."

I thought about Aunt Prue showing up when she did — and where she did. "I bet Aunt Prue knew we needed the maps. We had just entered the *Loca silentia* when she gave them to us."

"But the map stops, and the Great Barrier isn't on it. So how is anyone supposed to find it?" Liv sighed.

"My mom could. She knew how to find it without the star." I wished she were here right now, even a ghostly vision of her made from smoke and graveyard dirt and chicken bones.

"Did you read that in her papers?"

"No. It was something John said to Lena." I didn't want to think about it, even if the information was useful. "Where are we again, according to the map?"

She pointed. "Right there." We had reached the long curving line that followed the inlets of the southern shore. Caster connections wove their way together and apart until they met at the edge of the water like nerve endings.

"What are these little shapes? Islands?" Liv chewed on the end of her pen.

"Those are the Sea Islands."

Liv leaned over me. "Why do they look so familiar?"

"I've been wondering that, too. I thought it was from staring at the map for so long."

It was true. I knew those shapes, curving in and out like a group of lopsided clouds. Where had I seen them before?

I pulled a handful of papers—my mother's papers—out of my back pocket. There it was, tucked between pages. The sheet of vellum covered with a strange Caster design that looked like weird clouds.

She knew how to find it, without the star.

"Hold on—" I slid the vellum on top of the map. It was like tracing paper, thin as an onion skin on Amma's cutting board.

"I wonder..." I slipped the translucent sheet into place over the map, the outlines of each shape on the vellum lining up perfectly with the shape on the chart beneath it. Except for one, which materialized in a sort of ghostly silhouette, only appearing when the partial outline of the map grid met the partial outline of the vellum. Without both the vellum and the map, the lines looked like meaningless scribbles.

But when you held them just right, it all came together, and you could see the island.

Like two halves of a Caster key, or two universes stitched together for one common purpose.

The Great Barrier was hidden in the middle of a Mortal coastal chain. Of course it was.

I stared at the ink on the page, and beneath it.

There it was. The most powerful place in the Caster world, appearing through pen and paper as if by magic.

Hidden in plain sight.

No One's Son

The door itself wasn't that unusual.

Neither was the Doorwell leading up to it, or the curving passage we had followed to find our way here. Twist after turn through corridors built from crumbling rocks and dirt and splintering wood. This is what tunnels were supposed to feel like—damp and dark and tight. It was almost like the day Link and I followed a stray dog into one of the runoff tunnels in Summerville.

I guess the strangest thing was how ordinary everything seemed, now that we had figured out the secret to the map. Following it was the easy part.

Until now.

"That's it. It has to be." Liv looked up from the map. I stared past her to where a wooden staircase led up to streaks of light, forming the outline of a door in the darkness.

"You sure?"

She nodded and slid the map into her pocket.

"Then let's see what's out there." I climbed the steps to the door.

"Not so fast, Short Straw. What do you think is on the other side of that door?" Ridley was stalling. She looked as nervous as I felt.

Liv studied the door. "According to the legends, old magic, neither Light or Dark."

Ridley shook her head. "You have no idea what you're talking about, Keeper. Old magic is wild. It's infinite. Chaos in its purest form. Not exactly the combination for a happy ending to your little quest."

I moved closer to the door. Liv and Link were right behind me. "Come on, Rid. You want to help Lena or not?" Link's voice echoed off the walls.

"I was just saying…" I could hear the fear in Ridley's voice. I tried not to think about the last time she sounded this scared, when she faced Sarafine in the woods.

I pushed the door and it creaked, the worn wood bending and straining. Another try and it would open. We would be there, wherever there was. The Great Barrier.

I wasn't scared. I don't know why. But I wasn't thinking about entering a magical universe when I forced the door open. I was thinking about home. The wooden panel wasn't all that different from the Outer Door we found at the fairgrounds, under the Tunnel of Love. Maybe it was a sign—something from the beginning reappearing at the end. I wondered if it was a good omen or a bad one.

It didn't matter what was on the other side of the door.

Lena was waiting. She needed me, whether she knew it or not.

There was no turning back.

I leaned against the panel, and it swung open. The crack of light opened into a blinding field of white.

I stepped into the harsh light, the darkness behind me now. I could barely see the steps below me. I breathed in the air, heavy with salt and sour with brine.

Loca silentia. Now I understood. The moment we emerged from the darkness of the Tunnels into the broad, flat reflection of the water, there was only light and silence.

Slowly, my eyes began to adjust. We were on what looked like a rocky Lowcountry beach, covered in a spread of gray and white oyster shells, framed by an uneven row of palmettos. A splintered wooden walkway stretched along the perimeter of the shoreline facing the islands. We stood there now, the four of us, listening to what should have been the waves or the wind or even a gull in the sky. But the silence was so thick, it stopped us in our tracks.

The scene was perfectly ordinary and incredibly surreal, as vivid as any dream. The colors were too bright, the light too light. And in the far shadows beyond the shore, the dark was too dark. But everything was somehow beautiful here. Even the darkness. It was how the moment *felt* that silenced us. Magic was unfolding between us, encircling us like a rope, tying us to one another.

As I started toward the walkway, the rounded shores of the Sea Islands emerged in the distance. Beyond that was only dense, flat fog. Tufts of swamp grass rose from the water to form long, shallow banks rising in and out of the coastal mud. Along the beach, weathered wooden docks stretched out into the unbroken blue water until they disappeared into the black deep. The docks faded down the coast like weathered wooden fingers. Bridges to nowhere.

I looked up at the sky. Not a star in sight. Liv looked down at the selenometer whirring on her wrist, and tapped it. "None of these numbers mean anything anymore. We're on our own now." She unfastened her watch and slid it into her pocket.

"Guess so."

"What now?" Link bent to pick up a shell with his good arm and chucked it into the distance. The water swallowed it without a sound. Ridley stood next to him, streaks of pink hair whipping in the wind. On the far edge of the dock in front of us, the flag of South Carolina—with the silhouette of a palmetto and a crescent moon on a field of midnight blue—looked like a Caster flag as it fluttered from a spindly flagpole. When I looked at the flag more closely, I realized it had changed. This one had a seven-pointed star in the sky, next to the familiar crescent moon and palmetto silhouette. The Southern Star, right there on the flag, as if it had fallen out of the sky.

If this really was the seam where the Mortal and the magical touched, there was no sign of it here. I don't know what I was hoping for. All I had now were one too many stars on the state flag and a feeling of magic as thick as the salt in the air.

I joined the others at the far edge of the walkway. The wind had picked up, and the flag was whipping around the pole. It didn't make a sound.

Liv consulted the folded map. "If we're in the right place, it has to be between that island, beyond the buoy, and where we're standing."

"I think we're in the right place." I was sure of it.

"How do you know?"

"Remember that Southern Star you were telling me about?" I pointed to the flag. "Think about it. If you followed the star the whole way here, the star on the flag is exactly what you would be looking for. Some kind of sign you're at the right spot."

"Of course. The seven-pointed star." She examined the flag, touching the fabric as if she was allowing herself to believe it for the very first time.

There wasn't time for that. I knew we had to keep moving. "So what are we even looking for? Land? Or something man-made?"

"You mean this isn't it?" Link looked disappointed and shoved his garden shears back into his belt.

"I think we still have to cross over the water. It makes sense, really. Like crossing the river Styx to get to Hades." Liv flattened the map against her palm. "According to the map, we're looking for some kind of connector that will take us across the water to the Great Barrier itself. Like a sandbar or a bridge." She held the vellum over the map, and we all looked.

Link took them out of her hands. "Yeah, I see it. Kinda cool." He flipped the vellum up and down across the map. "Now you see it, now you don't." He dropped the map, and it fluttered into a mess of pages on the sand.

Liv bent to pick it up. "Careful with that! Are you completely mental?"

"You mean, like a genius?" Sometimes there was no point in Link and Liv talking at all. Liv pocketed Aunt Prue's map, and we started walking again.

Ridley picked up Lucille Ball. She hadn't said much since we left the Tunnels. Maybe now that she had been declawed, she preferred Lucille's company. Or maybe she was scared. She probably knew better than the rest of us the dangers that lay ahead.

I could feel the Arclight burning in my pocket. My heart began to pound, and my head began to spin.

What was it doing to me? Since we crossed over into the no man's land the map called *Loca silentia*, the light had stopped illuminating our path and started illuminating the past. Macon's past. It had become a conduit for the visions, a direct line I couldn't control. The visions were coming intermittently, interrupting the present with fragmented bits and pieces of Macon's past.

An old palmetto frond snapped loudly under one of Ridley's shoes. Then something else, and I felt myself slipping away—

Macon could feel it immediately when his shoulder snapped—the intense pain of his bones cracking. His skin tightened, as if it could no longer hold whatever was lurking inside him. The breath was sucked from his lungs, like he was being crushed. His vision began to blur, and he had the sensation he was falling, even though he could feel the rocks tearing at his flesh as his body seized on the ground.

The Transformation.

From this moment forth, he would not be able to walk among Mortals in the daylight. The sun would singe the flesh from his body. He wouldn't be able to ignore the urge to feed on the blood of Mortals. He was

*one of them now—another Blood Incubus in the long
line of killers on the Ravenwood Family Tree. A predator walking among his prey, waiting to feed.*

I was back again, as suddenly as I had gone.

I stumbled toward Liv, my head reeling. "We've got to get
going. Things are getting out of control."

"What things?"

"The Arclight—the things in my head," I said, unable to
explain it any better than that.

She nodded. "I thought it might get bad for you. I wasn't sure
if a Wayward would react more strongly to an intensely powerful place, being as sensitive to the pull of certain Casters as you
are. I mean, if you really are…" If I really was a Wayward. She
didn't have to say it.

"So you're saying you finally believe the Great Barrier is real?"

"No. Unless…" She pointed out past the farthest dock on
the horizon, where the skinniest, most splintered dock extended
past the others, so far that we couldn't see where it ended, except that it disappeared into fog. "That could be the bridge we're
looking for."

"Not much of a bridge." Link looked skeptical.

"Only one way to find out." I walked ahead of them.

As we picked our way across rotting boards and oyster
shells, I found myself slipping over and over. I was there, and I
wasn't. In and out. One minute, I could hear Ridley's and Link's
voices echoing as they bickered. The next, the fog blurred
around the edges, and I was pulled back into visions of Macon's

past. I knew there was something I was supposed to gain from the visions, but they were coming so quickly now it was impossible to figure out.

I thought about Amma. She would have said, "Everythin' means somethin'." I tried to imagine what she would have said next.

P. O. R. T. E. N. D. Seven down. As in, you be sure to pay attention to the *what now*, Ethan Wate, because that's gonna point the way to the *what's next*.

She was right, as usual—everything did mean something, didn't it? All the changes in Lena would have added up to the truth, if I had been able to see it. Even now, I tried to piece together my glimpses of the visions, to find the story they were trying to tell.

I didn't have time, though, because as we reached the bridge, I felt another surge, the walkway started to sway, and Ridley's and Link's voices faded—

The room was dark, but Macon didn't need light to see. The shelves were lined with books, as he had imagined they would be. Volumes on every aspect of American history, particularly the wars that had shaped this country—the Revolutionary War and the Civil War. Macon ran his fingers over the leather spines. These books were of no use to him now.

This was a different kind of war. A war among the Casters, waged within his own family.

He could hear footsteps above, the sound of the crescent key fitting into the lock. The door creaked, a slice of light escaping as the hatch in the ceiling opened. He wanted to reach out, offer his hand to help her down, but he didn't dare.

It had been years since he had seen or touched her.

They had only met in letters and between the covers of the books she left for him in the Tunnels. But he hadn't seen her or heard her voice in all that time. Marian had made sure of that. She stepped through the door cut into the ceiling, the light spilling into the room. Macon's breath caught in his throat. She was even more beautiful than he remembered. Her shiny brown hair was held away from her face by a pair of red reading glasses. She smiled.

"Jane." He hadn't said her name aloud in such a long time. It was like a song.

"No one's called me that since..." She looked down. "I use Lila now."

"Of course, I knew that."

Lila was visibly nervous, her voice shaky. "I'm sorry I had to come, but this was the only way." She avoided his eyes. It was too painful to look at him. "What I have to tell you—it's not something I could leave for you in the study, and I couldn't risk sending a message through the Tunnels."

Macon had a small study in the Tunnels, a reprieve from the self-induced exile of his solitary life in Gatlin. Sometimes Lila pressed messages between the pages of the books she left for him. The messages were never personal. They always related to her research in the Lunae Libri—possible answers to the questions they were both asking.

411

"It's good to see you." Macon took a step forward, and Lila stiffened. He looked hurt. "It's safe. I can control the urges now."

"It's not that. I—I shouldn't be here. I told Mitchell I was working late in the archive. I don't like to lie to him." Of course. She felt guilty. She was still as honest as Macon remembered.

"We are in an archive."

"Semantics, Macon."

Macon drew a heavy breath at the sound of his name from her lips. "What is so important that you would risk coming to me, Lila?"

"I've found something your father kept from you."

Macon's black eyes darkened at the mention of his father. "I haven't seen my father in years. Not since—" He didn't want to say what he was thinking. He hadn't seen his father since Silas had manipulated Macon into letting Lila go. Silas and his twisted views, his bigotry against Mortals and Casters alike. But Macon didn't mention any of that. He didn't want to make it harder for her. "The Transformation."

"There is something you need to know." Lila dropped her voice, as if what she was about to say could only be spoken in whispers. "Abraham is alive."

Macon and Lila didn't have time to react. There was a whirring sound, and a figure materialized in the darkness.

"Bravo. She really is much smarter than I had anticipated. Lila, is it?" Abraham was clapping loudly. "A tactical error on my part, but one your sister can correct easily enough. Wouldn't you agree, Macon?"

Macon's eyes narrowed. "Sarafine is not my sister."

Abraham adjusted his string tie. With his white beard and Sunday suit, he looked more like Colonel Sanders than what he was — a killer.

"There's no need to be nasty. Sarafine is your father's daughter, after all. It's a shame you two can't get along." Abraham walked casually toward Macon. "You know, I always hoped we would have a chance to meet. I'm sure once we talk, you'll understand your place in the Order of Things."

"I know my place. I made my choice and Bound myself to the Light long ago."

Abraham laughed loudly. "As if such a thing were even possible. You're a Dark creature by nature, an Incubus. This ridiculous alliance with the Light Casters, defending Mortals — it's inane. You belong with us, with your family." Abraham looked at Lila. "And for what? A Mortal woman you can never be with? One who is married to another man?"

Lila knew it wasn't true. Macon hadn't made his choice solely because of her, but she knew she was part of the reason. She faced Abraham, mustering all the courage she possessed. "We're going to find a way to end all that. Casters and Mortals should be able to do more than just coexist."

Abraham's expression changed. His face darkened, and he no longer looked like an aging Southern gentleman. He looked sinister and evil as he smiled at Macon. "Your father and Hunting — we hoped you would join

us. I warned Hunting that brothers are often a disap-
pointment. As are sons."

Macon turned his head sharply, his face changing to
mirror Abraham's. "I am no one's son."

"At any rate, I can't have you or this woman inter-
fering with our plans. It's unfortunate, really. You
turned your back on your family because you loved this
filthy Mortal, and yet she will die because you dragged
her into this." Abraham vanished, materializing in front
of Lila. "Oh, well." He opened his mouth, baring his
gleaming canines.

Lila covered her head with her arms and screamed,
waiting for the bite that never came. Macon materialized
between them. Lila felt the weight of his body as it
slammed into hers, throwing her backward. "Lila, run!"

For a second she was paralyzed, as the two of them
thrashed at each other. The sound was violent, as if the
earth was tearing itself apart. Lila watched as Macon
threw Abraham to the ground, his guttural cries rip-
ping through the air. Then she ran.

The sky swirled around me slowly, like someone hit REWIND. Liv
must have been talking to me, because I could see her mouth forming words, but I couldn't make them out. I closed my eyes again.

Abraham had killed my mother. She may have died by
Sarafine's hand, but it was Abraham who ordered it. I was sure
of it.

"Ethan? Can you hear me?" Liv's voice was frantic.

"I'm okay." I pushed myself up slowly. All three of them were staring down at me, and Lucille was sitting on my chest.

I was sprawled out on the rotting walkway. "Give it to me." Liv was trying to pry the Arclight out of my hands. "It's acting as some kind of metaphysical channel. You can't control it."

I didn't let go. It was a channel I couldn't afford to close.

"At least tell me what happened. Who was it now? Abraham or Sarafine?" Liv put her hand on my shoulder to steady me.

"It's fine. I don't want to talk about it."

Link stared down at me. "You okay, man?"

I blinked a few times. It was as if I was underwater, watching them through ripples. "I'm fine."

Ridley stood up a few feet away, wiping her hands on her skirt. "Famous last words."

Liv picked up her backpack and stood staring at the end of the almost endless dock. I pulled myself up next to her.

"This is it." I looked at Liv. "I can feel it."

I shivered. That's when I noticed she was shaking, too.

Sea Change

It felt like we had been walking forever, as if the bridge in front of us only got longer the closer we got. The farther we went, the less we saw. The air became brighter and heavier and wetter, until suddenly my feet came to the edge of the weathered planks—and what appeared to be an impenetrable wall of fog.

"Is this the Great Barrier?" I squatted down, touching the place where the wood ended. My hand felt nothing. No invisible Caster stairwell. Nothing.

"Wait, what if this is like a dangerous force field or some kind of poisonous smoke?" Link pulled out his shears and gently pushed them into the mist, then yanked them back, perfectly intact. "Or maybe not. Still, pretty creepy. How do we know if we go through that we're going to be able to come back?" As usual, Link was only saying what the rest of us were thinking.

I stood at the end of the bridge, facing the nothingness. "I'm going through."

Liv looked insulted. "You can barely walk. Why you?"

Because this whole thing is my fault. Because Lena was my girlfriend. Because I might be a Wayward, whatever that is.

I looked away and found myself looking at Lucille, her claws digging into Ridley's shirt. Lucille Ball was no fan of the water. "Ouch!" Ridley put her down. "Stupid cat."

Lucille took a few deliberate steps across the wood, turning to look at me. She cocked her head.

With a flick of her tail, she took off and was gone.

"Because." Turns out, I couldn't explain. Liv shook her head, and without waiting for anyone else, I followed Lucille into the clouds.

I was in the Great Barrier, between universes, and for one second I didn't feel like a Caster or a Mortal. All I felt was magic.

I could feel it and hear it and smell it, the air thick with sound and salt and water. The shore at the end of the bridge was pulling at me, and I was overwhelmed with an unbearable sense of longing. I wanted to be there with Lena. More than that, I just wanted to *be there*. I didn't seem to have a reason or logic for it, apart from the intensity of the longing itself.

I wanted to be there more than anything else.

I didn't want to choose one world. I wanted to be part of both. I didn't want to see only one side of the sky. I wanted to see it all.

I hesitated. Then I took a single step and walked out of the fog and into the unknown.

Out of the Light

Cold air hit me, sending goose bumps up my arms.

By the time I opened my eyes, the brightness and the fog had disappeared. All I could see was a blur of moonlight pouring into a hole in the jagged cave in the distance. The full moon was clear and luminous.

I wondered if I was looking at the Seventeenth Moon.

I closed my eyes and tried to experience the intense rush I'd felt the moment before, when I was between worlds.

It was there, behind everything else. The feeling. The electricity of the air, as if this side of the world was full of life I couldn't see but could sense all around me.

"Come on." Ridley was behind me, pulling Link, whose eyes were squeezed shut. Ridley let go of his hand. "You can open your eyes now, Super Stud."

Liv appeared after them, breathless. "That was brilliant."

She came up beside me, barely a golden hair loose from her braids. She watched the waves crash against the rocks in front of us, her eyes sparkling. "Do you think we're —"

I answered before she had a chance to finish. "We've crossed into the Great Barrier."

Which meant Lena was here somewhere, and so was Sarafine.

And who knows what else.

Lucille was sitting on a rock, casually licking her paw. I saw something next to her, snagged between two rocks.

It was Lena's necklace.

"She's here." I bent down to pick it up, my hand shaking un- controllably. I had never seen her without it, not once. The silver button was shining through the sand, the wire star caught in the loop where she had wrapped the red string. These weren't just her memories. They were our memories, everything we had shared since we met. The evidence of every happy moment she'd ever experienced in her life. Tossed aside like all the other lost bits of broken shells and tangled seaweed that washed up on the beach.

If it was some kind of sign, it wasn't good.

"Did you find something, Short Straw?"

Reluctantly, I opened my hand and held it out for them to see. Ridley gasped. Liv didn't recognize the necklace. "What is it?"

Link looked at the ground. "It's Lena's necklace."

"Maybe she lost it," Liv said innocently.

"No!" Ridley's voice was rising. "Lena never took it off. Not once in her whole life. She couldn't have lost it. She would've noticed the second it slipped off."

Liv shrugged. "Maybe she noticed. Maybe she didn't care."

Ridley lunged at Liv, Link holding her back by her waist. "Don't say that! You don't know anything! Tell her, Short Straw."

But even I didn't know anymore.

As we picked our way along the shore, we approached a rocky line of uneven coastal caves. Tidewater pooled in their sandy floors, and jagged rock walls kept everything in shadow. The pathway between the rocks seemed to be leading us toward a particular cave. The ocean crashed around us, and I felt like it could wash us away in a second.

There was real power here. The rock was humming under my feet, and even the light of the moon seemed alive with it.

I jumped from one rock to the next until I was high enough to see past the rocky outcroppings of the coastal caves. The others climbed after me, trying to keep up.

"There." I pointed at a large cavern, just beyond the caves surrounding us. The moon was shining directly above it, illuminating an enormous jagged crack in the ceiling.

And something else.

In the moonlight, I could barely make out figures moving in the shadows. Hunting's Blood pack. There was no mistaking them.

No one said anything. This wasn't a mystery to solve anymore. It was quickly becoming reality. It was a cave most likely filled with Dark Casters, Blood Incubuses, and a Cataclyst.

All we had was each other and the Arclight.

The realization hit Link hard. "Face it. The four of us are dead." He looked down at Lucille, who was licking her paws. "With one dead cat."

He had a point. From what we could see, there was only one

way in or out. The entrance to the cave was heavily guarded, and what waited inside was likely to be an even more formidable threat.

"He's right, Ethan. My uncle's probably in there with his boys. Without my powers, we're not going to survive the Blood pack again. We're useless Mortals. All we had going for us was that stupid shiny stone." Ridley kicked at the wet sand, as hopeless as ever.

"Not useless, Rid." Link sighed. "Just Mortals. You'll get used to it."

"Shoot me if I do."

Liv stared out at the sea. "Maybe this is as far as we can go. Even if we could get past the Blood pack, to take on Sarafine would be…" Liv didn't finish, but we all knew what she was thinking.

A death wish. Insanity. Suicide.

I looked out into the wind, the darkness, and the night.

Where are you, L?

I could see the moonlight pouring into the cave. Lena was out there somewhere waiting for me. She didn't answer, but that didn't stop me from reaching for her.

I'm coming.

"Maybe Liv's right, and we should think about goin' back. Gettin' some help." I noticed Link's breathing was labored. He had been trying to hide it, but he was still in pain.

I had to own up to what I was doing to my friends, the people who cared about me. "We can't go back. I mean, I can't."

The Seventeenth Moon wasn't going to wait, and Lena was running out of time. The Arclight brought me here for a reason. I thought about what Marian said at my mother's grave when she gave it to me.

In Light there is Dark, and in Dark there is Light.

It was something my mom used to say. I pulled the Arclight out of my pocket. It was turning a brilliant green, incredibly bright. Something was happening. As I turned it over and over in my hands, I remembered everything. It was all there, looking back at me from the surface of the stone.

Sketches of Ravenwood and Macon's family tree, spread across my mother's table in the archive.

I stared at the Arclight, seeing things for the first time. As I did, images rose to the surface of my mind, and the stone.

Marian handing me my mother's most treasured possession, standing between the graves of two people who finally found a way to be together.

Maybe Ridley was right. All we had going for us was this stupid shiny stone.

Then a ring, twisting on a finger.

Mortals alone were no match for Dark power.

A picture of my mother, in the shadows.

Could the answer have been in my pocket all along?

And a pair of black eyes that reflected back my own.

We weren't alone. We never were. The visions had laid it all out for me from the beginning. The images vanished as suddenly as they had appeared, replaced by words, the second I thought them.

In the Arc there is power, and in the power there is Night.

"The Arclight—it's not what we thought." My voice echoed off the rock walls surrounding us.

Liv was surprised. "What are you talking about?"

"It's not a compass. It never was."

I held it up so they could all see. As we watched, the Arclight shone, brighter and brighter, until it was eclipsed in a perfect circle of light. Like a tiny star. I could no longer see the stone within the light.

"What is it doing?" Liv breathed.

The Arclight, which I took so innocently from Marian at my mother's grave, wasn't an object of power, not for me.

It was for Macon.

I held the Arclight up higher. In the iridescent moonlight of the shallow tidal cave, the dark water around my feet glittered. Even the tiniest flecks of quartz studded in the rock walls caught the light. In the darkness, the sphere seemed to ignite. I could see the glow of the round, pearlized surface revealing the swirling colors of a hidden interior. Violet churned into somber greens, then burst into vibrant yellows, which deepened into oranges and reds. In that second, I understood.

I wasn't a Keeper, or a Caster, or a Seer.

I wasn't like Marian or my mother. It wasn't for me to keep the lore and the history or protect the books and the secrets that made up so much of the Caster world. I wasn't like Liv, charting the uncharted, measuring the immeasurable. I wasn't Amma. It wasn't for me to see what no one else could or to communicate with the Greats. More than anything, I was nothing like Lena. I couldn't eclipse the moon, bring down the skies, or kick up the earth. I could never convince anyone to jump off a bridge, like Ridley could. And I was nothing like Macon.

In the back of my mind, I had been searching for how I fit into the story, my story with Lena. Hoping I could fit into it at all.

But my story had found its way to me through all of them. Now, at the end of what seemed like a lifetime in the darkness and confusion of the Tunnels, I knew what to do. I knew my part.

Marian was right. I was the Wayward. It was my job to find what was lost.

Who was lost.

I rolled the Arclight to my fingertips and released it. The stone hung in the air.

"What the—" Link staggered closer.

I pulled the folded yellowed page out of my back pocket. The one I had ripped from my mother's journal and carried all this way, without a reason. Or so I thought.

The Arclight cast a silver light around the cave as it hovered. I stepped closer to it and held up the paper so I could speak the Cast from the page of my mother's journal, even though it was in Latin. I pronounced the words carefully.

"In Luce Caecae Caligines sunt,
Et in Caliginibus, Lux.
In Arcu imperium est,
Et in imperio, Nox."

"Of course," Liv whispered, moving closer to the light. "The Cast. *Ob Lucem Libertas.* Freedom in Light." Liv looked at me. "Finish it."

I turned the paper over. There was nothing on the other side.

"That's all there is."

Liv's eyes widened. "You can't leave it undone. It's incredibly dangerous. The power of an Arclight, let alone a Ravenwood Arclight, it could kill us. It could kill..."

"You have to do it."

"I can't, Ethan. You know I can't."

"Liv. Lena's going to die—you, me, Link, Ridley—we all

424

are. We've come as far as Mortals can go. We can't do the rest alone." I put my hand on her shoulder.

"Ethan." She whispered my name, just my name, but I heard the words she couldn't say almost as clearly as I heard Lena's voice when we Kelted. Liv and I had a connection all our own. It wasn't magic. It was something very human, and very real. Liv might not like what had unfolded between us, but she understood it. She understood me, and a part of me believed she always would. I wished things could have been different, that Liv could have everything she wanted at the end of all this. The things that had nothing to do with lost stars and Caster skies. But Liv wasn't where my road was taking me. She was part of the path itself.

She looked past me to the Arclight, still glowing in front of us. Her silhouette was framed in light so bright it looked like she was standing in front of the sun. She reached for the Arclight, and I remembered my dream, the dream of Lena reaching out to me from the darkness.

Two girls who were as different as the sun and the moon. Without one, I could never have found my way back to the other.

In Light there is Dark, and in Dark there is Light.

Liv touched the Arclight with a single finger and began to speak.

> *"In Illo qui Vinctus est,*
> *Libertas Patefacietur.*
> *Spirate denuo, Caligines.*
> *E Luce exi."*

She was crying, watching the ball of light as tears streaked down the sides of her face. She forced out every word, as if they were being etched into her, but she didn't stop.

"In the One who is Bound
Freedom will be Found.
Live again, Darkness,
Come out of the Light."

Liv's voice faltered. She closed her eyes and spoke the final words slowly into the night between us.

"Come out. Come—"

The words broke off. She held her hand out to me, and I took it. Link limped over to us, and Ridley clutched his arm on the other side. Liv's entire body was shaking. With every word, she was falling farther from her sacred duty and her dream. She had taken a side. She had Cast herself into the story that was only hers to Keep. When this was over, if we survived, Liv would no longer be a Keeper-in-Training. Her sacrifice was her gift, the one thing that gave her life meaning.

I couldn't imagine how that would feel.

We became four voices. There was no turning back.

"*E Luce exi!* Come out of the Light!"

The blast was so cataclysmic, the rock beneath my feet shot into the wall behind me. All four of us were thrown to the ground. I could taste the wet sand and the saltwater in my mouth, but I knew. My mom had tried to tell me, but I hadn't been able to hear.

In the cave, framed by rock and moss and sea and sand, was a being made of nothing more than a mist of shadow and light. At first, I could see the rocks behind it, as if it was an apparition. The water washed through it, and it didn't touch the ground.

Then the light stretched into a shape, the shape into a form, the form into a man. His hands became hands, his body became a body, and his face, a face.

Macon's face.

I heard my mother's words. *He's with you now.*

Macon opened his eyes and looked at me. *Only you can redeem him.*

He was dressed in the burnt clothes from the night he died. Only something was different.

His eyes were green.

Caster green.

"It's good to see you, Mr. Wate."

Flesh and Blood

Macon!"

It was all I could do not to fling my arms around him. He, on the other hand, looked at me calmly, brushing off some of the burnt grit from his dinner jacket. His eyes were unsettling. I was used to the glassy black eyes of Macon Ravenwood the Incubus, the eyes that regarded you with nothing but your own reflection. Now he was standing in front of me, as green-eyed as any Light Caster. Ridley stared, but didn't utter a sound. It wasn't often you saw Ridley speechless.

"Much obliged, Mr. Wate. Much obliged." Macon rolled his neck back and forth, uncoiling his arms, as if he was waking up from a long nap.

I bent down and picked up the Arclight, lying in the sandy dirt. "I was right. You were in the Arclight all along." I thought about how many times I'd held it in my hand and relied on it to guide me. How familiar the warmth of the stone had felt.

Link was having trouble coming to grips with the idea that Macon was alive, too. Without thinking, he reached out to touch him. Macon's hand flew up and grabbed Link's arm. Link flinched. "So sorry, Mr. Lincoln. I'm afraid my reflexes are a bit — reflexive. I haven't gotten out much lately."

Link rubbed his arm. "You didn't have to do that, Mr. Ravenwood. I just wanted, you know, I thought you were —"

"What? A Sheer? A Vex, perhaps?"

Link shivered. "You tell me, sir."

Macon extended his arm. "Go ahead, then. Be my guest."

Link stuck out his hand tentatively, as if he was about to hold it over a candle on a birthday dare. His finger came within a millimeter of Macon's ragged jacket and stopped.

Macon sighed, rolling his eyes, and tapped Link's hand against his chest. "See? Flesh and blood. Something we have in common now, Mr. Lincoln."

"Uncle Macon?" Ridley crept up to him, finally ready to face him. "Is it really you?"

He looked deep into her blue eyes. "You've lost your powers."

She nodded, her eyes brimming with tears. "So have you."

"Some of them, yes, but I suspect I've gained others." He reached for her hand, but she pulled away. "It's impossible to tell. I'm still in the midst of it." He smiled. "Sort of like being a teenager. Twice."

"But your eyes are green."

Macon shook his head, flexing his hands. "True. My life as an Incubus is over, but the Transition is not complete. Although my eyes are those of a Light Caster, I can still feel

Darkness within me. It has not been fully exorcised, yet."

"I'm not Transitioning. I'm nothing, a Mortal." She said the word like it was a curse, and the sadness in her voice was real. "I don't have a place in the Order of Things anymore."

"You're alive."

"I don't feel like myself. I'm powerless."

Macon weighed this in his mind, as if he was trying to determine her present state as much as she was. "You may be in the midst of a Transition of your own, unless this is one of my sister's more impressive tricks."

Ridley's eyes lit up. "Does that mean my powers might come back?"

Macon studied her blue eyes. "I think Sarafine is too cruel for that. I only meant that you might not be fully Mortal yet. Darkness does not leave us as easily as we would hope." Macon pulled her awkwardly to his chest, and she buried her face in his jacket, like a twelve-year-old. "It's not easy to be Light when you've been Dark. It's almost too much to ask of anyone."

I tried to quiet the torrent of questions racing through my mind, and settled for the first. "How?"

Macon turned from Ridley, his green eyes burning into me with their newfound light. "Could you be more specific, Mr. Wate? How am I not resting in twenty-seven thousand distinct fragments of ash in an urn within the Ravenwood family vault? How am I not rotting under a lemon tree in the sodden prestige of His Garden of Perpetual Peace? How did I come to find myself imprisoned in a small crystalline ball in your grimy pocket?"

"Two," I said without thinking.

"I beg your pardon?"

"There are two lemon trees over your grave."

"How very generous. One would have sufficed." Macon smiled tiredly, which was pretty remarkable, considering he'd spent four months in a supernatural prison the size of an egg. "Or are you perhaps wondering how is it that I died and you lived? Because I have to tell you, as far as *how*s go, that's a story your neighbors on Cotton Bend would be talking about for a lifetime."

"Except you didn't, sir. Die, I mean."

"You are correct, Mr. Wate. I am, and have always been, very much alive. In a manner of speaking."

Liv stepped forward tentatively. Even though she would probably never become a Keeper now, there was still a Keeper inside her seeking answers. "Mr. Ravenwood, may I ask you a question, sir?"

Macon tilted his head slightly. "Who might you be, dear? I imagine it was your voice I heard calling me from the Arclight."

Liv blushed. "It was, sir. My name is Olivia Durand, and I was training with Professor Ashcroft. Before…" Her voice dwindled.

"Before you Cast the *Ob Lucem Libertas*?"

Liv nodded, ashamed. Macon looked pained, then smiled at her. "Then you gave up a great deal to save me, Miss Olivia Durand. I am in your debt, and, as I always repay my debts, I would be honored to answer a question. At the very least." Even after being trapped all those months, Macon was still a gentleman.

"Obviously, I know how you got out of the Arclight, but how did you get in? It's impossible for an Incubus to imprison himself, especially when, by all accounts, you were dead." Liv was right. He couldn't have done it alone. Someone had to have helped him, and the minute the ball released him, I knew who it was.

It was the one person we both loved as much as Lena, even in death.

My mother—who had loved books and old things, nonconformity and history and complexity. Who had loved Macon so much she walked away when he asked her to, even though she couldn't bear to leave him. Even though a part of her never had.

"It was her, wasn't it?"

Macon nodded. "Your mother was the only one who knew about the Arclight. I gave it to her. Any Incubus would have killed her to destroy it. It was our secret, one of our last."

"Did you see her?" I looked out at the sea, blinking hard.

Macon's expression changed. I could see the pain in his face. "Yes."

"Did she seem..." What? Happy? Dead? Herself?

"Beautiful as ever, your mother. Beautiful as the day she left us."

"I saw her, too." I thought about Bonaventure Cemetery and felt the familiar knot in my throat.

"But how is that possible?" Liv wasn't trying to challenge him, but she didn't understand. None of us did.

Macon's face was full of grief. It wasn't any easier for him to talk about my mom than it was for me. "I think you'll find the impossible is possible more often than we think, particularly in the Caster world. But if you would care to take one last trip with me, I can show you." He opened his hand to me, offering Liv the other. Ridley stepped forward and closed her hand around mine, and hesitantly Link limped over, completing the circle.

Macon looked over at me, and before I could read his expression, the air was filled with smoke —

Macon tried to hold on, but he was blacking out. He could see the ebony sky above him, streaked with orange flames. He couldn't see Hunting as he fed, but he could feel his brother's teeth in his shoulder. When Hunting had his fill, he let Macon's body drop to the ground.

When Macon opened his eyes again, Lena's grandmother, Emmaline, was kneeling over him. He could feel the heat of her healing power as it coursed through his body. Ethan was there, too. Macon tried to speak, but he didn't know if they could hear him. Find Lena, that's what he wanted to say. Ethan must have heard him, because he took off into the smoke and fire.

The boy was so much like Amarie, so stubborn and fearless. He was so much like his mother, loyal and honest, and bound for the heartbreak that came from loving a Caster. Macon was still thinking about Jane when his mind faded.

When Macon opened his eyes again, the fire was gone. The smoke, the roaring of flames and ammunition — it was all gone. He felt himself drifting in the darkness. It wasn't like Traveling. This void had weight. It was pulling him through. Yet when he reached out, he could see that his hand was hazy, only partially materialized.

He was dead.

Lena must have made the Choice. She had chosen to go Light. Even in the darkness, knowing the fate of an

Incubus in the Otherworld, a sense of calm washed over him. It was finished.

"Not yet. Not for you."

Macon turned, recognizing her voice immediately. Lila Jane. She was luminous in the abyss, shimmering and beautiful. "Janie. There's so much I have to tell you."

Jane shook her head, her brown hair falling over her shoulder. "There's no time."

"There's nothing but time."

Jane stretched out her hand, her fingers glimmering. "Take my hand."

As soon as Macon touched her, the darkness began to bleed into colors and light. He could see images, familiar shapes and forms swimming around him, but he couldn't anchor them. Then he realized where they were. The archive, Jane's special place.

"Jane, what's happening?" He saw her reach out, but everything was blurry and unclear. Then he heard the words, the words he had taught her.

"In these walls with no time or space, I Bind your body and from this Earth erase."

There was something in her hand. The Arclight. "Jane, don't do it! I want to be here with you."

She was floating before him, already beginning to fade. "I promised if the time came, I would use it. I'm keeping my promise. You can't die. They need you." She was gone now, a voice, nothing else. "My son needs you."

Macon tried to tell her everything he had failed to say in life, but it was too late. He could feel the pull of

the Arclight already, impossible to break. As he spun
into the abyss, he heard her seal his fate.

"Comprehende, Liga, Cruci Fige.
Capture, Cage, and Crucify."

Macon dropped my hand, and the vision released us. I held it in my mind, unable to let her go. My mom had saved him, using the weapon Macon had given her to use against him. She had given up the chance for them to finally be together, because of me. Had she known he was our only chance?

When I opened my eyes, Liv was crying, and Ridley was trying to pretend she wasn't. "Oh, please. Enough with the drama." A tear leaked onto her cheek.

Liv wiped her eyes, sniffling. "I had no idea a Sheer was capable of anything like that."

"You would be surprised what we are capable of when the situation warrants it." Macon clapped his hand on my shoulder. "Isn't that right, Mr. Wate?"

I knew he was trying to thank me. But as I looked around our broken circle, I didn't feel like I deserved thanks. Ridley had lost her powers, Link was wincing in pain, and Liv had destroyed her future. "I didn't do anything."

Macon's hand tightened on my shoulder, forcing me to face him. "You made yourself see what most would have overlooked. You brought me here; you brought me back. You accepted your fate as a Wayward and found the way here. None of that could have been easy." He looked around the cave at Ridley, Link, and Liv. His eyes lingered a moment on Liv, and then his eyes locked on mine. "For anyone."

Including Lena.

I almost couldn't stand to tell him, but I wasn't sure if he knew. "Lena thinks she killed you."

Macon didn't speak for a second, but when he did, his voice was even and controlled. "Why would she think that?"

"Sarafine stabbed me that night, but you died. Amma told me. But Lena can't forgive herself, and it's...changed her." I wasn't making sense, but there was so much Macon needed to know. "I think she may have made a choice in her heart without realizing it."

"She didn't." Macon dismissed me.

"It was *The Book of Moons*, Mr. Ravenwood." Liv couldn't help herself. "Lena was desperate to save Ethan, and she used the Book. It made a trade, your life for his. Lena had no way of knowing what would happen. The Book can't be properly controlled, which is why it's not meant to be kept in Caster hands." Liv sounded even more like a Caster librarian than usual.

Macon tilted his head slightly. "I see. Olivia?"

"Yes, sir?"

"With all due respect, we've no time for a Keeper. This day will require certain actions best left unkept. At the very least, untold. Do you understand?"

Liv nodded. Her expression said she understood more than he knew.

"She's not a Keeper, not anymore." Liv had saved his life and destroyed her own in the process. She deserved Macon's respect, at the very least.

"Not likely, after this," she sighed.

I listened to the waves crashing, wishing they could carry my thoughts out to sea with them. "Everything's changed."

Macon's eyes flickered again to Liv, then returned to me. "Nothing's changed. Nothing important. It could, but it hasn't yet."

Link cleared his throat. "But what can we do? I mean, look at us." Link paused. "They've got a whole army a Incubuses and who knows what else down there."

Macon took stock of us. "What do we have? A powerless Siren, a renegade Keeper, a lost Wayward, and...you, Mr. Lincoln. A motley but resourceful crew, indeed." Lucille meowed. "And yes, you, Ms. Ball."

I realized what a train wreck we were, hammered, dirty, and exhausted.

"Yet, somehow you made it this far. And you released me from the Arclight, which was no small feat."

"Are you sayin' you think we can take them?" Link had the same look on his face as the one he had when Earl Petty started a fight with the whole Summerville High football team.

"I'm saying we don't have time to stand here and chat, as much as I enjoy your fine company. I have more than a few things to take care of, my niece being first and foremost." Macon turned to me. "Wayward, show us the way."

Macon took a step toward the mouth of the cave, and his legs collapsed under him. A cloud of dust rose where he fell. I looked at him, sitting in the dirt in his charred dinner jacket. He hadn't recovered from whatever happened in the Arclight. I hadn't exactly called in the Marines. We needed a plan B.

⊰ 6.20 ⊱

Army of One

Macon was insistent. He was in no condition to go anywhere, but he knew we didn't have a lot of time, and he was determined to go with us. I didn't argue, because even a weakened Macon Ravenwood was more resourceful than four powerless Mortals. I hoped.

I knew where we had to go. The moonlight was still pouring through the ceiling of the coastal cave in the distance. By the time Liv and I helped Macon navigate the shoreline leading to the moonlit cave, one painstaking step at a time, he had finished asking me his questions and I was asking him mine. "Why would Sarafine call up the Seventeenth Moon now?"

"The sooner Lena is Claimed, the sooner the Dark Casters will have secured their fate. Lena is growing stronger every day. They know the longer they wait, the more likely she is to make up her own mind. If they know the circumstances surrounding my *demise*, I imagine they want to take advantage of Lena's vulnerable state."

I remembered when Hunting told me that Lena killed Macon. "They know."

"It's of the utmost importance that you tell me everything."

Ridley fell into step alongside Macon. "Ever since Lena's birthday, Sarafine's been summoning power from the Dark Fire to become powerful enough to raise the Seventeenth Moon."

"You mean that crazy bonfire she started back in the woods?" The way Link said it, I was pretty sure he imagined a trash can burning by the lake at night.

Ridley shook her head. "That wasn't the Dark Fire. It was a manifestation, like Sarafine. She created it."

Liv nodded. "Ridley's right. The Dark Fire is the source of all magical power. If Casters channel their collective energy back into the source, it becomes exponentially more powerful. A sort of supernatural atomic bomb."

"You mean it's gonna blow up?" Link didn't look as sure about hunting down Sarafine now.

Ridley rolled her eyes. "It won't blow up, Genius. But the Dark Fire can do some serious damage."

I looked up at the full moon and the beam of moonlight creating a direct path into the cavern. The moon wasn't feeding the fire. The power of the Dark Fire was being channeled into the moon. That's how Sarafine called the moon out of time.

Macon was watching Ridley carefully. "Why would Lena agree to come here?"

"I convinced her, me and this guy John."

"Who is John, and how does he fit into all this?"

Ridley was biting her purple nails. "He's an Incubus. I mean, a hybrid, anyway. Part Incubus and part Caster, and he's really powerful. He was obsessed with the Great Barrier and how everything would be perfect if we got here."

"Did this boy know Sarafine would be here?"

"No. He's a true believer. Thinks the Great Barrier will solve all his problems, like it's some kind of Caster Utopia." She rolled her eyes.

I could see the anger in Macon's eyes. The green reflected his emotions in a way the black never had. "How is it that you and a boy who isn't even a full-blooded Incubus were able to talk Lena into something so absurd?"

Ridley looked away. "It wasn't hard. Lena was in a bad place. I think she believed there was nowhere else for her to go." It was hard to look at the blue-eyed Ridley without wondering how she felt about the Dark Caster she was only a few days ago.

"Even if Lena felt responsible for my death, why would she think she belonged with the two of you, a Dark Caster and a Demon?" Macon didn't say it with spite, but I could tell the words stung Ridley.

"Lena hates herself and thinks she's going Dark." Ridley glanced at me. "She wanted to go to a place where she wouldn't hurt anyone. John promised he'd be there for her when no one else would."

"I would have been there for her." My voice echoed off the rock walls surrounding us.

Ridley looked right at me. "Even if she went Dark?"

It all made sense. Lena was guilt-ridden and tormented, and John was there with all the answers, in ways I couldn't be.

I thought about how long he and Lena had been alone together, how many nights, how many dark Tunnels. John wasn't a Mortal. Her touch wouldn't kill him with its intensity. John and Lena could do anything they wanted—all the things Lena and I could never do. An image crept into my mind, the two of them curled up together in the darkness. The way Liv and I had been in Savannah.

"There's something else." I had to tell him. "Sarafine didn't do this alone. Abraham has been helping her."

Something passed across Macon's face, but I couldn't pin it down. "Abraham. That's no surprise."

"The visions have changed, too. When I was in them, it seemed like Abraham could see me."

Macon lost his footing, nearly tripping me. "Are you certain?"

I nodded. "He said my name."

Macon looked at me the way he had the night of the winter formal, Lena's first dance. As if he felt sorry for me, the things I had to do, the responsibilities that fell to me. He never understood I didn't care.

Macon kept talking, and I tried to focus. "I had no idea things had progressed so quickly. You must exercise extreme caution, Ethan. If Abraham has established a connection with you, then he can see you as clearly as you can see him."

"You mean, outside of the visions?" The idea of Abraham watching my every move wasn't a comforting thought.

"At this point, I don't have an answer. But until I do, be careful."

"I'll get right on that. After we fight an army of Incubuses to rescue Lena." The more we talked about it, the more impossible it felt.

Macon whipped around to face Ridley. "Is this boy John involved with Abraham?"

"I don't know. Abraham's the one who convinced Sarafine she could raise the Seventeenth Moon." Ridley looked miserable and exhausted and filthy.

"Ridley, I need you to tell me everything you know."

"I wasn't that high on the food chain, Uncle Macon. I never even met him. Everything I know came from Sarafine." It was hard to believe Ridley was the same girl who almost convinced my father to jump off a balcony. She looked so sad and broken.

"Sir?" Liv's voice was tentative. "Something's been bothering me ever since we met John Breed. We have thousands of Caster and Incubus family trees in the *Lunae Libri*, hundreds of years of history. How is it that this one person comes along out of nowhere, and there's no record of him? Of John Breed, I mean."

"I was wondering precisely the same thing." Macon started walking again, leaning heavily to one side. "But he's not an Incubus."

"Not strictly speaking," Liv answered.

"He's as strong as one." I kicked at the rocks under my feet.

"Whatever. I could take him." Link shrugged.

Ridley fell into step next to us. "He doesn't feed, Uncle M. I would have seen it."

"Interesting."

Liv nodded. "Very."

"Olivia, if you don't mind—" He held out his arm to her. "Have there been any cases of hybrids on your side of the Atlantic?"

Liv slipped her shoulder underneath Macon's arm, taking my place. "Hybrids? I should hope not...."

As Liv continued along the rocks with Macon, I lagged behind. I pulled Lena's necklace out of my pocket. I let the charms

442

roll around in my palm, but they were tangled and meaningless without her. The necklace was heavier than I imagined, or maybe it was the weight of my conscience.

We stood on a cliff above the entrance to the cave, surveying the scene. The sea cave was huge, formed completely from black volcanic rock. The moon was so low, it looked like it could drop right out of the sky. A pack of Incubuses guarded the mouth of the cave as waves crashed on the black rocks in front of them, sending shallow rushes of water across their boots.

The moonlight wasn't the only thing attracted to the cave. A host of Vexes, swirling black shadows, flowed up from the water and down from the sky. They were cycling through the cave's entrance and the opening in the ceiling, forming some kind of supernatural waterwheel. I watched as one Vex rose up from the water, a whirling shadow reflected perfectly in the sea below.

Macon pointed to their ghostly forms. "Sarafine is using them to fuel the Dark Fire."

An army. What chance did we have? It was worse than I thought, and the possibility of saving Lena more hopeless. At least we had Macon. "What are we going to do?"

"I'm going to try to help you get inside, but from there you'll have to find Lena. You are the Wayward, after all." Help us get inside? Was he joking?

"You're making it sound like you aren't going with us."

Macon slid down the rock until he was sitting on the overhang. "That assumption is correct."

I didn't try to hide my anger. "Are you kidding? You said it yourself. You think we're gonna save Lena without you—a Siren who's lost her powers, a Mortal who never had any, a librarian, and me? Against a pack of Blood Incubuses and enough Vexes to take down the Air Force? Seriously? Tell me you have some kind of a plan."

Macon looked up at the moon. "I am going to help you, but it will be from here. Trust me, Mr. Wate. This is the way it has to be."

I stood there staring at him. He was serious. He was going to send us in alone. "If that was supposed to be reassuring, it wasn't."

"There is only one battle that awaits down there, and it doesn't belong to me or to your friends. It's yours, son. You're a Wayward, a Mortal with great purpose. You've been fighting as long as I've known you—the self-serving ladies of the DAR, the Disciplinary Committee, the Sixteenth Moon, even your friends. I have no doubt you will find a way."

I had been fighting all year, but it didn't make me feel any better. Mrs. Lincoln might look like she could suck the life right out of you, but she couldn't actually do it. What waited below us was a different story.

Macon drew something out of his pocket and pressed it into my hand. "Here. This is all I have, as my recent trip was rather unexpected, and I didn't have time to pack." I stared down at the small square of gold. It was a miniature book, held shut with a clasp. I pressed on it, and it sprang open. Inside, there was a picture of my mother, the girl from the visions. His Lila Jane.

He looked away. "It happened to be in my pocket, after all this time. Imagine that." But the charm was worn and scratched, and I knew without a doubt it was in his pocket today because it was every day, as it had been for who knows how many years. "I believe you'll find this is an object of power for you, Ethan. It always has been for me. Let's not forget, our Lila Jane was a strong woman. She saved my life, even from the grave."

I recognized the look on my mother's face in the photo. It was one I thought she saved for me. It was the look she gave me the first time I read the road signs out loud through the car window, before she realized I could read. It was the look she gave me when I had eaten one of Amma's buttermilk pies by myself and slept in her bed with a stomachache as fierce as Amma herself. It was the look she saved for my first day of school, my first basketball game, my first crush.

And here it was again, staring out from inside the tiny book. She wouldn't abandon me. And Macon wouldn't either. Maybe he did have some kind of plan. He had cheated death. I pushed the book into my pocket, next to Lena's necklace.

"Wait a second." Link walked over. "I'm glad you have that little gold book and all, but you said the whole Blood pack was gonna be in there, plus Vampire Boy, and Lena's mom, and the Emperor, or whoever this Abraham guy is. And last time I checked, Han Solo wasn't around. So don't you think we need more than a little book?"

Ridley was nodding behind him. "Link's right. You may be able to save Lena, but not unless you can get to her."

Link tried to bend down next to Macon. "Mr. Ravenwood, can't you come with us and take out a couple a guys for us?"

Macon lifted an eyebrow. This was the first real conversation he'd ever had with Link. "Unfortunately, son, my incarceration has weakened me...."

"He's Transitioning, Link. He can't possibly go down there.

He's incredibly vulnerable." Liv was still holding Macon up, for the most part.

"Olivia is right. Incubuses possess incredible strength and speed. I'm no match for any of them in my present state."

"Luckily, I am." The voice came out of nowhere, and she ripped through the darkness even faster. She was wearing a long black coat with a high neck and wrecked black boots. Her brown hair was blowing in the wind.

I recognized the Succubus from the funeral right away. It was Leah Ravenwood, Macon's sister. Macon was as shocked as the rest of us to see her. "Leah?

She slid her arm across his back, supporting him, looking deep into his eyes. "Green, eh? That will take some getting used to." She laid her head on his shoulder, the way Lena used to.

"How did you find us?"

She laughed. "You're the talk of the Tunnels. Word on the street is my big brother's taking on Abraham. And I heard he isn't too pleased with you."

Macon's sister—the one Arelia took to New Orleans when she left Macon's father. The Sisters had mentioned her.

"Dark and Light will be what they are."

Link caught my eye from behind them, and I knew the question. He was waiting for me to make the call. Fight or flight. It wasn't clear what Leah Ravenwood wanted from us or why she was here. But if she was like Hunting, and she fed on blood instead of dreams, we had to get away fast. I looked at Liv. She shook her head, almost imperceptibly. She wasn't sure either.

Macon smiled one of his rare smiles. "Now, what are you doing here, my dear?"

"I'm here to even the odds. You know I love a good family

feud." Leah smiled. She fluttered her wrist, and a long staff, made of polished wood, appeared in her hand. "And I carry a big stick."

Macon was at a loss. I couldn't decide whether he looked relieved or concerned. Either way, he was stunned. "Why now? You don't usually concern yourself with Caster affairs."

Leah reached into her pocket and took out a rubber band, pulling her hair into a ponytail. "This isn't just a Caster battle, not anymore. If the Order is destroyed, we may be destroyed with it."

Macon gave her a meaningful look. I recognized it as his *not in front of the children* expression. "The Order of Things has stood since the beginning of time. It will take more than a Cataclyst to bring about its destruction."

She smiled and swung her staff. "And it's about time someone taught Hunting some manners. My motives are pure, like the heart of a Succubus." Macon laughed at the thought. From where I was standing, it didn't sound so funny.

Dark or Light—Leah Ravenwood could go either way, but it didn't matter to me. "We need to find Lena."

Leah picked up her stick. "I was waiting for you to say that."

Link cleared his throat. "Um, I don't wanna be rude, ma'am. But Ethan says Hunting's down there with his Blood pack. Don't get me wrong, you seem pretty badass and all, but you're still just a girl with a stick."

"This"—in a split second, Leah extended the rod straight out, inches from Link's nose—"is a Succubine Staff, not a stick. And I'm not a girl. I'm a Succubus. When it comes to our kind, the females have the advantage. We are quicker, stronger, and more clever than our male counterparts. Think of me as the praying mantis of the supernatural world."

"Aren't those the bugs that bite off the heads of the males?" Link looked skeptical.

"Yes. Then they eat them."

Whatever reservations Macon may have had about Leah, he seemed relieved she was going with us. But he did have some last minute advice. "Larkin has grown up since you last saw him, Leah. He's a powerful Illusionist. Be careful. And according to Olivia, our brother keeps his mindless hounds with him, a Blood pack."

"Don't worry, big brother. I have a pet of my own." She looked up at the ledge above us. Some kind of wild mountain lion, about the size of a German shepherd, lounged on the rocks, its tail hanging over the side. "Bade!" The cat leaped to its feet and opened its jaws, flashing rows of razor-sharp teeth, and jumped down beside her. "I'm sure Bade can't wait to play with Hunting's pups. You know what they say about cats and dogs."

Ridley whispered to Liv. "Bade is the voodoo god of wind and storms. Not one you wanna screw with." It reminded me of Lena, which made me feel a little better about the hundred and fifty pound cat staring down at me.

"Stalk and ambush is her specialty." Leah rubbed the cat behind its ears.

At the sight of the wild cat, Lucille ran over and swatted her playfully. Bade nudged Lucille with her muzzle. Leah bent down and picked her up. "Lucille, how's my sweet girl?"

"How do you know my great-aunt's cat?"

"I was there when Lucille was born. She was my mamma's cat. My mother gave Lucille to your Aunt Prue so she could find her way around the Tunnels." Lucille rolled around between Bade's paws.

I hadn't been so sure about Leah, but Lucille had never let me down. She was a good judge of character, even if she was a cat. A Caster cat. I should have known.

Leah tucked the staff under her belt, and I knew the time for talk was over. "Ready?"

Macon reached out his hand, and I took it. For a second, I could feel the power in his grip, as if we were in some kind of Caster conversation I couldn't comprehend. Then he let go, and I turned toward the cave, wondering if I would ever see him again.

I led the way and, motley or not, my friends were right behind me. My friends, a Succubus, and a mountain lion named after a volatile voodoo god. I only hoped it was enough.

Dark Fire

When we reached the base of the cliff, we hid behind a rock formation a few yards from the cave. Two Incubuses were guarding the entrance, talking in low tones. I recognized the scarred one from Macon's funeral. "Great." Two Blood Incubuses, and we weren't even inside. I knew the rest of the pack couldn't be far away.

"Leave them to me, but you may not want to watch." Leah signaled Bade, who loped to her side.

- The staff flashed through the air like lightning. The two Incubuses never saw it coming. Leah had the first Incubus on the ground in seconds. Bade lunged, catching the other by the throat and pinning him. Leah rose, wiping her mouth on her sleeve, and spat, a bloody spot marking the sand. "Old blood, seventy, a hundred years. I can taste it."

Link's mouth hung open. "Is she expecting us to do that?"

Leah bent at the neck of the second Incubus for barely a minute before she was waving us on. "Go."

I didn't move. "What do we—what do I do?"

"Fight."

The entrance to the cave was so bright, the sun could have been shining inside. "I can't do this."

Link looked into the cave nervously. "What are you talkin' about, man?"

I looked at my friends. "I think you guys should go back. This is too dangerous. I shouldn't have dragged you into this."

"Nobody dragged me anywhere. I came to—" Link looked at Ridley, then turned away awkwardly. "To get away from it all."

Ridley flipped her muddy hair dramatically. "Well, I certainly didn't come here because of you, Short Straw. Don't flatter yourself. As much as I like hanging out with you dorks, I'm here to help my cousin." She looked at Liv. "What's your excuse?"

Liv's voice was quiet. "Do you believe in destiny?"

We all looked at Liv like she was crazy, but she didn't care. "Well, I do. I've been watching the Caster sky for as long as I can remember, and when it changed, I saw it. The Southern Star, the Seventeenth Moon, my selenometer that everyone at home teased me about—this is my destiny. I was supposed to be here. Even if...no matter what."

"I get it," said Link. "Even if it wrecks everything, even if you know you're gonna get busted, sometimes you gotta do it anyway."

"Something like that."

Link tried to crack his knuckles. "So what's the plan?"

451

I looked at my best friend, who had shared his Twinkie with me on the bus in second grade. Was I really going to let him follow me into a cave to die? "There's no plan. You can't come with me. I'm the Wayward. This is my responsibility, not yours."

Ridley rolled her eyes. "Obviously the whole Wayward thing hasn't been explained to you properly. You don't have any superpowers. You can't leap over tall buildings in a single bound or fight Dark Casters with your magic cat." Lucille peeked out from behind my leg. "Basically, you're a glorified tour guide who's no better equipped to face a bunch of Dark Casters than Mary P. over here."

"Aquaman," coughed Link, winking at me.

Liv had been quiet until now. "She's not wrong. Ethan, you can't do this alone."

I knew what they were doing—or more like *not* doing. Leaving. I shook my head. "You guys are idiots."

Link grinned. "I'd have gone with 'brave as hell,' myself."

We stayed pressed against the cavern walls, following the moonlight pouring through the crack in the ceiling. As we rounded a corner, the rays became impossibly bright, and I could see the pyre below us. It rose from the center of the cave, golden flames encircling it and licking up the pyramid of broken trees. There was a stone slab, which almost resembled some kind of Mayan altar, balanced on top of the pyre as if suspended from invisible wires. A set of weathered stone stairs led up to the altar. The snaking circle worn by Dark Casters was painted on the cave wall behind it.

Sarafine's body was lying on top of the altar, just as it had been when she had appeared in the woods. Nothing else was the same. Moonlight streamed through the roof and hit her body, radiating outward in all directions as if refracted by a prism. It was like she was holding light from the moon she was calling out of time—Lena's Seventeenth Moon. Even Sarafine's golden dress looked like it was stitched together from a thousand shining metallic scales.

Liv breathed. "I've never seen anything like it."

Sarafine seemed to be in some kind of trance. Her body rose a few inches above the stone, the folds of her dress cascading down like water, past the edges of the stone altar. She was amassing some serious power.

Larkin was at the base of the pyre. I watched as he moved closer to the stone stairs. Closer to—

Lena.

She lay collapsed, her hands extended toward the flames, her eyes shut. Her head was in John Breed's lap, and she looked unconscious. He looked different—blank. Like he was in a trance of his own.

Lena was shaking. Even from here, I could feel the biting cold radiating from the fire. She must have been freezing. A circle of Dark Casters surrounded the pyre. I didn't recognize them, but I could tell they were Dark by their crazed yellow eyes.

Lena! Can you hear me?

Sarafine's eyes flashed open. The Casters began to chant.

"Liv, what's happening?" I whispered.

"They're calling a Claiming Moon."

I didn't need to understand what they were saying to know what was happening. Sarafine was calling the Seventeenth Moon so Lena could make her choice while she was under the influence of some sort of Dark Cast. Or the weight of her guilt, a Dark Cast of its own.

"What are they doing?"

"Sarafine is using all her power to channel the Dark Fire's energy, and her own, into the moon." Liv was fixated on the scene as if she was trying to memorize every detail, evil or not. It was the Keeper in her, compelled to record history in the making.

Vexes whipped around the cavern, threatening to bring down the walls — spiraling, gaining strength and mass. "We need to get down there." Liv nodded, and Link grabbed Ridley's hand.

We made our way down the side of the cavern, keeping to the shadows until we reached the wet, sandy cave floor. I realized the chanting had stopped. The Casters were silently transfixed, watching Sarafine and the pyre, as if they were all under the same mind-numbing spell.

"Now what?" Link looked pale.

A figure stepped into the center of the circle. I didn't have to guess who it was, because he was wearing the same Sunday suit and string tie from the visions. His white summer suit made him look even more out of place among the Dark Casters and the helix of Vexes.

It was Abraham, the only Incubus powerful enough to summon this many Vexes from below. Larkin and Hunting stood behind him, and every Incubus in the cavern fell to one knee. Abraham raised his hands up toward the vortex. "It's time."

Lena! Wake up!

The flames surrounding the pyre surged higher. In front of the pyre, John Breed gently lifted Lena to wake her up.

L! Run!

Lena looked around, disoriented. She didn't react to my voice. I wasn't sure if she could hear anything. Her movements were unsteady, as if she didn't know where she was.

Abraham reached out toward John and lifted his hand slowly. John jerked, then picked Lena up in his arms, rising as if being pulled by a string.

Lena!

Lena's head fell to the side, her eyes closing again. John carried her up the stairs. The cocky attitude was gone. He looked like a zombie.

Ridley pushed her way closer. "Lena's totally disoriented. She doesn't even know what's happening. It's an effect of the fire."

"Why would they want her to be passed out? Doesn't Lena have to be conscious to Claim herself?" I thought that was a given.

Ridley stared at the fire. Her voice was uncharacteristically serious, and she was avoiding my eyes. "The Claiming requires volition. She'll have to make the Choice." Ridley sounded strange. "Unless..."

"Unless what?" I didn't have time to try to interpret Ridley.

"Unless she already has." By leaving us behind. By taking off the necklace. By running off with John Breed.

"She hasn't," I said automatically. I knew Lena. There was a reason for all of it, everything. "She hasn't."

Ridley looked at me. "I hope you're right."

John reached the top of the altar, Larkin following behind him. Larkin bound Sarafine and Lena together under the light of the Seventeenth Moon.

I felt my heart pounding. "I have to get Lena. Can you help me?"

Link grabbed two chunks of rock, big enough to do some damage if he could get close enough to use them. Liv flipped through her notebook. Even Ridley unwrapped a lollipop and shrugged. "You never know."

I heard another voice behind me. "You aren't gonna be able to get up there unless you're fixin' to take care a all those Vexes on your own. And I don't remember teachin' you how to do that." I smiled before I turned around.

It was Amma, and this time she had brought some of the living with her. Arelia and Twyla stood nearby, and together the three old women looked like the Three Fates. Relief washed over me, and I realized part of me had thought I'd never see Amma again. I crushed her in a hug, which she returned, straightening her hat. That's when I saw Gramma's old-fashioned lace-up boots, as she stepped out from behind Arelia.

Make that Four Fates.

"Ma'am." I nodded to Gramma. She nodded back, as if she was about to offer me tea on the veranda at Ravenwood. Then I panicked, because we weren't at Ravenwood. And Amma and Arelia and Twyla weren't the Three Fates. They were three ancient, brittle-boned Southern ladies who were probably about two hundred and fifty years old between them—wearing support hose. And Gramma wasn't much younger. These Four Fates, in particular, had no business being on a battlefield.

Come to think of it, neither did this one Wate.

I slipped free from Amma's grip. "What are you doing here? How did you find us?"

"What am I doin' here?" Amma sniffed. "My family came to

456

the Sea Islands from Barbados before you were a thought in the Good Lord's mind. I know these islands like my kitchen."

"This is a Caster island, Amma. Not one of the Sea Islands."

"'Course it is. Where else would you hide an island you can't see?"

Arelia put her hand on Amma's shoulder. "She's right. The Great Barrier is hidden among the Sea Islands. Amarie may not be a Caster, but she shares the gift of Sight with my sister and I."

Amma shook her head so hard I thought it was going to fly off. "You didn't really think I was gonna let you wade knee-deep in quicksand on your own, did you?" I threw my arms around her and hugged her again.

"How did you know where to find us, ma'am? We had trouble findin' this place ourselves." Link was always a step ahead or a step behind. The four of them looked at him like he was a fool.

"Bustin' open that ball a trouble the way you boys did? With a spell older than my mamma's mamma? Might as well have dialed up the Greater Gatlin Emergency Phone Tree." Amma took a step toward Link, who took a step backward, out of pointing range. She didn't let go of me, though. That's how I knew what she was really saying: I love you and I couldn't be prouder. And you'll be grounded for a month when we get home.

Ridley leaned closer to Link. "Think about it. A Necromancer, a Diviner, and a Seer. We didn't stand a chance."

Amma, Arelia, Gramma, and Twyla turned to Ridley as soon as she spoke. She reddened, lowering her eyes respectfully.

"I can't believe you're here, Auntie Twyla." She swallowed. "Gramma."

Gramma held Ridley by the chin and stared into her bright blue eyes. "So it's true." She broke into a smile. "Welcome back, child." She kissed Ridley on the cheek.

Amma looked smug. "Told you. It was in the cards."

Arelia nodded. "And the stars."

Twyla scoffed, dropping her voice to a low whisper. "Cards only show da surface a things. What we have here, this is cut deep, past da bone and out da other side." A shadow crossed over her face.

I looked at Twyla. "What?" But she smiled, and the shadow was gone.

"You need some help from La Bas." Twyla waved her hand back and forth over her head. Back to the business at hand.

"The Otherworld," Arelia translated.

Amma knelt down, unwrapping a cloth filled with small bones and charms. She might as well have been a doctor preparing her surgical tools. "Callin' the sorta help we need's my specialty."

Arelia took out a rattle, and Twyla sat down and got comfortable. Who knew what she was going to have to raise. Amma spread out her bones and struggled with one of her mason jars. "South Carolina graveyard dirt. Best there is. Brought it from home." I took the jar from her and opened it, thinking about the night I followed her into the swamp. "We can take care a those Vexes. Won't stop Sarafine or Melchizedek's good-for-nothin' brother, but it'll cut off some a her power."

Gramma looked up at the dark cyclone of Vexes fueling the fire. "My goodness, you weren't exaggerating, Amarie. There are

458

a lot of them." I saw her eyes move from Sarafine's motionless body to Lena, in the distance, and the lines in her brow deepened. Ridley let go of her hand, but didn't leave her side.

Link let out a sigh of relief. "Man, I'm goin' back to church next Sunday for sure." I didn't say anything, but what I was thinking wasn't that far off.

Amma looked up from the dirt she was spreading below her feet. "We're gonna send them back down where they belong."

Gramma adjusted her jacket. "Then I'll deal with my daughter."

Amma, Arelia, and Twyla sat cross-legged on the damp rocks and joined hands. "First things first. Let's get rid a those Vexes."

Gramma stepped back and gave them some room. "That would be lovely, Amarie."

The three women closed their eyes. Amma's voice was strong and clear, despite the whirring of the vortex and the humming of Dark magic. "Uncle Abner, Aunt Delilah, Aunt Ivy, Grandmamma Sulla, we are in need a your intercession once more. I call you now to this place. Find your way into this world and banish the ones that don't belong."

Twyla's eyed rolled back in her head, and she began to chant.

> "*Les lois*, my spirits, my guides,
> Tear apart the Bridge
> That carries these shadows from your world
> into the next."

Twyla raised her arms above her head. *"Encore!"*

"Again," Arelia spoke the word in English.

> "*Les lois*, my spirits, my guides,
> Tear apart the Bridge
> That carries these shadows from your world
> into the next."

Twyla continued to chant, mixing her French-Creole with Amma and Arelia's English. Their voices overlapped like a chorus. Through the crack in the cavern ceiling, the sky darkened around the ray of moonlight, as if they had summoned a thundercloud to bring on a storm all their own. But they weren't calling a thundercloud. They were creating a different kind of vortex, darkness spiraling above them like a perfectly formed tornado touching down in the center of their circle. For a second, I thought the enormous spiral was only going to get us killed faster, attracting every Vex and Incubus within sight of it.

I should have known better than to doubt the three of them. The ghostly figures of the Greats began to emerge: Uncle Abner, Aunt Delilah, Aunt Ivy, and Sulla the Prophet. They were forming from the sand and dirt, their bodies being woven from it bit by bit.

Our Three Fates kept spinning.

> "Tear apart the Bridge
> That carries these shadows from your world
> into the next."

Within seconds, there were more spirits from the Otherworld, Sheers. They were being born from the spiraling earth, like butterflies from a cocoon. The Greats and the spirits attracted the Vexes, causing the shadowy creatures to rush toward

460

them with the horrible scream I remembered from the Tunnels.

The Greats began to grow. Sulla was so big, her rows of necklaces looked like ropes. All Uncle Abner needed was a thunderbolt and a toga, and he could've been Zeus looming above us. The Vexes shot out from the flames of the Dark Fire, black streaks tearing across the sky. Just as quickly, the shrieking streaks disappeared. The Greats inhaled them, as Twyla had seemed to inhale the Sheers that night in the cemetery.

Sulla the Prophet glided forward, her heavily ringed fingers pointing at the last of the Vexes, turning and screaming in the wind. "Tear apart the Bridge!"

The Vexes were gone, leaving nothing except a dark cloud overhead and the Greats, Sulla in the forefront. She was shimmering in the moonlight as she spoke her final words. "Blood is always Blood. Even time cannot Bind it."

The Greats disappeared, and the dark cloud dissipated. Only the billowing smoke from the Dark Fire remained. The pyre was still burning, and Sarafine and Lena were still tied to the slab.

The vortex of Vexes was gone, and something else had changed. We were no longer silently watching, waiting for an opportunity to make our move. The eyes of every Incubus and Dark Caster in the cave were on us, canines bared and yellow eyes blazing.

We had joined the party, whether we liked it or not.

Seventeen Moons

The Blood Incubuses reacted first, dematerializing one by one, and reappearing in pack formation. I recognized Scarface, the Incubus from Macon's funeral. He was in the front, his black eyes calculating. Hunting was predictably nowhere in sight, too important for simple slaughter. But Larkin was standing in front of them, a black snake coiled around his arm. Second in command.

They surrounded us in seconds, and there was nowhere to go. The pack was in front of us, and the cave wall behind us. Amma pushed her way between the Incubuses and me, as if she planned to fight them off with her bare hands. She didn't get the chance.

"Amma!" I called out, but it was too late.

Larkin was standing inches from her tiny frame, wielding a knife that didn't look anything like an illusion. "You're a real pain in the ass for an old lady, you know that? Always pokin' around where you don't belong and callin' up your dead relatives. About time you joined them."

Amma didn't move. "Larkin Ravenwood, you're gonna be ten kinds a sorry when you try to find your way outta this world and into the next."

"Promise?" I could see the muscles in Larkin's shoulder move as he pulled back his arm, preparing to lunge at Amma.

Before he could strike, Twyla threw her hand open, and white particles flew through the air. Larkin cried out, dropping the knife and rubbing his eyes with the back of his hands.

"Ethan, watch out!" I could hear Link's voice, but everything was happening in slow motion. I saw the pack coming at me, and I heard something else. A humming sound that started low and rose slowly, like the crest of a wave. A green light flew up in front of us. It was the same pure light the Arclight emitted when it spun in the air in front of us, right before we released Macon.

It had to be Macon.

The hum grew louder, and the light surged forward, hurling the Blood Incubuses backward. I looked around to see if everyone was all right.

Link was bent over, with his hands on his knees like he was going to puke. "That was close." Ridley patted his back a little too hard and turned to Twyla.

"What did you throw at Larkin? Some kind of Charged Matter?"

Twyla smiled, rubbing the beads on one of the thirty or forty necklaces she wore. "Don't need Charged Matta, *cher*."

"Then what was it?"

"*Sèl manje*." She spoke the words in her thick Creole accent, but Ridley didn't understand.

Arelia smiled. "Salt."

Amma whacked me on the arm. "Told you salt could keep away evil spirits. Evil boys, too."

"We have to move. There isn't much time." Gramma rushed toward the stairs, carrying her cane in her hand. "Ethan, come with me." I followed Gramma up to the altar, the smoke from the fire creating a thick haze around me. It was intoxicating and suffocating at the same time.

We reached the top of the stairs. Gramma held her cane out toward Sarafine, and immediately it began to glow with golden light. I felt a wave of relief. Gramma was an Empath. She had no powers of her own, except the ability to use the powers of others. And the power she was taking now belonged to the most dangerous woman in the room—her daughter Sarafine.

The one channeling the energy of the Dark Fire to call the Seventeenth Moon.

"Ethan, get Lena!" Gramma called. She was in some sort of psychic holding pattern with Sarafine.

It was all I needed to hear. I grabbed for the ropes, loosening the knots that bound Lena and her mother together. Lena was barely conscious, her body resting on the freezing stone. I touched her. Her skin was ice cold, and I felt the choking grip of the Dark Fire as my body started going numb.

"Lena, wake up. It's me." I shook her, and her head rolled from side to side, her face red from the icy rock. I lifted Lena's body, wrapping my arms around her, giving her what little warmth I had.

Her eyes opened. She was trying to speak. I held her face in my hands. "Ethan—" Her lids were heavy, and her eyes shut again. "Get out of here."

"No." I kissed her as I held her in my arms. No matter what happened, it was worth this one moment. Holding her again.

I'm not going anywhere without you.

I heard Link scream. One Incubus had escaped the powerful wall of light that was holding the rest of them at bay. John Breed was behind Link, with his arm around Link's neck, canines bared. John still had the same glazed expression, like he was on autopilot. I wondered if it was an effect of the intoxicating fumes. Ridley turned and threw herself onto John's back, tackling him. She must have taken him by surprise, because Ridley wasn't strong enough to take him down on her own. The three of them fell to the ground, grappling for the upper hand.

I couldn't see more than that, but it was enough to make me realize we were in serious trouble. I didn't know how long the supernatural field would hold, especially if Macon was the one generating it.

Lena had to end this.

I looked down at her. Her eyes were open, but she looked past me, as if she couldn't see me.

Lena. You can't give up now. Not when—

Don't say it.

It's your Claiming Moon.

It's not. It's her Claiming Moon.

It doesn't matter. It's your Seventeenth Moon, L.

She stared up at me, her eyes empty.

Sarafine raised it. I didn't ask for any of this.

You have to choose, or everyone we care about could get killed here tonight.

She looked away from me.

What if I'm not ready?

You can't run from this, Lena. Not anymore.

You don't get it. It's not a choice. It's a curse. If I go Light, Ridley and half my family will die. If I go Dark, Gramma, Aunt Del, my cousins — they'll all die. What kind of choice is that?

I held her tighter, wishing there was a way I could give her my strength or absorb her pain.

"It's a choice only you can make." I pulled Lena to her feet. "Look at what's happening. People you love are fighting for their lives right now. You can stop it. Only you."

"I don't know if I can."

"Why not?" I was shouting.

"Because I don't know what I am."

I looked into her eyes, and they had changed again. One was perfectly green, and one was perfectly gold.

"Look at me, Ethan. Am I Dark, or am I Light?"

I looked at her, and I knew what she was. The girl I loved. The girl I would always love.

Instinctively, I grabbed the gold book in my pocket. It was warm, as if some part of my mother was alive within it. I pressed the book into Lena's hand, feeling the warmth spread into her body. I willed her to feel it — the kind of love within the book, the kind of love that never died.

"I know what you are, Lena. I know your heart. You can trust me. You can trust yourself."

Lena held the tiny book in her hand. It wasn't enough. "What if you're wrong, Ethan? How can you know?"

"I know because I know *you.*"

I let go of her hand. I couldn't bear to think of anything happening to her, but I couldn't stop it from coming. "Lena, you have to do it. There's no other way. I wish there was, but there isn't."

We looked out over the cavern. Ridley looked up, and for a second I thought she saw us.

Lena looked at me. "I can't let Ridley die. I swear she's trying to change. I've already lost too much."

I already lost Uncle Macon.

"It was my fault." She clung to me, sobbing.

I wanted to tell her he was alive, but I remembered what Macon said. He was still Transitioning. There was a possibility he still had Darkness within him. If Lena knew he was alive and there was a chance she could lose him again, she would never choose to go Light. She wasn't capable of killing him a second time.

The moon was directly over Lena's head. Soon the Claiming would begin. There was only one decision left to make, and I was afraid she wasn't going to make it.

Ridley appeared at the top of the steps, breathless. She hugged Lena, taking her from me. She rubbed her face against Lena's wet cheek. They were sisters, for better or worse. They always had been. "Lena, listen to me. You have to choose." Lena looked away, pained. Ridley grabbed the side of her cousin's face, forcing Lena to look at her. Lena noticed right away. "What happened to your eyes?"

"It doesn't matter. You need to listen to me. Have I ever done anything noble? Have I ever let you sit in the front seat of the car a single time? Have I ever once saved you the last piece of cake, in sixteen years? Ever let you try on my shoes?"

"I always hated your shoes." A tear rolled down Lena's cheek.

"You loved my shoes." Ridley smiled and wiped Lena's face with her scraped and bloody hand.

"I don't care what you say. I'm not doing it." Their eyes were fixed on each other.

"I don't have a selfless bone in my body, Lena, and I'm telling you to do it."

"No."

"Trust me. It's better this way. If I still have some Darkness inside me somewhere, you'll be doing me a favor. I don't want to be Dark anymore, but I'm not cut out to be a Mortal. I'm a Siren."

I could see the recognition in Lena's eyes. "But if you're a Mortal, you won't—"

Ridley shook her head. "There's no way to know. Once there's Darkness in your blood, you know..." Her voice broke off.

I remembered what Macon said. *Darkness does not leave us as easily as we would hope.*

Ridley hugged Lena tight. "Come on, what am I going to do with seventy or eighty more years? Can you really see me hanging around Gat-dung, making out with Link in the back of the Beater? Trying to figure out how the stove works?" She looked away, her voice faltering. "Can't even get decent Chinese in that crappy town."

Lena held tight to Ridley's hand, and Ridley squeezed it, then gently pulled her hand away, one finger at a time, and placed Lena's hand in mine.

"Take care of her for me, Short Straw." Ridley disappeared back down the steps before I could say a word.

I'm scared, Ethan.

I'm right here, L. I'm not going anywhere. You can make it through this.

Ethan—

You can, L. Claim yourself. No one has to show you the way. You know your own way.

Then another voice joined mine, from a great distance and also from within me.

My mother.

Together we told Lena, in the one stolen moment we had, not what to do but that she could do it.

Claim yourself, I said.

Claim yourself, my mother said.

I am myself, Lena said. *I am.*

Blinding light surged from the moon, like a sonic boom, shaking the rocks loose from the walls. I couldn't see anything but the moonlight. I felt Lena's fear and her pain, pouring over me like a wave. Every loss, every mistake, was seared into her soul, creating a different kind of tattoo. One made from rage and abandonment, heartbreak and tears.

Moonlight flooded the cave, pure and blinding. For a minute, I couldn't see or hear anything. Then I looked over at Lena, tears running down her cheeks and shining in her eyes, which were now their true colors.

One green, one gold.

She flung her head back to face the moon. Her body twisted, her feet hovering above the stone. Below her, the fighting stopped. No one spoke or moved. Every Caster and Demon in the room seemed to know what was happening, that their fates hung in the balance. Above her, the brightness of the moon began to vibrate, the light pulling, until the whole cave was one ball of light.

The moon continued to swell. Like a moment from a dream, the moon split into two halves, dividing in the sky directly over where Lena stood. The moonlight behind her seemed to form a giant, luminous butterfly, with two brilliant, glowing wings. One green, one gold.

A cracking sound echoed across the cave, and Lena screamed. The light disappeared. The Dark Fire disappeared. There was no altar, no pyre, and we were back on the ground.

The air was perfectly still. I thought it was over, but I was wrong.

Lightning sliced through the air, splitting into two distinct paths, hitting its targets simultaneously.

Larkin.

His face twisted in terror as his body seized, then started to blacken. He seemed to be burning from the inside out. Black cracks crawled along his skin until he turned to dust, blowing across the cave floor.

The second bolt traveled in the opposite direction, hitting Twyla.

Her eyes rolled back in her head. Her body fell to the ground, as if her spirit had stepped out and tossed it aside. But she didn't turn to dust. Her lifeless body lay on the ground as Twyla rose above it, shimmering and fading until she became translucent.

Then the haze began to settle, the particles rearranging until Twyla looked more as she had in life. Whatever she had left behind in this life, it was finished. If she had business here again, it would be because she chose to. Twyla wasn't tethered to this world. She was free. And she looked peaceful, as if she knew something we didn't.

As she rose up through the crack in the cave ceiling toward the moon, she stopped. For a second, I wasn't sure what was happening as she hovered there.

Good-bye, cher.

I don't know if she really said it, or if I imagined it, but she reached out a luminous hand and smiled. I lifted my own hand toward the sky and watched as Twyla faded into the moonlight.

A single star appeared in the Caster sky—a sky I could see, but only for a second. The Southern Star. It had found its rightful place, back in the sky.

Lena had made her choice.

She had Claimed herself.

Even if I wasn't sure what that meant, she was still with me. I hadn't lost her.

Claim yourself.

My mom would be proud of us.

Darkness and Light

Lena stood straight and tall, a dark silhouette against the moon. She didn't cry, and she wasn't screaming. Her feet had settled on the ground, on either side of the giant crack that now marked the cave, splitting it almost entirely in two.

"What just happened?" Liv was looking at Amma and Arelia for answers.

I followed Lena's eyes across the great expanse of rocks and understood her silence. She was in shock, staring at one familiar face.

"It appears Abraham has been interfering with the Order of Things." Macon stood in the cave entrance framed by light from a moon that was beginning to stitch itself back together. Leah and Bade were at his side. I wasn't sure how long he'd been standing there, but I could tell from the look on his face he had seen everything. He walked slowly, still adjusting to the feeling of his feet touching the ground. Bade kept pace with him, and Leah kept one hand on his arm.

Lena softened at the sound of his voice, a voice from the grave. I heard the thought, barely a whisper. She was afraid to even think it.

Uncle Macon?

Her face went white. I remembered how I felt when I saw my mother at the cemetery.

"An impressive little trick you and Sarafine managed to pull off, Grandfather. I'll give you that. Calling a Claiming Moon out of time? You've outdone yourself, really." Macon's voice echoed in the cavern. The air was so still, so quiet, you couldn't hear anything except the low churning of the tides. "Naturally, when I heard you were coming, I had to make an appearance." Macon waited, as if he was expecting an answer. But when he didn't get one, he snapped. "Abraham! I see your hand in this."

The cave began to shake. Rocks fell from the jagged crack in the ceiling, beating down onto the floor. It felt like the whole cavern was about to collapse. The sky above grew darker. The green-eyed Macon—the Light Caster, if that's what he truly was—seemed even more powerful than the Incubus he was before.

A rumbling laugh echoed off the rock walls. Down on the watery cave floor, where the moon no longer shone, Abraham stepped out of the shadows. With his white beard and matching white suit, he looked like a harmless old man instead of the Darkest of Blood Incubuses. Hunting stayed at his side.

Abraham stood over Sarafine, whose body was lying on the ground. She had turned completely white, covered in a thick layer of frost, an icy cocoon.

"You call on me, boy?" The old man laughed again, sharp and quick. "Ah, the hubris of youth. In a hundred years, you will learn your place, Grandson." I tried to mentally calculate the generations between them—four, maybe even five.

"I am well aware of my place, Grandfather. Unfortunately, and this is exceptionally awkward, I believe I'll be the one to send you back to yours."

Abraham smoothed his beard deliberately. "Little Macon Ravenwood. You were always such a lost boy. This is your doing, not mine. Blood is Blood, just as Dark is Dark. You should have remembered where your allegiances lie." He paused, looking at Leah. "You would have done well to remember that, too, my dear. But then, you were raised by a Caster." He shuddered.

I could see the anger in Leah's face, but I could also see the fear. She was willing to try her luck with the Blood pack, but she didn't want to challenge Abraham.

Abraham looked at Hunting. "On the subject of lost boys, where is John?"

"Long gone. Coward."

Abraham whipped around to face Hunting. "John isn't capable of cowardice. It's not in his *nature*. And his life means more to me than yours. So I suggest you find him." Hunting lowered his eyes and nodded. I couldn't help but wonder why John Breed was so important to Abraham, who didn't seem to care about anyone.

Macon watched Abraham carefully. "It's touching to see how concerned you are about your boy. I certainly hope you find him. I know how painful it is to lose a child."

The cavern started to shake again, and rocks fell around our

474

feet. "What have you done with John?" In his rage, Abraham seemed less like a harmless old man and more like the Demon he truly was.

"What have I done with him? I think the question is what have you done *to* him?" Abraham's black eyes narrowed, but Macon only smiled. "An Incubus who can walk in the sunlight and retain his strength without feeding...it would require a very specific coupling to produce those qualities in a child. Wouldn't you agree? Scientifically speaking, you would need Mortal qualities, yet this boy John possesses the gifts of a Caster. He can't have three parents, which means his mother was—"

Leah gasped. "An Evo." Every Caster in the room reacted to the word. The surprise spread like a ripple, a new kind of coldness in the air. Only Amma looked impassive. She folded her arms and fixed her eyes on Abraham Ravenwood as if he was just another chicken she was planning on plucking, skinning, and boiling in her banged-up pot.

I tried to remember what Lena told me about Evos. They were metamorphs, with the ability to mirror human form. They didn't just step inside a Mortal body, like Sarafine. Evos could actually become Mortals for short periods of time.

Macon smiled. "Precisely. A Caster that can take on human form long enough to conceive a child, with all the DNA of a Mortal and a Caster on one side and an Incubus on the other. You have been busy, haven't you, Grandfather? I didn't realize you were matchmaking in your spare time."

Abraham's eyes grew blacker. "You are the one who muddied the Order of Things. First, with your infatuation with a Mortal, and then by turning on your own kind to protect this girl." Abraham shook his head, as if Macon was nothing more than an impetuous boy. "And where has it left us? Now the Duchannes child has cleaved the moon. Do you know what this means? The threat she poses to all of us?"

"The fate of my niece is none of your concern. You seem to have your hands full enough with your own science experiment of a child. Although, I have to wonder what you're doing with him." Macon's green eyes glowed as he spoke.

"Be careful who you speak to that way." Hunting took a step forward, but Abraham put up his hand, and Hunting stopped. "Killed you once, I'll kill you twice."

Macon shook his head. "Nursery rhymes, Hunting? If you are planning a career as Grandfather's minion, you're going to have to work on your delivery." Macon sighed. "Now then, tuck your tail between your legs and follow your master home like a good dog." Hunting's expression hardened.

Macon turned to Abraham. "And Grandfather, as much as I would love to compare lab notes, I think it's time you leave."

The old man laughed. A cold wind began to circle around him, whistling between the rocks. "You think you can order me around like an errand boy? You will not call my name, Macon Ravenwood. You will cry my name. You will bleed my name." The wind grew around him, blowing his string tie awkwardly across his body. "And when you die, my name will still be feared, and yours will be forgotten."

Macon looked him in the eye, without the slightest hint of fear. "As my mathematically gifted brother clarified, I've already died once. You're going to have to come up with something new, old man. It's getting tiresome. Allow me to see you out."

Macon fluttered his fingers, and I heard a ripping sound as

the night opened behind Abraham. The old man hesitated, then smiled. "My age must be catching up with me. I almost forgot to collect my things before I leave." He reached out his hand, and something emerged from behind one of the crevices in the rock. It vanished, reappearing in his hand. I held my breath for a second when I saw it.

The Book of Moons.

The Book we believed had burned to ash, in the fields of Greenbrier. The Book that was a curse all its own.

Macon's face darkened, and he held out his hand. "That doesn't belong to you, Grandfather." The Book twitched in Abraham's hand, but the darkness surrounding him deepened, and the old man shrugged with a smile. A second ripping sound echoed across the cavern as he disappeared, taking the Book and Hunting and Sarafine with him. By the time the echo died, the shallow tides washed away even the imprint of Sarafine's body in the sand.

At the sound of the rip, Lena started to run. By the time Abraham was gone, she was across the rocky cave floor and halfway to Macon. He leaned against the rough wall until Lena threw herself into his chest, and Macon swayed as if he was going to fall.

"You're dead." Lena spoke into his dirty, ripped shirt.

"No, sweetheart. I'm very much alive." He drew her face up to look at him. "Look at me. I'm still here."

"Your eyes. They're green." She touched his face, shocked.

"And yours are not." He touched her cheek, sadly. "But they are beautiful. Both the green and the gold."

Lena shook her head in disbelief. "I killed you. I used the Book, and it killed you."

477

Macon stroked her hair. "Lila Jane saved me before I crossed over. She imprisoned me in an Arclight, and Ethan released me. It wasn't your fault, Lena. You didn't know what would happen." Lena began to sob. He stroked her wild black curls, whispering, "Shh. It's all right now. It's over."

He was lying. I could see it in his eyes. The black pools that kept his secrets were gone. I didn't understand everything Abraham had said, but I knew there was truth in it. Whatever had happened when Lena Claimed herself wasn't the solution to our problems, but a new problem all its own.

Lena pulled away from Macon. "Uncle Macon, I didn't know this was going to happen. One minute I was thinking about Dark and Light—about what I really wanted. But all I could think about was that I don't belong anywhere. After everything I've been through, I'm not Light or Dark. I'm both."

"It's all right, Lena." He reached out for her, but she stood on her own.

"It's not." She shook her head. "Look what I've done. Auntie Twyla and Ridley are gone, and Larkin..."

Macon looked at Lena as if he was seeing her for the first time. "You did what you had to do. You Claimed yourself. You didn't pick a place in the Order. You changed it."

Her voice was hesitant. "What does it mean?"

"It means you are yourself—powerful and unique—like the Great Barrier, a place where there is no Dark or Light, only magic. But unlike the Great Barrier, you are both Light and Dark. Like me. And after what I saw tonight, like Ridley."

"But what happened to the moon?" Lena looked at Gramma, but it was Amma who spoke up, from the rocky ledge.

"You split it, child. Melchizedek's right, the Order a Things

478

is broken. Can't say what'll happen now." The way she said *broken* made it clear that broken wasn't something we wanted the Order to be.

"I don't understand. You're all here, but so were Hunting and Abraham. How is that possible? The curse—" Lena faltered.

"You possess both Light and Darkness, a possibility the curse did not account for. None of us did." There was pain in Gramma's voice. She was hiding something, and I sensed things were more complicated than she was letting on. "I'm just glad you're all right."

The sound of water splashing echoed through the cavern. I turned in time to see Ridley's blond and pink hair whip around the corner. Link was right behind her.

"Guess I really am a Mortal." Ridley said it with her usual brand of sarcasm, but she looked relieved. "You always have to be different, don't you? Way to go and screw things up again, Cuz."

I heard Lena's breath catch, and for a second she didn't move.

It was all too much. Macon was alive, when Lena believed she'd killed him. She had Claimed herself and remained both Dark and Light. As far as I could tell, she had broken the moon. I knew Lena would fall apart moments from now. When she did, I would be there to carry her home.

Lena grabbed Ridley and Macon, practically strangling them in her own kind of Caster circle, seeming neither Light nor Dark. Just very tired, but no longer very alone.

The Way Back Home

I couldn't sleep anymore. I had crashed hard last night, on the familiar pine-board floor of Lena's room. We had both passed out, still wearing our clothes. Twenty-four hours later, it was weird to be in my own room, in a bed again, after sleeping between tree roots on muddy forest floors. I had seen too much. I got up and shut my window, in spite of the heat. There were too many things out there to be afraid of, too many to fight.

It was a wonder anyone in Gatlin slept at all.

Lucille didn't have that problem. She was kneading a pile of dirty clothes in the corner, fluffing up her bed for the night. That cat could sleep anywhere.

Not me. I flipped over. I was having a hard time getting comfortable with comfortable.

Me, too.

I smiled. Floorboards creaked, and my door swung open.

Lena was standing in my doorway, in my faded Silver Surfer T-shirt. I could see the tip of pajama shorts underneath. Her hair was wet and she was wearing it down again, the way I liked it best.

"This is a dream, right?"

Lena closed the door behind her, the slightest twinkle in her gold and green eyes. "Do you mean your kind of dream or mine?" She pulled up the covers and climbed in next to me. She smelled like lemons and rosemary and soap. It had been a long road for both of us. She tucked her head under my chin and leaned against me. I could feel her questions and her fears, beneath the covers with us.

What is it, L?

She burrowed deeper into my chest.

Do you think you'll ever be able to forgive me? I know things won't be the same —

I tightened my arms around her, remembering all the times it felt like I'd lost her forever. Those moments wound themselves around me, threatening to crush me under their weight. There was no way I could be without her. Forgiving her wasn't a question.

Things will be different. Better.

But I'm not Light, Ethan. I'm something else. I'm ... complicated.

I reached under the covers and brought her hand to my mouth. I kissed her palm where the swirling black patterns hadn't disappeared. It almost looked like Sharpie, but I knew it would never fade.

"I know what you are, and I love you. Nothing can change that."

"I wish I could go back. I wish..."

I pressed my forehead against hers. "Don't. You're you. You chose to be yourself."

"It's scary. My whole life, I've grown up with Dark and Light. It feels strange not to fit in anywhere." She flopped onto her back. "What if I'm not anything?"

"What if that's the wrong question?"

She smiled. "Yeah? What's the right one?"

"You're you. Who is that? Who does she want to be? And how can I get her to kiss me?"

She raised herself on her arms and leaned over my face, letting her hair tickle me. Her lips touched mine, and it was back—the electricity, the current that ran between us. I had missed it, even as it burned my lips.

But something else was missing.

I leaned over and opened the drawer of my nightstand, reaching inside. "I think this belongs to you." I let the chain fall into her hand, her memories spilling between her fingers—the silver button she had fastened on a paper clip, the red string, the tiny Sharpie I gave her on the water tower.

She stared into her hand, stunned.

"I added a couple of things." I untangled the charms so she could see the silver sparrow from Macon's funeral. It meant something so different now. "Amma says sparrows can travel a long way and always find their way back home. Like you did."

"Only because you came to get me."

"I had help. That's why I gave you this."

I held up the tag from Lucille's collar—the one I carried in my pocket while we were searching for Lena and I was watching her through Lucille's eyes. Lucille looked at me calmly, yawning from the corner of the room.

"It's a conduit that allows Mortals to connect with a Caster animal. Macon explained it to me this morning."

"You had it all this time?"

"Yeah. Aunt Prue gave it to me. It works as long as you have the tag."

"Wait? How did your aunt end up with a Caster cat?"

"Arelia gave Lucille to my aunt so she could find her way around the Tunnels."

Lena started to untangle the chain, untying the knots that had formed since she lost it. "I can't believe you found it. When I left it behind, I never thought I'd see it again."

She hadn't lost it. She had taken it off. I resisted the urge to ask her why. "Of course I found it. It's got everything I've ever given you on it."

Lena closed her hand around it and looked away. "Not everything."

I knew what she was thinking about—my mother's ring. She had taken off the ring, too, but I hadn't found it.

Not until this morning, when I discovered it lying on my desk, as if it had always been there. I reached into the drawer again and opened Lena's hand, pressing the ring into it. When she felt the cool metal, she looked up at me.

You found it?

No. My mom must have. It was sitting on my desk when I woke up.

She doesn't hate me?

It was a question only a Caster girl would ask. Had the ghost of my dead mother forgiven her? I knew the answer. I found the ring lying inside a book Lena loaned me, Pablo Neruda's *Book of Questions*, the chain serving as a bookmark under the lines "Is it true that amber contains / the tears of the sirens?"

My mother had been more of an Emily Dickinson fan, but Lena loved Neruda. It was like the sprig of rosemary I found in my mom's favorite cookbook last Christmas—something of my mother's and something of Lena's, together, as if that was always how it was intended to be.

I answered Lena by fastening the chain around her neck, where it belonged. She touched it and stared into my brown eyes with her green and gold ones. I knew she was still the girl I loved, no matter what color her eyes were. There was no one color that could paint Lena Duchannes. She was a red sweater and a blue sky, a gray wind and a silver sparrow, a black curl escaping from behind her ear.

Now that we were together, it felt like home again.

Lena leaned into me, grazing my lips gently at first. Then she kissed me with an intensity that sent heat buzzing up my spine. I felt her find her way back to me, to our curves and our corners, the places our bodies fit together so naturally.

"Okay, this is definitely my dream." I smiled, running my fingers through her incredible mess of black hair.

I wouldn't be so sure about that.

She ran her hands across my chest as I breathed her in. My mouth wandered down her shoulder, and I pulled her closer until I could feel her hipbones digging gently into my skin. It had been so long, and I had missed her so much—the taste of her, the smell of her. I held her face in my hands, kissing her even more deeply, and my heart began to race. I had to stop and catch my breath.

She looked into my eyes, leaning back on my pillow, careful not to touch me.

Is it any better? Are you—am I hurting you?

No. It's better.

I looked at the wall and counted silently, steadying my heart.

You're lying.

I slid my arms around her, but she wouldn't look at me.

We'll never really be able to be together, Ethan.

We're together now.

I ran my fingers lightly down her arms, watching goose bumps spring up under my touch.

You're sixteen, and I'll be seventeen in two weeks. We have time.

Actually, in Caster years, I'm already seventeen. Count the moons. I'm older than you now.

She smiled a little, and I crushed her in my arms.

Seventeen. Whatever. Maybe by eighteen we'll figure it out, L.

L.

I sat up in bed, staring at her.

You know, don't you?

What?

Your real name. Now that you're Claimed, you know it, right?

She tilted her head to the side, with a half-smile. I grabbed her up into my arms, my face hovering just above hers.

What is it? Don't you think I should know?

Haven't you figured it out yet, Ethan? My name is Lena. It's the name I had when we met. It's the only name I'll ever have.

She knew it, but she wasn't going to tell me. I understood why. Lena was Claiming herself again. Deciding who she was going to be. Binding us back together with the things we had shared. I was relieved, because she would always be Lena to me.

The girl I met in my dreams.

I pulled the cover up over our heads. Though none of my dreams went remotely like this, in a matter of minutes, we were both sound asleep.

New Blood

For once I wasn't dreaming. It was Lucille's hissing that woke me up. I rolled over, Lena curled up next to me. It was still hard to believe she was here and she was safe. It was the thing I had wanted most in the world, and now I had it. How often did that happen? The waning moon outside my bedroom window was so bright, I could see her eyelashes touching her cheek as she slept.

Lucille leaped off the bottom of my bed, and something moved in the shadows.

A silhouette.

Someone was standing in front of my window. It could only be one person, who wasn't actually a person at all. I bolted upright in bed. Macon was standing in my room, and Lena was under the covers in my bed. Weakened or not, he was going to kill me.

"Ethan?" I recognized his voice the second I heard it, even though he was trying to be quiet. It wasn't Macon. It was Link.

"What the hell are you doing in my room in the middle of the night?" I hissed, trying not to wake Lena.

"I'm in trouble, man. You gotta help me." Then he noticed Lena curled into a ball next to me. "Oh, jeez. I didn't know you were — you know."

"Sleeping?"

"At least someone can." He was pacing, full of nervous energy, even for Link. His arm was in a cast, and it was swinging erratically. Even with only the dim light from the window, I could see his face was sweaty and pale. He looked sick, worse than sick.

"What's up with you, man? How did you get in here?"

Link sat down in the old chair by my desk, then stood up again. His T-shirt had a hot dog on it and said BITE ME. He'd had it since we were in eighth grade. "You wouldn't believe me if I told you."

The window was open behind him, the curtains blowing inside as if the breeze was being drawn into my room. My stomach was beginning to twist into a familiar knot. "Try me."

"Remember when Vampire Boy grabbed me on Hell Night?" He was talking about the night of the Seventeenth Moon, which would always be Hell Night to him. It was also the title of the horror movie that scared the crap out of him when he was ten.

"Yeah?"

Link was pacing again. "You know he could've killed me, right?"

I wasn't sure I wanted to hear where this was going. "But he didn't, and he's probably dead, like Larkin." John disappeared that night, but no one actually knew what happened to him.

"Yeah, well, if he is, he left a partin' gift. Two actually." Link leaned over my bed. Instinctively I jumped back, bumping into Lena.

"What's going on?" She was half asleep, her voice deep and gravelly.

"Relax, man." Link reached past me and switched on the light next to my bed. "What does it look like to you?"

My eyes adjusted to the dim light, and I saw two small puncture wounds on Link's pasty neck, the distinct mark made by two evenly set canines.

"He bit you?" I jerked away from him, pulling Lena off the bed and pushing her against the wall behind me.

"So I'm right? Holy crap." Link sat down on my bed, dropping his head in his hands. He looked miserable. "Am I gonna turn into one a those bloodsuckers?" He was staring at Lena, waiting for her to confirm what he already knew.

"Technically, yes. You're probably already Turning, but it doesn't mean you're going to be a Blood Incubus. You can fight it, like Uncle Macon, and feed on dreams and memories instead of blood." She pushed her way out from behind me. "Relax, Ethan. He's not going to attack us, like a vampire in one of your lame Mortal horror movies where all witches wear black hats."

"At least I look good in hats." Link sighed. "And black."

She sat down next to him on the edge of my bed. "He's still Link."

"You sure about that?" The more I checked him out, the worse he looked.

"Yeah, I gotta know this sorta stuff." Link was shaking his head, defeated. It was pretty obvious he had been hoping Lena was going to tell him there was some other explanation. "Holy crap, my mom's gonna throw me outta the house when she finds out. I'm gonna have to live in the Beater."

"It'll be okay, man." It was a lie, but what else could I say? Lena was right. Link was still my best friend. He had followed me into the Tunnels, which was the reason he was sitting here now with two holes in his neck.

Link ran his hands over his hair nervously. "Dude, my mom's a Baptist. You think she's gonna let me stay in the house when she finds out I'm a Demon? She doesn't even like Methodists."

"Maybe she won't notice." I knew it was a stupid thing to say, but I was trying.

"Sure. Maybe she won't notice if I never go out durin' the day because my skin'll fry off." Link rubbed his pale arms as if he could already feel his skin beginning to peel.

"Not necessarily." Lena was working something out in her mind. "John wasn't your average Incubus. He was a hybrid. Uncle M is still trying to figure out what Abraham was doing with him."

I remembered what Macon said about hybrids when he was arguing with Abraham at the Great Barrier, which already seemed like a lifetime ago. But I didn't want to think about John Breed at all. I couldn't forget seeing him with his hands all over Lena.

At least Lena didn't notice. "His mother was an Evo. They can Morph—transmutate into virtually any species, even Mortals. That's why John could walk around during the day, while other Incubuses have to avoid sunlight."

"Yeah? So I'm what, like, a quarter bloodsucker?"

Lena nodded. "Probably. I mean, I can't be certain of anything."

Link shook his head. "That's why I wasn't sure at first. I was out all day and nothin' happened. Figured it meant I was in the clear."

"Why didn't you say something right away?" It was a stupid question. Who would want to tell their friends they were Transforming into some kind of Demon?

"I didn't realize he bit me. Just thought I got worked over in the fight, but then I started feelin' weird and saw the marks."

"You'll have to be careful, man. We don't know much about John Breed. If he's some kind of hybrid, who knows what you can do?"

Lena cleared her throat. "Actually, I knew him pretty well." Link and I turned and looked at her at the same time. She twisted her necklace nervously. "I mean, not that well. But we were in the Tunnels together for a long time."

"And?" I could feel my blood rising.

"He was really strong, and he had some kind of weird magnetism that drove girls crazy everywhere we went."

"Girls like you?" I couldn't help myself.

"Shut up." She nudged me with her shoulder.

"This is startin' to sound better already." Link cracked a smile, in spite of himself.

Lena was going down the list of John's attributes in her mind, a list I was hoping wasn't too long. "He could see and hear and smell things I couldn't."

Link inhaled deeply, then coughed. "Dude, you really need a shower."

"You've got superpowers now, and that's the best you can do?" I shoved him. He shoved me back, and I flew off the bed onto the floor.

"What the hell?" I was used to being the one throwing him on the ground.

Link looked at his hands, nodding with satisfaction. "That's right, fists a fury. Like I always said."

Lena picked up Lucille, who had backed herself into a corner. "And you should be able to Travel. You know, materialize wherever you want. You won't need to use the window, even though Uncle Macon says it's more civilized."

"I can walk through walls, like a superhero?" Link was cheering up considerably.

"You'll probably have a great time, except..." Lena took a breath and tried to act casual. "You won't really eat anymore. And assuming you plan to be more like Uncle Macon than Hunting, you'll have to feed off people's dreams and memories to sustain yourself. Uncle Macon called it eavesdropping. But you'll have plenty of time because you won't sleep anymore."

"I can't eat? What am I gonna tell my mom?"

Lena shrugged. "Tell her you've become a vegetarian."

"A vegetarian? Are you insane? That's worse than bein' a quarter Demon!" Link stopped pacing. "Did you hear that?"

"Hear what?"

He walked over to the open window and leaned out. "Seriously?" There were a few banging sounds on the side of the house, and Link hoisted Ridley through my window. I looked away dutifully, since most of Ridley's underwear showed at one point or another during the climb over the windowsill. It wasn't the most graceful entrance.

Apparently, Ridley had cleaned up and gone back to looking like a Siren, whether she was actually one or not. She pulled her skirt down and shook out her blond and pink streaked hair. "Let me get this straight. The party's here, but I'm supposed to stay in my cell with the dog?"

Lena sighed. "You mean my bedroom?"

"Whatever. I don't need the three of you hanging out together, talking about me. I have enough problems as it is. Uncle Macon and my mom have decided I should go back to school, since apparently I'm not a danger to anyone anymore." It looked like she was about to burst into tears.

"But you're not." Link pulled out my desk chair for her.

"I'm plenty dangerous." She ignored him, flopping down on my bed. "You'll see." Link grinned. He hoped so, that much was clear. "They can't make me go to that backwoods dump you call a school."

"Nobody was talking about you, Ridley." Lena sat down on the bed, next to her cousin.

Link went back to pacing. "We were talkin' about me."

"What about you?" He looked away, but Ridley must have already seen something because she was across the room in a second. She grabbed the side of Link's face. "Look at me."

"What for?"

Ridley zeroed in on him like a Sybil. "Look at me."

As Link turned, his pale, sweaty skin caught what little light the moon cast into the room. But it was enough light to see the puncture marks.

Ridley was still holding his face, but her hand was shaking. Link put his hand on her wrist. "Rid—"

"Did he do this to you?" Her eyes narrowed. Even though they were blue now, instead of gold, and she couldn't convince anyone to jump off a cliff, she looked like she could throw someone off one. It was easy to imagine her sticking up for Lena at school when they were kids.

Link took her hand and pulled her toward him, slinging his arm around her shoulders. "It's no biggie. Maybe I'll get some homework done once in a while, now that I don't need any sleep." Link cracked a smile, but Ridley didn't.

"This isn't a joke. John is probably the most powerful Incubus in the Caster world, aside from Abraham himself. If Abraham was looking for him, there's a reason." I could see her biting her lip, staring out into the trees outside my window.

"You worry too much, Babe."

Ridley shrugged off Link's arm. "Don't call me Babe."

I leaned back against my headboard, watching the two of them. Now that Ridley was a Mortal and Link was an Incubus, she would still be the one girl he couldn't have—and probably the only one he wanted. Junior year was going to be interesting.

An Incubus at Jackson High.

Link, the strongest guy in school, driving Savannah Snow crazy every time he walked into the room without a single lick from one of Ridley's lollipops. And Ridley, the ex-Siren, who I was pretty sure would find her way back to trouble, with or without the lollipops. Two months until September, and for the first time in my life, I could hardly wait for the first day of school.

Link wasn't the only one of us who couldn't sleep that night.

Sunrise

"Can't you dig any faster?"

Link and I glared at Ridley from where we stood, a few feet down in Macon's grave. The one he'd never spent a minute in. I was already dripping, and the sun wasn't even up yet. Link, with his newfound strength, had yet to break a sweat.

"No, we can't. And yes, I know you're totally grateful we're doin' this instead a you, Babe." Link waved his shovel at Ridley.

"Why does the long way have to take so long?" Ridley looked at Lena, disgusted. "Why are Mortals so sweaty and boring?"

"You're a Mortal now. You tell me." I tossed a shovelful of dirt in Ridley's direction.

"Don't you have a Cast for this sort of thing?" Ridley flopped down next to Lena, who sat cross-legged beside the grave, looking through an old book about Incubuses.

"How did you guys manage to get that book out of the *Lunae*

Libri, anyway?" Link was hoping Lena could find out something about hybrids. "It's not a bank holiday." We'd gotten in enough trouble in the *Lunae Libri* during the past year.

Ridley shot Link a look that probably would've brought him to his knees when she was still a Siren. "He has a lot of pull with the librarian, Genius."

As soon as she said it, the book Lena was holding caught fire. "Oh, no!" She yanked her hands back before they were burnt. Ridley stomped on the book. Lena sighed. "I'm sorry. It just happens."

"She meant Marian," I said defensively.

I avoided her eyes and busied myself with my shovel. Lena and I were back to being, well, us. There wasn't a second I didn't think about the proximity of her hand to my hand, her face to mine. There wasn't a moment when we were awake that I could bear to have her voice out of my head, after I'd lost it for so long. She was the last person I spoke to at night and the first person I reached for in the morning. After everything we had been through, I would've traded places with Boo if I could. That's how badly I never wanted to let her out of my sight.

Amma had even started setting a place for Lena at the table. At Ravenwood, Aunt Del kept a pillow and a comforter folded next to the downstairs couch for me. Nobody said a word about curfews or rules or seeing too much of each other. Nobody expected us to trust the world with each other if we weren't together.

The summer had gone beyond that. You couldn't un-happen things. Liv had happened. John and Abraham had happened. Twyla and Larkin, Sarafine and Hunting—they weren't people

I could just forget. School would be the same if you ignored the fact that my best friend was an Incubus and the second hottest girl in school was a declawed Siren. General Lee and Principal Harper, Savannah Snow and Emily Asher, they would never change.

Lena and I would never be the same.

Link and Ridley were so supernaturally altered, they weren't even in the same universe.

Liv was hidden in the library, happy to be safely tucked away in the stacks for a while. I had only seen her once since the night of the Seventeenth Moon. She was no longer training to be a Keeper, but she seemed okay with it.

"We both know I would never have been happy watching from the sidelines," she'd said. I knew it was true. Liv was an astronomer, like Galileo; an explorer, like Vasco da Gama; a scholar, like Marian. Maybe even a mad scientist, like my mom.

I guess we all needed to start over.

Plus, I got the feeling Liv liked her new teacher as much as her old one. Liv's education had been turned over to a certain former Incubus who spent his days out of sight—in Ravenwood or his favorite study, an old haunt in the Caster Tunnels—with Liv and the Head Caster Librarian as his only Mortal companions.

It wasn't how I expected the summer to turn out. Then again, when it came to Gatlin, I never knew what was going to happen. At some point, I had stopped trying.

Stop thinking and start digging.

I dropped my shovel and pushed up against the side of the grave. Lena leaned over on her stomach, her ratty Converse kicking up behind her. I put my hands around her neck and pulled her mouth to mine until our kiss made the graveyard spin.

"Kids, kids. Keep it clean. We're ready." Link leaned on his shovel and stood back to survey his handiwork. Macon's grave was open, not that there was a coffin down there.

"Well?" I wanted to get this over with. Ridley pulled a small bundle of black silk out of her pocket and held it in front of her.

Link pulled back as if she had shoved a torch in his face. "Watch it, Rid! Don't get that thing anywhere near me. Incubus kryptonite, remember?"

"Sorry, Superman, I forgot." Ridley climbed down into the hole, holding the bundle carefully with one hand, and placed it in the bottom of Macon Ravenwood's empty grave. My mom may have saved Macon with the Arclight, but we saw it for what it was—dangerous. A supernatural prison I didn't want to see my best friend trapped inside. Six feet under was where the Arclight belonged, and Macon's grave was the safest place any of us could think of.

"Good riddance," Link said as he pulled Ridley up out of the grave. "Isn't that what you're supposed to say when good defeats evil at the end of the movie?"

I looked at him. "Have you *ever* read a book, man?"

"Dig." Ridley rubbed dirt off her hands. "At least, that's what I say."

Link piled shovelful after shovelful of dirt over the bundle while Ridley watched, without taking her eyes off the grave.

"Finish it," I said.

Lena nodded, jamming her hands in her pockets. "Let's get out of here."

The sun began to rise over the magnolias in front of my mom's grave. It didn't bother me anymore, because I knew she wasn't there. She was somewhere, everywhere else, still watching out for me. Macon's hidden room. Marian's archive. Our study at Wate's Landing.

"Come on, L." I pulled Lena by the arm. "I'm sick of the dark. Let's go watch the sunrise." We took off, running down the grassy hill like kids—past the graves and magnolias, past the palmettos and oaks tangled in Spanish moss, past the uneven rows of grave markers and weeping angels and the old stone bench. I could feel her shivering in the early morning air, but neither of us wanted to stop. So we didn't, and by the time we reached the bottom of the hill, we were almost falling, almost flying. Almost happy.

We didn't see the eerie golden glow pierce through small cracks and fissures in the dirt shoveled over Macon's grave.

And I didn't check the iPod in my pocket, where I might have noticed a new song in the playlist.

Eighteen Moons.

But I didn't check, because I didn't care. No one was listening. No one was watching. No one existed in the world but the two of us—

The two of us, and the old man in the white suit and string tie, who stood at the crest of the hill until the sun began to rise and the shadows fell back into their crypts.

We didn't see him. We only saw the fading night and the rising blue sky. Not the blue sky in my bedroom, but the real one. Even though it might look different to each of us. Only now I wasn't so sure the sky looked the same to any two people, no matter what universe they lived in.

I mean, how could you be sure?

The old man walked away.

We didn't hear the familiar sound of space and time rearranging as he ripped into the last possible moment of night—the darkness before the dawn.

Eighteen Moons, eighteen spheres,
From the world beyond the years,
One Unchosen, death or birth,
A Broken Day awaits the Earth...

⊰ AFTER ⊱

Siren's Tears

Ridley stood in her room at Ravenwood, the room that used to belong to Macon. But nothing remained the same except the four walls, a ceiling, and a floor, and possibly the paneled bedroom door.

Which she shut, with a heavy click, and bolted. She turned to face her room, her back against the door. Macon had decided to take another room at Ravenwood, though he spent most of his time in his study in the Tunnels. So this room belonged to Ridley now, and she was careful to keep the trapdoor leading down into the Tunnels locked under thick pink shag carpeting. The walls were covered with spray painted graffiti, black and neon pink mostly, with shots of electric green, yellow, and orange. They weren't words, exactly—more like shapes, slashes, emotions. Anger, bottled in a can of cheap spray paint from the Wal-Mart in Summerville. Lena had offered to do it for her, but

Ridley insisted on doing it herself, Mortal-style. The reeking fumes made her head ache, and the splattering paint made a huge mess of everything. It was exactly what she wanted and exactly how she felt.

She'd made a mess of everything.

No words. Ridley hated words. Mostly, they were lies. Her two-week incarceration in Lena's room had been enough to make her hate poetry for a lifetime.

Mybeatingheartbleedingneedsyou —

Whatever.

Ridley shuddered. There was no accounting for taste in the family gene pool. She pushed herself away from the door and walked over to the wardrobe. With the slightest touch, she opened the white wooden doors, revealing a lifetime's careful collection of clothing, the hallmark of a Siren.

Which, she reminded herself, she wasn't.

She dragged a pink footstool to the shelves and climbed up on it, her pink platform shoes slipping back and forth over her pink striped knee socks. It had been a Harajuku kind of a day, not often seen around Gatlin. The looks she got at the Dar-ee Keen were priceless. At least it had passed the afternoon.

One afternoon. Out of how many?

She felt along the top of the shelf until she found it, a shoe box from Paris. She smiled and pulled it down. Purple velvet four-inch peep-toes, if she remembered. Of course she remembered. She'd had some damn fine times in those shoes.

She dumped the contents of the box onto her black and white bedspread. There it was, half-shrouded in silk, still covered with crumbling dirt.

Ridley slumped down on the floor next to her bed, resting

her arms on the edge. She wasn't stupid. She just wanted to look, as she had every night for the past two weeks. She wanted to feel the power of something magical, a power she would never have again.

Ridley wasn't a bad girl. Not really. Besides, even if she was, what did it matter? She was powerless to do anything about it. She'd been tossed aside like last year's mascara.

Her cell phone rang, and she picked it up from her nightstand. A picture of Link popped up on the screen. She clicked it off and tossed it into the endless pink shag.

Not now, Hot Rod.

She had another Incubus on her mind.

John Breed.

Ridley settled back into place, tilting her head to the side as she watched the sphere begin to glow a subtle shade of pink.

"What am I going to do with you?" She smiled because, for once, it was her decision to make, and because she had yet to make it.

three

The light grew brighter and brighter until the room was bathed in a wash of rose-colored light, which made almost everything else disappear like thin pencil lines that had been only partly rubbed out.

two

Ridley closed her eyes—a little girl blowing out a birthday candle, to make a wish—

one

She opened her eyes.

It was decided.

Acknowledgments

Writing a book is hard. It turns out, writing a second book is twice as hard. Here are the people who got us through the many phases of our Seventeenth Moon:

OUR BELOVED AGENTS, SARAH BURNES AND COURTNEY GATEWOOD, WITH HELP FROM REBECCA GARDNER, FROM THE GERNERT COMPANY, *who continue to shepherd Gatlin County to new and faraway places no piece of pecan fried chicken has ever seen.* SALLY WILCOX AT CAA, *for bringing Gatlin County to a town where nobody would ever touch a piece of fried anything.*

OUR BRILLIANT TEAM AT LITTLE, BROWN BOOKS FOR YOUNG READERS: OUR EDITORS, JENNIFER BAILEY HUNT AND JULIE SCHEINA, OUR ART DIRECTOR, DAVID CAPLAN, OUR MARKETING GURU, LISA ICKOWICZ, OUR QUEEN OF LIBRARY SERVICES, VICTORIA STAPLETON, OUR PUBLICITY GURU, MELANIE CHANG, AND OUR PUBLICIST, JESSICA KAUFMAN, *who are as good at what they do as Amma is at crossword puzzles.*

OUR AMAZING FOREIGN PUBLISHERS AND EDITORS, ESPECIALLY AMANDA PUNTER, CECILE TEROUANNE, SUSANNE STARK, MYRIAM GALAZ, AS WELL AS THOSE WE HAVE YET TO MEET, *who have welcomed us into their houses and their countries.* OUR #1 SPANISH FAN, AUTHOR JAVIER RUESCAS, *who not only blurbed our book in Spain but spread the word.*

OUR FAVORITE READER, DAPHNE DURHAM, *who gets us and, more important, Ethan and Lena. There isn't a cream-of-casserole big enough to show her how we feel. Even with cornflakes or tiny fried onions or mashed-up potato chips on top.*

OUR RESIDENT TEEN CLASSICIST, EMMA PETERSON, *who translated Latin Casts while cramming for AP Vergil.* OUR FRIGHTENING TEEN EDITOR, MAY PETERSON, *who no doubt will go on to terrify many other writers in the future.*

OUR BOSS PHOTOGRAPHER, ALEX HOERNER, *whose photo of us looks nothing like us, so we love it.* VANIA STOYANOVA, *for her beautiful trailer, amazing photos, and her work as co-administrator of our U.S. fansite.* YVETTE VASQUEZ, *for reading our drafts a hundred times, blogging our tour, and acting as co-administrator of our U.S. fansite.* THE CREATORS OF OUR INTERNATIONAL FANSITES IN FRANCE, SPAIN, AND BRAZIL. ASHLY STOHL, *who designed bookplates and invites, built websites, and took photos that brought the South to life for readers around the world.* ANNA MOORE, *for building our* Beautiful Creatures *site 2.0.* AUTHOR GABRIEL PAUL, *who creates all the brilliant online games for our tours and promotions.*

OUR CASTER GIRLS 12, 13, 14, 15, 16, 17, 18, AND 25. *You are the heart of* The Caster Chronicles *and always will be.*

OUR YA WRITING MENTORS, WP AUTHORS, BOOK BLURBERS, TRAILER MAKERS, FANSITE DESIGNERS, FELLOW DEBUT AUTHORS, BLOGGERS, NING/GOODREADS FRIENDS, AND, OF COURSE, OUR TWEETHEARTS. *Like Gatlin's postmaster, Carlton Eaton, we hear all our news from you first. And whether good or bad, it's better to hear it from one of your own. Nobody will ever know how much fun you make even the Cave o' Revisions.*

OUR FAMILIES
ALEX, NICK, AND STELLA GARCIA AND LEWIS, EMMA, MAY, AND KATE PETERSON AND ALL OUR RESPECTIVE MOMS, DADS, SISTERS, BROTHERS, NIECES, NEPHEWS, SISTERS-IN-LAW, PARTY-THROWING COUSINS, AND FRIENDS. FROM AUNT MARY TO COUSIN JANE, *you have always been there for us.* STOHLS, RACCAS, MARINS, GARCIAS, PETERSONS: BY *now you have every right to hate us, but oddly you don't.*

DEBY LINDEE AND SUSAN AND JOHN RACCA, *for housing us on our many Southern field trips.* BILL YOUNG AND DAVID GOLIA, *for being our knights in shining armor.* INDIA'S AND NATALIA'S DADDY, *for helping us when we were supposed to be helping him.* SAUNDRA MITCHELL, *for everything, as always.*

OUR READERS, TEACHERS, AND LIBRARIANS, THE CASTERS AND OUTCASTERS, *who discovered* Beautiful Creatures *and loved it enough to take another trip through the Tunnels with us. Without you, they're just (so many) words.*

OUR MENTOR, MELISSA MARR, AND OUR THERAPIST, HOLLY BLACK. *They know why.* DR. SARA LINDHEIM, *our Keeper, who knows our Casts better than we do.*

AND FINALLY, MARGARET MILES, LIBRARIAN AND YOUTH SERVICES DIRECTOR AT THE NEW HANOVER COUNTY LIBRARY, IN WILMINGTON, NORTH CAROLINA. *Because Marian Ashcroft isn't the only Caster Librarian, after all.*